TAKEN

GODS AMONG US TRIQUETRA PROPHECY
BOOK TWO

MELODY GRACE HICKS

TAKEN

For information contact :

http://www.melodygracehicks.com

Book and Cover design by Melody Grace Hicks

Paperback ISBN: 978-1-0689324-5-8
Hardcover ISBN: 978-1-0689324-6-5

10 9 8 7 6 5 4 3 2 1

CONTENTS

DESCRIPTION

When captured by the Wild Hunt, this mortal-scientist-turned-goddess doesn't wait for her prince to rescue her. Shannon's not some helpless princess in a damn tower. She'll save herself and her unborn son.

When Loki's worst fear comes true, Asgard's Black Prince will stop at nothing to rescue his pregnant consort and soulmate. Yet, not even the threat of Asgard's forces looming in the skies over Alfheim can force the Unseelie Winter Realm elves to return Shannon when she's disappeared from her cell. Nightmares of his past haunt Loki as he searches for her. He'll do anything to find her before she gives birth.

A feisty, new Elven goddess, Shannon isn't the type to wait for rescue. On a strange planet with her soulmate bond muted by a Dwarven iron cuff, she's surrounded by enemies and doesn't know who to trust. Less than thirteen weeks remain in her pregnancy, and the Fates don't play fair. She must rely on her wits and limited, dwindling energy resources that are critical for her and her child's survival. Yet the cost to save her son may be more than her heart can bear.

Some truths are hard to swallow.

And even for a scientist-turned-goddess, some laws of the universe can't be fought.

PREFACE

Welcome to the Gods Among Us Universe. It's inspired by an amalgamation of world mythologies including Norse, West Coast First Nations, Mesoamerican, Celtic, Greek, Roman, Mesopotamian, Egyptian, and Asian, blended with our current modern world, and expanded to other worlds across multiple solar systems within this created universe. I take copious liberties with world mythologies, twisting them as needed to serve the interests of my stories. No disrespect is intended to any original ancient sources, cultures, or religions associated with these world mythologies.

World mythology pre-dates modern usage in popular culture. Characters in my fiction created from these mythologies share some traits and occasional backstory elements with popular culture characters since both are sourced from the same ancient material. Reference to popular world culture provides a sense of the *real world* in the Earth-based scenes and would be familiar to characters living in a version of our modern world. Points to readers who catch my pop culture references and specific mythology legends.

The Gods Among Us Universe is diverse, with a wide range of abilities, appearances, mental states, and gender expressions, and sexualities, including a shapeshifting genderfluid race. While the main romance in the Triquetra Prophecy is predominately heterosexual, with the ability to shapeshift, genderfluid characters transition physically in addition to socially such that their chosen gender identity and biological sex assignment matches. This author's choice to present gender fluidity tied with shapeshifting should not in any way be construed as disrespecting real world individuals of their gender choice, whether cis or trans to their biological sex.

This first trilogy, the Triquetra Prophecy, is focused on three main characters. *Taken* is a direct sequel to *Hidden*, picking up immediately where *Hidden* left off. Tropes included in *Taken* are: he-falls-first, altered heroine, ancient-beings-find-love, soulmates, dangerous secrets, love triangle, touch-her-and-die, the quest, damsel in distress, feisty heroine, and fish-out-of-water. For information on trigger warnings within *Taken*, please see my website (www.melodygracehicks.com). As this is book two of the trilogy, it does end with unanswered questions.

Since this author is Canadian, this book is written in Canadian English, which means there is a 'u' in colour, a 'z' in realize, and 'll' in tunnelling. These and other variations from strictly UK English or strictly American English are not spelling errors, but rather reflect the unique combination that is Canadian English.

PART 1

Captivity & Confrontation

"Courage is resistance to fear, mastery of fear, not
absence of fear."

Mark Twain

Chapter 1

MARKED FOR HARVEST

Two Nights Ago (Earth Calendar)

It began as a wisp of fog. The silver-grey substance danced like the flickering of a flame in a breeze. Gaining strength, it swirled and thickened, becoming a dense column that suddenly burst outward. In the heart of the disturbance, a darker sphere appeared, pulsed and expanded into an eerie, blue shimmering haze that filled the space within the ancient stone ring.

Hidden within its dense cloak of silver-grey fog, a tall, gaunt shape took form. Covered in shades of grey and black, he blended with the washed-out colours of the night. As he stepped through the border of the stone ring, the mist encompassed him, slinking with him, and the blue shimmering haze winked out.

Making his way through the quiet of the night with no more sound than the fog creeping along the ground, he stalked the nearby town. Locked doors were no impediment to his entry. With a flick of long, bony fingers, each metallic security gave way to the push of air on deadbolt or tumblers. Like a demonic wraith, he prowled silently through every home, making note of those that met the sacrificial criteria.

First-born children, but only if they were still untouched by adult desires, were added to his list for harvest. Destroying their innocence made the blood sacrifice that much more powerful, more effective in harvesting energies the Unseelie realm needed to function. King Cernunnos and Queen Mene preferred to corrupt the young for the quarterly ritual.

But not him. No, Crom Cruach relished the dual sacrifice of innocence and fertility in a dark perversion of his former fertility god powers. Pregnant women were his favourite ritual prey. The flavour of power he received when their energies were absorbed made him shiver with an unholy lust. Anticipation surged at what awaited him on the upcoming Lughnasadh hunt.

Home after home he invaded throughout the summer night, desecrating every mortal residence in the area with his foul presence. Each victim was left with a wisp of unnatural fog clinging invisibly to him or her, marking them for the Wild Hunt's harvest when the sun set and the veil between worlds thinned in a measly rotation and a half of this planet.

As dawn brightened the sky on the sleepy English town, Crom made his way back towards the stone circle. Yet, some instinct sent him detouring through the nearby hills. Disguised within his cloak of mists and blending with the natural fog that clung to the hilltops, he spotted three women.

A tall curly redhead, bright hair shining in the sunlight, fought with a pair of short swords against a curvaceous sprite with blue hair swaying in a high ponytail, wielding a longsword and dagger. The speed and skill of the women curled his lip into a sneer. Damn Asgardians. He'd fought enough Valkyrie to know their style of combat anywhere, and he recognized that cursed redhead. It was the third woman that held him transfixed. An immortal—she must be to accompany Valkyrie—but her skills were not as polished as she practiced an elemental magic. Even with her back towards him, her curse as her seidhr went astray was audible.

An adult immortal that hadn't yet mastered their skills?

A sadistic grin stretched his lips. Younger than she appeared or newly immortal—it was the only explanation. If the Wild Hunt could separate her from the Valkyrie, she'd make a better sacrifice than any of the mortals. What he'd give to get some payback, some—

The woman turned, peering into the hills towards him with a hand resting on... empty air?

4

He sucked in a gasp.

Pregnant! She had to be with a stance like that.

Blood surged hotly within him, and he fought the shuddering arousal inflaming his senses, almost blinding him to his surroundings. A weak, pregnant immortal. By Danu, what a gift! She was worth more than all the other prey combined.

And oh, how he would enjoy her.

He'd make her torture last many long months. Her eventual ritual sacrifice when she was finally used up would provide the realm energy for years. She would be utterly delicious. The thought of her screams as she fought and clawed had him groaning and spilling his seed on the rocky hilltop, his eyes fixed on his unwitting prey.

The Present (Earth Calendar)

Prince Loki, Asgardian God of Chaos, Stories, and Song, rubbed his chest as he surveyed the London Pinewood Studios soundstage and set of his hit movie sequel, *The Assassin's Reward*. The uncomfortable sensation had begun as two riggers hooked him into the wire harness for an upcoming stunt.

"Good to go, Tod," the blond-haired rigger said, giving Loki a thumbs up.

The second rigger, a Scot by his accent, gave Loki a thumbs up and muttered under his breath about working on the first of August, a holiday in Scotland but not elsewhere in the United Kingdom.

In his mortal guise as Tod Corvus, Loki flashed both men a smile, eyed the cables above him, and returned the thumbs up. "Thanks. And mate, you get the holiday later this month while your pals back home work. Their turn to be mithered."

The Scot reddened slightly, shrugged a shoulder, and laughed. "Aye. True enough."

The hairs on Loki's body stood as his uneasiness deepened. He frowned, glancing around again. Even if something went wrong with the rig, his immortal strength would easily carry him through the two-story jump between the mock-up brownstone roof and the nearby balcony. The stunt coordinator talked with the director, gesturing wildly with his hands in his usual fashion. The camera crew checked their settings. Nothing in particular set off Loki's instincts.

Still, like an itch he couldn't deny, something wasn't right.

His heartbeat quickened.

Nothing *here*, at least. He pressed a fist to his breastbone where he most felt the soulmate bond with his consort. The sensation was coming from Shannon.

Focusing inward and tuning out the surrounding conversations, his heart raced as his consort's emotions switched to alarm, then frustration and anger. What was happening? With Kara and Mist there to protect Shannon on her girls' weekend, surely it couldn't be serious? They only had to call on the Bifrost if the Valkyrie couldn't handle whatever it was. Heimdall would evacuate them in a couple of heartbeats.

He exhaled and rolled his shoulders.

And really, how much trouble could they get into at a spa in the Lake District? Yggdrasil's roots, it was all rolling hills, some forest, and lakes. Keswick was barely five thousand people. Mortals were no danger to Shannon.

But... Elise was with them.

The mortal woman wasn't aware of the immortal worlds or that Shannon was an Elven goddess. Was Shannon angry on Elise's behalf? Loki took a few measured breaths, trying to calm his thundering pulse.

Yet the sensations didn't dissipate, and his muscles tensed as his chest squeezed tighter.

Should he contact Shannon?

Another wave of frustrated fury hit him.

Unable to hold back, he sent a telepathic query. *<Shannon?>*

His fingers tightened on the brick at the lack of response.

She'd come far in her defensive training, both fighting and using her goddess powers. And the way she'd defeated Isis only days ago... no, Isis wasn't likely to have returned after that trouncing. Even if she had, the two Valkyrie and Shannon were more than a match for his grief-crazed sister-in-law. But if his consort needed so much concentration that she didn't answer, didn't acknowledge his call—

By the Nine, what was happening?

Did he dare try again? It might be dangerous to distract her.

Brick crumbled beneath his fingertips. Damn it. He had to stay in control. He drew in an unsteady breath and released it slowly. She'd call if she needed him. And she had Mist and Kara with her. There was nothing to worry about.

As the stunt coordinator came over and gave his final instructions, Loki tried to pay attention. But before they called action, fear crept through the bond, then grew stronger, sharper, and overwhelming. His system flooded with adrenaline, senses sharpening as Shannon's fear spiked. Unable to resist any longer, he sent his consciousness through the bond, desperate to reach her, to see what was happening.

<*LOK*—> she shouted.

Agony exploded through his body, nerves searing as her telepathic cry cut off and their bond severed, his mind snapping back.

"*NO!*" Loki screamed, grabbing his head and collapsing to his knees on the painted wooden roof.

"Tod? *Tod!* What's wrong?" asked the stunt coordinator.

Barely able to breathe through the agony—fuck, was his body was being torn apart?—Loki forced himself to his feet. "Off. Get these off. I've got to go. I've got to leave." Blindly, he clutched at the wires, fumbling to undo them as he stumbled. Hands helped, and as soon as he was free, he teleported the few kilometres to the rooftop garden of his London flat.

"Heimdall!"

The swirling rainbow-hued wormhole swept Loki up and deposited him on the white stone platform of Asgard's Bifrost chamber. Staggering, he barely caught his balance.

"Where is she?" he forced out through the pain short-circuiting his nervous system. He thrust his hand out as he sent the mental call to Laevateinn, the sword he'd forged with Helheim's death runes.

Heimdall's hand steadied him. "I'm sorry, Prince Loki. The Wild Hunt attacked them."

Loki's heart clenched, horror filling his mouth with bile.

"The Bifrost was blocked by whatever portal the Unseelie were using. Without a lock, I couldn't extract them before Princess Shannon disappeared from my sight." Even unable to see Asgard's guardian and gatekeeper properly through pain-ridden eyes, the frustration and anger in Heimdall's deep voice was clear as it rumbled and echoed in the stone chamber. "Although I can't see your consort, I can send you to Mist and Kara."

Laevateinn's black-and-silver hilt slapped into Loki's palm, and he tightened his grip. "Yes. Now. Tell Thor," he bit out as the lights swirled around him again.

When the Bifrost's vortex dissipated, Loki was in the midst of a thunderstorm. Rain poured in blinding sheets and wind buffeted him, almost knocking him off his feet. Lightning flashed, illuminating the utter disaster in front of him. A vehicle with a crumpled left side and missing door tilted into a partially-flooded ditch, off the far side of a road. Mist sprawled unconscious on the ground, a pool of blood surrounding her silvery face, despite the rain's attempt to wash it away. She bled from a nasty head wound that turned blue braids to black. On her hands and one knee with determination in every movement, Kara crawled toward her fellow fallen Valkyrie, dragging a leg with one thigh mangled and missing flesh. There was no sign of Shannon or Elise.

Loki dashed to Kara, sheathing his sword on his back to free his hands. "Where is Shannon?" he shouted, pain harshening his voice as he conjured bandages to bind her leg.

"They took her through a stone ring portal, my prince." The Valkyrie wept bloody tears down her scratched and bleeding face. "I failed you. I'm so sorry!"

"She is still alive?" he demanded. He tightened a tourniquet at the top of her thigh—the best he could do to stop the blood loss with the gaping bites. Cursed hellhounds.

Golden eyes widened as she shook her head. "Yes! Absolutely, yes. They bound her with Dvergr iron. Shannon's not dead."

Relief weakened his knees, and he collapsed, gasping. Tears streamed down his face unheeded in the stinging rain. The fuckers had bound her magic. The Dwarven metal prevented the soulmate bond from connecting with him, but she wasn't dead.

Shannon wasn't dead.

It fucking hurt to not feel their connection, but he had to keep telling himself that she wasn't dead.

She wasn't dead.

Shannon was alive.

Alive.

And he *would* save her.

"Who? Who took her?" Relief was torn away by explosive white-hot rage. Someone had *dared* to take his soulmate. They dared! He would rain chaos and bloody death on their heads. He'd rip them apart and obliterate their atoms.

"Crom Cruach and Llew with the Wild Hunt. They must have reactivated the circle." Kara waved a hand toward the ancient stone ring standing in windswept grasses a short distance from the modern roadway.

"Her fucking *Uncle*?" he roared, fists clenching gravel. "Oh, that tree-fucking goatspawn is dead. We should have killed them before. He's going to wish I'd killed him in the last war."

Kara stared at him, wide-eyed and unblinking.

"Shannon won't know that's her bloody uncle. She only heard his name once when she met Manannan a few weeks ago. Filthy, sadistic Unseelie." He rose, glaring at the ancient portal site. "At least I know where to get her back. If those dark elves or any of their twisted creatures have harmed her, there won't be anywhere on Alfheim that escapes my wrath," Loki snarled, already plotting his next steps. Needing to think clearly, he gritted his teeth and shoved a mental block around the pain of the missing bond.

"I want to come with you," Kara demanded, trying to rise despite her damaged thigh.

"Don't worry, my fierce Valkyrie. I will ensure you get your chance. In the meantime, let's get you and Mist back to Asgard's healers. Wait, where is Elise?" Eyes narrowed against the rain, he glanced around again. Had those fuckers taken the mortal wife of his close friend?

"She missed all the action. She's in the car and got knocked out when they drove us off the road."

"Okay, let's get you over to Mist so Heimdall can extract you both at once. I'll get Elise out of the car, and see if she needs medical attention."

Gently, he gathered Kara in his arms and strode to Mist. "Heimdall? If you would please get these two to the healers?" he instructed, as he laid the Valkyrie down carefully beside her fellow warrior, trying not to hurt her more than necessary, and stepped back. Within seconds, they disappeared in a swirl of rainbow lights.

Loki hurried over to the car and then around to the driver's side tilted into the ditch. The water level was rising, but not yet threatening her inside the vehicle. Elise appeared to be out cold, eyes closed and mouth slack. That certainly made things easier. If he could avoid needing to tamper with her memories on top of any injuries from the crash, it would be better for her. Mortal minds were fragile.

The driver's door was pinned in the ditch. No way was he getting in from there. Even attempting it would flood Elise's seat. Loki moved back to the ripped-open passenger's side and crawled inside to reach the trapped woman. He briefly checked her over—she had a mild concussion he could repair with his meagre healing abilities. Thank the Norns. One less thing to worry about. With a search through her recent memories, easier with her unconscious and unresisting, he located the cottage where the girls were staying, then teleported Elise directly there. Loki laid her on a bed, healed her, implanted memories of returning here, and left her sleeping while he called Harry.

"Hey, mate. The girls got caught in a thunderstorm, and a stag knocked them off the road. Elise is fine and back at the cottage, resting, but Shannon needs to go to the hospital. Kara and Mist are on the way with her now. I'm driving out to meet them. Can you come get Elise at the cottage? Your RAV4 is done for, I'm afraid." Using a vocal illusion, he kept his voice calm for his friend's benefit, even as his rage surged, howling at the fraying leash of his control.

"Bloody hell! Of course, Tod. I'll leave now. Will you keep us updated on how Shannon is doing?"

"Absolutely." Loki didn't flinch at the bald lie as he hung up. Harry's friendship was important to him, but no way would Loki put the mortal in danger by introducing the man to immortal realities. Mortal lives were already fleeting.

And Loki couldn't afford any distractions.

Not with his precious Shannon and their unborn child missing. The phone crumpled in his grip. Taken by the dark elves, just as his previous wife, Sigyn, had been. Treaty or no treaty, the Unseelie would not get away with this atrocity. War was no excuse this time. His breath rasped in his lungs, pulse thundering. If they harmed her like they had Sigyn, used her in their sick sacrificial practices—

Unable to restrain himself further, he teleported into the nearby mountains. There, Loki uncaged the maelstrom inside him, surrounded by the rawness of the storm.

The pounding, rapid tempo of fiery rage in his veins heightened the flashes of lightning.

The furious trembling in his rigid muscles shook the earth.

The churning, sickening fear within his belly burst from his throat in dry heaves as his chaos exploded.

And in the aftermath, the screaming quiet in his soul where Shannon's absence left him colder than death. The resulting devastated landscape of broken forest, shattered rock, and cratered earth would no doubt leave mortals mystified for decades, but the expenditure gave him enough clarity to regain control.

Lethal calm restored, Loki called Heimdall. Asgard's Black Prince was going hunting. Nothing, and no one, would stop him from saving Shannon. If he had to set fire to the entire Norse-cursed universe, he wouldn't rest until he had her back in his arms.

Chapter 2

MY KINGDOM FOR A BOBBY PIN

S pine rigid with chest-tearing agony, Doctor Shannon Murphy, scientist, professor, and newly immortal Elven goddess, gasped as she swam to consciousness. Her eyelids were heavy weights, tears squeezed from the corners, and before she could lift them, the torment dragged her back under.

Breath-stealing pain greeted her anew the next time she woke, rubbing at dried crusts gluing her eyes closed. When she pried her eyes open, darkness surrounded her. Gods, everything hurt, her muscles and joints a wretched suffering. Before she took in her surroundings, again, the throbbing robbed her of her senses.

With her teeth gritted at the intense ache within her chest—a pulsing black hole devouring her soul—she was slower to open her eyelids the third time she woke, but once she did, the darkness wasn't so impenetrable. After a few blinks, her outstretched hand became visible in the dim glow.

She tried to shift positions. Pain flared, and she stifled a groan. Damn it to fucking hell. Even moving her fingers hurt. Why did everything ache like she'd been beaten?

Carefully probing with her hands, she couldn't detect any specific injuries on her skull or chest. Her heart was tender as if it had been held in someone's fist and squeezed until it almost burst. As she went to lift her head, she hissed. Spiking pain stabbed at her temples with every heartbeat.

A sudden kick in her abdomen had her grabbing her belly.

Holy crap, her baby!

Gasping, she ran her hands over the basketball-sized bulge. A relieved breath exploded at her son's second kick. Thank gods. At least he seemed fine.

But... where the hell was she?

Musty earth and an acrid bitter scent surrounded her, with the distinct waft of urine from her left. With a groan, she pushed to a sitting position and took in the rough stone-walled room with its dirt floor. A faint yellow light trickled in through a barred window in the black door. Hello, medieval times. Damn. What place had a room like this? Was she stuck in a castle basement? A dungeon?

Rustling noises and breathing echoed in the gloom. There were others in here. As Shannon squinted, she made out small unmoving bodies and some larger forms that blinked with wide, terrified eyes. Their shapes were oddly rounded, and she peered closer, then sucked in a breath—women, all pregnant women like her.

Frowning, she focused on the smaller shapes.

Her fists clenched as she made out a little face. The fucking bastards had taken kids. The children were unconscious, sprawled on the floor in heaps. Like they'd been dumped and left in whatever position they'd landed.

But who...

Memory returned in a cacophony of pain, sound, and fear that brought a metallic taste to her tongue. The Wild Hunt attack. The troll. The hellhounds, redcaps, and headless dullahan. Heart thundering in her chest, Shannon shuddered as she recalled a huge white stag with eyes of flame and an old cruel-looking man on an odd-shaped black stallion.

Something was wrong with her leg. It was abnormally heavy, and pain radiated up from her ankle.

Had she twisted it? Broken it? Struggling to make out details in the faint light, she spotted a dark iron cuff around her leather boot. The last memory she had from the attack was that old man coming towards her, and then searing agony when he snapped the metal onto her leg. With her fingertips, she probed the cuff and tried to create some illumination to see it better.

Nothing happened. No light.

Her pulse pounding, she tried to summon water.

Nothing happened.

What the fuck? Her abilities were gone... or blocked. Swallowing against the fear, she glared at the metal on her ankle, then wrapped her arms around herself, trembling. Shannon took a few shaky breaths before smoothing them out. Right, time to call in the cavalry.

<Loki?>

No answer to her mental call. Her breath froze.

<Loki!>

Again, no response, and that warm glow of their soulmate bond in her chest was gone. Instead, pain was a vise around her heart, an agonizing emptiness. Clenching and unclenching her hands, she focused on her breathing as a chill rippled down her spine.

Don't panic. Don't. Panic.

It must be the fucking cuff, whatever it was.

But her armour remained in place, covering her to mid-thigh. Shannon had called it up before the cruel bastard put the cuff on her. Quickly, she patted her body down. Damn it. Her throwing knives and sais were gone.

Her hand flew up. She still had the Valkyrie communicator clipped to her ear.

"Kara? Mist?" she murmured.

Dead silence. Shit. Must be out of range.

"Heimdall?"

No rainbow Bifrost lights to swirl her away.

Where was she that neither Heimdall nor Loki could hear her?

Nothing around her gave any solid clues. Despite her pain and the sharp tang of fear saturating the air, she inhaled deeply and exhaled slowly until her pulse didn't thunder in her ears and she'd controlled the trembling in her limbs. She couldn't give in to panic. Not now. Not with her baby to think of.

After a few more measured breaths, she considered what she knew.

Maybe not Earth? From what Queen Frigga had taught her, the Wild Hunt was Unseelie Sidhe, part of Svartalfheim, the Winter Realm of Alfheim, ruled by dark elves. The Sidhe had been banned from Earth in their last war with Asgard so they wouldn't have lingered, risking Asgard's detection and reprisal.

Which meant... she was somewhere on Alfheim, most likely.

Damn, but she wished she'd asked Frigga more questions.

Growing up thinking she was human hampered so much of Shannon's knowledge of the immortal worlds. She pinched the bridge of her nose. It wasn't like she'd known she'd get kidnapped, but still... Ugh, focusing her lessons on Asgard and not the rest of the Nine Realms had clearly been a mistake.

What *did* she know about Alfheim, the home of the elves?

She scrubbed her hand over her face. Very little, unfortunately. Ironic, given she'd probably been born on the dratted planet. Yet she had no memories of her life here. Of course, she didn't. Mom—still weird to think of Rose as her adoptive mother instead of birth mother—said Shannon had been around a year old when given to her. But Shannon's birth parents were most likely here somewhere. If Manannan Mac Lir was to be believed, her father, Dylan, was a light elf from the Summer Realm.

But who was Shannon's mother? An elf for certain, given the Asgardian healers said she was one hundred percent Sidhe, but what kind? Shannon leaned her head back against the cool stone wall behind her, closing her eyes and rubbing at her aching chest.

Manannan warned her about the Unseelie, her Winter Realm relatives on her father's side. If he was right, and Shannon had no reason to doubt him when Loki vouched for the Elven sea god, then she couldn't trust her uncle or paternal grandparents. Even without Manannan's and Loki's warnings, she wouldn't trust the damn Unseelie. They'd fucking kidnapped her.

What did the dark elves want with her?

Manannan had been adamant that Shannon shouldn't let the Unseelie know she was pregnant. Her gaze skittered over her fellow captives. Why? What was the sea god worried about? Had he guessed they'd kidnap her? For what purpose? Her fingers ran through her hair, pushing the long tangled red-brown strands from her face, and drew up her knees to cradle her belly. If only she'd asked more questions.

Unease rippled down her spine. There had to be almost ten women and twice the number of children in this hellish dungeon with her. Why did the Unseelie want pregnant women and children? Slavery? Worse?

In the gloom, her fingertips patted the floor, searching for something, anything useful to pry this damn cuff off her leg. It felt like there was a keyhole in the metal. Gods, if only she was one of those women who wore bobby pins in their hair. With the loss of her knives, Shannon had nothing useful to pick a lock. Her questing hands found dirt, little stones, and absolutely nothing helpful.

Something shifted under her vambrace and she jiggled her wrist. Her charm bracelet slid out from underneath the silver metal. Perhaps one of the charms might be useful? She fingered the platinum set of movie reels with diamonds, the shot glass with a chunk of amber, and the coyote with its glittering emerald eyes until she located the representation of Yggdrasil, the world tree. Could she straighten one of the filigree branches?

Her fingernail scratched the soft metal... shit, of course it was gold. Way too soft to pick a lock.

Raised voices echoed off the stone walls. As they approached, getting louder with each step, she distinguished two separate individuals and made out a few words. At least she retained the ability to understand all languages, even if she couldn't sense her goddess powers.

"I don't care... Crom and... want. They kill... too... a waste. Let them expend... the mortals. I want... immortal... better use..." said the first voice in the harsh cacophony of rock tumbling down a hillside.

Shannon's breath caught, fist clenching. Were they talking about her?

"But... Queen... wants... Didn't Arianrhod say...?" said a second whinier, higher-pitched voice.

Arianrhod! Did she know Shannon was her granddaughter yet? Would she help—

Shannon recalled the sneer on the woman's face when they'd met and Manannan's warning. No, grandmother or not, she couldn't rely on Arianrhod for assistance.

"I don't care who she is. I'm taking her, and you aren't going to squeal. We'll keep her hidden, powering our forges for as long as she lasts," the deeper voice insisted, finally close enough to hear clearly. "They'll never find her."

The metal lock rattled, followed by a scratching.

"Hurry up. Do you know what you are doing?" squeaked the higher voice.

A meaty thud hit the door.

"Shaddup. We have plenty of time still with this masking potion," the deeper voice grumbled as the lock clanged open. Two huge shapes entered. Women whimpered in fear, flinching away.

Not giving in to her racing pulse or the chill washing over her skin, Shannon glared at the hulking forms and grabbed dirt and pebbles in her fists. Powering their forges didn't sound like a long future for her or her child. In the low light, they reminded Shannon of the troll that had snatched her. Huge, with dark grey skin, they had ugly misshapen faces, small beady eyes, and straight dark shaggy hair.

After looking around, they headed right for her. Fuck. Of course, they did.

She kicked at their hands, threw the dirt and pebbles, and desperately tried to fight, despite the throbbing pain and weakness of her limbs. Shannon would not make it easy for these creatures. They slapped at her feet, catching them in their large hands. As she twisted and turned, struggling to free herself from their grasp, they dragged her out of the cell on her back.

Damn it. Without her powers, they were just too strong. While one took her feet, the other picked her up with an arm wrapped under her armpits. Another hand was slapped over her mouth, ignoring her attempts to bite him as they carted her down a tall, wide passage that seemed to be carved from rock, with strata layers visible on the smooth surfaces. It was tall enough that another of the creatures could have stood on the shoulders of the first and still not brushed his head on the ceiling. Bioluminescent vines grew along the ceiling, clinging and providing a greenish-yellow light.

Since her struggles were getting her nowhere, she paid attention to her surroundings. Maybe she'd see something to help her escape. She had to escape. There was no damn way she was dying here.

After several turns and a good thirty minutes of walking through similar smooth-walled tunnels, they came to a vertical shaft that dropped straight down. The creatures didn't even hesitate. Her heart leapt into her throat as they stepped in. Yet they didn't fall. Instead, some kind of invisible air platform held them aloft. They descended what had to be the equivalent of at least two hundred floors before stopping in mid-air to step into another passage. The air was hotter at this level. Shit, she really was being taken to hell.

Again, they walked through tunnel after tunnel for over an hour, making more turns than Shannon could remember before reaching a second vertical shaft. This time, they descended about half the distance, then exited into a rough-hewn corridor with a smooth floor but jagged walls and ceiling—the first she'd seen that resembled the careless craftsmanship of the cell she'd woken in.

A short walk, maybe twenty minutes, and they passed through an archway into a massive cavern. Heat and sulphur filled her lungs, and she coughed against the hand still covering her mouth. Streams of molten lava flowed in channels with graceful stone bridges over them, bathing everything in a red glow. Their pathway crisscrossed with others and eventually reached the far side that held archways at various points.

Passing through one, they entered what appeared to be a suite of rooms and a workshop. Tools lie on bench tops and three forges glowed against one wall. They carried her to an empty black stone wall and dropped her to the floor.

A stab of pain jolted up her spine when she hit the hard surface, and she couldn't hold back her yelp.

Quickly, one of them grabbed Shannon's wrist and attached a cuff that dangled from the wall on a chain. It was connected to some silver-black contraption with dials. A second cuff was snapped around her other wrist. Once he had her secured, he bent to her ankle and removed the iron cuff.

The intense ache in her chest dissipated, but it wasn't entirely gone. Only muted. Instead of the rush of her abilities, only the faintest trickle of power returned. And she still couldn't sense her bond with Loki. Tears pricked at her eyes, but she blinked them back. No, she wasn't willing to give them the satisfaction. Instead, fists clenched and jaw tight, Shannon glared her hatred. These fuckers would regret taking her.

The creature turned some dials and grunted, seemingly pleased, before walking away.

When she stood, she couldn't reach the dials on the wall. Her efforts to summon enough air to lift her barely stirred the air.

Still, maybe it was enough.

<Loki? Loki!> She held her breath, waiting for an answer.

When none came, a tear escaped, and she swiped at it impatiently. With her arms stretched, she tried to reach the nearest benchtop and tools that might help her escape, but she couldn't get within a metre of it. Not even with her boots. Snorting in disgust, she sat on the stone floor with her back against the wall, then watched the two creatures move around the workshop for hours.

They weren't graceful or attractive. Surely, these weren't elves. Were they trolls? Their size and dark grey skin suggested they might be. In the brighter light of the workshop, she was better able to distinguish between them. The one with the higher-pitched voice was shorter and rounder, with its belly protruding over its thick black belt and black pants. It wore a ragged grey tunic with sweat stains under the armpits. The other was less corpulent, but thick muscles stretched its equally tattered garments. A scar bisected one dark eye and carved into its cheek. But it was the constant scowl on its face that sent a shiver down her back.

Still, she could only hold her curiosity back for so long. "Who are you? What are you?" she finally called out.

"Rude! What do you mean, *what* are we?" said the shorter creature. "How can you be an immortal and not know what a dwarf is? Seriously? Are you stupid?"

Dwarves... shit, she was on Nidavellir? Not Alfheim?

But wait—it was the Wild Hunt that captured her.

And these dwarves had discussed the Unseelie.

Was the home of the dwarves beneath the surface of Alfheim? Below the Winter Realm? They hadn't passed through any portals during her descent to this hellishly hot workshop. Fuck a damn duck, it had to be. Why hadn't she known that? She resisted the urge to thump her head back into the wall and drew in another ash-laden breath, keeping her frustration off her face. Gods, what she'd give to be able to ask Frigga questions right now. There needed to be an immortal internet... a freaking google for immortal newbies.

The mean-looking dwarf rolled its eyes and grumbled, "I'm Fjalar and that's Galar."

"No, not stupid, but I am a relatively new immortal." If they underestimated her and thought she was weak, all the better. Maybe they'd be careless if they assumed she was no threat.

"Get used to your new life. You won't be leaving, ever," Fjalar said in a flat tone as he pinned her with a glare.

She ducked her head, hiding her need to glare back. "Why? What do you want with me?" Eels squirmed in her belly as she waited for his answer. Still, better to know. Knowledge was power, and every bit helped with an escape plan.

"Your energy now powers our magic," Fjalar stated with a cruel grin. "Cooperate and your existence will be tolerable."

Galar clapped his thick hands together. "We'll take good care of you, much better than the Winter Court would have. You can have a long life with us. The Unseelie would have expended your life's energy in ritual sacrifice." He snorted as he peered into a noxious mixture, added granules from a tin, then added, "As an immortal, you're worth more than that. You'll continue recharging and supplying energy as long as we keep you alive. It's a waste to kill you with the mortals."

Her chest tightened, nausea rising. Oh gods. All those children. Bastard hadn't even looked at her when dropping that bomb. She gripped the chain in her fists, swallowing down acidic bile. Those women and their babies. She swallowed again. No wonder Manannan and Loki were so worried about the dark elves—sick fuckers.

Still, she played along. "I guess I'm grateful you took me." What could she do? She had to get free to rescue them, to help them. Damn it, she couldn't help anyone chained up here.

Fjalar thumped a jug of water and a mug on the floor beside her. "Help yourself."

She eyed it, swallowing painfully. Between the nausea, the heat, and the harsh fumes, her throat burned. If they really wanted to keep her alive, it should be safe. She poured a glass and drank deep, revelling in the liquid, even if it tasted of lukewarm ash.

"I'll bring you food in a little while," he grumbled. "If you behave, we'll get you a bed."

Wow. A fucking bed. With effort, she kept her sarcasm to herself and stifled her eye roll.

Galar set a chamber pot down with a leer. "I'm sure you'll need that at some point. Wouldn't want you making a mess you'd have to clean up, right?"

Disgusting pig. Despite the bile climbing her throat, Shannon maintained her neutral expression and nodded in agreement. They needed to think she was grateful. The more things they gave her, the more she had to work with to plot her escape.

Chapter 3

FAMILY TIES

When the lights of the Bifrost dissipated around Loki, Thor was waiting, thick arms crossed and a thunderous expression on his square-jawed face. Lightning sparked in his brother's ice-blue eyes and flickered along his silver scale armour to the silver-black metal of Mjolnir, the double-headed war hammer resting on his back. Good. Thor was ready to hunt those fucking elves who'd dared, *dared*, to take Loki's goddess.

Clapping him on the shoulder, Thor said, "We won't rest until we get her back, brother," in a deep rumble rolling across storm-tossed plains.

"No, we won't. Let's talk to our parents before I break Asgard's treaties," Loki snarled. "I'll meet you in the throne room." While he appreciated his brother's support, Loki didn't have the patience to walk. Besides, Thor would get there faster flying, anyway.

As he teleported twice to reach the guarded antechamber that was the closest point to the magically shielded throne room, blackness washed over Loki's vision. Gritting his teeth, he fought to reign in the molten fury blazing through his veins that had his chaos, his black seidhr lashing out. Sweat dampened his brow. The pain of his and Shannon's temporarily severed bond was a knife blade through his soul, eating away at the chains he'd attempted to put on his emotions.

Only temporary. It was only temporary. Just until he got that cursed Dwarven cuff off her.

Fuck. If he wanted his father to set aside the treaty for Shannon, Loki needed to be logical and reasonable in his arguments, not lost to fury and emotion. Even if he craved unleashing his chaos. No... he'd already lost control once. With a snarl of concentration, Loki reinforced the mental block he'd put on the agony, lashing it down and clearing his head.

He took a breath, held it, then blew it out.

Court attire. Right. Even in a crisis, he wasn't exempt from throne room protocol. He scowled at the costume from his film set. Fake body armour and fake throwing knives wouldn't help him get his goddess back, not that he needed anything else with Laevateinn on his back. With a ripple of midnight power, he shed the bright auburn hair, fuller face, and ice-blue eyes of his mortal identity to don his taller, black-haired and green-eyed Asgardian body. After an annoyed twitch of his shoulders, he settled his silver-black liquid-scale armour and black battle leathers onto his body, adding the golden chest plate with the royal crest of Yggdrasil in silver to meet the minimum court requirements.

Thor landed with his usual loud flourish beside Loki. Stealthy, his brother was not. Hand on Loki's shoulder, his sibling gave him a reassuring squeeze. Together, they strode past the guards and into the throne room. Odin and Frigga sat on their thrones. When the brothers reached the base of the stairs, Thor and Loki bowed their heads, waiting for their parents to acknowledge their presence.

"My sons, we will *not* tolerate the kidnapping of our daughter and grandson!" Odin's voice ripped through the silence like a crack of thunder, echoing in the space. His rage was a tangible predator stalking the room. "I have demanded the presence of the Sidhe Ambassador. Ogma will show himself within the day. We will have satisfaction, or it will be war!"

Loki's gut clenched in raw, visceral reaction. His father's tone so echoed Loki's own feelings. The tightness in his chest eased slightly as his father's fury soothed an unspoken need for acceptance and validation. Bor's beard, he'd not been sure if he'd have to fight to convince Odin. In all his childhood lessons, his father had emphasized the importance of peace, of upholding hard-fought-for treaties. Not that they hadn't warred when necessary.

Loki inclined his head in appreciation. "Thank you, Father. I know you don't threaten war lightly." Especially after two wars with the Sidhe and various skirmishes with the Jotuns, Lilu, and Dragar already within Loki's thousand Asgardian years. Yggdrasil's roots, he'd barely gained control of his abilities as a young male of only two hundred before Freya's War pitted Asgard against the elves in the former Asgardian consort's selfish bid for revenge after Odin cast her aside, using Baldur's death as an excuse. Norns knew, she was a piece of work.

The reminder of his older brother further dampened Loki's churning chaos, settling his pulse. Asgard's population had yet to recover from the tragic death toll of those wars, thanks to the low birth rate of immortals. Just being their prince didn't give him the right to spend their lives carelessly. Especially not when he'd already caused Baldur's death.

Calmer now, his mind flew through ramifications, making rapid connections between different bits of information he'd been unable to focus on in his rage. "Kara said it was Crom Cruach and Llew with the Wild Hunt. They must have taken advantage of the thinning of barriers between the realms on Lughnasadh, which means they have likely also been taking advantage on Samhain, Imbolc, and Beltane, as we suspected with Gwydion's and Arianrhod's presence in London around Beltane."

"Once we have Shannon back, we will look into it further. I won't have the elves sneaking to Midgard, perverting the mortals into life force generators again. The Winter Realm can solve their waning energy issues some other way than disgusting ritual sacrifice and torture," Odin growled, his power lashing the air and sparking off the silver-and-gold fixtures and white stone walls.

Loki winced as a potential complication occurred to him. "There is also a family connection that Shannon and I discovered last week while visiting Thor." His gaze met his brother's. "We encountered Manannan Mac Lir while exploring the Great Barrier Reef. He helped us when we ran afoul of a herd of bunyip."

Thor frowned at him. "Why didn't I hear about this?"

"I didn't have a chance to tell you when Amelia wasn't around."

Thor tilted his head in understanding and extended a hand for Loki to continue.

"Shannon's Midgardian mother said her birth father's name was Dylan Connolly. I wasn't familiar with a Sidhe of that name, but Manannan told us that Dylan is a sea god, the Elven God of Selkies. His brother is Llew."

"Her *uncle* kidnapped her?" Frigga exclaimed, green eyes widening, then narrowing as her mouth turned down.

"Yes," Loki confirmed, as disgusted as his mother with that fact.

Odin's eye narrowed with his white eyebrows drawn into a scowl. "Do they know of the family connection, or is it only Shannon and Manannan who are aware?"

Slowly, Loki shook his head. "No, I don't believe they know. Until Manannan told us, I wasn't aware that Arianrhod and Gwydion are Llew's and Dylan's parents and Shannon's paternal grandparents." His lip curled at the unfortunate family connection. Thankfully, his goddess was nothing like them. She had a hard time even telling the white lies all immortals needed to hide their worlds and existence from the Midgardians, let alone committing the treachery of her paternal relations.

Frigga tapped her lips with two fingers as she gazed off in thought. "Arianrhod and Gwydion are Winter Court, although I believe Gwydion plays both sides. As one of their stronger mages, they welcome him to both courts. Llew is also Winter Court. Do we know where Shannon's father's allegiance lies?" Mother asked, meeting Loki's eyes.

Loki waggled his fingers in a teeter-totter of uncertainty. "According to Manannan, Dylan is Summer Court. The sea god actually warned Shannon to avoid her paternal grandparents and uncle in the Winter Court."

Asgardians didn't interact with sea gods with any frequency, it being a rare ability within Aesir or Vanir as only small saltwater seas were present on Asgard and Vanaheim. None of the Elven sea gods had participated in the wars between realms. The infrequent contacts had remained politely cordial, even friendly, across the years. That Manannan was so forthcoming with Shannon, considering her safety even at such a brief acquaintance, reinforced Loki's positive opinion of him.

"Still, it will make it sticky to negotiate if they realize they have a familial claim. They could try to say she isn't a prisoner, but a welcomed member of the family that they have returned home," Odin warned, the lines deepening in his forehead and around his mouth.

"Given that her father is Seelie, I believe we would have the support of the Summer Court in that argument. The light elves don't have any great love for the dark elves, especially after so many Sidhe lives were lost in the last war against us," Frigga mused, rising to pace with her hands clasped behind her. "Although it really depends on who her mother is. Do we have any idea?"

"No," Loki answered with a wince. Damn. Why hadn't he thought to ask if Dylan had any known matings? "We never asked Manannan if he knew, or if Dylan has a consort. The sea god did offer aid to Shannon if she ever needed it."

"Wait and see how our meeting with Ambassador Ogma goes." Odin's fingers drummed the arm of his throne. "Since Manannan has taken a liking to Shannon, I may send you to speak with him and enlist his aid. It bodes well for him helping to retrieve her. Unlike us, he can move through all the realms of Alfheim relatively unimpeded."

"How soon is the Ambassador expected?" Thor asked from where he leaned against a gleaming white pillar.

"I haven't had a reply yet, nor has Heimdall spotted him in the few areas of Alfheim that aren't shrouded by those benighted mists. I sent Sigrdrífa and Thjalfi to escort Ogma here. They are waiting on Alfheim's treaty plains," Odin replied.

The distraction of planning waned. Restless energy surged through Loki's limbs. Constantly stilling his les, not fidgeting with his clothes, tugging at his hair, or keeping himself from pacing along with his mother, was wearing on him. He couldn't get rid of the excess energy welling from the soul-deep instinctual demand to do something. Anything. Bor's beard. At a minimum, he needed to move.

"In the meantime, I'd like to check on Kara and Mist. Kara took it very hard that Shannon was kidnapped under her watch," Loki said.

Frigga met his gaze, her sympathetic eyes flicking over his face. "Yes, it would have taken more than Kara, Mist, and Shannon to counter the full force of the Wild Hunt, despite how well-trained and fierce our Valkyrie are." She flicked her fingers with a small smile. "Go reassure Shannon's friends that they will get the chance to help get her back."

Odin nodded and also waved a hand to dismiss him.

With a bow, Loki left the throne room to head down the two flights of stairs and long hallway to the healers' wing. Upon entering the archway, he sought the green-robed form of the palace's Masterhealer, Healer Moja.

"Prince Loki," the diminutive woman called. Turning, he found Moja at the entrance to a treatment room off to his right. "Are you looking for Kara and Mist?"

"Yes, Healer."

"In here." She waved him over, and Loki followed her inside.

Mist was awake and sitting in a chair—no sign of the head injury as even her blue braids were clean of blood—but Kara was on a treatment bed, unconscious, as another healer worked at rebuilding the muscle of the Valkyrie's thigh by manipulating the multi-armed tissue generators that laid strand-by-strand of muscle fibre, blood vessels, and nerves in the gaping thirty-centimetre wound held in a green stasis field. His fists clenched. She'd recover fully, thank the Norns, but those fuckers would pay.

Mist jumped to her feet, long braids swinging when she spotted him. "Did you get Shannon back?" she asked, hope in her wide, tri-coloured blue eyes.

"No. We are waiting for the Sidhe Ambassador to arrive. The All-Father is furious and has given them a day before we invade to take her by force," Loki said, controlling his voice and stilling the growl that wanted to erupt. The Healer Hall was not a place for fury when they manipulated delicate energies. No way would he set back Kara's healing.

"Good! I'm ready to go. They healed my concussion and the few scrapes and bruises I had. Kara is much worse off. Those damn hellhounds took quite a chunk out of her. Almost to the bone." Mist shuddered and scowled.

Healer Moja snorted, crossed her arms, and raised a brown brow. "Mist, I wouldn't call a fractured skull, three cracked ribs, a broken collarbone and ulna, and multiple stab wounds *nothing*. You were a bit of a mess yourself."

Mist shrugged with a toss of her braids and grinned at Loki. He couldn't help but smile back. Their Valkyrie were fierce indeed, and Shannon's friends had fought overwhelming odds. Frankly, it was astounding they were still alive. The Wild Hunt was vicious, comprised of any combination of hellhounds, trolls, redcaps, banshees, dullahan, kelpies, and other creatures, depending on what the hunt leader called to him. Loki would have hated to rescue Shannon, only to tell her that her friends had died trying to prevent her kidnapping.

Loki turned to Healer Moja. "How long will it take before Kara is back on her feet?"

"At least a day. I'd like two, but I don't know if I can keep her down that long. As you see, we are literally rebuilding her leg, but the Valkyrie are nothing if not stubborn."

"Thank you, Healer Moja. I promised Kara could come when we get Shannon back."

She placed a hand on his shoulder, kind brown eyes rising to meet his gaze. "If you need a healer along, I'll come. I'm worried about Shannon and the baby, given the notorious rough handling of the Unseelie."

Loki was surprised, but he shouldn't have been. In her two short months here—in truth, barely more than six weeks—Shannon had won over the hearts and minds of their people. That the Masterhealer would risk herself when she'd never left Asgard before brought a lump to his throat. He patted Moja's hand. "Thank you. We appreciate the offer. I will let you know." His voice came out ragged and hoarse.

Mist stood and hugged him tightly when Healer Moja stepped away. Unexpected, but Loki hugged her back gratefully. "We will get her back, Loki. No other outcome is possible!" she said, her tone fierce with determination.

"Yes, yes we will. Even if we have to burn all of Alfheim to the ground to find her," he vowed.

Chapter 4

AMBASSADOR OGMA

Mother's tall, elegant form appeared in the healing room. "We've received word Ambassador Ogma is on his way. Come back to the throne room, son."

Loki's fists clenched, and his pulse leapt. Finally. He nodded as her projection dissipated. "Come with me, Mist. We may want your eyewitness account when we speak to Ogma."

"Of course, my prince. Anything I can do. Absolutely anything," she offered as she accompanied him out of the room.

He glanced sideways, taking in the stubborn set to the petite Valkyrie's usually mobile and laughing face. "You know I may need to access your mind?" The same diminutive height as his consort—both women barely reaching the middle of his chest—she'd demonstrated her loyalty in numerous ways over the weeks since she'd befriended Shannon, taking his soulmate under her wing, training her in hand-to-hand combat, and aiding Shannon's adjustment to life on Asgard. He was loath to hurt the Valkyrie, even unintentionally.

Mist didn't flinch, but her jaw tightened. "As I said, absolutely anything, Loki. A bit of discomfort as you project my memories is a tiny price for getting Shannon back," she replied, fierceness in her tone.

They hurried up the sets of carved granite stairs and through the gleaming white stone halls until they reached the throne room. Additional guards in their golden armour with Yggdrasil emblazoned on their chest plates had been stationed along the marble-and-gold-veined walls in anticipation of the presence of the Sidhe ambassador.

On their golden thrones, Odin and Frigga represented balance—Odin, the All-Father, in his black leather overlaid with golden-hued liquid scale armour, his golden eye patch, and snow-white braided beard and hair representing Asgard's military and technological prowess while Frigga, the All-Mother, in her silver-and-emerald gown, high ponytail of sleek ebony hair, and green eyes that missed nothing representing Asgard's fairness, families, and interconnectedness with the natural world. Together, they never failed to take advantage of an opportunity to emphasize Asgard's multiple strengths to political visitors from other realms.

As his mother had said numerous times during his childhood, nothing was fiercer and more motivated than a mother protecting her children... and all of Asgard belonged to her. While many feared Odin's wrath and obvious power, only a fool would underestimate Frigga's. She smiled as she destroyed Asgard's enemies with a stealthy intelligence, and they thanked her, not realizing they were already dead. Loki rolled his shoulders and blew out a breath. His mother loved Shannon. There was nothing she wouldn't do to help him get his soulmate back. She'd help him plan when emotion clouded his thinking.

Reminded of his family's support, the tightness in his lungs eased slightly as he joined Thor at the steps at the base of the thrones, then bowed, with Mist following suit. At Odin's gesture, they stood to the side so they would surround the ambassador when he arrived. That fucker wasn't getting out of this room without giving them answers.

"Mist has agreed to allow me to project her memories of the event so the ambassador can't deny the presence of The Wild Hunt, Crom Cruach, and Llew," Loki announced, attempting to control the fury surging through his veins as he said their names. Bor's beard, he wanted to grab the bloody ambassador by the throat and squeeze until the sly politician returned Shannon—the first, but certainly not the last, to pay for her kidnapping.

"Is this true, Mist?" asked Odin, his single ice-blue eye unblinking.

With a quick jerk of her head, she replied, "Yes, All-Father. Anything to help Princess Shannon."

Frigga gave her a gentle smile. "Thank you, Mist. I'm aware it is an uncomfortable invasion."

Mist inclined her head and glanced at Loki, meeting his eyes briefly before the doors opening behind them drew his attention.

Sigrdrífa and Thjalfi entered, leading a squad of six palace guards surrounding the tall, lean, golden-haired Elven ambassador. Approaching the steps to the throne, they bowed to Odin and Frigga, then stepped to the side.

As Ambassador Ogma strode forward with a polite smile and bowed, waiting to be acknowledged, Loki fought to keep the sneer off his face. How dare that bastard smile at them?

"Ambassador Ogma, we have called you to Asgard to answer for the kidnapping of our daughter, Princess Shannon, consort of Prince Loki." Odin's voice was a threatening rumble, his fury filling the space with dangerous potential.

Ogma's eyes widened. "King Odin, All-Father. I bring greetings from the Sidhe and congratulations to Prince Loki on his mating." His gaze darted to meet Loki's, who glared back at him before the ambassador returned his attention to Odin. "I am appalled to hear his consort has gone missing. However, I am at a loss why you think the Sidhe would have knowledge of your daughter?" The smarmy politician's answer was careful, with his grating voice measured and polite in the face of Odin's anger.

Loki's fists clenched, heartbeat increasing as he gritted his teeth. Yggdrasil's roots, never mind throttling the fucker—Loki wanted to tear the lying elf's head from his neck in an explosion of visceral bloody rage. How dare he act as if he didn't already know?

"Valkyrie Mist was with Princess Shannon when she was taken. Prince Loki will project her memory of the events that took place on Midgard, near the town of Keswick and the Castlerigg stone circle in the United Kingdom," Odin stated, growling as he pinned Ogma with his gaze.

Ambassador Ogma frowned but inclined his head in agreement.

Loki fought back his snort. As if the bastard had a choice. Still, Loki flexed his hands a couple of times and took a couple of breaths to rein in the churning chaos within him. There was too much at stake. He couldn't lose control. Not now. Not when he was going to see—

He shut that thought down. He couldn't think of it. Not if he was going to do this. And by all the Nine Realms, he was damn well going to do this.

He stepped closer to Mist. With a final harsh exhale, he placed one hand on her forehead and held his other out to the empty space between where the Ambassador stood on the stone floor tiles that depicted the World Tree, Yggdrasil, and the Nine Realms, and the start of the stairs leading to Odin and Frigga.

"This will hurt less if you bring up the memory so I don't have to search your mind for it," Loki told Mist quietly as he met her nervous gaze. She was several hundred years younger than him, and he'd never had the occasion to need to speak telepathically or obtain a memory from her after a mission. While he'd known of her abilities, as he did all the Einherjar and Valkyrie—a prince of Asgard needed to know the assets under his command, after all—they'd never fought together during the last war or in sparring sessions. It was only Shannon's training and friendship with her that had really brought Mist into his personal orbit.

Chewing her lip, she nodded, and Loki delved into her mind, allowing the imagery to flow through him as he projected it for all to see.

He watched as the SUV was driven into a ditch and Shannon yanked from the vehicle by the massive grey form of a river troll. Mist lost sight of Shannon briefly while the Valkyrie crawled out between the seats, then saw Shannon bravely trying to battle the troll as it held her off the ground, shaking her like a child with a doll. Long red-brown hair flew as the storm-driven rain soaked it into ropey lengths that whipped about her silver-blue armour-clad body, emphasizing the troll's violent movements.

It took every iota of Loki's strength and rigid willpower to continue to project the image. Rage howled within him like Jotunheim's dire wolves. At least Shannon had managed to call her battle leathers and her armour, protecting her torso and their child from Unseelie weapons and their foul creatures' teeth and claws. If only he'd—

With clenched teeth and straining muscles, Loki remained in place and forced the thought away. He had to stay in control to do this, to protect Mist as he projected her memories.

Tears poured down Mist's face as she continued to remember. The Valkyrie was driven away from Shannon by a pair of bloody redcaps swinging their pikestaves and grinning maniacally. Watery blood spattered Mist as she fought, getting in her mouth and obscuring her vision. Headless dullahan galloped on their black horses. She ducked as their gruesome spinal column whips lashed the air, then rolled to escape their rearing demon stallions. Powerful hooves kicked at her short swords, the impacts reverberating up her arms as she regained her feet.

Kara emerged from the car and was set upon first by a dullahan, then a trio of spectral Cŵn Annwn white hellhounds. Additional dullahan galloped around them, striking both Valkyrie with their sharp-edged whips.

Mist told Shannon to use sunlight and saw the troll shake Shannon violently at the first glimmer of light. Her cries of pain as her head was whipped to and fro had helpless agony spearing Loki's heart. Ragged breaths sawed in and out of his lungs as black rage darkened his vision. If he could explode the troll from here, he would have. Obsidian seidhr trickled from him, and he fought his chaos back under control.

In the remembered memory, Mist took down a redcap, lopping off its head with its bulging red eyes and fangs. The crack of a bone whip lashed her neck. A large white stag with flaming eyes, the favourite animal form of Llew, appeared out of the sheets of rain. Shaggy Cŵn Cyrff, the black hellhounds, stood on either side of him, snarling and baring massive bloody jaws.

The skeletal figure of Crom Cruach on his nuckalavee mount, a black demonic stallion comprised of raw flesh with glowing red eyes and exhaling toxic gases, pulled to a stop beside Llew. Behind them, numerous trolls and dullahan carried captive women and kids.

At the sight of Llew and Crom, Mist fought even harder to reach Shannon, unable to get past the redcaps when three more of the fierce goblin-like creatures joined the battle against her. She took a blow to the head when two dullahan whips yanked her off balance, knocking her to the ground. As she fended off the pikestaves pummelling her, she caught glimpses of Crom approaching Shannon with a black Dwarven cuff.

Shannon screamed, then went limp, sagging in the troll's massive grip like a wilted flower. The beast gave her one more shake, sniffed her, then tossed her over its shoulder.

Loki bit the inside of his cheek hard, the pain helping him retain enough control to continue to project Mist's memories as the copper taste of blood filled his mouth. Chaos burned in his veins. They would pay. As soon as he had his beloved consort back, they would all pay.

With ominous howls from the black hellhounds, Llew led the Wild Hunt into the nearby stone circle. Frantically, Mist fought to rise and reach Shannon, as Kara was taken down by the pack of snarling white hellhounds. Her last memory was the cruel smile on Crom's face as the troll carrying Shannon disappeared through the cloaking mists into a shimmering blue portal held open in the stone circle.

Mist continued to cry silent tears as Loki ended the projection and withdrew from her mind.

His brother put his hand on Loki's back as Loki battled to control his surging rage now that he wasn't using his magic. His lungs heaved, nostrils flaring as he clenched and unclenched his fists, black swirls of energy flowing around them. Shudders racked his spine. As fast as he chained his energies down, chaos broke it wide open again, fed from the blackest depths of churning agony within his soul. Dead. He wanted every last fucking Unseelie *dead*. Destroyed. Obliterated.

"Tell us again, *Ambassador*, that the Sidhe have *no knowledge of my daughter!*" roared Odin, shaking the throne room with the wave of his power. Explosions of light burst like firecrackers throughout the room, blinding with their intensity.

Ambassador Ogma appeared shocked and pale, his usual eloquence missing. He swallowed, an audible gulp, then pleaded, "All-Father, the Seelie, the light elves of the Summer Realm, have no need for such barbaric practices. I am appalled and disgusted at this breach of treaty and kidnapping of your daughter by our dark brethren, the Unseelie of the Winter Realm. Give me leave to rectify this immediately."

"You have twenty-four hours to bring my daughter back, unharmed, or it will be war between us," Odin demanded. "Sigrdrífa and Thjalfi, escort the ambassador back to Alfheim and wait there for either the return of our princess or for our legions to join you."

With a deep bow, the ambassador backed away from the steps, then followed the two warriors out of the throne room, still surrounded by the squad of six guards.

Once they were well out of earshot, Loki couldn't contain his rage and pain any longer. A soul-deep scream roared from his throat, and a burst of telekinesis hit everyone around him as he fell to his knees.

In a fog of misery, Loki heard Odin clear the throne room of guards, and his father's black boots appeared in front of him. A hand clasped Loki's shoulder tightly, energy pouring into him.

"My son, I'm so sorry. We will get Shannon back, I swear to you. I'm incredibly proud of how you handled yourself. To have held your control to show Mist's memories like that. If it had been your mother that was taken, I don't know that I could have managed it."

Loki sensed his father attempting to take some of his pain and anguish, returning strength to him, and Loki gazed up at him through blurred, tear-covered vision.

"I swear, Loki. We will get her back," Odin reassured Loki, no other possibility allowed in the All-Father's expression.

"Thank you, Father," Loki choked out, grateful for his unwavering support.

"I noticed Shannon did not appear pregnant in Mist's memory, and you did not mention our grandson," Frigga commented, holding out her hands to coax Loki back to his feet.

"Shannon was wearing a ring I'd made her to provide visual illusions, allowing her to hide her pregnancy while on Midgard. It won't hold up to physical touch, though," Loki said, choking on his words. *Norns, please protect her until I can save her.* He had to save her. Had to save his son. Any other possibility... no, he couldn't lose them. He couldn't.

"Shannon kept the spell activated throughout our girls' weekend since Elise didn't know about the pregnancy," Mist confirmed.

"Would the Dvergr cuff deactivate the spell?" Thor asked.

"No, Dwarven iron can't take magic away. Instead, it prevents Shannon from accessing the energy. That includes the soulmate bond, which is why both of you feel the pain of being cut off. Any spells that were active will remain active, such as the illusion and her armour," Frigga confirmed.

Loki exhaled, a tiny frisson of relief that Shannon had called her armour before that cursed cuff had been put on her, armour he'd had a hand in advancing since the last war with the Sidhe. Those fucking Unseelie would find it impossible to get through unless they had Helheim-runed blades—an exceptionally rare and difficult weapon to forge, with only a few weaponsmiths capable of the feat across the Nine Realms.

Still, the armour didn't cover her whole body. It could, but she hadn't practiced envisioning it as a full-body suit. Instead, the way she'd called it protected the most vulnerable parts of her upper arms, torso, and down to her hips. Vambraces covered her forearms and leather covered her legs to her boots. Why hadn't he taught her to cover her entire body? Bor's beard, he was such a fool.

"So they may not know she is pregnant, which is why I didn't mention our grandson. I won't give them any further information or weaknesses to use against her, if they don't know already," Odin explained.

Frigga nodded. "Wise choice."

"Thor," Odin continued, "prepare the Einherjar and Valkyrie for war."

Chapter 5

UNFORESEEN CONSEQUENCES

From his throne of interwoven, black branches in the heart of the Winter Realm, King Cernunnos of the Unseelie elves asked, "Successful hunt?"

The huge white stag with flaming eyes snorted, before a rolling silver wave revealed a tall, slender snow-pale elf with long dark hair, dressed in black boots, black leather pants, silver tunic and silver cape. Llew bowed in a graceful, outstretched sweep of his arms. "Extremely, my king. More than enough to get us through until Samhain's hunt."

"How did my babies do?" Cailleach asked, as the ancient hag lavished attention on the large black or white hellhounds that pushed and shoved to get close to her at the edges of the inner court glade.

Llew smirked. "They were very effective. Even took a decent bite out of a Valkyrie."

"That's not amusing, Llew," snapped Queen Mene, ascending the dais in a swirling mist of black feathers to join her husband. After sitting on her throne, her long blood-red nails tapped on the black wood with her crimson lips pressed into a tight line.

"It wasn't meant to be," Llew snarled, his green eyes narrowed as he met her glare. "We encountered a couple of Valkyries and an immortal Crom decided to take. They were literally metres outside the circle, travelling in one of those metal death traps the mortals are so fond of these days. We couldn't have avoided them, and I have no idea how they happened to be there at the exact right time."

"What idiocy has Crom Cruach done this time? I'm fed up with his poor choices." Cernunnos banged a fist on the arm of his throne. "Drawing Asgard's attention to us is foolish. What was so special about that one immortal that he'd risk the entire Winter Realm to take her? He could have kept the Hunt cloaked in mist until you'd retreated through, even with the Asgardians so close."

"I don't know, but Arianrhod recognized her when she was brought in. The female is Elven and was with Asgard's princes when she and Gwydion encountered them on Litauī last month during Beltane," Mene hissed, a red flush rising on her silver cheeks.

Cernunnos' eyes widened as he met Mene's furious expression. Opening his mouth, he started to speak, then stopped, a frown creasing his forehead as a disturbance back near the glade's entrance drew his attention.

Wind and fog whipped around Crom's skeletal form in a swirling tempest as the wizened elf elbowed his way past courtiers to face the king and queen on their dark thrones.

"*Who* took my prize? She was *mine*!" Crom's ancient face twisted to match the snarl in his voice as spit coated his scraggly white beard.

"Good of you to join us, Crom Cruach," drawled King Cernunnos, narrowing his eyes. "We were just discussing you. Why have you drawn Odin's eye over a single immortal?"

Crom drew up short, a frown deepening the wrinkles of his pale forehead. "Oh, come on. It's not that bad." He waved a dismissive, bony hand. "The Asgardians won't care if a couple of Valkyrie get hurt and they lose one woman. She can't be that important. They'll threaten and bluster, but Odin will back down. He doesn't want another war that will cost the lives of his people. Especially not over some temporary sheet-warmer."

A tall golden-haired elf in a sleek sky-blue gown slit up to upper thigh entered from the back of the glade, swayed seductively through the courtiers, stepped to the side of the king's throne, and raised a golden eyebrow. "As if *you* know what Odin would or wouldn't do. Without knowing who this woman is and why she was with the princes, you have no idea." Freya placed a well-manicured hand on Cernunnos' shoulder. "If you draw my brother into another bloody conflict with my ex-husband, I might just help Odin and kill you myself."

"Thank you for your support, sister," Cernunnos said, patting her hand. "Let's sit and devise a strategy to deal with Asgard if they come looking for the woman."

A tall, lean blond-haired elf in an emerald tunic over white pants with an emerald cape trimmed in snow rabbit's fur thrown over one shoulder pushed through the courtiers to reach the throne. "I'm afraid it's already too late. Asgard just gave our ambassador an ultimatum."

"Danu's tits." Cernunnos glared at Crom, then waved an elegant, long-fingered hand at the newcomer. "What news do you bring, Gwydion?"

Gwydion turned, his green eyes narrowed as he sneered at Crom. "You took Loki's consort, you senile old fool! If you weren't ruled by your cursed cock, you wouldn't have put us in this position. Odin has given us twenty-four hours to return her, or they are declaring war. Ogma saw the entire attack through the memory of a Valkyrie. The Summer Court has already washed their hands of this. They will not aid us. We'll face the might of Asgard alone."

Crom staggered, eyes widening and face blanching.

Queen Mene rose from her throne, her steps ominously graceful as she strolled to stand in front of Crom. "As much as it pains me, since I know it will hurt my sister, we have no choice but to appease Asgard. As you've noticed, the moon-cursed woman is now missing."

In a blur of motion, her hand cracked across Crom's face, the force knocking him to the hard slate-covered ground of the inner court. When he raised his head, four bleeding gashes marked him from ear to mouth.

"Lock him up," she snarled to the guards. "If we can't find the woman, we'll have to give them Llew and Crom."

"*No!* Sister! Don't do this!"

Mene looked away from Crom to see her twin, Badb, pushing her way through the gawking courtiers.

"Please, sister. Give them Crom, but not my husband," pleaded Badb as she reached out a hand to kneel in front of Mene. "Please! Don't give them Llew!"

Mene looked down at the dark-haired beauty in front of her and shook her head slowly. "I'm sorry. I'm so sorry Badb, but we can't go to war with Asgard.

Without the support of our Summer Court cousins, we don't stand a chance. Odin has proof Llew and Crom led the Wild Hunt."

Another elf, her black hair pooling on the flagstone floor as she knelt to put an arm around Badb, tried to comfort her. "We'll ask Cailleach to use her hounds to search for the woman."

Cailleach met Mene's gaze, then nodded and ushered her hellhounds into the surrounding forest.

Tears streamed down Badb's face as she sobbed, one fist pounding the unyielding slate. "It's *not enough*, Nemain. It's not enough. I can't lose Llew. Not after losing our sons to those *butchering* Asgardians. I can't lose Llew, too. I can't."

"Don't worry. I have an idea. Help me take her to my chambers," Mene told Nemain. They each put an arm around Badb, drawing her to her feet. Together, they led her away through an archway in the trees.

Chapter 6

BLOOD MEAD

Although it was some hours later, the dwarves kept their word and brought Shannon a bowl of stew. She didn't recognize what was in it, but she was hungry enough to not be picky—despite the alarming red colour, chunks of unknown meat, and what she took to be vegetables.

She scooped up the last spoonful and held out her bowl. "Could I have more?" Weird or not, food was fuel, after all.

"More? Where do you put it? You are skinny and half the size of us!" Galar complained, even as he refilled her bowl and returned with another jaw-breaking biscuit.

Skinny? Frowning, she took the bowl and biscuit from him as she eyed the pronounced curve of her belly. Mid-bite, her heart skipped a beat when realization struck. The illusion hiding her pregnancy still worked! They couldn't see her baby.

She fought back the need to rest a hand on her abdomen and instead, finished chewing and swallowed. Tightness constricted her throat—the food a hard lump that almost didn't go down. How long would the illusion last if she couldn't renew it? It must be starting to fade if she could see the swell of her abdomen. She drank her ash-tasting water, fingers trembling.

Energy. She stared down at the biscuit and stew. Food and rest, that was what she needed. Any energy she got, she'd put into the illusion to hide her son.

After dunking the biscuit to make it easier to chew, she ate in small, quick bites, despite the anxiety churning in her belly. She had to protect her child.

"Well, for a small thing, she is putting out twice the life force energy I would have expected," Fjalar said with a glance at some dials on an intricate set of glass piping flowing into various jars on the closest workbench. "Definitely worth the extra food she consumes."

Galar grunted. "Good investment. Get her a bed, then?"

Fjalar nodded, and Galar left the workshop.

"With you putting out so much energy, we don't need to draw quite as much." Fjalar stepped over to the wall beside her and turned a dial on the device attached to Shannon's chains. "No need to waste, after all."

A little more power returned to her, and the ache in her joints lessened. Oh, thank gods. Immediately, she sent energy to the ring Loki had given her, strengthening the illusion hiding her son until she no longer saw her rounded belly. Her shoulders slumped, breath whooshing out. At least her son was safe, was hidden.

"Hmm... that gives me an idea though." Fjalar walked to a workbench that held chemistry apparatus, several large cauldrons, and casks with cork stoppers. After picking up a large silver-black tankard and dagger, he returned.

"I've been wanting to try this since a Jotun visitor told me about the possibility a century ago, but I haven't had a strong immortal to try it on." Before she could react, he grabbed her arm and slashed the unprotected part of her forearm above her armoured vambrace.

"Hey!" Shannon jerked at the stinging pain, but couldn't free herself from his thick calloused fingers. "That hurt!" He held her arm over the empty tankard, catching the streaming blood. "What are you doing?" Fuck. She should have covered her entire arm with her scaled armour. Too late now unless she could save a bit more energy.

"Supposedly, it's possible to harvest your powers. I want to test the theory. Don't worry. I want to keep you alive so I won't take *that* much."

Damn bastard. She banged his hand with her other fist, trying to tug her arm free.

"Stop struggling, girl." He slashed her arm again, and she yelped. "It's not that bad," he scoffed as he continued to fill the tankard with her blood.

Shannon grew dizzy, and her gaze started to lose focus, darkening at the edges. "I'm not that big! I don't have that much." The tankard had to hold at least two litres and was already three-quarters full. Fucking leech.

"All right, all right. I'm done. Bandage it up." He threw a dirty cloth at her. "You're immortal. You'll heal soon enough."

Although she'd yanked her arm away, she struggled to catch the rag, misjudging its trajectory. Her head spun as if she'd downed five shots of tequila. It fell to the floor, and she leaned over to get it. Weakness plagued her. Finally snagging it, she eyed the stains and smears of unknown chemicals. Damn it, the fucking thing was as likely to give her an infection or some weird rash as stop her from bleeding. Still, she wrapped the cleanest part over her wounds and awkwardly tied it with her teeth. When it soaked through right away, she re-tied it tighter. Worn out by her efforts, she leaned against the stone wall and closed her eyes.

"Get up, girl." Galar kicked her in the leg, jolting her awake and adding to the ache in her limbs.

He'd returned with a small twin-sized bed in a metal frame. Clumsily, she struggled to her feet by bracing against the wall.

After shoving her over as far as the chains would allow, he dropped the bed and pushed it into the corner. With an ungainly flop, Shannon fell onto the mattress, then dragged herself to the far side and leaned against the wall. Although the bed wasn't the softest, it was a definite improvement over the hot stone floor.

Fjalar returned from one of the adjoining rooms with an armload of blankets and pillows and dumped them on the bed.

"Thank you," she mumbled as she made a nest of the blankets and pillows. Despite the earlier nap, exhaustion dragged at her, like a weight pulling her into the depths. But whether it was from the blood loss, the stress of the situation, being pregnant, or the energy they were draining, she wasn't sure. Maybe a combination of all of them. Barely able to keep her eyes open, Shannon tried to watch what Fjalar was doing with her blood. Why would he mix it with honey?

Shouting from one of the adjoining rooms off the main workshop woke her.

"They are looking for her!" Something slammed. A door?

"What? Why would they care about one girl amongst all the captives they took?"

A hollow thump, like a fist hitting a wooden stool, echoed. "Asgard is threatening war. She's Loki's mate!"

"Bah! All talk. Odin wouldn't go to war over Loki's mate. He doesn't even like Loki that much. I'd be more worried if she belonged to Thor."

"I'm telling you, that elf I sold the potion to said the Summer Court is willing to go to war with the Winter Court to prevent Asgard from invading Alfheim."

"What do we care? They are always fighting. Foolish elves. It doesn't affect us here. Our kings will keep Nidavellir out of it, like they did the last two wars." A dull thump pounded. "Besides, do you know how many dwarves hate Loki? The sons of Ivaldi would love to get revenge after he tricked them."

Galar's tone was less panicked, losing its strident note. "Still, Loki has friends. The builders' guild would turn us over in a heartbeat."

A loud bang echoed and crashed, like metal thrown to the stone floor. "So we make sure they don't find out. We weren't going to parade her around, anyway."

"This is dangerous, Fjalar. I don't like it."

"Shut up. Stop worrying so much. It's going to be fine. We can always sell her to Hreidmar if it looks too risky to keep her. You know he'd buy her to get revenge for the death of his son. He's crazy enough to take on Asgard, and since his brother, Fafnir, can turn into a dragon, they are damn tough dwarves. I wouldn't want to pick a fight with that family." Fjalar laughed and another loud crash sounded, followed by a whoosh. "Remember that idea Suttung told us about? Try this mead I made."

"By the first forge! Did you just shoot fire from your hands? That's incredible! It actually works! I thought that giant was full of spent coal. Give me some!"

"Easy now. We can't take too much of her blood at a time. This has to last us for a while. Only a shot."

As their voices calmed, Shannon couldn't make out as many words. Closing her eyes, she almost smiled at hearing Asgard was coming for her. She knew Loki would move heaven and earth to find her, but hearing Odin's threat of war sparked a warm glow in her chest. It meant Loki had the full support of the All-Father. She just had to hold out until she could escape, or they found her.

Damn it, she had to get out of these chains.

Opening her eyes, she tried to spot anything she could use that might be left within reach. Her ceramic spoon and bowl were no help. Maybe if they gave her a fork in the future, she could bend a tine. Since she was alone, she got off the bed and checked the metal frame for any removable screws or parts thin enough to fit the keyholes in the cuffs. The underside of the bed had metal bars to hold the mattress in place but they were welded to the frame. Crap. There was nothing remotely useful.

Lethargic, Shannon sat back on the bed. Her limbs were leaden weights. Was gravity different on this planet? Or was she just that exhausted? Again, she sent every bit of magic she had into the ring to reinforce the illusion spell. Not much, barely a trickle, but her curved belly hadn't reappeared, so it worked.

Even though she couldn't see her son, he squirmed and flipped around. She tried to send reassuring thoughts to him as she rubbed where he kicked. <*Daddy is coming for us, son. We just have to hold on and escape. He'll find us if we don't find him first.*>

Chapter 7

PRISONERS

Loki dragged his hand through his shoulder-length hair as he paced the stables. Bor's balls, surely it couldn't be much longer? His stallion, Hulda, was saddled and ready, but Loki had too much energy to sit. Not when they might get Odin's approval to invade at any moment. Thor was outside on his stallion, Magni, talking to the Valkyrie with their winged steeds. His brother would tell him when it was time to leave.

They'd given the Sidhe their day to get Shannon back. The bloody elves were giving excuses. Yeah, Loki was fucking done with excuses and done with waiting. By Yggdrasil's gnarliest knotted bark, he wanted Shannon back *now*. Politics be damned. His fists clenched. If he had to kill every single one of them himself, he'd get Shannon back. Losing her the way he'd lost Sigyn was *not* an option.

Kara entered the stables, the hitch in her stride only given away by the extra wobble of her red curls piled into a top ponytail. She wasn't willing to wait the extra day the healers wanted, but Loki wouldn't order her to stay behind. As the Goddess of The Hunt and Battle Strategy, she was a formidable warrior, even with a limp. Besides, her loyalty to Shannon meant she'd simply follow if he tried to forbid her. Loki wouldn't deny her this.

"We are ready, my prince. The All-Father has given Thor the go-ahead to proceed," she called out.

"Finally!" Loki leapt up on Hulda and followed Kara out of the stable. She mounted her flying horse, a palomino she'd named Sigrun.

"To the Bifrost!" boomed Thor, pointing Mjolnir towards the rainbow bridge.

They rode swiftly across, several legions of Einherjar following behind, with the Valkyrie in the air above.

When Heimdall activated a wide beam of the Bifrost, the swirling light swept them to Alfheim. The Asgardians appeared on the treaty plains that bordered the land between the eternally bright Summer Realm and the dark, gloomy Winter Realm. The angle and odd perpendicular spin of the planet meant only one side ever fully faced the star that provided its light to Alfheim, although the three moons continually reflected a small amount onto the Winter Realm.

Sigrdrífa and Thjalfi met them with the message that representatives of both Sidhe courts were on their way.

Ambassador Ogma appeared first out of the mists from the Summer Realm.

After approaching Thor and Loki astride their steeds, Ogma bowed deeply. "Prince Thor, Prince Loki, King Nuada and Queen Aine of the Seelie Summer Realm bid you welcome. With the assistance and agreement of King Cernunnos and Queen Mene of the Unseelie Winter Realm, they have captured Llew and Crom and will turn the oath-breakers over to you for Asgardian justice."

Loki shifted in his seat, his hands tightening on the reins. What the fuck did he care about the cursed prisoners? They weren't his damned priority, other than they needed to fucking die. "*Where* is Princess Shannon?" he ground out, unable to keep the violence from his tone.

The ambassador hesitated, swallowed, and then blurted. "Although there were several witnesses who agree Princess Shannon was brought to the Winter Realm, she seems to have gone missing. Despite sending out search parties, they can't find her. It is possible she escaped, but no one has yet been able to locate her."

"You *LOST* my consort?" Loki's rage caused Hulda to rear, his hooves flashing with lethal intent.

The ambassador paled, stumbling out of the way.

"Did you send out the hellhounds of The Wild Hunt to track her?" Thor's tone was an ominous rumble. Lightning crackled in the sky above, but he kept his temper in check.

Ogma swallowed audibly. "Yes, Prince Thor. We were unable to find her. They go to the chamber where she was held, but can find no trace of her beyond that. I, myself, have observed the hounds' difficulty."

Un-fucking-believable. "The Norns curse you all! I want to see for myself!" Loki roared. Liar. Fucking liar. No way did they lose her. Clenching and unclenching his fists, it was everything he could do to not lash out with his power churning and surging inside him at hurricane intensity. Trickles of black seidhr swirled around his fingers. What fucking game were they playing?

The ambassador bowed, eyes fixed on Loki's hands. "Yes, Prince Loki. I have been given leave to take you to see if you can find any sign of her."

"Hold up, brother. Mist, Kara, and I will accompany you once we have secured the prisoners," Thor told Loki.

With a disgusted growl, Loki flicked a hand to let Thor know he'd wait. Those damn prisoners could fucking drop dead, frankly. He chafed at the additional delay.

Norns, but he was tempted to just kill the bloody bastards with his telekinesis. Odin's treaty and his unwavering support were the only things that restrained him. A waste of time and space—they fucking deserved to die.

Six light elf warriors in white armour emblazoned with a golden sun and six dark elf warriors in grey-and-brown camouflage armour with a stylized black thorn crown on their chests surrounded Llew and Crom as they approached out of the mists. The two prisoners were bound in black Dwarven chain. At least the Sidhe were taking this part seriously.

But how the fuck did they lose Shannon? Bullshit. They had to have her hidden somewhere.

The procession was led by Math Mathonwy of the Summer Court and Cailleach of the Winter Court. Both representatives gave brief nods of greeting.

Math's perennial smile was missing, replaced by a downward tilt to his lips at odds with the laugh lines creasing his burnished walnut cheeks and brown eyes. "Prince Thor, Prince Loki, it has been some time. Truly, I wish we were meeting under better circumstances."

In the past, Math and Loki had been friends and spent many a pleasant hour comparing the differences between Sidhe and Asgardian seidhr. Amongst other things. But Loki had no desire to recollect their times together, given the current circumstances. Instead, he just glared at the elf.

"Let's get this done," snarled Cailleach, her craggy face twisted by its hag-like appearance. "We are turning these two over under protest, Princes. We expect them to be treated as befits nobles of the court."

A harsh breath escaped Loki, and his brother's hand reached out to grip his arm.

Clenching his teeth, Loki pressed his lips together to still the biting remark he wanted to make to this arrogant elf. How *dare* she ask for anything when Shannon hadn't yet been returned to him? His chaos strained to strike her down where she stood, the black fire within his soul fed by the yawning, empty pit of his missing soulmate.

They were lucky he was willing to abide by Asgardian justice. The fuckers should be dead. Obliterated. Just a small burst of his chaos. Not lounging around in the Asgardian dungeons. He could kill every fucking elf here and not bat an eye.

Thor's grip tightened on Loki's arm, almost like his brother had heard Loki's thoughts. The irony of Thor being the calm one was not lost on Loki.

"They will be treated according to the guidelines of the treaty, despite their failure to uphold their oaths to it," Thor rumbled, warning in his tone. He turned to the Asgardians behind them. "Sigrdrífa, take a cadre each of Einherjar and Valkyrie to escort Crom and Llew to the dungeons. Please update the All-Father as to our status in finding Princess Shannon. Roskva, Thjalfi, take charge of the legions of Einherjar and Valkyrie and await our return. Mist, Kara, leave your mounts here."

Thor dismounted and handed his reins to Thjalfi, while Loki did the same and handed his reins to Roskva, who also held the reins for Kara's and Mist's winged horses.

When the swirling lights of the Bifrost disappeared with Sig, the prisoners, and escorting cadres, Loki, Thor, and the two Valkyrie faced the ambassador. Thor gestured for him to lead on.

"This way, please, Princes," Ogma said as they started into the mists leading to the Winter Realm. Besides Mist and Kara, Math and Cailleach joined the party.

After a short walk into the mists, they passed through a grey stone archway with a shimmering silver portal and found themselves in a subterranean hallway. Glowing greenish yellow vines grew on the ceiling and partly down the walls, providing light to the smooth-walled carved stone corridor. Every so often, the corridor branched but Ogma did not hesitate in his path and continued on the route Loki recalled from the war four hundred years ago, when they'd broken through the Unseelie's defenses to rescue Sigyn... too late to save her, to save their child. Loki bared his teeth. That was not happening this time. Not again.

Once through a second portal archway, they entered a dark forest within an enormous cavern. The ceiling was far above, with more glowing vines providing light to the gloom. A well-trodden trail led through the towering mix of silver deciduous trees with palm-sized pale green leaves and dark green pines and firs, their long needle-filled branches spreading wide. Paths headed off in various directions. After taking one to the right, they walked for at least twenty minutes, the forest eerily silent around them, then took another path that veered off to the right. Coming to the edge of the forest, they entered another stone-carved corridor. Within ten minutes or so, they turned left to a corridor with a series of barred doors.

Opening the third one on the right, Ogma gestured to the room. "This is where she was when she was brought from Litaui."

Loki's jaw clenched as he stepped off the stone path and onto the dirt floor of the empty cell. The scent of blood, waste, and fear from its recent inhabitants was thick on his tongue. Amongst that miasma, he couldn't detect any hint of Shannon. They'd kept his consort, his beautiful goddess *here*, in this filth? As if he didn't have enough reasons to kill them—

Thor caught Loki's arm.

Loki dragged his raging chaos back under control until the black waves of seidhr stopped pulsing around him. Fuck. He couldn't lose it now.

"Call the hounds," Thor demanded. "I want to see how they react."

As Cailleach called her hellhounds, Loki reached out, astral projecting multiple invisible copies of himself to search nearby rooms and hallways. Everywhere he looked, he failed to find any sign of her. A few Sidhe were able to detect Loki's presence, even though they couldn't see him, but he passed by them, searching as wide as he could.

Farther and farther he searched with copies of himself, skirting the edge of the throne room itself, hidden in the heart of the forest they'd walked through.

No sign of her, anywhere.

Not even a hint.

Not only that, but he didn't find any trace of the other prisoners they'd seen in Mist's memory. Where were they hiding the mortals? Norns curse them, surely the Unseelie hadn't sacrificed them all in the three days since their capture?

Unaware of his presence, Loki listened to conversations of Sidhe as they speculated about Shannon's fate. Rumours were as plentiful as weeds along a roadside, but no actual leads.

Cailleach's massive black shaggy hounds arrived.

"Dormarth, Grim, find the Princess," she said after showing them where Shannon had been.

She sent them out, and although the hounds went up and down the hallways, and into all the nearby rooms, never once did they give off the howling bay that indicated they had found her scent.

"As you see, they can't find any sign of her," she said.

"Call them back and let them try with this," Loki demanded, holding out a hair tie that held Shannon's scent. Who knew what fucking scent Cailleach had just sent the hounds after? If he couldn't detect where Shannon had been in that cell, if she'd even been in that particular one, how could Cailleach?

Cailleach shook her head, scowling, but did as Loki asked and sent the hounds out again.

Still, they did not indicate they'd found her scent. Fuck.

"Unfortunately, it is as we told you. We can't figure out where she has gone," Ogma said, spreading his hands apologetically.

Loki glared at him. He couldn't tell if the sly fucker was lying or not. "Any ideas, Mist? Kara?" His thoughts circled and spun—the disappointment and frustration surging like a toxic wave. It swamped his ability to strategize while expending most of his energy astral projecting so many copies of himself. It was too much feedback... too many directions. Bor's beard, what he'd give to be able to just kill them all and let Hades sort them out after.

Mist shook her head. "No, my prince. With the Dwarven cuff on, she couldn't have masked her presence herself. The only answer is someone who could hide her scent took her."

"Who would have that ability?" Thor asked.

"Anyone who can manipulate air could do it," Mist replied.

"Or who had a cloaking spell, could teleport, or create a portal," Kara added.

"Unfortunately, there are too many options," Loki reluctantly concluded. A sharp ache in his head and the onset of exhaustion hit. He'd reached his limit and withdrew his astral selves. He couldn't afford to show weakness in front of the Sidhe. Despite penetrating deep into the Unseelie territory, he hadn't found any trace of Shannon or anyone who had a real lead on what had happened to her. If it was a conspiracy by the Winter Court, it was extremely well executed. Their nobles appeared as clueless as the rest.

Nor had he found the other captives. But fresh blood stained the court runes. He ground his teeth. No doubt the fucking elves had slaughtered the mortals. Sadistic bastards. And if even a drop of that blood was Shannon's... nothing in the Nine Realms would save them from his vengeance. He wouldn't stop until he found out where she was, or proved they'd been behind her death.

After sharing a look of frustration with Thor, Loki allowed the Sidhe to guide them back to the treaty plains where their legions of Einherjar and Valkyrie waited. His empty soulmate bond screamed in his chest with every step.

Part of him wanted to attack the elves to make the Unseelie pay... pay for the death of the mortals... pay for kidnapping Shannon in the first place. But it was a purely emotion-driven impulse he knew Odin wouldn't support. Not when Asgard had the kidnappers in their dungeon. Attacking the Sidhe was pointless without a single lead of where Shannon was. When every elf he'd eavesdropped on seemed clueless. When there was no proof Shannon had died at their hand.

Yet, the Asgardians weren't going to simply leave.

After forcing the elves to agree to allow cadres of Einherjar and Valkyrie to join their search parties throughout the Winter and Summer Realms, Thor and Loki sent them off with their Sidhe counterparts. No way did Loki trust the Sidhe to tell the truth in their search for Shannon, given they had taken her in the first place.

And not after Sigyn. Loki would never trust the Unseelie. Not ever.

Secrets had a way of coming to light, and the two Elven realms spied on each other. No doubt the Summer court would find out the truth of how Shannon disappeared from her cell. Some elf had to either know something or had have seen something.

As much as he wanted to join the searchers here on the ground, he needed information, a clue, some logical way forward. There were other avenues he and his brother could pursue. And if those didn't pan out? He flashed the ambassador a toothy glare. Well, he could always return to capture and torture Unseelie, even if it would infuriate his father.

Still, it was with leaden feet and an aching heart that Loki mounted his horse. Every part of his soul pulled at him to stay, but after telling Ogma they'd be expecting updates on the searches, they withdrew to Asgard.

Loki couldn't help but feel defeated by the lack of progress. Who had Shannon? Was she even still on Alfheim? How could he save her if he couldn't find her?

Chapter 8

JUST LIKE THE ONE RING

Each day, Shannon grew noticeably weaker. Or at least, what she presumed to be a day. With no distinction between night and day, she'd lost track of time. Unfortunately, she'd left the inter-realm watch Loki made her at the rental cottage when she'd toured castles with Kara, Mist, and Elise as part of their girls' weekend. She mourned its loss. Her best guess was she'd been chained in this hellish workshop for somewhere around two weeks. Gods, it was hard to be sure. Exhaustion plagued her, and despite her efforts to come up with an escape plan, she kept falling asleep.

Fjalar had harvested her blood five more times. Each time, it took longer for the wounds to heal, seeping for hours, and she slept longer afterwards, hardly able to stay awake long enough to eat. Although they used the blood-infused mead sparingly for themselves, it seemed the blasted bastards were selling casks of it. Disgusting, but she couldn't stop them. Fuck, she could barely raise the water jug to her lips. Twice now, Galar had left the workshop with a small wagon of altered mead, returning the next day to crow with Fjalar about how much they had made in trade.

Shannon's eyelids were so heavy, like weights pulling her down to the ocean's depths. At times, she wondered if she'd fall asleep and not wake again.

"Why are you so tired, girl?" Fjalar demanded. "You should recover faster. Are you a goddess of anything?"

"Ocean, forest," she mumbled. No way would she tell him she was a fertility goddess, too. Given the way they'd treated her thus far, she wasn't willing to risk them getting the idea to use sex to revive her. Shannon was not that liberal with her affections, nor did she trust they wouldn't sell her body in addition to her blood. Especially since Frigga had told her sex wasn't an unusual aspect of Sidhe rituals. Who knew what dwarves thought about such things?

"Ocean, huh?" He walked into one of the adjoining rooms and brought out a large metal tub, easily twice the size of Shannon. He dropped it beside the bed with a loud clang on the stone floor that had her wincing despite her fatigue. At the workbench with chemistry supplies, he picked up a box and dumped the contents into the tub. After moving down the wall, he uncoiled a hose and started pouring steaming water into the tub.

When it was three-quarters of the way full, he gestured to it and told her to help herself before he walked away to work at a bench.

Reaching over to feel the water, it was warm, almost hot. Nothing seemed to be even remotely cool this deep in the planet, so she shouldn't have been surprised. She took a deep breath—the tang of salt surrounded her and brought tears to her eyes. With a hand swiping at her eyes, she inhaled again. Her nose had gotten used to the sulphuric fumes in this gods-forsaken workshop, but the reassuring scent wasn't an illusion.

Eying Fjalar, he seemed occupied with whatever he was working on. He never paid much attention to her anyway, more interested in the blood mead he was creating. Galar was the one she had to watch out for, the one who leered at her when she used the chamberpot. But the perverted dwarf had left a while ago and hadn't yet returned.

She couldn't get her armour to recede with as little power as she had—she continued to use every bit to charge the ring and hide her baby. Nor did she want to chance not being able to bring her armour back after her bath. Saltwater wouldn't hurt the Asgardian alloy, but her boots and leather pants wouldn't fare as well. After slipping them off, she stepped into the tub, still wearing everything else. Quickly, she sunk under the water. Her skin tingled. A deep breath slowly escaped as the water's energy soaked into her starved cells.

Gods, it was amazing. For the first time in so many days, her heavy exhaustion lifted. Without the overwhelming weight on her chest, she could breathe again. Hell, she could think again. Even her heart felt like it pumped easier, her blood not syrup-like in her veins. Seeming to also enjoy the influx of energy, her son kicked and squirmed. He'd been still of late, and his vigorous movements erased the fear that had gripped her heart in unrelenting, icy, talon-tipped clutches.

Made for the much larger dwarves, the tub was plenty big enough that she submerged her body entirely, laying spread-eagle on the bottom and staring up through the water. Her arms stopped throbbing as they finally healed from the most recent blood-lettings. Would that she'd never have to get out.

Fjalar's face appeared over the edge of the tub, looking down. Reluctantly, she lifted her head out of the water.

"Well, you look more lively and alert. I'll make sure you can have a soak in saltwater after we harvest from you each time. It seems to do wonders for you," he mused. A sneer twisted his lips. "Plus, it will keep you from stinking."

Fucking asshole. He returned to his workbench, and she bit her tongue to keep herself from growling at the insult. She didn't ask to get chained to a wall with no opportunities for personal hygiene, so if she smelled, that was on them, not her. If she could access more of her power, she'd be able to clean herself.

With that thought, an idea twigged that hadn't earlier with her mind in such an exhausted fog. She'd been trying to find some way of picking the locks on the cuffs. But if she could access more of her power, she could use water to freeze the locks and break the cuffs.

She gazed up through the water at the contraption on the wall. Could she reach the dials that controlled the pull on her energy to get more back?

She needed to wait until neither dwarf was in the workshop. It wasn't often they left her alone. They didn't seem to sleep at the same time. Perhaps that was a product of no real night or day down here. They simply slept when they got tired.

How would she reach the dials? With as dizzy as she'd been, she hadn't tried standing on her bed, but if she climbed onto the metal frame of the headboard, she should be able to reach. If the bed didn't work, could she use the chains to ascend the wall? That might be possible.

Still deep in her thoughts, Fjalar startled her when he returned to tell her to get out of the water and tossed a large towel on the bed. After rising, she lifted a foot to step out when his shout froze her in place.

"How in the first forge did you hide that?" he yelled.

Her heart pounded. What—What did he mean?

"How many months pregnant are you?" he demanded.

Oh. Shit.

Her lungs almost seizing, she felt for the ring and found a bare finger. Since her capture, she'd lost too much weight, and crap, she'd forgotten to clench her fist as she rose. Like everything else she wore except the armour that automatically adjusted to her size and movements, the ring was too big for her now and had slipped off in the water.

Tears pricked her eyes. *Damn it to hell.* The one thing she was trying so hard to hide was now out in the open. Far too late, she crouched into the water, patted along the bottom until she found the ring, and slid it back onto her finger.

"Oh no, you don't," Fjalar demanded, wrenching her out of the water.

She shrieked, fighting for balance and almost falling on the edge of the tub.

"Answer me!" he growled.

Panting, she swallowed and tried to think past the thundering in her ears. "I'm about twenty-nine weeks now." Maybe? If she hadn't completely lost track of time.

"How long is gestation for you?"

Her chest tightened. "Forty weeks," she managed in a breathless wheeze.

"*This* is why you have been so tired, despite eating lots, and putting out extra life force energy. No wonder Crom wanted you."

He released her.

Shannon took the two steps to the bed, snatched up the towel and wrapped it around her hips and legs as she climbed onto the bed. Whoever Crom was, he couldn't have her, damn it. What the fuck were these damned dwarves planning now?

"Is the kid Loki's?"

Her stomach churned, and she fisted the towel as she held it tighter. Was it better to tell the truth or not? "Yes," she finally answered.

"Well, damn. Asgard will never stop looking for you or the kid. You are carrying Odin's forge-be-damned grandchild."

"Yes." Her voice cracked. Shit, she should have lied. She didn't dare look away from the dwarf as he pounded a fist on the nearest workbench, glassware rattling. Gods, she had to get out of here.

"Oh, great! Keeping you is like carrying leaking dynamite on a Jotun road. I'd rather not be present for the eventual explosion." He glared at her as he picked up a jar and threw it at one of the glowing fireplaces. It shattered, and a flare of noxious fumes wafted through the room. "Galar is right. You *are* trouble."

A fine tremor started in her limbs, and she fidgeted with the tinkling charms on her bracelet. "If you let me go, I won't tell them who had me." She was ready to beg or promise almost anything if it meant he'd let her go.

"Yeah, right. I'm not that gullible. I'm selling you to Hreidmar. He'll give me a good price and won't care about the trouble you'll bring him." Fjalar laughed and gave her a twisted grin before scowling again. "Yeah, he'll like that. Probably torture you and kill your kid just to get back at Loki."

Shannon didn't respond, ducking her head as tears fell onto her lap. There was no point. She was out of time. She needed to escape immediately.

Fjalar continued to stomp around the workshop, muttering angrily to himself.

She dried off, including her tears, then pulled her pants and boots back on. At the first opportunity, she needed to be ready to go. She sipped at the ashy water and waited, watching. Even if her hands still shook, and her stomach churned.

When Galar returned several hours later, Fjalar pulled him into another room and soon, angry shouting erupted.

Taking advantage of their distraction, Shannon blew out a shaky breath and climbed onto the frame of the headboard to stretch up the wall. Damn it. She still couldn't quite reach the dials.

She drew another breath in, then exhaled while trying to calm her racing heart. With one foot braced on the wall and another on the top of the headboard, she pulled on the chains and lifted herself further up the wall.

With even more force on the chains, she lifted her foot off the headboard and stepped up the wall. Carefully leaning, while maintaining pressure against the wall with her feet and pulling on the chains, she reached up, stretching, straining, holding her breath until she could just touch the dial with her fingertips.

When she moved it slightly clockwise, it pulled more energy from her, and sagging, she almost lost her grip. Quickly, she flicked it back counter-clockwise and the surge of energy hit her like a bolt of lightning. Twisting it all the way, Shannon was lightheaded as her energy returned.

Hurry, have to hurry. She summoned water into the locks on the chain. It took a minute, but she finally sensed the locks were saturated. *Please... please work.* Focusing, she froze the water.

As the cuffs released her wrists with a loud snap that echoed in the stone-walled workshop, she gasped and almost lost her grip on the wall. Adrenaline surged.

Free!

Moving fast, she scrambled down and wrapped a shield of air around her to bend the light and make herself invisible—a skill she'd been working on with Mist. Although it wasn't perfect, in the low red glow of the workshop, it should be sufficient.

Fjalar and Galar rushed into the room, searching for the source of the sound. When they spotted the broken cuffs, they swore.

Shannon's pulse leapt into her throat. Every boom of her heart sounded like thunder. Yet she didn't even want to breathe. Careful to not bump anything or jiggle her charm bracelet and give herself away, she hid behind a bench as she watched them search, then run out the entrance.

She exhaled a long, shaky breath. Thank gods. They assumed she'd taken off right away.

But if she was going to make a run for it—she rubbed her swollen abdomen—she needed supplies. With an eye on the entrance to make sure they didn't return and spot her, she took a large cloth and filled it with a loaf of bread, fruit, nuts, and hard cheese. She dumped out a small flask with a potent alcohol and filled it with the ashy water. Better than nothing if she didn't have the energy for her powers to gather water. The cloth-wrapped bundle was as much as she could easily carry tied to her armour and still keep her hands free. Nerves jangling and skin prickling, she didn't want to delay any longer. She needed to get out of there now.

While focusing on her armour, Shannon visualized her throwing knives, sais, and daggers, and their sheaths strapped to her body. Her breath caught when they appeared, and she almost let out a cheer as relief surged. She'd assumed she'd lost them for good. After changing her filthy, damp clothes to new fighting leathers that better protected her body and fit her leaner physique, she crept out of the workshop and into the massive cavern.

Unable to remember which way they'd come, she headed to the left. Anywhere had to be better than here.

PART 2

IF AT FIRST YOU DON'T SUCCEED

"Our greatest glory is not in never falling, but in rising every time we fall."

Confucius

Chapter 9

RUMOURS

Loki had never appreciated how much of Midgard was covered with water until he tried to find one sea god in the vastness of Earth's oceans. While barely four weeks passed on Asgard, it was a long four and three-quarter months by the Midgardian calendar that he and Mist searched the oceans to find Manannan Mac Lir.

At least the intelligent sea life aided their quest, particularly the playful, curious dolphins. But despite starting with the Great Barrier Reef and oceans around Australia where Loki and his beloved Shannon had last spoken to the elf, the local pods hadn't seen the sea god recently. With each new pod the Asgardians encountered, they left the message that if the dolphins saw Poseidon—the name the sea creatures usually referred to Manannan as—to let him know Loki sought him on Shannon's behalf. If Loki wasn't convinced that the sea god could scour vast areas of Alfheim faster than the current search parties who continued to fail to find her, he'd have given up trying to locate the elf and returned to hunt for her himself.

Yet Manannan was their best hope to finding her before their son was due.

Visions of Shannon alone, struggling, in danger, and labouring with their son haunted Loki whenever he closed his eyes. He did his best to not think about it. Worse were the nightmares where his memories of Sigyn's ravaged body blended into Shannon's, leaving Loki to wake screaming, sweat-soaked, with terror a thick coat on his tongue. When he let himself dwell on his fears, he couldn't function. Hunting for Manannan gave Loki a concrete goal to get through each minute, each hour, each day as the weeks dragged on.

And thank the Norns for Shannon's best friends. While Kara tracked down other leads and kept him apprised of the search teams' progress, Mist accompanied Loki, keeping him on target and from losing his mind.

At least the time difference between realms worked for them. Every five or six days on Midgard, the pair returned to Asgard for a daily update. Ambassador Ogma claimed there was still no sign of Shannon. Unfortunately, the Einherjar and Valkyrie embedded with the searching Sidhe confirmed the lack of progress. The teams hunted methodically, but it was a big planet and the network of portal doorways spanned vast distances, making it impossible to narrow the search to a single localized area.

As the days piled up without any tangible proof of his soulmate's wellbeing or location, Loki fought against the rising tide of despair. Barely functioning, he couldn't afford to let the lack of progress get to him. If he was paralyzed by anxiety, he wouldn't be able to find Shannon. He *had* to find her, find her and save her.

With judicious use of hypnosis, he'd cleaned up his mess on his Midgardian film set. Being able to clone himself allowed him to finish filming. And every bit of godly energy the acting gave him, Loki used to continue his hunt for Manannan and to stave off sleep. But filming wrapped a month ago, leaving him fighting exhaustion and his need for sleep.

Shoving his worry from his mind and attempting to lock the nightmares away, Loki focused on today's destination. He nodded to Heimdall to activate the Bifrost. He and Mist were heading to the waters surrounding the Isle of Man. The swirling lights of the wormhole set them down on a patch of unoccupied honey-coloured beach in an isolated cove. After wading into the cold Irish Sea, Loki changed shape and plunged his dolphin body into the dark waters, emitting clicks to locate a local pod. Mist tracked him by running above the waves.

He sped through the depths, searching. When a response came, he swerved in that direction. They were travelling at a good clip when the soul-deep ache plaguing him for so long disappeared.

Shocked at the lack of pain, he stopped swimming and tumbled through the water.

Shannon! Shannon was alive! She was a warm thrum in his chest. Oh, thank the Norns!

If he hadn't been in the water and in dolphin form, the relief would have dropped him to his knees. As it was, he arched out of the water in a gleeful leap that had Mist halting.

Heart pounding, he sent a telepathic call. *<Shannon, can you hear me?>*

Sharp claws of disappointment raked his chest when there was no reply. He swallowed, tail flexing. Still... some exchange, some aspect of the link was active again.

Mist's voice drew him back to the surface.

He shifted back to humanoid and treaded water. "Something has happened. The bond doesn't hurt anymore. I can't feel Shannon exactly, but we aren't cut off anymore." He rubbed his chest, struggling to explain what he sensed through the lump of emotion choking his throat. A sob escaped as he rubbed at his welling eyes. "She's alive, Mist. Shannon's alive."

She blinked tri-coloured blue eyes that filled with tears, then nodded slowly as she discretely wiped the moisture away and exhaled a shaky breath. "Do you want to try to find Manannan today, or should we head back to Asgard to see if they know anything?"

He sniffed, then scooped water over his face as he weighed their options. Bor's balls, if only he could talk to Shannon. Yet, other than knowing she was alive, nothing else had changed. Manannan was still their best bet for searching the surface and subterranean seas of Alfheim. "We're already here. A pod answered my call. Let's look first, then head to Asgard."

"Okay. Ready when you are."

After shifting back to a dolphin, he dove, renewed power and determination in every flex of his sleek grey form. When he sent out a series of clicks, the pod answered, closer now.

They were headed to meet him.

When Loki and Mist reached the seven male juvenile Bottlenose dolphins, Loki asked if they'd seen the sea god.

With excited chatter, they offered to take the pair to where the sea god was today. A wave of anticipation blasted through him as Loki relayed their words to Mist. Finally. Finally, some progress. He and Mist followed as the dolphins swerved and leapt their way towards the blue-haired elf swimming amongst a kelp forest, trident and sword strapped to his back. Powerfully built like Thor, the sea god wore a navy skinsuit and a finely scaled armour that shimmered iridescent in shades of blue.

As they approached, Manannan called out, "Why, Prince Loki, you make a handsome dolphin. Who is your Valkyrie friend, and where's the lovely Princess Shannon?" as he raised a hand in greeting and smiled, pleasure in his ocean-blue eyes.

The three rose to the surface, with Loki shifting back to his humanoid form again to answer. "This is Mist."

"We've met, but it was when I was still a child, Manannan." She nodded at the elf's greeting.

Loki shoved his wet hair back out of his eyes as he treaded water. "We've come seeking your aid, Manannan. Shannon was taken by Crom Cruach and Llew with the Wild Hunt in a Lughnasadh raid through the Castlerigg stone circle near Keswick almost five months ago by Midgard's calendar. Somehow, they lost her on Alfheim when she disappeared from an Unseelie holding cell without a trace." The reminder had a toxic mix of frustration and rage surging, choking his voice as he said, "With my own eyes, I watched the hellhounds unable to track her, and my search of the Winter Court found no hint of her."

Manannan's expression darkened, his brow creasing and scowl building. "Those thrice-brained idiots! Feckless fools and their sick sacrifices! Have Crom and Llew been apprehended?"

"Yes, the Summer Court forced the Winter Court to turn them over to us. They are enjoying the hospitality of our dungeons on Asgard." Mist cocked her head and eyed the sea god with slightly raised eyebrows. "Unfortunately, they have been no help in determining who took her on Alfheim or her current location."

"That is too good for them," growled Manannan. "Does Llew know Shannon carries his nephew?"

Loki shook his head. "No. As far as we're aware, they didn't learn of her pregnancy. I gave her a ring to hide it." Thank the Norns for that small mercy.

"Smart precaution. You absolutely do not want him to know." Manannan's face twisted in disgust as he shook his head, before his expression cleared and he stared off in the distance, fingers caressing his square jaw. "There have been no ripplings through the waters of Litauī." He returned his gaze to the two Asgardians. "And I haven't been to Tír na nÓg since I last saw you. But I will spread the word immediately through the water realms of Midgard and Alfheim to search for her and provide aid if she is found. The summoning shell I gave her hasn't been used, or at least its call hasn't yet reached me if she's used it on Tír na nÓg."

The tightness in Loki's chest eased. "Thank you. I am in your debt." He'd hoped the sea god would help them, but he hadn't been sure. With Manannan searching in the water, surely Loki would be able to find and save Shannon that much faster.

"No, Prince Loki, there is no debt between us. Princess Shannon is also one of mine, an Elven sea goddess, and I will not allow other Tuatha Dé Danann to take advantage of her youth and current vulnerability," Manannan insisted, holding Loki's gaze.

"Thank you, Manannan," Mist interjected. "Shannon is important to many of us."

Manannan turned to her with an admiring smile and glance that took in all the Valkyrie's assets. "You, my gorgeous Valkyrie, are as loyal and honourable a friend as you are a talented and fierce warrior."

She narrowed her eyes. "Are you flirting with me, Sea God?"

His deep, resonant chuckle surrounded them. "If you have to ask, I'm clearly out of practice."

Mist raised a speculative eyebrow. "Perhaps we can discuss your rusty skills after we have rescued Princess Shannon."

Still grinning, Manannan inclined his head. "Indeed. I'll leave you now so that I can start my search." He cupped his hands briefly and a familiar glow filled them. Opening his hands, two silver and blue spiral sea shells sat on his palms, just like the one he'd given Shannon. Did she still have it? Loki took one from him as Mist collected the other.

"When you have need of me, go to the nearest saltwater body, focus on the shell and speak. I will hear you and find you, whether it be here on Litauī or on Tír na nÓg," Manannan promised. "If I find out anything, I will call out to Heimdall, and he can pass on the message. I know he can hear me here, and I can get my message through the fáeth fiada, the cloaking mists of Tír na nÓg, well enough."

"Thank you," Loki said as Manannan disappeared below the waves. Rising to stand on the surface of the waves, Loki called to Heimdall, and the Bifrost's wormhole brought the pair back to Asgard.

"Any news, Thor?" Loki asked as he and Mist joined his brother for lunch in their usual warriors' lounge off the training grounds.

Thor forked up another heaping spoonful of thick brown stew with chunks of root vegetable and braised auroch and waved a hand at the laden self-serve buffet tables. The food was replenished throughout the day by palace kitchen staff. "Yes. Grab something to eat and pack. I waited for you to return. We're heading to Jotunheim."

"Why Jotunheim?" Loki asked as he made a roast game bird and bacon sandwich on sourdough. Shannon had gotten him hooked on them. It was one of her favourite lunches. Even with them apart, it made him feel closer to her to eat the familiar sandwich. Norns, he hoped she was eating enough, was keeping her energy up. She had to be okay. She had to be. He rubbed his chest where the bond hummed, reassuring himself that she lived. *Hang on, darling. I'm coming.*

"One of the Bergrisar has been boasting about a divine mead that gives the drinker god-like powers, specifically creating fire, wind, or rain," Thor explained.

Loki's jaw dropped, and it took him a second to respond. "Yggdrasil's roots! You don't think a mountain giant took her and is making a mead potion from her blood?" Stomach churning, his body flooded with barely leashed chaos as he thunked his silver plate on the scarred wooden table across from Thor. Even the idea of such a barbaric practice was disgusting. Blood magic was crass, primitive, and unpredictable. Only someone completely inept in the application of seidhr would use blood. Fury boiled in a roiling, ravenous need for revenge. Like a snarling feral beast barely restrained. The metal plate bent, twisting as his fingers clenched.

"Certainly worth looking into. Given Shannon is an elemental goddess, someone drinking a potion with her blood would get that potential combination of powers," Mist agreed, even as she wrinkled her nose in distaste. As she took a seat beside Loki, she snarled, "If it's true, he's dead, Thor. We aren't bringing him back as a prisoner."

Loki bared his teeth in a fierce grin. Yet another reason he liked this friend of Shannon's. And he agreed. He wasn't about to be denied his prey this time. Not with something like this as the crime. If someone had used Shannon that way, the fucker wouldn't live to see the inside of Asgard's dungeons. Not this time.

Thor smiled, a tight pressing of his lips, with lightning flashing in the depths of his eyes as he met Loki's gaze. "Don't worry, brother. I have no intention of stopping you, and Father agrees. It is entirely your call. I've asked the twins to join us. Thjalfi will scout, and since we're dealing with the mountain giants, Roskva can pry them out of their damn rock if need be."

"Yeah, you aren't leaving Kara and I behind if we have a lead on Shannon," Mist said as she finished her sandwich. Another roast game bird and bacon on sourdough. Shannon really had influenced all of them.

Thor inclined his head. "I wouldn't even try. Kara is with the twins, gathering the provisions we'll need for the six of us."

Pacified at the knowledge he had Father and Thor's full support, Loki stilled the growls he hadn't realized were coming from him until he spoke. "Yes, I just need to talk to Mother for a minute. Something has changed with the bond, and I want her input before we leave." He flexed his hands on the nimbus of black seidhr swirling around his fingers. He had to stay in control, at least until he had the fuckers in his sights. Then, all bets were off.

"We'll meet you at the palace gates in thirty minutes. Is that enough time?" Thor asked.

"Perfect." Loki stuffed the last bite of sandwich into his mouth, then shoved back from the scuffed bench and table and headed to Mother's garden. At this time of day, it was her favourite place to have tea.

Sure enough, Frigga appeared lost in thought, sitting at a wrought-iron and glass table with her usual silver teapot and cup resting within arms reach as she gazed out at the riot of colourful blooms climbing and draping over trellises, metal towers, and stone sculptures when Loki entered the terrace. But he knew she'd marked his presence. Mother was never caught unprepared. Her sorcery skills were far too perceptive for that. She'd taught him, after all.

"Are you ready to leave for Jotunheim?" she asked as he approached, her back still to him. Ebony tresses piled on her head in an intricate coil that left her neck bared and seemingly vulnerable, the silver-and gold dress she wore hid the warrior mage he knew his mother to be. Only a fool would underestimate Asgard's queen. Even his father stepped lightly when Frigga was roused to fury.

"Yes, I'm meeting Thor at the gates shortly. Mist and I were successful at finding Manannan today. He's more than willing to search for Shannon and put out word that she is to be assisted if she finds herself in the seas of Alfheim or Midgard."

She turned to face him and tilted her head curiously as Loki sat. "That's excellent news. But you wouldn't seek me out to tell me that when you have a trail to pursue in Jotunheim. What is preying on your mind, my son?"

"The feeling of the bond has changed. Ever since that cuff was put on her, it was a deep, painful ache. Today, for the first time, it doesn't hurt. Instead, there's a hum of her presence but anything more seems to be muted. I tried reaching her telepathically, but there was no response. It's more like when she deliberately blocked me." Loki bit back the fears that wanted to tumble out.

Frigga smiled gently, giving him a knowing look. "The good news is it tells us she is still alive. Shannon wouldn't be blocking you. Not now. I'm certain she wants to be found. If she is still within the veil of the fáeth fiada, the cloaking mists of concealment on Tír na nÓg, then they could block the bond between the two of you just as it blocks Heimdall's sight. I have a theory that the dimensional matrix Heimdall uses to see such distances is the same one that holds the energy ribbons for soulbonds. If I'm correct, then it would explain the blockage. I doubt the Sidhe considered the impact on soulmate bonds when they hid themselves from the Bifrost's reach in Freya's War."

Breath he hadn't realized he was holding expelled in a whoosh. "Thank you, Mother. It's what I suspected, but I wanted your opinion."

Frigga reached over and put her hand on his cheek, green eyes so like his own pinning him in place. "Shannon loves you, Loki. Do not doubt it. Not even for a second."

How clearly his mother saw him, even when he had trouble seeing himself. She cut right through to the heart of his insecurities to reassure him. He hadn't wanted to admit his fear, even to himself.

Loki smiled, taking her pale hand and placing a kiss on her slender fingers. "Thank you."

"Go see what you can discover about Shannon from this boastful giant on Jotunheim. Bring my daughter back." Frigga shooed him away with a smile and a flick of her fingers.

"I love you, Mother," he said as he left the garden terrace.

"I love you too, son," she called after him.

Stopping by his rooms, Loki gathered his sword, Laevateinn. Although he could manifest weapons, for anything truly hard to kill, he wanted the sword that had taken him a full year to craft. Inscribed with Helheim death runes with the assistance of Hades, and chaos seidhr from his half-Jotun heritage, it could even pierce dragonscale. Embedded with his essence, just as Mjolnir responded to Thor's call, Laevateinn responded to Loki's, crossing dimensional boundaries and realms to return to his hand.

If that giant had taken Shannon's blood, there would be no mercy. Politics be damned. Odin could deal with their king to smooth things over afterwards. Immediately after that thought, Loki smirked. Whether the Jotun king would survive the exchange depended on whether he knew of his giant's culpability. Father had impressed Loki with the depths of his fury at Shannon's kidnapping, and while Mother had kept her calm, her temper less obviously volatile than Odin's, her justice was all the more deadly in its stealth.

Refocused on his task, Loki considered what else he might need. Most things he'd be able to conjure, but he packed travel rations, healing salves and potions, and a few spelled medallions for bribing locals. Not always relying on his powers was wise, especially given their destination. Even the God of Chaos, Stories, and Songs wasn't completely immune to Jotunheim's chaotic influences on seidhr. Dimensional energies were in flux in that realm, making outcomes somewhat unpredictable.

With his packing finished, he teleported to the palace gates to find Thor and the others already waiting.

"Ready?" his brother asked, spinning his double-sided hammer in one powerful fist. The runes on the silver-black metal glowed, betraying Thor's mood despite the outwardly calm set to his face.

"Yes." Loki strode through the cobblestone avenues and the towering city gates towards the stone and metal bridge seething with spectral dimensional energies that fed the Bifrost chamber. "Do we have the name of the giant?" Loki asked as Thor fell in step beside him.

"Suttung. We'll start at Thrymheim, mountain stronghold of the giant Thiazi. I'm hoping he will have a location for Suttung."

"Doesn't Thiazi hate you?" asked Thjalfi, laughter in his tone and dancing blue eyes as he side-eyed them.

Thor sighed and shoved his best friend's shoulder with a hard thump, drawing a grunt and stagger from the less brawny male. "Yes, but I'm hoping that Loki's silver tongue will be enough to get the information from him."

Loki rolled his eyes.

It was never that simple. Just because he usually considered his words before he spoke and used complex multi-dimensional tactics to beat his brother in the strategy games Father had them play, Thor assumed Loki could convince anyone of anything. Or maybe it was because Loki could convince his brother of almost anything.

Loki snorted to himself.

Yeah, he'd gotten them into a lot of mischief over the years that Thor probably wouldn't have gotten into on his own. He smirked. Okay, who was he kidding? Thor definitely wouldn't have caused nearly as much trouble without Loki's influence.

Still, while that ability to think before leaping made Loki the better diplomat, Thor was no slouch in the political arena. As the crown prince since their older brother's death, Thor had hundreds of years of experience dealing with ambassadors of different realms beyond the Nine Realms that Asgard regularly monitored and influenced in order to protect not just Asgard, but the far more vulnerable and interstellarly naïve Midgard. Not that Loki didn't deal with ambassadors and representatives of other ruling realms as well, but more often, the duty fell to Thor.

Well, unless it was some particularly sticky situation Odin wanted handled with delicacy, like the demons of Muspelheim. For the last five hundred years, they'd always been Loki's burden to negotiate with. The two brothers had learned from each other, and Thor wasn't nearly as quick-tempered as he'd been in their youth.

"Well, if I can't, I'm sure you can beat some sense into him," Loki teased, lips quirking.

Just because his brother was far more clever than he let on, it didn't mean it wasn't fun to tease Thor about only ever using his fists or hammer to resolve any difficulties. What was the point of being a younger brother if he couldn't annoy his older sibling? Loki hid his smirk behind his hand when Thor glared.

Kara snorted, amused at their banter.

"This is going to go well," Ros added in a dry tone, elbowing her twin. Thjalfi grinned.

When they reached the Bifrost chamber, Heimdall let them know the closest he could get them to Thrymheim was the start of the Skogsdunge forest that surrounded the Gudbrandsdal mountain range.

"The dimensional energies of Jotunheim are flaring, interfering with the connection of the Bifrost, particularly near their cities and homes, so be well clear by a good fifty kilometres at least or I won't be able to get you," Heimdall warned. "If you call for me and I don't answer, you need to get farther away from any of their seidhr-built structures and into the wilderness."

The Skogsdunge.

Shiiiit.

Loki exchanged a scowl with Thor. That Norns-cursed forest was where the brothers had run into snow griffins that had almost killed them as young immortals. Jotunheim was a forbidding and frequently deadly destination for unwary travellers. Giants weren't the only predators there. Indeed, they weren't even the most dangerous inhabitants of Jotunheim.

At least they'd be arriving during the day when the largest, meanest predators slept.

As the swirling lights of the Bifrost dissipated, Loki and the Asgardians had been deposited at the edge of a rocky, desolate, wind-swept grassland and the start of a towering dark forest of pine and spruce.

At night.

He cursed under his breath. The quest to seek Suttung so he could rescue Shannon was starting off with as much luck as he'd expected. Fucking none.

Dual moons cast a pale light that failed to penetrate the close canopy of trees as Loki walked between the dark trunks. The others spread out, moving as quietly as possible. There was no actual path through the forest, but they needed to head uphill. If they could get through the foothills of the mountains covered by Skogsdunge forest, they would be above the tree line. At that point, they'd pick up the trail to Thrymheim.

The deep, harsh hoots of a snowy owl echoed from the left, with another replying from farther away. Dry snow crunched under their boots, and Thor winced as a twig snapped under his foot. They weren't as silent as Loki would like, although Mist, Ros, and he left no footprints or sounds of their passing.

Thjalfi scouted ahead, using his speed to search for the best route through the forest and keep an eye out for danger. On his way back to them, he flushed several rabbits startled by his passing. A flash of wings and the panicked squeaks abruptly cut off. The owls would eat well tonight. Hopefully, they were the only predators aware of their presence.

"There is a steep ravine ahead. It'd be better to go around than to climb down and up the far side. If we got pinned in there, we'd be sitting ducks," Thjalfi advised. "We should veer north to get around it."

As they shifted direction to avoid the upcoming obstacle, the deep resonant howl of a wolf echoed from farther up the mountain.

Chapter 10

POSITION ON THE FOOD CHAIN

Loki drew Laevateinn and extended his senses.

"Damn. Was that a dire wolf or one of the smaller timber wolves?" Kara murmured, gaze scanning their surroundings as she held her recurve bow cocked with a blacksteel-tipped arrow at the ready.

"I don't—" Another echoing howl pierced the air. This time, from the direction Thjalfi had just scouted. "Dire wolves," Loki confirmed, pulse thrumming. "It's too deep for the timber wolves." *Damn it.*

"I didn't see any wolves," Thjalfi said, eyes wide and alert.

From behind them, back along their trail, another spine-tingling howl resonated through the trees. Bor's balls, it was even closer. How had the bloody wolves tracked them so quickly?

"They've surrounded us." Mist drew her swords with the swish of metal on leather. "We need to run or fight."

"Have you seen the size of dire wolves? They're huge, clever, and resistant to magical attacks." Loki shook his head. With Laevateinn, he'd be fine, and Thor had Mjolnir. Kara might be able to take them out with her rune-enhanced bow, but the others... He eyed Mist's swords, Thjalfi's knives, and Roskva's long sword. Fine Asgardian weapons wielded by excellent warriors, but if the pack surrounded them in large numbers, it would get dicey, fast. "Even the Bergrisar avoid tangling with them. It's why the mountain giants build above the tree line instead of down here in the forest. A pack can take down the massive short-faced bears and woolly mammoths in this part of Jotunheim. We do *not* want to fight them."

The spine-tingling howls were getting closer.

Thor lifted Mjolnir, pointing to the sky through the forest canopy. "Kara? Do you want to fly with me? Or risk running with Thjalfi?"

"Norns curse it, I hate flying with you." She uncocked her bow and wrapped an arm around him. "Don't drop me."

Loki teleported to an upper branch and shifted to a raven, beckoning for the others to join him. There was no time to waste. Mist and Ros flew up beside him, buoyed on air and a wave of dirt, respectively, and Loki took flight to circle around them but stayed near the tops of the trees.

Just as Thor and Kara rose off the ground, an enormous grey-and-black dire wolf leapt through the trees at their backs. Loki cawed a warning. Cursing, Kara twisted and kicked it in the muzzle, knocking the beast sideways. The wolf tumbled as it hit the forest floor, regained its footing, and snarled at its lost prey with gleaming white fangs. Thor took them higher and out of reach.

Thjalfi took off, his speed allowing him to dodge the razor-sharp claws of another leaping wolf. Two more raced after him as several stared up, howling their displeasure.

With a viscous growl, another scrambled up the wave of soil and rock that Roskva was using to fly. She levitated some boulders, then smashed the wolf back down. It yelped and didn't rise again.

Above the treetops, the Asgardians flew towards the distant craggy mountain peaks, over the ravine Thjalfi had warned them about. Loki ruffled his feathers, relaxing into the motion of his wingbeats as he confirmed the Einherjar warrior was at least twice as fast as the wolves that tried to track him. He'd hate to lose his drummer, after all. He huffed out an amused breath. Okay... and Thor's best friend.

For an hour they continued in the air with Thjalfi keeping pace beneath them. Still, Loki kept them as low and close to the trees as possible, travelling a good seventy-five kilometres over the rising foothills before landing to join

Thjalfi in a small rocky meadow. They didn't dare continue further in the air. It was too dangerous as they approached the mountains.

Sharp-eyed snow griffins hunted the wintery skies of the colder mountain regions of Jotunheim. Even with the dire wolves, it was safer in the trees and on the ground than fending off the blade-like talons of those fierce aerial predators. Frankly, Loki would rather take on a bloody dragon than a snow griffin, but then, being a quarter fire giant from his birth father made him resistant to dragonfire, so perhaps he had an unfair advantage.

"There should be a traveller's stone hut we can take refuge in once we reach the trail that runs between Thrymheim and Gastropnir," Loki said as they trekked upwards through the trees.

Of the six of them, only Thor, Kara, and Loki had travelled extensively in Jotunheim. Mist, Ros, and Thjalfi hadn't been to this region before. The planet's chaotic nature and inherent dangers meant it was not a realm commonly travelled by Asgardians, except to the capital city of Utgard. High King Thrym of the sea giants ruled Utgard from the more hospitable, warmer latitudes of the planet.

After another six hours of steadily climbing in elevation, they finally came to the forest's edge and upper timberline. The light from the double moons shone brighter, reflecting off the rocky landscape. Above a long rock scree slope, the trail was a visible ribbon in the landscape as it wound along two kilometres higher on the mountain.

Before Loki could warn him, Thjalfi dashed up the fine scree and screamed as he fell into an antlion trap. Loki teleported to the edge of the shallow pit that had given way under Thjalfi's weight. Bor's balls. Two thin fang-like jaws had pierced Thjalfi's right leg, through the leather and boot, and deep into his calf. The predator was already sucking blood at a rapid rate.

"Don't move and try to stay silent," Loki warned, even as Thjalfi attempted to stifle his screams. "Mist, Ros, I could use your help here. Either stand on the edge of the pit like I am, or keep hovering so you don't accidentally trigger another one. These scree slopes are their favourite nest-building sites."

Thor eyed the scree warily and held Kara back with a hand on her shoulder as the other two Valkyrie joined Loki.

"We have to stun the antlion in its burrow before we can remove the jaws. Ros, use the earth to keep it immobile in its burrow. I'll need to pry the jaws out of Jal's calf without touching them, or it will eject poisonous needles. Mist, once I have him free, pull him up and hold him off the ground. Take him to the trail above us, but don't step on any of the scree. If Ros releases this antlion too soon, it will come after us and trigger a wave of others to burst from their burrows to attack as well." Loki waited to be sure they understood the instructions, both Valkyrie nodding, before he waved a hand at Ros to hit the burrow with her power.

Golden seidhr flowed from her and sank into the small jagged rocks. "Got it," she said, staring down, blue eyes narrowed in concentration.

Working quickly, Loki removed the leather and boot from around the punctures with a flick of power, then forced the foot-long sickle-shaped jaws apart with his telekinesis and held them wide to draw them all the way out of Thjalfi's leg. The fuckers had gone deep. Thjalfi screamed, slumping into Mist's arms as Loki painstakingly withdrew the tips. Rich, red blood poured from the punctures in twin dark rivulets down Thjalfi's calf and the metallic scent perfumed the area.

"Now, Mist," Loki murmured, glancing around. Hopefully, those damned wolves didn't pick up on the scent of Jal's blood. His eyes flicked skyward. Or another predator.

With her arm around Thjalfi's waist and fog wrapping around them, Mist lifted the injured Einherjar, towing him up to the trail.

Thor flew Kara and himself up, leaving just Ros and Loki to join them.

"Okay, I'm going to let go of the jaws now, Ros. Then I'll grab you and teleport us," Loki said, with another scan of their surroundings.

She met his gaze and flashed the Valkyrie hand sign for agreement.

As soon as he released the creature's jaws, the earth squeezed tighter around the antlion in a visible shudder. The beast squirmed, screeching, but couldn't get free. When she nodded, Loki reached for her shoulder, teleporting them up to the trail.

Sure enough, the antlion burst from its burrow—its fat, metre-long, dark-grey body spinning and searching. But without prey nearby that it could detect with its limited vision and no vibrations to trigger its sensitive hearing, it reluctantly retreated below. Loki let out a slow breath, tension easing from his chest. They were vicious little blood-suckers.

"How is he?" Loki crouched beside Kara as she sealed Thjalfi's wounds with a thick green healing balm and self-adhesive bandage.

"He'll be fine. The balm should take away the effects of the neurotoxin and his body will deal with the remaining injury within the next twenty-four hours. Until he heals the punctures, he won't be running. It would put too much strain on the healing blood vessels. If we can rest soon, perhaps have a meal, that would help," she recommended, pressing the edges of the dressing to form a bond to the surrounding skin.

"Thank you," Thjalfi said, subdued. As he started limping up the path, Roskva tucked herself beside her twin and draped his arm over her shoulder to help him walk.

"Now that we are on the trail, it shouldn't be too far before we come to one of the shelters. They build them every few hours along the trail so it's never too far to hide from predators," Thor said as they set off behind Thjalfi and Roskva, with Mist scouting ahead.

Sure enough, an hour later, a stone hut came into view. Once they reached the sturdy single-level shelter with its thick stone walls and stone roof, they unlatched and pushed open the heavily reinforced wood door. Firewood was stacked against one wall near a fireplace with a cooking frame that could be swung into the heat.

After conjuring a pot with water, Loki set it on the cooking frame and set a charm on the chimney stones that would dissipate the smoke and scent of food to keep from Jotunheim's creatures from investigating their hut. Kara opened a pack and pulled out provisions for stew, adding them to the pot, while Thor started the fire with a cascade of sparks onto a pile of kindling and dried moss.

"How's the leg, Jal?" Loki asked as Ros helped her twin to the stone table and benches.

Narrow lips twisted in a self-deprecating frown, the lean male hung his silver head. "I'll live. Sorry, I just feel like a fool."

"No, I'm sorry that I didn't warn you." Loki said, patting him on the shoulder. "Jotunheim is a dangerous realm, with more wild creatures, particularly large predatory creatures, than almost any other. Each of its regions have their own risks. It's why we issue so few travel approvals here. Without a knowledgeable guide, this planet is lethal."

"So I'm finding out. I won't make that mistake again."

Loki smiled and met his brother's gaze from across the room. He and Thor had made their share of mistakes when they first started coming to Jotunheim. "Nothing like experience for a teacher, right?"

Thjalfi snorted and nodded.

Mist handed out mugs of stew and hardtack, the hard biscuits that travelled well but were hell to chew unless dunked in some kind of soup or stew. No one complained about the basic fare. It was hot and filling—good enough to warm them as they relaxed.

After helping clean up and insisting on the first watch, Loki sat with his back against the cold stone wall as the others fell asleep.

Thjalfi's light snore echoed in the enclosed space.

Loki shook his head, a little grin twisting his lips, and cast a sound barrier over the hut. No sense announcing to the far-too-clever predators that tasty snacks were waiting inside the stone structure.

But all too soon, his dark amusement faded. With the light of the banked fire flickering over his fellow Asgardians, he considered the rumour they were chasing. Would it provide a real lead to Shannon's location?

He swallowed against the fears forming a lump in his throat, the nightmares that had him avoiding sleep. Even with the change in the bond reassuring him Shannon lived, it was far too easy to imagine the worst. Over and over, he saw her fighting the Wild Hunt and being taken through the portal. Too easily did his mind imagine the ravages that could be visited on her, with her yet living. Sigyn's suffering had lasted weeks before Loki had located her, only for the sick bastards to kill her and his unborn daughter mere hours before the Asgardians broke through the dark elves' defenses to rescue his wife. And she hadn't been the only victim. Loki had seen numerous horrors Unseelie did to their captives, especially immortals, during the last two wars with them.

He had to rescue Shannon. He had to. No way could he fail again.

<Shannon?>

The heavy silence answering his telepathic call ate at him. With his arms wrapped around his middle, Loki clung to the knowledge that the bond was still there. She was alive. He'd find her and rescue her. He needed to take hope in that.

Listening to the sounds of the night, he waited until it was time to wake Kara.

Chapter 11

TRIALS

The sun was rising over the horizon when Loki and the others left the sparse stone hut. They steadily climbed the packed stone trail that wove back and forth into the mountains and ever higher. Surrounded by rocky slopes with their scrubby heather, clumps of hearty grasses and cold-tolerant mosses, thyme, and lichen-covered boulders, it took another four hours before the Asgardians reached the gates to Thrymheim.

The stronghold had been built where meltwater flowed off a hanging glacier. A bright green lake drained over a massive waterfall to form a river several hundred metres below. Built into the mountainside, Thrymheim wasn't particularly easy to spot. It blended into the surrounding stone. The location gave the stronghold the strategic advantage of steep cliffs rising at its back and falling at its front and right sides, as well as a ready water source for the inhabitants.

Hulking guards, easily two-and-a-half metres tall, about Heimdall's height, were camouflaged against the granite mountainside until they stepped away from hidden nooks beside the tall stronghold gate. The guards escorted Loki and his party through an enormous tiled courtyard. A central fountain, gardens along one long wall, stables adjacent to the gate and guard barracks gave way to a multi-story central stone building with turrets and defensive positions. Smooth, grey-marbled rock formed the ceiling, walls, and floor. After a short hall that branched left and right, they were guided through another tall, carved stone door and into a great hall with soaring ceilings. Positioned high in the walls, windows built to catch the arc of Jotunheim's red dwarf star lit the room with plenty of daylight. Two rows of long grey stone tables and benches filled either side wall, partially occupied by giants who stopped eating at the Asgardians' entrance.

Silence filled the space as conversation and the clink of cutlery on plates died out. Centred at the far end of the room sat Thiazi, Lord of Thrymheim and the mountain giants dwelling within its protection, at his own table. A platter of roasted meat and vegetables sat on the stone table, and he picked at them with thick fingers and a short, gleaming knife.

"Prince Thor, Prince Loki, to what purpose do you come to Thrymheim and disrupt my midday meal?" the lord demanded in his deep, gravelly voice. Like most Bergrisar, he was on the shorter side for a Jotun, barely a head and shoulders taller than Thor, but extremely heavyset. His dark hair and penetrating black eyes were a striking contrast to silver, almost translucent marbled skin that resembled the stone of his home.

"Good Lord Thiazi, we seek the giant Suttung. We understand he is one of your Bergrisar and come to ask for your assistance in locating him," Loki replied in his smoothest diplomatic tone. The giant was a prickly bastard, but appealing to his ego often swayed him.

Thiazi's eyes narrowed, and he put down the tuber he'd speared with his knife. "I may or may not have a giant of that name in my region. What is your purpose for finding Suttung?"

A roar of elation swamped Loki for a second—their quarry was nearby. Loki stiffened his spine, fighting to not show what the giant had revealed. "Suttung may have information to help locate my consort, Princess Shannon. She was kidnapped just over a month ago."

The giant's brows flew up, and he thumped the table in front of him with a palm, the sound splitting the air and echoing off the stone walls. Next to Loki, Mist flinched, and he stilled her with a discrete hand on her arm. They couldn't show weakness or the giants would attack.

"Some idiot was bold enough to kidnap a Princess of Asgard? Do you suspect Suttung?" Thiazi asked, staring unblinkingly.

So the news hadn't yet reached this part of Jotunheim. Loki wouldn't have thought the elves had managed to keep that gossip from travelling far and wide, given the number of search parties and degree of commerce between the realms. But then, Thrymheim was far from the capital and the more hospitable trading routes. The nearest spaceport was a three-week walk to the plains around Suttgard, although the mountain giants rode woolly mammoths and towed multiple hovercarts to make the distance in a fraction of that time.

Still, Loki needed to proceed carefully and without giving away information that left Asgard appearing vulnerable. Thiazi was their best chance of finding Suttung quickly—it was clear he knew the giant's location—but Asgard's strength was what kept the peace across the Nine Realms and protected the still developing Midgard. Humans were not ready to join the rest of the galaxy and could not defend themselves or their planet.

Loki also couldn't risk the Jotun lord thinking he needed to protect Suttung. Better to not tell the giant that if Suttung had mead made with Shannon's blood, then kidnapper or not, that fucker was dead.

"No, Lord Thiazi. We have the initial perpetrators in Asgard's dungeons where they will regret that decision for the rest of their lives. However, Princess Shannon was taken from the kidnappers by unknown individuals. Suttung has been boasting of a source of unusual divine mead. We want to know his supplier, as we believe they may be the secondary kidnappers," Loki explained, playing on Thiazi's need to be the most powerful in his region. He wouldn't like one of his giants to become a threat to his rule.

"I have heard of the claims Suttung has made," Thiazi answered thoughtfully, and raising his knife, he took a bite of the yellow tuber, chewing slowly. He was quiet for a few minutes, continuing to eat while staring off with an unfocused gaze. Loki started to wonder if the giant was going to reply when Thiazi finally spoke again. "I don't want to stand in the way of your quest or fight with Asgard. However, I cannot be seen giving away information on my giants. You will have to win the knowledge by competing in three trials. After each successful win, I will give you one of the three clues you need to find Suttung. If you fail to win a trial, you will not get that clue."

Loki met his brother's gaze. Thor nodded. It was the best deal they were going to get and wasn't the first time they'd had to make such a bargain with a giant. Jotuns did love their games.

"Very well, we agree," Loki told Thiazi. "What are the trials?"

"Each one will test something different. You may choose any of you to complete a trial, but only one gets to attempt it. The first trial will test strength. Which of you will take on the challenge?" Thiazi asked, jagged silver teeth bared as he smiled widely at each of them.

As if it was even a question. Loki turned to his sibling. Thor would volunteer.

"I will," Thor stated. "What do I need to do?"

"Hrungnir is the strongest of my giants. Outside our gates, up the left side of the mountain, each of you will have the chance to use your weapons to see who can create the largest break in the ground with one blow." Thiazi rose from his stone throne and led the way out into the courtyard. A procession of giants followed them from the great hall.

In a booming voice, the lord summoned Hrungnir from the guard barracks—a giant twice the size of Thor in both height and girth. Hrungnir had long grey hair and skin that appeared to be grey, white, and black granite. He held a large shield and a thick, black metallic club with spikes.

After following Thor and Hrungnir out the gates and to the side of the mountain by the deep lake, everyone stood well back as Hrungnir walked quite a distance away toward the sheer cliff that held the glacier. He stopped halfway between the cliff and the lake. With a roar, the massive giant swung his club and slammed it into the ground.

A tremendous cacophony shook the mountain. Rock dust flew into the air. With an ear-splitting crack, a chunk of blue glacier calved off the cliff and broke into a shattered heap at the base of the stream, further feeding the stronghold's freshwater lake. As the icy wind blew the grit-filled cloud away, a large crater—a good fifty metres across and ten metres deep—stood where the giant had impacted the ground.

Backing away with a satisfied smirk, he gestured for Thor to try.

"Yeah, that's a nice little pothole," Thor taunted, and then walked even closer to the glacier and half a kilometre from where everyone watched.

Loki held his breath. His brother would win. Of course he would. Still, Loki's heart pounded.

Thor rose into the air, Mjolnir lifted high, and yelled a battle cry as he descended to smash the ground with a thunderous *crack*. Massive chunks of rock, smaller debris, and dust flew up into the air. Another crack echoed as the glacier lost a second huge shard of ice.

It took a while for the debris to fall and settle. Mist and Roskva shielded and diverted the larger chunks of rock and dirt away from landing on the group. Thor strutted back with a pleased grin. But when the air finally cleared, only a small crevice appeared in the ground, partially hidden by the displaced chunks of rock.

Thiazi smirked. "It doesn't appear that you caused a very large break in the ground, Thor."

Loki frowned in disbelief. No way had his brother dislodged that much debris to cause only a small crevice. He was about to intervene, but Ros beat him to it.

"Excuse me, Lord Thiazi," Roskva interrupted. "I believe you are mistaken."

She sent a wave of golden seidhr over the ground, and the illusion of the rock chunks disappeared, showing a large ravine now in its place. At its widest, it was at least two hundred metres across and a depth of fifty metres. The broken ice had tumbled in, water rapidly filling the new topography.

"Trying to cheat, Lord Thiazi?" Loki asked in a mild tone, an eyebrow raised. The damned giant wouldn't find the Asgardians easy prey.

Thiazi scowled, apparently not expecting them to see through his illusion. "Very well. Your first clue is Gunnlod, Suttung's daughter, guards his so-called divine mead in an underground chamber in the centre of his mountain home."

"What is the second trial?" Loki asked, maintaining his polite tone as his fists clenched. What kind of lame ass clue was that? It told them nothing about how to locate Suttung. Yggdrasil's roots, they could find all the damned hidden chambers themselves once they found the fucker's home.

Thiazi gave him a sly grin. "A test of speed. Pick your fastest runner to race against my swiftest messenger to the base of the waterfall and back here again."

"I can do it," Thjalfi offered, lifting a hand. "My leg is healed."

"Are you sure?" Mist asked, glancing down at his calf.

"Yes, it's completely healed," he said confidently.

"You are the fastest," Loki agreed. Jal should easily beat any mountain giant, even if his injured leg wasn't fully healed yet. Bergrisar were strong, not fast.

"Who will I be racing?" Thjalfi asked.

"Hugi!" Thiazi shouted and a surprisingly lean giant jogged out into the courtyard, joining them at the gates.

No way was Hugi a Bergrisar. With his extra height, standing half a metre taller than everyone else, and the tracework of green running through his dark brown skin, he had to be a Fyririsar, a forest giant known for their speed and agility. Loki swallowed. Hugi had a clear advantage with much longer legs than Thjalfi, but the Einherjar warrior ran like the wind. It would be close.

The two speedsters lined up at the gates, and with a sharp drop of his arm, Thiazi gave them the signal to race.

Off they went, neck and neck, flying down the stone trail, over the bridge and to the base of the waterfall. After turning at the bottom, they sped back up the trail, still within a step of each other. Thjalfi's silver hair blew straight back, but Hugi's long dark strands didn't seem to be affected by any wind.

Mist frowned and gestured—the wind disappeared. Pleased she'd also noticed the deception and intervened, Loki patted her on the back.

Thjalfi drew ahead of Hugi for a few steps, then stumbled only a few metres from the finish. Crying out in pain and grabbing his calf, Thjalfi fell behind. Hugi raced through the gate first, smiling.

Blood streamed down Thjalfi's calf to pool on the grey stone as he stopped beside Loki, raising devastated blue eyes to gasp out, "I'm sorry. I'm so sorry, Loki."

Kara bent down beside him to pull up his pant leg. It was the same calf the antlion had pierced. The punctures must not have been as healed as Thjalfi had thought. Loki bit back a curse, and acknowledged his friend's apology with a nod and clasp of the warrior's shoulder. None of the remaining Asgardians would have come close to beating Hugi. Jal had done his best.

The Jotun lord smiled and bared his teeth, beady eyes gleaming. "You lost that clue."

Loki's teeth ground together as he fought his temper. He could just extract the information from the damn giant if he didn't care about diplomacy. Fucking politics. Fucking treaties.

"What is the last trial?" Mist asked, her hand on his arm. Had he growled out loud?

Thiazi smirked. "A test of intelligence."

"I'll do it. What do I have to do?" Loki narrowed his gaze at the sly giant. No tricks were going to cheat him out of the last clue he needed.

"You must correctly answer these three riddles. For the first riddle, what day comes three days after the day, which comes two days after the day, which comes immediately after the day, which comes two days after Mánadagr?"

Jotunheim used the same days of the week Asgard did. It was a simple matter of counting backwards. Loki didn't see any trick in it. Still, he took the time to figure it out twice. It wouldn't due to make a sleep-deprived mistake. Not when his soulmate and son were missing.

"Tysdagr or Tuesday."

Thiazi scowled. "Yes." He gave a disgruntled grunt. "The second riddle is I disappear if you say my name. What am I?"

Loki grinned, taking but moments for the answer to come to him. Even with his exhaustion, this trial wasn't challenging. "Silence."

Thiazi huffed and glared. "Fine! In Utgard, there are five wooden homes, each built using a different tree of Jotunheim. In each home lives a different race of giant. Each giant drinks a particular beverage, has their own unique hobby, and keeps a specific type of pet. None have the same pet, same hobby, or drink the same beverage."

Loki nodded and gestured for Thiazi to continue.

The Jotun lord smirked, his silver teeth shining. "The fire giant lives in the burning ash home. The frost giant has a jackalope as a pet. The forest giant drinks honey mead. The ironbark home is on the left of the blue spruce home. The giant who lives in the ironbark home drinks nutty ale. The giant who creates jewellery raises cockatrices. The giant in the weeping papyrus home draws for fun. The giant living in the centre home drinks autumn wine. The sea giant lives in the first home, closest to the docks. The giant who collects round, shiny pebbles lives next to the giant who has a pet raven. The giant who raises sithcats lives next to the giant who draws. The giant who collects ornaments drinks starlight splash. The mountain giant knits jumpers. The sea giant lives next to the redwood home. The giant who collects round pebbles has a neighbour who drinks grog." Pinning Loki with narrowed black eyes, he asked, "Who owns the phoenix?"

Although Loki had expected something more difficult, he wasn't about to say so. "The mountain giant," he answered, trying not to smile. He didn't need to antagonize the Jotun lord right before he obtained the information he needed.

Thiazi grumbled, stomped, and waved a thick arm. With a frustrated sigh, he said, "Very well. Suttung's home is located halfway up a mountain, with his farm in the narrow valley between the two peaks. He has no neighbours."

Loki gave a slight bow to express his appreciation. "Thank you, Lord Thiazi. We won't impinge on your hospitality any longer."

The Jotun waved them off as he stomped back through his courtyard, grumbling in an undertone, and disappeared into his great hall.

The Asgardians hiked down until they reached the main stone trail.

"Do we head through the mountains towards Gastropnir or in the other direction towards Suttgard?" Thor wondered aloud, looking back and forth between the opposite directions.

Loki ran a hand through his hair and considered what he knew of the giant lord's territory. "Thiazi's territory only extends another day's walk in this direction before the trail descends to the forest and eventually rejoins the plains, whereas it extends a good fifteen days' travel towards Suttgard. Without the other clue, we'll have to check this way first, then if it doesn't pan out, try towards Gastropnir."

Thjalfi hung his head, hands clasped on the back of his neck as he looked down, kicking a rock on the trail. "I'm so sorry, Loki. It's my fault we don't have that third clue."

Loki patted his friend on the back. "None of us could have beaten him. We'll find Suttung." He led the group towards Suttgard, setting a brisk pace. The coiling tension in his gut had him pushing the others to make the best speed they could, eating meals as they walked. Not stopping when night fell despite the lethal nocturnal predators, they continued onward. Thjalfi ignored his injury and insisted on scouting ahead. As dawn rose the next morning, the warrior returned to tell them he'd spotted where the trail entered the forest, yet there was still no single farm in a valley between two mountain peaks.

"Bor's hairy damn balls!" Thor growled as the group spun to retrace their steps.

Loki wanted to join his brother in shouting his frustration at the mountainside, but drawing attention would only bring dangerous beasts down upon them. A tension headache pounded in his temples, and his jaw ached from clenching his teeth.

By early evening, they passed the hut they'd stayed at the night before last and continued on past the scree slope with the antlion burrows. In the dark, they picked their way carefully along the trail with a meagre glow Loki cast, trying to not attract attention. Once the first of Jotunheim's moons rose, reflecting off the snow and pale rock, it was easier to travel. He extinguished his light.

The second moon had risen when they stopped at another traveller's hut. Thor and Thjalfi sliced up a loaf of bread and cheese, while Mist dug out fruit and nuts from the packs. After a cold meal, Loki conjured a blanket and curled up in a corner, resigned to another sleepless night of his imagination haunting him.

Up a few short hours later, they hiked the trail as the sun finally rose over the mountain peaks. An uneventful day of travelling while covering a considerable distance, it made for a pleasant change compared to the challenges of the previous three days. Pushing onward, they continued through the night again, with no one complaining when Loki asked them to keep going.

The pale light of both moons reflected off the rocky surface of the trail when Roskva collapsed. Her twin caught her before she hit the ground.

"Ros? What's wrong?" he demanded as he held her waist.

"Nothing. I'm fine. Why are you holding me?" she slurred.

When Loki reached them from his position further down the trail, a suspicious, wet, viscous pink-tinged gel fell from Ros' back as Thjalfi held her up.

"Kara! Thor! Check everyone for Hirudo worms!" Loki shouted back to them, alarm raising his voice despite the risk. Kneeling beside Thjalfi and Ros, he tugged up the back of her jacket and tunic.

"What is it? What's wrong with her?" Thjalfi asked, blue eyes pleading. Roskva had lost consciousness. Blond braids splayed across the ground and her head lolled to the side as her twin held her up.

Loki swore when he got the tunic up enough to see her lower back. Six of the flesh-eating worms were latched on, their fifteen-centimetre-long flat grey-brown undulating bodies engorged a dark red from feasting on Roskva's body. The clear viscous fluid they secreted from their serrated, sucker-like mouths to keep the host desensitized and unaware dripped down in thick streams, soaking the waistband of her trousers and turning the light brown leather a dark black. The faintest hint of blood had escaped their mouths to colour the fluid in a few spots. If left unchecked, the worms would continue to feed until they reached their full half-metre length, killing her as they ate through her.

"We're all clear. We just need to check you and Thjalfi," Kara said, as they caught up.

"Yggdrasil's twisty branches! Those things are gross!" exclaimed Mist. She bent down to stare at Ros's back. "How do we get them off?"

"Fire or ice works, but don't touch them. Their skin contains a nerve agent that paralyzes, leaving you vulnerable to them if you try to take them off," Thor warned, catching Mist's reaching fingers and drawing her hand back.

After removing her weapons, pack, and jacket, Loki tore the tunic from Roskva's back and dropped it to the trail. "Fortunately, we don't need to touch them." Drawing Laevateinn and using his quarter frost giant heritage, Loki channelled ice down its length. Careful to avoid Ros' skin, he pressed the frozen tip of his sword to the side of one worm's circular mouth. It flinched, drawing back. Loki pressed further, and the worm detached its mouth hooks. Before it could re-attach itself to her body, he flicked his wrist, flinging the worm to the rocky trail. Channelling flames inherited from his other quarter fire giant nature down the blade, he incinerated the squirming worm and her tunic.

"Nasty. They stink." Mist crinkled her nose at the repulsive dead carrion smell as it burned.

Loki returned to Roskva's back, working on removing and incinerating the next worm.

Thor tugged up the back of his brother's tunic. "You and Thjalfi are clear as well. It's just Ros that has them." Thor let the fabric and leather of Loki's tunic and coat fall back into place.

"That's good. We're going to need to stop to treat her wounds. They fed deeply on her." Loki removed and incinerated the third worm.

Thor bent to look at her back. "Damn. They sure did. Do we have poultices for that?"

"I've got some that Healer Moja gave me." Kara dug into her pack.

Loki removed and incinerated the last three worms. "If the poultice doesn't work for her, I have some healing salves we can try." Conjuring a cloth, he wiped the worms' thick excretions from Ros' back, then dropped the cloth to incinerate it on the trail. With the thick fluid gone and the worms no longer feeding, the deep wounds wept dark rivers of blood, but he didn't see the pink of organs. The creatures hadn't made it through the muscles into her abdominal cavity, thank the Norns. The air stunk of burnt flesh mingled with the copper scent of blood.

"Tip her onto her stomach," Kara instructed.

Thor and Thjalfi turned Ros, cradling her while Kara applied poultices, packed the wounds and covered them with bandages. In the meantime, Loki cleaned his sword, heating the blade to remove any taint from the worms.

Mist eyed their surroundings. "Where would she pick them up?"

"Most likely the stream and waterfall area we stopped at for lunch." Loki wrinkled his nose as he reshealthed Laevateinn on his back. "They nest around moist areas and wait for animals to stop to drink. They tend to go for hard to reach areas where they can stay out of sight since that allows them to latch on without notice. Nasty bastards."

"I'll say! Getting eaten alive by those things is horrible." Mist shuddered in revulsion, rubbing her hands over her arms.

With Thor carrying Roskva's upper body wrapped in her jacket and Thjalfi carrying her legs to avoid the wounds on her back, they made their way to the next traveller's hut to stop for the remainder of the night. She hadn't regained consciousness by the time they laid her on her bedding.

Anxious to reach Suttung and find out what the giant knew about Shannon, Loki couldn't help but wonder how far they still had to travel. They'd come across several cottages and farms, but none like Thiazi had described. As his companions fell asleep around him, Loki sat with his back against the wall, head on his knees and hands at the back of his neck, trying to avoid imagining what tortures Shannon might be enduring at the hands of those who would turn her blood to mead.

Every second stretched into an eon.

Chapter 12

A TRAIL TO FOLLOW

W hen Thor took over the watch, Loki attempted to sleep. After tossing and turning, he eventually gave up and prepared breakfast. Fortunately, the poultices Healer Moja had supplied seemed to work for Roskva. Already the wounds were filling in, and although disgusted by Mist's descriptions of the worms, Ros was awake and recovering well. Still, she wasn't moving with her usual fluidity but could at least walk on her own. No one complained when Loki rushed them through the meal and back onto the trail as the sun rose, seemingly as anxious as he to continue.

Every day, hour, minute, and second brought Shannon closer to her due date. The ticking clock pressed on Loki like a mammoth sitting on his chest. She'd been missing more than four-and-a-half weeks. Assuming she was on either Alfheim or Jotunheim, less than eight weeks remained in her pregnancy.

But if she had somehow made it back to Midgard, their son would already be born. Not likely, given Loki still couldn't get a reply to his telepathic attempts to reach her through their soulmate bond. Unable to resist, he'd tried again last night, to no avail.

Was she okay? Was their child okay? Or—he swallowed against the lump rising in his throat—was she being tortured, her blood continually harvested for this sick mead? If only he could sense her emotions, something more than simply her presence within him. His hand shook as he shoved his hair back from his face, then rubbed at his chest. Norns, he had to find her, had to save her.

As often as Loki tried to push those thoughts away, they remained, like a Hirudo worm relentlessly eating his brain. Angry and vengeful emotions he could deal with. But this helplessness kept him huddled into himself, unable to join in the quiet conversation with the others as they hiked.

Shannon would be increasingly vulnerable as her due date approached. His heart squeezed, thundering in his chest every time he thought of her giving birth, alone... or worse, in captivity where her kidnappers could steal their son from her. He didn't know what to do with that fear. It roiled in his gut like a poisonous brew. There was too much time to think as they walked. Too much time to feel.

When Thjalfi returned from scouting ahead to say they'd reached a valley with a farm and cottage that fit the description they sought, energy surged through Loki and his senses sharpened. Finally, a chance for information, a clue, a way forward.

After shifting to a raven, he flew ahead to examine the location and entrance to the mountain home. Wheeling on the updrafts, Loki circled the stone house built into the mountain. Smoke wafting from the chimney suggested someone was inside. The fields further down the valley were empty of Jotuns, but the crops and livestock were well-tended.

He flew back to the others, changed back to humanoid, and relayed what he'd seen.

Kara crossed her arms. "We need a plan of attack."

"Thor knocks down the door, then you and he hold the giant in place while I take the information from his mind. Assuming it's Suttung, I don't plan to be nice. Nor am I in any mood to be patient." Loki met their gazes. "I've used up my patience. Diplomacy be damned. We've wasted enough time just finding him." Smiles and nods greeted Loki's growled words, and he continued, "While we question him, Jal and Mist can deal with the daughter and get the mead. Given you aren't back to full mobility, keep watch from outside, Ros. If anyone tries to escape from a door we don't know about, you can trap them in rock."

Thor chuckled, slapping Loki on the shoulder. "That sounds more like my plans than your usual finesse, brother. I approve!"

After a chorus of agreement, they crept within a few hundred metres of the home.

At Loki's nod, Thor threw Mjolnir. With a crash, it knocked the stone door off its hinges. The deafening boom echoed off the craggy mountain peaks.

The Asgardians charged through the broken doorway and into the dark depths of the house. An abrupt bellow of rage and a brief blast of fire announced the presence of the stout, pale giant, but Loki turned the flames back at the Jotun before any reached his friends and brother. After a brief struggle, Thor and Kara pinned the giant to the sturdy kitchen table.

Thjalfi and Mist sped behind Loki and into a passageway carved into the mountain like a dark, ominous, gaping mouth.

Loki approached the giant as he fought against Thor's and Kara's hold.

"Are you Suttung?" Rage turned Loki's voice deceptively calm.

"What's it to you? Who are you?" the giant demanded, even as his eyes darted nervously between Thor, Kara, and Loki. Sweat began beading on his speckled brow.

Yeah, Loki was done with this fucking polite shit when the giant's behaviour professed his guilt. No damned Bergrisar wielded fire. Instead of answering, he pressed his fingers to the Jotun's forehead and dove into his memories. At the same time, Loki projected what he saw into the room so the others could view it as well.

This was definitely Suttung.

Loki saw the daughter sitting in a dimly lit cave, working a loom to create rugs while guarding three light brown casks of mead. Following the path of those memories to where the giant acquired the mead was the image of a dwarf. Not one Loki knew, but the dwarf had their race's large, powerful stature, typical dark grey skin, misshapen face, small beady eyes, and straight shaggy hair.

This dwarf crowed about his success at following Suttung's directions for making a divine mead using a captive immortal. Suttung asked who the immortal was, but the dwarf, Galar, waved the question away. Once Suttung tasted the mead and experienced its power, he bought the three casks Galar had to sell and told the dwarf he'd be back to buy more.

"Where do we find Galar?" Loki demanded.

Suttung fought Loki's control, cursing. Ruthlessly, the prince cut further into the giant's mind, forcing the memories forward. Blood poured from

Suttung's nose, ears, and eyes as he fought Loki's telepathic probe. The damned giant was dead either way. No way would Loki allow the fucker to live after he'd told dwarves how to make a blood mead and drank another immortal's powers, some of their life's essence, whether or not that immortal was Shannon.

Loki dug deeper.

There was a spaceport, then a massive market with a mix of races and Dwarven craftsmen with their booths. It was Eternity Market, the space base run by the dwarves on the largest of Alfheim's moons and used for all their off-planetary trade with the galaxy's space-faring races. But this Galar hadn't had his own storefront. He'd sold the mead from a portable cart. With a snarl, Loki dug for Suttung's earlier memories. If the fucker had taught the dwarf how to make the mead, then he'd interacted with Galar before. There was the bright blue beam of a dwarven teleport, then carved tunnels, and a workshop off a massive cavern with rivers of lava.

Loki recognized Nidavellir.

Of course.

Nidavellir was deep below the surface of Alfheim, not aligned with either the Summer or Winter Elven Courts, but a separate realm ruled by the four Dwarven kings. Asgardians accessed the dwarves of Nidavellir directly through the Bifrost to a reception area controlled by each Dwarven king or on Eternity Market, but never from the Elven realms or from Alfheim's surface. Yet there must be access tunnels that linked the two Elven realms to Nidavellir.

It never even occurred to Loki to search Nidavellir. Dwarves were miners, craftsmiths, weapons makers, and engineers. They brewed fine ales and meads. Unless their kings had been hiding behind the cloak of the Unseelie, they weren't known for taking prisoners—aside from the few wars they'd fought. Dwarves didn't practice ritual sacrifice, or any kind of blood magic. They had no need when their realm provided so richly for their lifestyle. Their goods, indeed their craftsmasters of all fields, were widely sought and welcomed across the galaxy, not just by the races of the Nine Realms.

Either way, Loki had a location and a name to pursue. The immortal this Galar held captive might not be Shannon, but Loki would find out.

Thjalfi and Mist returned, carrying the three casks Loki had seen in Suttung's mind. They placed them by Loki, and he stepped away from the giant, releasing his telepathic control.

Ignoring Suttung's renewed struggles and blood flowing in thick, dark ribbons down the giant's face, Loki focused on the casks. His fingers trembled as he removed the cork from one. The sweet scent filled the room. Gut churning, Loki sent a tendril of black seidhr inside.

The mead sung with Shannon's essence, saturated with her life force and power.

Savage rage, burning so fiercely, coldly pure that it was the lethal calm of death, flashed instantly into a towering fiery inferno. It hazed Loki's mind, snapping the leash of conscious control. Screaming, he incinerated the casks and chopped off Suttung's head, Laevateinn flaming in his hand, before anyone realized Loki had moved.

Splattered in blood from the headless body he and Kara let drop, Thor held out a hand to calm his sibling. "We will find her, brother. The dwarf will die."

"Is the daughter who guarded that disgusting abomination dead?" Loki growled in a barely articulate snarl.

"Yes, Loki. She didn't give it up willingly," Mist said, no regret in her tone.

"Then let's get out of this fucking Norns-forsaken realm and rescue Shannon from these butchers," Loki ground out, ready to take on all of Nidavellir if he needed to. After burning off the polluting blood and sheathing his sword, he punted Suttung's head out of the way. It splatted against the far wall. The giant's death had been far too fast for his crimes, but Loki refused to waste time with the fucker when he had a lead on Shannon's location.

Ushering the others ahead of him as he left, Loki released a blast of chaos. He didn't look back as a landslide wiped out all evidence that a home had ever resided there. Instead, he led the group back down the mountain.

Instead of turning to follow the trail, Loki continued over it and into the forest below. He wanted the first available location far enough from the chaos energy that infused all Jotun-built roads, trails, and structures so the Bifrost could lock on and transport them. Shannon had waited long enough for his rescue.

Steadily over the next six hours, the quiet party sped their way through the gloomy forest, heading downhill toward the grasslands. The forest wasn't as foreboding during the day. The occasional bird chirped. Trees swayed in the light breeze, creaking. A rodent, similar to Midgardian chipmunks, but dark grey with big ears, chittered as it scampered amongst the branches.

Yet no one spoke. The only evidence of their passing was the occasional crunch as they hit a patch of snow or a fallen branch with a careless footfall.

Until Thjalfi raced back towards them from his position, scouting ahead. "Stampede! There's an auroch stampede headed our way!"

Loki met Thor's gaze—their eyebrows rising in unison. The massive cattle were grassland dwellers and not particularly aggressive, although their long curved horns could do damage. Still, at four thousand pounds with sharp horns, the Asgardians did not want to be caught amongst the aurochs' enormous bodies.

"Why would they come into the forest?" Thor eyed their surroundings as the first rumble of hundreds of hooves striking the ground reached them.

"It's got to be a predator spooking them. We should be safe in the trees until they pass. Everyone, up a tree!" Loki climbed a large nearby pine and looked over as the others also quickly scrambled up thick trunks. Even Ros, despite a few winces and muttered curses, had made it partway up a tree before her golden seidhr petered out, and the soil wave she'd been using fell back. It left her lower than he'd like.

The thundering sound grew until it was deafening. The vibration shook his tree, pine needles falling as the cattle appeared. Eyes wide with panicked breaths, they swerved around tree trunks. Their scared bellows echoed in the landscape and mixed with the rhythm of their hooves. It was a fast-moving stream of reddish-brown hides with flashing, deadly white horns.

The steady flow of bodies underneath the Asgardians started to decline as the bulk of the stampede passed uphill. Silently, Loki swore as he got his first glimpse at what had panicked the cattle. Using Valkyrie hand signals, he warned Mist and Ros, the nearest to his tree, telling them to pass it on. They needed to be absolutely silent.

A sleek black-and-tan form leapt gracefully onto the back of an auroch, slashing its throat, before jumping to a nearby tree to avoid the flashing horns as the cow writhed in its death struggles. Another predator pounced from farther away, taking down its own prey.

Ros let out a startled curse when a thousand-pound leaping saber-tooth jaguar landed on a thick branch immediately below her, the tree swaying with the impact. The huge head whipped up. It snarled, ears flattened, swatting a massive paw tipped with lethal claws at her. She tried to climb out of reach, and the cat followed in a far more nimble display, dragging the injured Valkyrie back down the trunk by her thick leather pants.

Mjolnir crashed through the tree, knocking the cat out of the tree before returning to Thor. "That won't keep the jaguar down for long! We need to get out of here!"

Loki winced. This was exactly what he'd hoped to avoid.

The Asgardians now had the attention of the entire hunting pride as predatory yellow eyes narrowed and fixed on them. The remainder of the cattle escaped, with only those the cats had already taken down dead or dying on the forest floor.

With Roskva's powers questionable as her energy went to healing the gaping wounds in her back, Mist would need to carry her. But while Mist knew how to make the most of her abilities, she didn't have the endurance to carry Roskva through the air for the remaining kilometres to the plains. As strong as his brother was, Thor couldn't carry two others when he flew.

And these damned cats wouldn't give up hunting them.

"Thor, we need to hold them off to let the others get out of here. We'll never make it if we try to run. They're already stalking us," Loki yelled back.

Mist floated in the air, firing blasts of air at the cat trying to reach Kara. Thjalfi had taken advantage of Thor's attack to drop from his tree and distract the cats from climbing after his twin. He ran with two cats in pursuit, twisting back and forth between the trees.

But there were too many of the relentless beasts, and more slunk toward the Asgardians.

"Go! Everyone, go! Downhill to the grasslands. Loki and I will join you there!" Thor boomed as he knocked another jaguar back with Mjolnir.

Ros scrambled out of her tree but couldn't move fast enough to avoid the claws that raked her from shoulder to wrist. Her armour took most of the impact, but she bit back her cry, cradling her arm where a gap between vambrace and shoulder armour left a gap for claws to tear flesh. Loki dove onto the cat gathering for another swipe.

"Go!" he yelled, even as he teleported the cat and himself away from her. It was a snarling, squirming mass of fangs and claws. After shoving it back to give himself space, Loki shifted into an equally massive black jaguar and roared in rage. The confused cat's ears flattened to its skull, and it backed away, body lowered. Its mouth opened to hiss at Loki, and he roared at it again.

Catching movement in his peripheral vision, Loki turned as another leapt for his throat. Swatting it with claws out and baring his fangs, Loki twisted away and then caught the cat, sinking his teeth into the thick fur of its nape. When he raked his claws down the jaguar's flank, it yowled in pain. The stink of copper filled Loki's nose. Damn it. He didn't want to kill the majestic animals, but he had to keep them from following.

"Loki! Stop wrestling and let's go!" Thor yelled.

After kicking away the jaguar he'd injured, Loki teleported to Thor as his brother hit several with lightning to discourage them. With a paw on him, Loki teleported them away from the fight, released his brother, and shifted to a raven. Together, they flew down the mountain to catch up with the rest of their party. The brothers reached the other Asgardians just as Thjalfi and Kara, with Roskva carried between them, broke out of the trees and into the plains of the grassland, still running full out. Mist ran through the air behind them, covering their retreat.

Loki shifted back to humanoid and landed. "We don't have a lot of time before those jaguar catch up."

"Heimdall?" Thor called.

The lights of the Bifrost descended and swirled around them. With less than their usual grace, they landed on Asgard's platform and the colours dissipated.

"I have informed Odin of your findings on Jotunheim and that you will be travelling to Nidavellir," Heimdall said, lifting his hand from the hovering holographic pad near the wall. "Do you know which of the four kings' territories you want to start with?"

"If I'm not mistaken, Sudri and Vestri's territories are the most likely to be under the Winter Court. Does that sound correct to you, Heimdall?" Loki asked.

"Yes, my prince."

"Brokkr and Eitri are in Sudri's territory, but the dwarves of the builder's guild are in Vestri's territory," Loki mused. "What do you think, Thor?"

"Let's try Brokkr and Eitri first. They know a lot of other dwarves, and we've had a good relationship with them for far longer than you've known the ones in the builder's guild."

"As long as it's not back to Jotunheim. Everything wants to eat us in that Norns-forsaken realm!" complained Thjalfi with a dramatic huff. Kara and Mist hid their laugh behind their hands as Ros smacked him on the back of the head, then staggered. She fell against a pillar. Blood dripped from the make-shift bandage covering her arm onto the marbled grey stone.

Thjalfi pulled out the green emergency kit from its concealed nook. He unwrapped the saturated bandage from his twin's forearm up to her biceps. As the pressure was released, a red gush sprayed from the ripped flesh of her elbow.

"Damn it. I think I need the healers. I'm just slowing you down like this, Loki." She winced as Thjalfi applied a temporary sealant.

Pale and sweating, her complexion told Loki everything he needed to know. Between the worms and the jaguars, she'd tapped her reserves. He'd pushed them hard to get to this point with little rest. Kara still had scratches on her face that hadn't yet healed despite her immortal healing. Mist was disheveled—her blue hair escaping her braids in a wild halo. Even his brother looked worn. But fuck, how could he delay now when they'd finally had a solid lead?

Thjalfi met Loki's gaze. "I'll take her. My calf isn't at full strength yet either so I could use a trip to the healer hall. The rest of you should continue on to rescue our princess. We'll catch up as soon as possible."

Loki shook his head, trying to not grit his teeth. "No, we'll take a six-hour break for a nap, meal, and healing, then meet back here to go to Brokkr and Eitri. I don't want exhaustion or injury to be the reason we fail to rescue Shannon." His fingers tightened on his pack. It was the wisest course of action, but by Yggdrasil's mighty roots, he was tempted to leave them all behind to go now.

<I'm coming, Shannon. Hang on, I'm coming.>

Chapter 13

PICK A DIRECTION

S hannon crept along, nerves sparking and flinching at every hiss and pop of lava. She tried to keep the wall of the massive cavern within sight as she detoured across a bridge of the fiery red rock when the flow blocked her path. Sweat poured down her brow, trickled down her spine and between her breasts as she was forced closer to the steaming, lethal molten rock. With the additional brightness of the crisscrossing lava streams, she wasn't sure how well her air-bending would hide her. Instead, she kept a wary eye out for Fjalar and Galar and picked out hiding places behind boulders and bridge edges.

At the first opening that wasn't another workshop, she left the cavern. The stone corridor headed down. Too hot as she was, no way did she want to go deeper. Backtracking, Shannon returned to the cavern and tried the next corridor.

This one sloped gradually upwards, and after a ten-minute walk, she spotted one of those air shaft elevators the dwarves had used. She poked her head in, peering up and down the vertical shaft. No controls. How did they work? She waved her hand and slapped the wall, but nothing happened. Using her powers, she stepped into the shaft and shot upwards. It was a long, long way, passing opening after opening, before she reached the top, stopping with a tired jerk just before she hit her head on the roof of the shaft. Gods, her reflexes were shot.

After floating out, Shannon released the air and dropped heavily onto her feet, grunting at the impact. Not exactly graceful. But then, little of her was graceful at present. Noticeably cooler compared to the constant heat so many levels below, she shivered and rubbed her hands over her arms while she adapted to the change. Starting to tire, especially after using that air shaft, she crept down the smooth stone tunnel. Whenever her feet slapped down, exhaustion getting the better of her, she hissed and stiffened, glancing around. She'd dropped the air-bending disguise, too worn out to use it. She had to conserve her waning energy until she found somewhere to hide and rest.

Some tunnels weren't smooth, but roughly hewn, as if they were still under construction. She checked each until she finally spotted a dead-end. Based on the haphazard rock piles, it didn't look as if anyone had been in it for a while. With her body tucked behind boulders near the dead-end, she closed her eyes. She let herself drift for a while, then jolted awake every so often to check her surroundings and any sounds suggesting someone might be approaching her hiding spot. Although her sleep wasn't particularly restful, her eyelids drooped regardless.

When she'd finally recovered enough that she didn't have to concentrate to keep her eyes open, Shannon ate a meal of cheese and bread. With a little more energy, she set out again. She had to get farther from her captors. Every once in a while, she heard the murmur of voices, but they never came down her tunnel. At each junction, she stopped to listen and chose the one with no voices or sounds of activity. Damn it, she knew so little about dwarves. She couldn't risk asking for help. What if she asked ones that hated Loki? Or others that also wanted to use her to power their forges?

No, she couldn't risk it.

After stumbling forward for hours, the air grew humid, and she gratefully sucked it in. Even with the faintest ashy tang, it was better than the heat that had baked her for weeks. Despite drinking constantly, her lips had become chapped and dry until that saltwater bath finally healed her.

Was there some kind of water source down here? Surely, dwarves needed water, too?

She started choosing her direction by the path that held more moisture but didn't have any voices. A day or so later, after finding several more sheltered nooks to nap and successfully avoiding anyone as she walked the endless tunnels, Shannon's luck ran out.

Shannon yelped as she turned a corner and came face-to-face with someone else.

The small being, barely tall enough to reach Shannon's waist, shrieked and fell backwards onto their butt.

Grey skin and dark hair back in two braids framed a small face. Was this... was this a Dwarven child?

Shannon held her hands out, trying to calm the child down. "Whoa! I won't hurt you!" With the kid's dark eyes wide and scared, Shannon did *not* want this young dwarf running to their parents, giving away where she was. "Please, it's okay. Really. I mean you no harm."

"Are... are you Seelie or Unseelie?" the child asked in a high, trembling voice.

It took Shannon a minute to understand the question. She didn't yet consider herself an elf. In her mind, she was still human. Despite the results of her genetic testing and goddess powers.

"Seelie," Shannon said, smiling as she held out a hand. The child took it, returning her smile. "What are you doing, off on your own?"

"I wanted to go play in the Howling Falls."

"Hmm... I've never played in the Howling Falls. Is it fun?" Shannon asked with deliberately wide eyes and a playful tone.

The child grinned, eyes lighting up. "Is it *ever*! You can jump on one of the mead barrels and shoot down the falls and then float the rumbling river all the way to the seaport cavern where they load the ships to trade with King Austri's territory."

"Wow, that *does* sound like fun! I would love to see you do that." She couldn't trust an adult dwarf, but a child? Surely, she could trust a child to not deliberately lead her into danger, and a seaport cavern sounded promising. There had to be a way to the surface from there.

"Sure!" The child tugged Shannon's hand and led her forward, turning several times before a rumble reached her ears. As they got closer, the sound became the more distinct roaring of water. The air grew saturated and misty spray floated through the air ahead.

The end of the corridor opened onto a stone platform, slick with water and moss. A graceful carved stone bridge led across a set of falls that sloped into uneven pools and drops of no more than ten metres each. Across the bridge on the far platform, several corridors led into the darkness, with metre-high barrels stacked in holding bins. On each side of the falls, wet, moss-covered stairs led up and down.

The child dropped Shannon's hand, dashed surefooted across the soaked bridge, pulled a brown barrel from a bin, and shoved it into the nearby pool. With a whoop and grin, the kid jumped in the pool and lay on the barrel, kicking with their legs until the barrel was poised to slip over the first step of the falls.

It looked dangerous. Should she should stop the child? Before Shannon could decide, the young dwarf and barrel tipped over the edge.

"Yeah!" the kid shouted, clearly loving it. The barrel bobbed in the pool after surviving the first fall unscathed. With no hesitation, the little dwarf pushed the barrel towards the next step of the falls.

After wrapping mist around her—surely, the child couldn't be unsupervised for long—Shannon crept down the stairs. The falls became shallower as she descended, gradually turning into a meandering stream after a few minutes of walking. Before the seaport came into view, the kid floated out of sight.

The smell of saltwater filled Shannon's senses as she approached the massive cavern, and her jaw dropped when she caught her first glimpse. Holy cow. It was an underground sea, with the ceiling far, far up above. Occasional wave-smoothed white stone pillars stretched from below the water's surface to the ceiling. She couldn't tell what it was, but some kind of glowing vegetation grew in patches along the ceiling. Was it the same as what grew in the tunnels? It provided a soft green light to the unusual scene.

A net stretched along the stream's mouth to catch barrels as they came downstream, and a stack of barrels was piled on one side. Sailless, mastless ships, shaped like large Viking long boats were tied to a stone wharf near the mouth of the stream. Dwarves loaded barrels onto one, heaving them effortlessly with their powerful builds. She'd yet to see a short, slender or weak dwarf, not counting the child. Shannon didn't spy any means of propulsion for the ships as she crept closer, careful to stay in the shadows with mist wrapped around her.

With a little air boost, she climbed onto the slate tile roof of a stone wharf-side building. She peered over the edge at the ships—some held metal ore and others held sacks of grain that were being unloaded onto wagons. Guided by a dwarf, a fully loaded wagon disappeared into a wide tunnel at the same level as the wharf, but like the ships, she couldn't spot any obvious form of propulsion.

After creeping back from the edge so she wouldn't be seen from below, she lay on her back and stared at the ceiling far above. This was the safest place she'd found to take a few minutes to consider her options.

If Heimdall couldn't see into most of Alfheim, including Nidavellir, because of the cloaking mist Frigga had mentioned, would he be able to see Shannon if she went to the surface? Did the mist veil the entire planet? All of Nidavellir? She didn't know for sure. Gods, what she'd give for an immortal version of Google. Was there a wiki-gods she didn't yet know about?

There had to be some places the Bifrost could connect to on this blasted planet. Asgardians travelled to the Summer Realm, and there was a Dwarven market that was popular. She'd heard some of the Valkyrie talking about it. Maybe she just needed to keep trying?

"Heimdall? Can you hear me?" she murmured, hoping none of the dwarves on the wharf below would hear. They were making enough noise that she didn't think her quiet words could be heard over the clanking of wagons, the thump of barrels, and shouted orders.

When the rainbow lights didn't sweep her up, she tried to ignore the sinking in her gut. Still, tears pricked her eyes, and she scrubbed at them. Picking through her small stash of food, she took out the nuts and nibbled on them while massaging her abdomen where her son kicked and stretched. He was elbowing her in the ribs on her left side—or maybe that was a knee or foot. Either way, it was uncomfortable. Gods, if only Loki was there to rub her belly and soothe their son.

She sniffed, fingering her charm bracelet. <*I miss you, Loki.*> Since getting rid of the chains, Shannon sensed the bond was there again, but she couldn't feel him and hadn't gotten any response whenever she tried to communicate. Still, she continued to send a telepathic message every so often.

Damn it, she felt so alone.

If she was going to ask for help, and it was looking like she'd have to at some point, as the probability of her stumbling into a location that Heimdall could see was slim, then she wanted to be far from Fjalar and Galar. Far from any of those dwarves Fjalar had threatened to sell her to.

Somehow, she needed to get out of Nidavellir and reach the planet's surface without running into the Unseelie or unfriendly dwarves. If what she'd overheard was true, Asgard's forces and Loki might be on the surface, searching for her. Or she could take her chances in the Summer Realm, if she could find it. Surely the Seelie would help her get back to Loki. Although, how would she know if an elf was Seelie or Unseelie? She snorted. If only light and dark meant something visible, tangible, instead of where their powers originated and which realm they'd sworn allegiance to. How inconsiderate of the bad guys to not look like bad guys. She rolled her eyes at herself.

How was she going to find the surface? Climbing to the planet's surface through Nidavellir's tunnels seemed to be just asking to get caught again. She sat up and glanced around. Could she get there from this underground sea? The Dwarven child said it connected with the other kings' territories, and there were four kings, if she was remembering correctly. There must be other ways to the surface.

Peeking over the side, Shannon confirmed there weren't any small boats, just the large ships that didn't have cabins. They were entirely open, with the cargo lashed in place along the centre of the ship. It didn't leave anywhere to hide on a ship if she wanted to stowaway on board.

But why did she need to stowaway? If her senses weren't lying, then it was saltwater. She'd be able to use her powers to propel herself without being drained. At least, she hoped so. Gods, she was exhausted all the freaking time now. Even a small use of her powers wore her out. Of course, she also had no idea what creatures might lurk in an underground ocean, but she did know what would happen if Fjalar and Galar recaptured her.

Decision made, she laid down and closed her eyes. Just a little more rest first.

Chapter 14

DON'T LOSE YOUR HEAD

K ing Sudri's palace reception chamber was a large cavernous space, with high carved marble pillars that depicted the line of previous kings. Although having a lifespan twelve times longer than Midgardians, dwarves had the shortest lives of the immortal races. Sudri was the third king of this territory that Loki had known in his years visiting their realm.

"Welcome Prince Thor, Prince Loki, and companions. To what do we owe the visit?" asked Einhenda, the Dwarven Ambassador for King Sudri, as she gave a respectful nod. Her massive build was encased in a sleek, brown-and-gold armoured hi-tech suit with a long, gold sleeveless duster, as if she'd just come from their off-world spaceport—the Eternity Galactic Market on Alfheim's largest moon, An Tsíorafocht. For the most part, dwarves kept their advanced technology hidden, unless it came to commerce. With few exceptions, visitors were restricted to the moons and not allowed down to Alfheim by the dwarves who controlled the spaceport and teleport technology, just as Asgardians restricted who could visit Asgard's planetary surface.

"We come seeking my consort, Princess Shannon. She was taken. We have intelligence that she has been held here in Nidavellir by a dwarf named Galar," Loki answered. His usual patience with formalities was nonexistent. He found himself having to still an unfamiliar urge to fidget. Politics was the last thing on his mind at present, even if a small kernel of curiosity bloomed. Who were the dwarves hosting that had their ambassadors attending the popular market?

"I am not aware of a dwarf by that name. Is he or she in this kingdom?" Einhenda's voice had turned cautious, dark eyes wide as she looked back and forth between Loki and Thor.

Loki frowned, glancing at his brother. The ambassador showed no surprise that Shannon had been taken. Why had the dwarves not reached out to aid Asgard if they knew Shannon was missing on Alfheim? Had relations between the two realms deteriorated and Thor not mentioned it?

"We don't know, but we will seek him across all four kingdoms if we must." Thor's expression was as dark as one of his storm clouds, with sparks of lightning in his eyes.

The ambassador swallowed, then asked, "You have proof that this Galar has, or had, your consort?"

Fed up with the delay, Loki bit back his snarl as he projected the memory he had taken from Suttung. When he finished, Einhenda was pale. Given the dark grey complexion of dwarves, it was an impressive feat.

Her voice trembled with suppressed outrage. "We do *not* abide by the twisted, depraved magic that has corrupted the Unseelie and some of the Jotun. I'll pass on the evidence to my king. We will not stop you from taking your revenge against this dwarf who has so clearly wronged you and your consort."

Loki blinked, gratified. That had been more of the response he'd expected. "Thank you, Ambassador Einhenda."

She bowed deeply as the Asgardians took their leave.

Exiting the chamber with impatient footsteps, the group set off on the four-hour journey to Brokkr and Eitri's workshop. It was an easy walk through the wide Dwarven tunnels. After taking an air chute down to the correct level, they wove their way through the three bustling market caverns of Dumgan, Highrim, and Obsidian where dwarves sold breads, grains, vegetables, livestock, preserved meats, metal ore, and other goods. Guild members sold products from the metalworkers, leatherworkers, gemworkers, artisans, builders, chemsmiths, and weaponsmiths. Ordinarily, the princes would have stopped to browse the selection of wares, always of the highest quality for the home market, but not today.

Upon leaving Obsidian, the last of the three markets, the Asgardians followed the wide wagon trail tunnel until it reached the Howling Falls wharves on the Sea of Lantia. Workers busied themselves loading and unloading the numerous ships that travelled back and forth between Dwarven kingdoms. After passing the bustling docks, the group worked their way along the rocky shoreline path to finally climb the steps to Brokkr and Eitri's workshop.

Thor banged on the heavy wooden door, and a shout echoed from inside.

"Hang on, hang on to your damn pants!" grumbled a low, rough voice as it got closer.

The door swung open, and Brokkr stood there. He blinked a couple of times at seeing the princes, and then a smile cracked his ugly face.

"Well! I'll be a spent chunk of coal! Asgardians at my door on this fine afternoon! Welcome!" He stepped aside to let them enter.

When they walked past him, they entered the main workshop. It was a large open space with multiple forges along one wall and benches, tools, and materials in the centre. Another wall held shelves with weapons' moulds and finished weapons. The third wall had doors that led to a couple of smaller workshops, several bedrooms, a bathroom, a lounge, and a kitchen.

Closing the door with a thump, Brokkr brushed his large bulk past the Asgardians and opened the door to the corridor leading to the lounge and kitchen. The group followed him and found Eitri sitting at a wooden table with a mug of ale, eating stew while drawing a design. He looked up at their entrance, then smiled with delight.

"Asgardians! Thor! Loki! It is so good to see you! Nothing wrong with Mjolnir, is there?" he asked in his deep but surprisingly pleasant voice.

Thor swung Mjolnir around. "Nope, it's as good as the day you made it, Eitri!"

"Ale?" asked Brokkr.

"Yes," Thor replied. "Oh, sorry. Introductions. This is Kara, Mist, and the twins Thjalfi and Roskva."

"I'm Brokkr," he said, pointing to himself. "This ugly face is Eitri," he pointed with his thumb.

"Hey! If I'm ugly, so are you, brother!" Eitri complained good-naturedly, dark eyes twinkling.

Brokkr filled mugs with ale and set them down in front of the Asgardians as they joined Eitri at the large table.

"So what brings Asgardians to our door? Are you commissioning more weapons?" Eitri asked, one heavy eyebrow quirking up.

"Nothing that pleasant," Loki growled, before taking a big gulp of ale. He didn't want to be rude to Eitri and Brokkr, but his fury every time he considered what Shannon was suffering had him grasping for control of his powers.

"Loki's consort, Princess Shannon, has been taken. First by the Wild Hunt, then by a dwarf named Galar," Thor explained. "Do you know of him?"

"Fouled melds," Brokkr swore. "Yes. He's a slimy journeyman for the chemsmith guild. Never could get his master's rank. You'd have to be desperate to buy or trade anything with that piece of spent coal. He's got a buddy he hangs with... Oh, what's his name?"

"Fjalar," Eitri said, looking equally disgusted as his brother. "What a worthless hunk of basalt. That murderer spent time in the lowest coal mines after killing another dwarf. And he's also a journeyman chemsmith. Useless, the pair of them."

"Do you know where their workshop is?" asked Mist.

"Yes. It's two, two and a half hours from here, down on one of the lowest residence levels right at the start of the lava fields, I think," Eitri answered. "What in the five hells are Galar and Fjalar doing with your consort, Loki?"

Loki's throat tightened. He couldn't respond. Instead, he projected Suttung's memory and their finding of the casks of mead for Eitri and Brokkr.

Both dwarves had their mouths hanging in shock when Loki was done. Brokkr was the first to recover.

"*Those foul, lava-licking fools!* I'll fucking kill them!" He got up and strode out towards the main workshop.

"Dead. Dead fucking dwarves walking," muttered Eitri as he followed his brother.

The Asgardians glanced at each other in surprise. Loki hadn't expected them to be almost as furious as he was. The dwarves didn't even know Shannon. After rising from their seats, the group rejoined the Dwarven brothers in the workshop.

Eitri picked up a heavy warhammer, and Brokkr pulled a double-bladed axe from a top shelf.

"Do any of you need weapons?" Eitri asked.

"No, we're good. We came prepared," Thor said.

"Thank you for the offer, though. We appreciate it," Loki answered with a respectful nod. Dwarves did not offer their weapons lightly. Especially master weaponsmiths who'd crafted every weapon here themselves by hand. It was a sign of great respect and trust.

Eitri grunted. "Least we can do. Right. Let's go get this done, then." He headed towards the door, opened it, and left.

The Asgardians followed, with Brokkr bringing up the rear.

Back down the steps, they returned along the shoreline of the Sea of Lantia until they reached the Howling Falls wharves. Retracing their steps, they strode up the tunnel with the numerous heavily laden wagons travelling to the Obsidian market cavern. They wove their way through the busy market and to the other side, but instead of the corridor that led back towards the next market cavern and the king's palace, Eitri took a passageway that turned to the right.

Although less busy, they still passed other dwarves heading in the opposite direction. They gave the Asgardians a curious look, but the scowl on Eitri and Brokkr's face didn't invite conversation. Anxiety built within Loki with every step. It was everything he could do not to break out in a run.

After another hour of walking, Eitri led the group to an air chute. It was a long, long way down, much farther than Loki had taken a chute previously. When they exited, the air was hotter with an eye-watering sulphur stench.

It was about fifteen minutes of walking through various tunnels before they entered an enormous cavern with crisscrossing streams of lava. Eitri led them on a twisted path around and over stone bridges as they made their way through the cavern, turning to head towards a far wall. He read the writing above each doorway, then stopped at a particular one and entered.

It was a workshop with several benches, forges on one side, and chemistry apparatus, casks, and cauldrons set up on the middle bench. Snarling, Eitri slammed his warhammer on the chemistry apparatus, shattering it. With another blow, he smashed the casks. The smell of mead and Shannon's blood filled the air.

Furious, Loki obliterated it all, including the workbench.

Eitri looked back at him and nodded. "Nicely done."

Thor and Brokkr disappeared into a room off of the workshop, while Thjalfi and Roskva took another, and Mist and Kara took a third. About to head to the fourth opening, Loki caught sight of something that halted him dead in his tracks.

In the far corner, hanging on the wall by a small bed, iron chains with cuffs dangled. The chains were attached to a device on the wall that connected to the forges. Loki stopped Eitri, reaching up to put a hand on the dwarf's shoulder, turning him towards the sight.

The dwarf sucked in a harsh breath. "*No!* They *didn't!*"

"Is this what I think it is?" Loki asked, horrified. Barely able to get the words out, nausea was a violent burn in his throat. By the Norns, he didn't want to accept what he saw.

"If you think it is one of the Unseelie's disgusting life force draining devices, then yes, it's exactly what you think it is," Eitri snarled with fury. He started ripping it apart.

"They have it connected to their forges?" Loki hissed, before he roared, "They had my consort powering their fucking workshop *like a Norns-cursed battery?*"

A turbulent storm of madness swept through him, wiping out rational thought. Only instinct remained. Swirling in the air around him, his power reflected the violent, chaotic inferno inside.

Destroy.

Destroy it *all*.

Whatever his chaos power touched disintegrated in an ever-widening, churning black circle as primal rage tapped into the well of his Jotun heritage.

Gone. He wanted it all gone. Erased out of existence.

The others raced back into the main workshop.

"Oh fuck," Mist said, her voice muffled to Loki's ears.

Thor roared when he saw the device Eitri was dismantling, heedlessly striding around the edges of Loki's swirling cloud of devastation to help Eitri rip it apart.

Seeing Thor almost in the path of his unleashed chaos jarred Loki's brain from its animalistic destruction. As reason returned, the potential of accidentally killing his brother, *another* brother, had Loki straining to rein it in. Chaos, once unleashed, wanted to grow.

With his chest heaving like he'd run the length of Asgard's central plains, he clawed back control, bit by ragged bit. Until, body trembling, he contained the last black tendrils of energy.

Two dwarves entered the workshop, took one glance and bolted. Like a leaping predator, Loki teleported in front of them, Laevateinn drawn and flaming, halting their flight. He wasn't about to let his prey escape. Pointing his sword at them, he forced them into the workshop.

Seconds later, the others joined Loki, restraining the two dwarves.

"Galar and Fjalar, I presume?" Loki glanced at Eitri when they stayed silent, and the dwarf nodded.

"We can do this the easy way or the hard way, but either way, you *will* tell me what I want to know." Loki's voice was a lethal knife's edge, deceptively soft. *Shred their brains, extract what you want and then obliterate them*, suggested his ruthless chaos-driven instincts. *There's no need to ask questions with such overwhelming guilt*. Loki shifted his shoulders, standing straighter as he further reinforced control over his powers and shoved those seductive thoughts back.

One dwarf glared around the room, staring at them with a mulish twist to his lips, while the other flinched and stared at his feet.

"Where is Shannon?"

"Don't know any Shannon," the defiant dwarf scoffed.

"The hard way it is, then," Loki said, smiling in teeth-baring delight. Restraining himself was getting harder by the second, especially after reining in his chaos earlier.

The other dwarf started speaking, his words tumbling together in his rush to get them out. "We don't know! She got away a few days ago. We haven't been able to find her!"

Slapping his fingers to the burbling dwarf's forehead, Loki sliced into the sick bastard's memories, uncaring how his telepathic powers cut into the soon-to-be-dead dwarf's brain. He was done with restraint. Screams erupted and blood bubbled from every orifice as Loki projected the dwarf's memories for everyone.

Huh. The asshole had told the truth.

Not waiting, Loki stepped to the no longer defiant dwarf who begged but gave no real answers. Loki tore into the dwarf's pathetic mind, ignoring the horrific screeches as blood poured from the bastard's eyes, ears, nose, and mouth. With ruthless efficiency, Loki hacked and slashed, but didn't get all the way through projecting the sick fucker's memories of Shannon before black rage took over and the dwarf's Norns-cursed head was on the stone floor, Laevateinn in Loki's hand.

That filthy, sadistic fucker had been the one to cut into Shannon, to steal her blood and make the mead. He'd *hurt* her! And once again, Loki had made the death too quick.

Muscles rigid, Loki howled his fury. By the Nine Realms, he wanted to revive the dwarf just to kill him again, achingly slow. Shaking with black seidhr swirling around him, Loki's telekinesis exploded the other dwarf's head as the bastard begged, choking on blood. Shannon had begged, too, asking them to stop cutting her, and yet this one had happily sold the mead and crowed about their profits.

"Gross, Loki. Effective, but gross," complained Kara, wiping blood and brain matter from her face.

With a snarl, Loki kicked the severed head into the nearest forge. *Four days!* We missed her by four fucking days!" he roared, kicking and stomping the two headless bodies.

Chapter 15

TEMPTING FRENEMIES

With a jolt, Shannon woke. She bit back a groan. Although she'd needed the rest after constantly fighting off exhaustion while wandering those tunnels for days, her muscles had stiffened from not moving. Sitting up was harder than it should have been, even with her pregnancy. Damn. How long had she slept? Hours at least and deep enough that she'd dreamt of Mist's and Kara's voices. Gods, if only.

Fortunately, she'd neither tumbled off the roof nor been spotted. Shannon rolled her eyes at herself. And wouldn't that have been an ignominious end to her escape attempt? Still, she thumped her thigh with a fist. She *had* to be more careful.

On hands and knees, she crept to the roof's edge. The wharf remained a hive of activity, but perhaps it always was. Without a change in light or a watch, she had no way of judging time. After backing away from the edge, she crawled toward the next building.

A small burst of air later and Shannon was on the next roof, then the next, making her way down the line until she reached the end of the buildings, abutted against the cavern wall. Only a single boat was tied up at a dock on this idle section of wharf. The owner was nowhere in sight. After climbing down in the shadow of the cavern wall, Shannon slunk towards the sea, keeping an eye out for anyone moving this way.

No one came.

Within a few minutes, she was submerged in the cool water. Despite the temperature, which she adjusted around her body with a thought, the saltwater created a prickling sensation across her skin that soon tingled deeper into her flesh. Holy moly, the energy felt awesome. She relaxed and simply breathed for several moments, letting the buoyancy of her pregnant belly relieve her aching back and sore muscles.

But as she gazed through the water back towards the docks, worry crept in. Could she still be spotted? With slow movements so as to not stir the water's surface, she swam out farther and deeper, following the rocky bottom with her fingertips until the metallic clanging, thumps, and hum of the wharf completely faded.

She continued onward in the dark depths for another stretch of time that seemed like an hour, then created a small yellow glow ahead of her to view her underwater surroundings. A mix of sand and rock greeted her. With the light to guide her, she shot through the water, swerving around stone pillars while keeping the Dwarven shoreline behind her. She stayed deep and kept an eye out for boats passing above her. The farther she got from her captors, the more the tenseness faded from her muscles until she finally smiled. The sensation of the saltwater streaming over her was like badly needed full-body massage.

As Shannon travelled further into the sea, she passed patches of glowing vegetation that seemed to act like a coral reef. These areas had a tremendous diversity of fish, shrimp, sea stars, and urchins. Gods, it was amazingly beautiful. If only she could share this rich bounty of underground sea life with some of her scientific colleagues, discussing the similarities and differences with Earth's oceans. Maybe some day. Having to hide her new knowledge and the advances she could make for human science was still one of the more painful adjustments of her becoming a goddess. It went against her every instinct as a researcher.

Shit. How would she explain her latest multi-month absence to her graduate students? At least she was still on leave from the university so they didn't expect her there in person or to teach any classes. Something to worry about after she got off this damned planet. She rubbed a hand over her belly. Saving her son had to be her priority.

The conversations of sea creatures she passed penetrated her thoughts. They revolved around the immediate needs of food, shelter, sex, and offspring. If only her life was so simple.

Still, it made her wonder. So far, all the sea life was on the small side, but there had to be larger predators out there somewhere. What was at the top of the food web in these seas? Even taking breaks and stopping to sleep, she'd swum for at least a day, as far as she could tell, but had yet to see anything threatening.

After passing a particularly extensive area of sea life that covered a winding set of underwater ridges, the sea didn't grow darker again as the ridge dropped away into much deeper depths. Instead, down in those depths, the green phosphorescent glow intensified.

Shannon dove to investigate but had only gone a handful of metres when a man, with midnight-black and brilliant silvery-white contrasting flesh tones she'd only ever seen on orca whales, darted in front of her, halting her. Eerily beautiful black with silver starburst eyes met hers. Some kind of scaled black-and-silver armour blended with his skin tones and he carried a trident. His unique colouration, paired with well-proportioned, strong masculine features surrounded by a halo of wavy black hair made for a handsome face that distracted her from noticing the decidedly hostile expression at first.

"Who are you, and what are you doing in our territory, elf?" he demanded, eyes narrowed and trident pointed at her.

Shannon blinked. Wow. Who peed in his cornflakes?

"Apologies. I didn't realize I was intruding. I was just swimming by and saw the light," she said calmly, hoping he would see she wasn't a threat. Although her ring hid her pregnancy and she wasn't as exhausted as she'd been when she'd escaped her captors, she didn't want to get into a fight if she could avoid it. Why did everyone have to be so cranky?

"You didn't answer my question. Who are you?" Those fascinating eyes glared as his voice deepened with aggression.

Seriously, dude? Gods, she didn't have the energy for this crap. "I'm Shannon. What's your name?" Still hoping to avoid a physical confrontation, she kept her tone polite.

"Prince Elatha of Atlantia. This is Fomorian territory, and you will come with me. Our queen will determine whether you are as innocent as you claim." The prince jabbed at her with the trident.

Shannon's jaw clenched. Nope. No fucking way. Not again. "I'm sorry but that's not going to work for me." She drew her sais from their thigh sheaths and deflected his trident. "While I'd love to meet your queen some day under better circumstances, I've had *quite* enough of being captured and held against my will."

Damned stubborn unfriendly man. No way did she have energy for a prolonged fight, but adrenaline fired her muscles. Shannon wasn't about to be taken again. Not again.

The prince growled, whirling the trident like a stave, trying to first hit her legs, then her head. Although slower in the water, she countered each strike and hit him with a pressure wave of water.

He wasn't expecting it, and it knocked him back. When he returned one her way, she split the wave to part harmlessly on either side of her.

Scowling, he fired a burst of white power from the end of the trident. Shannon blocked it with a shield of air that disrupted the burst, then shot back a concentrated beam of intense heat.

As it scalded him, he yelped.

"You are not an ordinary elf, Shannon!" he accused.

"I never said I was," she snapped, tired and irritated by his attack. For gods' sake, she just wanted to get home and leave all these fucking rude, pushy assholes behind. "I'm Princess Shannon of Asgard, Goddess of the Forests and Seas. And I was being *polite* until you attacked me, you bloody big brute."

At her words, he paused, eyes still narrowed. "Asgard. You are not of the Winter Realm? Not an elf?"

"Definitely *not* of the Winter Realm. Yes, I'm an elf, but also an Asgardian."

"A goddess of the sea?" Eyebrows raised, his tone was more careful now, less accusing.

"That's what Manannan Mac Lir told me. Oh, crap... I forgot I had this." She reached into the armoured pouch at her back and pulled out the tiny blue-and-silver spiral communication shell Manannan had given her when they'd met on Earth a few months ago.

Before she'd said anything further, the prince held up his hands.

"My deepest apologies, Princess Shannon, for this terrible misunderstanding. The Fomorians have no quarrel with Asgard, or with anyone that has the Sea God's favour."

Although surprised at his abrupt turnaround, Shannon wasn't about to complain. The fight had sapped the little energy she had. Despite the water's rejuvenation, her limbs dragged.

"I'll accept your apology if you can tell me how to get to the planet's surface from here? I'm trying to return to Asgard. Actually, Midgard would be fine as well."

A frown furrowed his brow. "I will escort you through our territory so you won't be accosted again and take you through the nearest tunnel system to the surface waters. But are you sure you want to go to the planet's surface to get to Asgard? The Dwarven kingdoms each have a reception chamber to receive Asgard's Bifrost. If I take you to King Sudri's kingdom, you could be back in Asgard tomorrow." He gestured back the way Shannon had come.

Shannon shuddered and shook her head. "No, I'm not sure which dwarves I can trust."

He frowned and eyed her oddly. "Okay... Well, the nearest water portal to Midgard is a three-week journey." The prince jabbed a thumb to his left.

"Three weeks is longer than I'd like to wait." Her hand strayed to her belly, and she forced her fingers to her hips instead. "The surface is my best option, I believe." Surely it had to be closer than three weeks?

"Very well, but it's still a four-day journey to reach the surface and another week to get to the treaty plains," the prince said as he started to lead the way through the water, lit by his trident. "With the cloaking mists everywhere, I think that's the only surface location that connects to the Bifrost."

Damn. Eleven days. But if the prince knew a location where the Bifrost worked, that was more than she'd had previously. Could she trust him?

"That's okay. I don't mind." As she followed, she considered the shell in her hand. If the nearest portal to Earth was so far away, perhaps she should wait. If this prince turned into an enemy, the closer she was to Manannan, the sooner he'd reach her. Just knowing she had a way to call for help settled the butterflies in her stomach. Carefully, she tucked the precious shell back into her pouch. "I've never heard of the Fomorians. Would you tell me about your people?"

"What do you want to know?" he asked cautiously.

"No secrets, just what you're willing to tell me. Are all Fomorians like you with silver-and-black colouration?"

Elatha smiled brilliantly, white teeth gleaming against his mostly black lips. Again, Shannon was struck by how unusually handsome he was with his strong jaw, sharp cheekbones, Grecian nose, and full lips. "Some are more white and black, some are white and silver, some are all black, and a few are all white or silver, but most of us are some pattern of silver and black."

"You remind me of orca whales." She followed him around a series of pillars. Despite herself, she couldn't help stealing glances at him, fascinated by the unusual appearance of his body and eyes.

"That's actually an apt analogy. I'm familiar with the orca of Litauī. They are quite playful when they are of a mind to be and extremely intelligent. I used to swim with them frequently when there were more water portals between Litauī and Tír na nÓg. With the nearest portal farther away now, I don't make the trip nearly as often. My brother spends most of his time on Litauī."

Oh, wow. Elation had her sucking in a quick breath. Swimming with the pod—definitely on her to-do list for the future. "I grew up by resident pods of orca. From my backyard dock, I watch them when they are in the inlet."

"You didn't grow up on Asgard?"

Elatha's question pulled Shannon back to her present surroundings, even as she longed for home. "No, I grew up near Vancouver, in Canada, on the west coast of North America. Are you familiar with current Midgardian geography and political boundaries?"

"Yes. As a prince of my people, I need to be aware of what goes on in the other realms. I must admit, though, that I didn't know that Asgard had a princess. I thought it was only Prince Thor and Prince Loki in the royal family." A small frown creased his brow, and Elatha gave her a sidelong glance. "I'm also a bit confused how a Princess of Asgard grew up on Litauī."

Shannon shrugged. "I didn't know I was a goddess until recently. I'm Prince Loki's consort."

The frown disappeared, and with a flash of teeth, a wide smile stretched his face. "Ah! Of course. Congratulations to you both on your binding. Prince Loki is a very lucky god to have such a beautiful, fierce, and courageous goddess as his consort." Based on the sparkle in those unusual silver eyes, she got the distinct impression he was flirting.

"Thank you. We're very happy. I can't wait to get back to him." Yeah, she didn't want any further misunderstandings with the far too handsome

Fomorian prince. Not that she was noticing. She dragged her eyes away from him and peered into the distance.

Prince Elatha eyed the Elven sea goddess. Of all the things he'd expected when he'd set out on an inspection of the recently seeded coral beds, this mysterious woman hadn't been one of them. Long water-darkened locks floated in the surrounding water instead of the braids Fomorian women usually preferred. Slender as a shoreline reed—except for full breasts he couldn't help but notice—with long delicate limbs like a brittle star gliding through the water, she had a graceful elegance to her movements. Decidedly lean she might be, but she was well armoured in fine, dark blue scales that flowed over her body as she swam and the blades strapped to her body. If it hadn't been for her halo of hair and the ripples she'd created in the water, he wouldn't have spotted her despite his keen sight—an unsettling thought with their people going missing.

Still, she carried Manannan's shell—a gift the sea god didn't give out lightly. Unlikely she had anything to do with the Fomorian disappearances.

And with that a risk in Tír na nÓg's waters, it was a good thing she moved with stealth. Although, her ferocity in defending herself also stood her in good stead. Deceptive. He shouldn't have judged her on her waif-like appearance. She'd surprised him with her skill in weaving water to her will.

Guilt stirred in his gut.

He'd *had* to question her presence in their territory, but shells, his first instinct had been to kiss her, not attack her. And wasn't that a puzzle? He, who hadn't been interested in anyone in the last seven years, found himself drawn to this alluring stranger with her cautious but vulnerable eyes, sharp cheekbones, and full lower lip she nibbled with those white teeth. Did he make her nervous?

As prickly as a sea urchin at first, everything about her fascinated now that they were talking, drawing him like a riptide. She'd lived such an unusual life. Imagine, thinking she was mortal? He wanted to ask her more, but well... he'd already discomforted her.

Would she be interested in a second consort if he could prove his worth?

Elves took multiple partners. Did Asgardians? He'd not met any, although he'd heard of Prince Loki and Prince Thor. Pleasant enough, as long as one dealt with them honestly and didn't prey on the Midgardians, if his older brother was to be believed. Elada worked with their outpost commanders on Litauī, the mortal realm, and had the occasional interaction with Thor over the past centuries. Asgardians didn't pick fights with the Fomorians, unlike the blasted Shen or the barnacle-blighted Unseelie.

Still, where was her consort? Who had dared capture her?

It had to be the foul dark elves. Only they would be so bold as to piss off someone as dangerous as Loki. Atlantia had stayed out of the last two wars between the Sidhe and the Asgardians, but even in the water's depths, Fomorians had heard tales of Asgard's Black Prince, who'd cut through the elves and their depraved creatures with ruthless, bloody abandon.

"I'm surprised Prince Loki isn't tearing Tír na nÓg apart to find you. You said earlier you were fed up with being captured and held against your will?" His tone was careful—he'd already attacked her, after all, and didn't wish to upset her further, yet he couldn't help but wonder why she was taking the long way back to her people. Should he be more wary, despite Manannán's shell? He had to know if there was some danger he wasn't aware of.

Shannon smiled, a fleeting flash before lines of strain appeared on her forehead and at the corners of her eyes. "Oh, I believe he is, which is why I'm trying to get to the surface to reach him."

Did Loki not know where she was? How had she ended up down here? With everything he learned about her and her situation, his questions replicated like an algal bloom. "Ah, that makes sense. Was it the Winter Realm? I'm not trying to pry," Elatha added quickly, raising a hand when she narrowed her eyes, suspicion in the green-gold depths. "I only ask because we've had our share of wars with them. The Unseelie have taken many of our people as slaves or as sacrifices to power their perverted magic." He winced and sent her an apologetic smile. "It's why I greeted you with such hostility."

She didn't seem to be holding a grudge. Her expression cleared, and she gave him a little answering smile. "Yes, the Wild Hunt kidnapped me from Earth, but then two dwarves stole me from the dark elves." Her face tightened, the muscle in her jaw working, and a fine tremor seemed to shake her body. "The bastards held me prisoner, siphoned my power and harvested my blood."

"Dwarves?" Elatha's lungs froze, and he stopped dead in the water, staring at her. "But we've never had any issues with the dwarves! We've never even thought to look at them to find any of our missing people. They've always been completely honourable in our dealings."

"I don't know how common it is, but they were well prepared with chains, cuffs, and a contraption to draw my power before they ever brought me to their workshop. They didn't craft it just for me."

She shuddered, her hauntingly beautiful face twisting in distress, and Elatha fought instincts that shouted he should wrap her in his arms, hold her, and comfort her. Shells, she'd been tortured for who knows how long... not that he was about to ask and make her relive it. No way would she want some strange male she'd just met touching her. Damn those shell-cracking bastards to the deepest, driest deserts.

But he had to think of his people, too, not only the sea goddess before him. He set out again, swimming faster. Clenching his fist, he said, "Sea squirts, this changes everything. If the dwarves have been playing us false, I need to tell my queen as soon as possible. I know you are in a hurry to get home, but we'll need to detour to one of our outposts so I can send a message. It won't add too much to our journey if we hurry."

"Okay," she agreed, but something in her tone had him blowing out a breath and shoving his hair back to subtly check her expression. He glimpsed her wincing when they quickly changed directions to swerve around a couple of pillars. Stiffening, he had to lock his muscles against the need to reach out to her. Was she injured and hiding it from him? After the way he'd acted, she wouldn't want to reveal a weakness.

Blasted barnacles.

His heart sank. And like a barracuda going after a sparkly treasure, he'd attacked her, piling onto what she'd already endured. He'd really stumbled into the sea urchin bed. Could she hurry without further injury? She'd been making decent progress, but perhaps a little caution would be in order. Trying to not be obvious, he slowed and let her set the pace.

Chapter 16

SO CLOSE, YET SO FAR

Still in the stinking workshop with the headless bodies of the dwarves Loki had killed, they debated the best way to proceed. He didn't regret the dwarves' deaths. In fact, his only regret was that he'd killed them too quickly and too painlessly. For what they'd dared do to Shannon, Loki should have tortured the fuckers endlessly. Over eons.

"If Shannon was here four days ago, we should be able to find her." Mist rubbed her fingers over her arms as she glanced around, eyes reddened and strained. "She can't have gotten that far, especially not with how emaciated she was. Norns, I'm scared for her. A strong wind would blow her over."

"I'll get the word out with our friends that we are looking for a missing Asgardian," Brokkr offered.

"Better make that Asgardian or elf. Shannon is also a light elf, so they might not recognize her as an Asgardian," Thor said.

"Yes, good thinking," Brokkr agreed as he strode out the door.

Revenge was a pale substitute for Loki's beautiful, intelligent goddess. The ache inside him wasn't appeased by the meagre offering, and remembering her frail state tormented his soul. Mist wasn't wrong. Shannon had to be suffering terribly. And their child... Norns, how was their child when Shannon was a shadow of herself? The urge to scream, rage, and cry was held in only by his overwhelming need to find her.

He had to find her, to save her, to save their son.

In the dwarves' memories, she'd appeared exhausted and dangerously thin when her pregnancy was revealed... a shocking change from what his ring illusion had shown. Until then, she'd merely appeared slender. If he hadn't known her beforehand, he wouldn't have suspected the massive, rapid weight loss. She must have been losing at least two pounds every single day to have gone from an ideal size to... He swallowed, remembering. Mist was right. Surely, Shannon couldn't have gotten far—not in her condition. He didn't know exactly how she had done it, but he was incredibly proud of her successful escape and evasion.

"Shannon will avoid dwarves. She doesn't know who to trust among them," he said as the thought occurred.

"So where does that leave her?" Roskva's fingertips trailed over a workbench, wrinkling her nose in distaste. "Shannon's never been to Alfheim, right?"

"Not that she remembers," Loki agreed.

"Jal, why don't you run as many corridors as you can cover to try to find her?" Roskva suggested.

Thjalfi nodded and left in a blur of speed. The healers had repaired the damage to his leg and his twin's back, even though the delay put them farther behind Shannon's trail. Where was she?

"That's a good idea, Ros." Exhaustion pulled at Loki—the numerous nights with little to no sleep catching up with him. Still, he'd wear himself to the bone if it meant finding Shannon. He replicated himself—only able to create five physical copies with his energy lagging—and sent the duplicates out to add to the search. "If she sees me, she'll come out."

"If Shannon doesn't trust the dwarves and doesn't trust the Winter Court, does she try to go to the Summer Realm?" Kara leaned against the workshop doorway, gazing out into the cavern.

Mist turned over a metal tub, nudging it with her toe. "Or does she go to the Atlanteans?"

Loki frowned and rubbed his lips. "I've never mentioned the Atlanteans to her. Have you?"

Mist shook her head. So did Kara and Thor.

"So I doubt that's an option," Loki mused. "She can't ask for help from people she doesn't know to look for."

"If her only real option is to get to the Summer Realm, how does she get there from here? Shannon probably knows the Winter Realm is above us since she was taken from there. Does she try to go up, anyway?" Kara wondered.

"There are only two ways to the surface from here. Up through Dwarven territory, to the Winter Realm, or across the Sea of Lantia, then the Sea of Uaithne, through the Glass Tunnels, and up to Ocean of Ceobhran," Eitri said, outlining the areas using spilled crystals on a workbench.

Mist pointed to one spot. "If she comes out on the Ocean of Ceobhran, where does that leave her?"

"Directly up from the Glass Tunnels, she'd end up in the area between the Winter and Summer Realms. The ocean is in twilight there, with a few scattered islands. The Winter Realm is closer in terms of the shoreline, within eyesight of where she'd come up, unless there's a storm. But, if she knows to go towards the light, she could reach the Summer Realm in a week. It's a damn long swim, though. She'd need powers to get through the tunnels and up to the surface of the ocean or she'd drown," Eitri explained, sketching more details on his rudimentary map.

"That's not a concern for her. Shannon's a sea goddess." Certainty filled Loki as he met their gazes. "She'd go to the water, the sea, if she can find it. It gets her away from dwarves faster when she doesn't know who to trust, and it would recharge her goddess powers."

"I agree, but Shannon doesn't have the information Eitri just gave us. If I were on my own, I wouldn't know there was a sea or how to get to the surface," Mist argued.

"Which is why Thjalfi and I need to search every corridor and pathway from here to the surface, while some of you go to the surface to intercept her. We also need to contact the Atlanteans, but none of us know the locations of one of their outposts or cities on Alfheim. I only know where a few are on Midgard." Loki turned to Eitri. "How do you contact them?"

He shrugged. "We don't. If the Atlanteans want something from us, they come here. It's rare that we see them."

"Damn." Loki could try to find an Atlantean outpost or city, but there was a lot of water to cover. Mist couldn't hold an air bubble in the water for long periods the way Shannon could. She also couldn't breathe underwater, so couldn't help him search the depths. It was a far more common ability with the Tuatha Dé Danann and the Shen. Asgardians, and even the Vanir, didn't have much of a presence in the water realms. Yggdrasil's roots, they didn't even have an ambassador or formal treaty with the Atlanteans—they'd never been in conflict.

"What about Manannan?" Mist suggested, withdrawing a blue-and-silver shell from a pouch in her armour. "He gave us these to call him if we needed him and said it would work here as well as Midgard."

"Brilliant, Mist! That's exactly what we will do. Let's head to the Howling Falls wharves now. It's the closest access to the Sea of Lantia, right?" Loki confirmed with Eitri.

He nodded.

"Wait up, brother. I think I should go with Roskva and Kara to the surface. We'll reunite with the Einherjar and Valkyrie we sent with the Sidhe search parties. Together, we can search the areas Eitri mentioned to see if Shannon is there, as well as wait to intercept her. Mist can try to contact Manannan while you and Thjalfi search here for Shannon," Thor suggested.

Loki slapped him on the back. "Sound plan. Thank you, brother." Thank the Norns everyone was coming up with good ideas. His mind continued to stray, to recall that horrifying image of Shannon, dangerously thin with his child so large on her slight frame, and his mouth dried as his heart pounded. He had to save her, to save them. He had to.

The group left the workshop, with Eitri giving Thor directions on the fastest route to the surface. After parting on one path as they moved through the massive cavern of lava streams, Loki, Mist, and Eitri returned the way they'd come, while Thor, Roskva, and Kara angled toward a different exit.

Throughout the walk back to the air chute, up the tall shaft, and out into the cooler air, Loki considered what he could be missing. He ground his teeth, inspiration failing him.

Halfway back to the Obsidian market, Brokkr found them again. "I may have a lead on your consort!" he shouted as he spotted them.

They ran to join him.

"A child told her mother that she'd met a nice light elf yesterday afternoon and took her to see the Howling Falls," Brokkr said.

"Can we talk to the child?" Anticipation surged and Loki fidgeted, eager to press on. Could they really be that lucky? Please, Norns, let it be true.

"Yes. The mother is waiting for me back at the Obsidian market. I said I'd bring you there."

Unable to wait a second longer, Loki and Mist started running, with Eitri and Brokkr still outpacing them with their longer legs. After returning to the market cavern in half the time, they had to slow when they hit the crowded stalls. They followed Brokkr as he weaved in and around the shopping dwarves.

Even so, it took a while to get through the crowds and across the cavern to where the woman waited. Loki blinked when he recognized the dwarf with the black braids.

"Delling?"

She smiled a wide and uneven grin. "Prince Loki! It is so good to see you!"

"Thank you. Your daughter may have seen my consort yesterday?"

"Let's go find out. She's at home." Delling led the way out of the cavern. "Our guild hall is the envy of all other guilds, you know."

Loki smiled, amused. "I'm glad I could help you build Lyr, but I really didn't do very much."

"Nonsense," she scoffed. "We wouldn't have the flames if it wasn't for you! That's why our hall is so envied."

"I feel I'm missing a story?" Mist asked as they followed Delling into an air chute and shot up a short distance.

"I'm in the builders' guild. We wanted our hall to reflect us. Loki helped us create magical flames that never go out and that we can manipulate to show different building designs on the sides of our hall. They create moving pictures. It's brilliant, the envy of all others," Delling said proudly.

Eitri nodded. "It's quite spectacular."

After another fifteen minutes, they reached Delling's home. She called for her daughter, who entered the room, ducking her head and not meeting their gaze.

"This is Prince Loki. The same Prince Loki that helped me build Lyr. He wants to see your memory of the elf you saw yesterday," Delling told her.

The girl nodded. "Okay, Ma. I'm happy to help. She was nice."

"Just picture her in your mind, okay? Try to push that memory to me," Loki told the girl. The more she was receptive to him seeing her memory, the less his telepathic probe would bother her.

Gently, he touched his fingers to her forehead. Loki didn't even have to search—it was right there. Shannon, again hiding behind the ring illusion, appeared tired but smiling at the child as they held hands, walking through a corridor to the falls. Then the child was on a barrel, shrieking in delight, waving up at Shannon standing on a bridge at the falls. That was the last time she'd seen his consort before the girl's barrel took her over the next set of falls.

Loki removed his fingers and smiled at the child. "Thank you. You did really well."

Nodding, he looked over at the others. "It was Shannon. She was at Howling Falls yesterday afternoon."

"Okay, she would have followed the water to reach the Sea of Lantia. She probably headed out through the water. We need to get there and try to contact Manannan." Mist grinned, slapping Loki on the back. "We're close, Loki. Hot on her heels!"

His pulse pounded in a desperate, urgent rhythm as he wordlessly agreed. Without knowing which direction to take, they couldn't follow her into the sea. Even if they went the right way, without the ability to contact her, Shannon could be below them in the water and they'd never know. To be so close, yet unable to reach her, to find her. He clenched his fists. Damn cloaking mists!

With a thanks to Delling and her daughter, Eitri and Brokkr led the Asgardians to Howling Falls. It was a short thirty-minute walk from Delling's home. After making their way down the slippery steps at the side of the tumbling sets of falls, they followed the path to the wharf. Methodically and rapidly, Mist checked the rooftops and Loki searched around the buildings and boats. Eitri and Brokkr questioned the Dwarven dockworkers and sailors.

Other than a stray nut shell on a rooftop, there was no sign of Shannon.

Loki stared out at the water. How long ago had she left?

"I'm going to try my ear cuff. If Shannon's still in range, she'll hear me, even in the water," Mist said.

Loki eyed the Valkyrie communicator. Norns curse it. Why hadn't they tried that earlier?

"Shannon? Can you hear me? It's Mist. I'm at Howling Falls wharf." She listened intently. Repeating the attempt, she waited, but then shook her head. "It's no use. She either doesn't have it anymore or she's out of range."

The kernel of hope that had sprouted in Loki's heart shrivelled. "It was still on her ear in the memory the child showed me yesterday. She must be out of range." Unbidden, tears sprang to his eyes, and he rubbed at his chest. A day... a single damned day. How could she have been so close, and he hadn't known? Fuck, they'd walked right past.

Mist moved down to the water, continued in, and pulled out the silver-and-blue seashell. "Manannan Mac Lir, we need your help. Shannon is here on Alfheim in the Sea of Lantia, making her way to the Ocean of Ceobhran. We can't follow her to tell her we are here without potentially missing her. We can't contact the Atlanteans to ask for their help." She touched the shell to the water. A pulse went out in all directions, rippling through the water.

"I guess the message is sent," Loki said. "Now, we wait." An illusion disguised the anguish in his voice and hid the salty trails coursing down his cheeks. His muscles trembled with the need to fling himself into the water to chase after his consort, even if he didn't know which direction to search. Yggdrasil's roots, he had to do *something*.

"You just need to remain near the sea?" asked Brokkr, laying a hand on Loki's shoulder.

"Yes." Fists clenched, Loki didn't think he could move away from the sea, knowing his goddess was held in its embrace somewhere.

"Then come stay with us while you wait," he offered.

Lightheadedness surged through Loki, and his vision started to tunnel. "Thank you. We appreciate it." The dwarves' home and workshop provided an ideal base to wait by the sea. Loki could sit on their steps and watch for Manannan's arrival.

As they walked with Eitri and Brokkr to their place, pain behind Loki's eyes and weariness had him pulling back his duplicates, save one to tell Thor what they'd found. Then, he located Thjalfi and sent him with Thor. Even pulling the Einherjar and Valkyrie from the useless Sidhe search parties, they'd have a lot of ground to cover if Loki and Mist didn't find Shannon in the seas. Those tasks done, Loki drew the last of his seidhr back within himself. His feet dragged, each step an effort. After the numerous expenditures, he'd hit his limit and needed rest or he'd burn himself out for days.

When Eitri showed him to a bedroom, Loki gratefully laid down, only to toss and turn, unable to sleep. Like a torture reel, over and over his mind replayed

Shannon's abuse by the dwarves and the number of times they slashed her open to steal her blood. The way she'd grown more and more tired, slurring her words, and hardly lifting her head. And her true energy-starved state revealed after the bath—sunken eyes and thin cheeks, and his child far too big on her ravaged, emaciated frame.

His fault.

By the Nine, he *never* should have let her go on that girls' weekend.

Foolish. He was so foolish to ignore the risks.

Turning his face into the bed, he let his tears soak into the sheets even as he choked back the sobs he was too tired to hold inside and had no more energy to disguise. He couldn't lose her. He couldn't. *Please, Norns. I'll do anything to save her, to bring her back home. Anything. Just let her survive until I can get to her. Please.*

PART 3

Don't Bet Against Darwin

"The world will not be inherited by the strongest, it will be inherited by those most able to change."

Charles Darwin

Chapter 17

CULTURAL DIFFERENCES

Shannon swam hard in the wake of the Fomorian as he cut through the water with his powers. After almost nine hours, a light appeared in the depths ahead. When Prince Elatha angled down toward it, she followed.

As they approached, the light resolved into a green energy field that created a bubble of air surrounding a series of graceful spiral towers on the sea floor shaped like conical shells. The outpost was arranged in a wheel with shorter buildings laid out in spokes, surrounding larger central towers. Momentarily forgetting the exhaustion and headache plaguing her, she stared open-mouthed at the beauty of it.

Elatha swam toward a metallic silver circle near the base of the bubble where it met the sea floor. He waited for her to join him, then entered a code on a virtual pad that appeared when his hand raised a spot on the side of the circle. The energy field pushed outward, over them, and to the edges of the silver circle, creating a bubble of air surrounding them and open to the inside. As they stepped inside onto a white gravel—or perhaps crushed shell—pad, the green energy field retracted and the water once again pressed against the original bubble wall.

The level of technology or magic was incredible. To hold back the pressure of that much water at more than a couple of kilometres in depth... she shook her head, eyes wide as she took it all in. As she'd learned on Asgard, magic was simply science she couldn't yet fully explain, and she had so much to learn to catch up to the level of scientific knowledge held by immortals. She'd expected Asgard to be advanced after seeing Loki's abilities and with the way the Bifrost had transported her with Thor that first time. But here... the prince hadn't shown her much other than his trident and the ability to move water. She'd started to believe that perhaps Alfheim was technologically inferior to Asgard after the primitive conditions of her cell in the Winter Realm and only the air chutes and Dwarven boat and wagon propulsion suggesting some kind of power or ability in Nidavellir. Her captors certainly hadn't had any advanced technology except the contraption they'd used to steal her energy.

But this outpost far surpassed her expectations.

Given their environment, she'd expected the air to smell like salt. Yet the air inside the dome was fresh, like after a spring rain. It reminded her of the temperate rainforests of home, a comforting and familiar scent, and she breathed deep, her chest loosening a little. With the surrounding air, she dried herself and her clothing, removing the salt. As much as she loved being in the water, she hated the way the salt felt gritty on her skin when it dried into a crust.

Prince Elatha watched her, one black eyebrow raised at the display of power. Once she'd finished, he nodded, seemingly in approval. Instead of drying himself, he shook his thick shoulder-length black hair, leaving it damp to curl appealingly around his face. His body, armour, and tight-fitting skinsuit visible on the unarmoured parts of his undeniably athletic body shed the water almost as fast, leaving a puddle on the dry, porous ground beneath him. Clearly, being wet didn't bother him. Although Shannon wished she hadn't noticed he looked even more attractive in the air than he had in the water.

"This way, Princess," Elatha said, his voice a richer baritone in the air as he nodded to the two Fomorians standing on either side of the bubble entrance—guards in white-and-black armour and black skinsuits, holding tridents—and then strode down the white path toward the large central buildings. It was a graceful collection of silver towers framed by fruiting trees, gardens of trellised and raised-bed vegetables and fruit, and green spaces with benches and round tables with curved shell-shaped seats surrounding them. Everywhere Shannon looked, it was clean and tidy, with the occasional Fomorian working in the gardens.

"How large is the Fomorian territory?" she asked, stumbling with her first step. The two guards eyed her, one stepping forward with an outstretched hand, but he dropped it when she gave him a small smile and shook her head. Elatha glanced back at her, and she forced her feet to cooperate and follow him. Despite his assistance thus far, she didn't want to give away her weakness. Instead, she gazed at the colourful garb of the people working in the gardens. While all of them wore skinsuits in varying colours, they also had some kind of flowing, sheer sleeveless overtunic that ranged from hip-length to swirling around the ground in bright colours like butterflies tending the plants.

"Atlantia has seven major cities spread across one hundred and twenty million square kilometres of lower sea territory. Hy-Brasil is our capital city. We also have numerous outposts throughout the edges of Fomorian territory, on the upper oceans, and a few still on Litauī."

Shannon blinked, his answer catching her off guard and distracting her from her admiration of the gardens. "You call your kingdom Atlantia?" A small grin crept onto her face. "So, by any chance, would one of those outposts on Midgard be Atlantis?" Of course! No wonder those ancient tales said the Atlanteans were advanced compared to the rest of Earth. Atlantean must be another name for Fomorian.

Elatha laughed, eying her with amusement. "Yes, yes it is. I can guess what your next question is going to be, right? Was Atlantis on the surface and sank?"

She nodded, following him into a central tower. The stories made so much sense in light of the technology she saw here. Those ancient humans would have been in such awe at the sight of Fomorian outposts. Hell, *she* was in awe.

"Our cities and outposts used to float on the surface, but after too many attacks by the elves and the Shen, we retreated under the water. So yes, Atlantis, our outpost in Litauī's Mediterranean Sea, sank below the waves but it was a defensive strategy, not a disaster."

Shannon shook her head. Her understanding of even her own planet's history was so biased towards humanity. How was she ever to catch up?

But these worries fled as they climbed several flights of gleaming silver stairs, and she focused on just drawing enough breath into her lungs so she didn't pass out. Between the pregnancy and captivity, her fitness had evaporated. Gods, she was in such terrible shape. Her legs were rubbery and lungs wheezing by the time they stopped at a room that held multiple screens, similar to the holographic control pad screens she'd seen on Asgard. Windows provided visibility into the nearby waters lit by the energy barrier and the bioluminescent plants. Several Fomorians in black skinsuits and white-and-black armour stood at different stations, monitoring read-outs.

When they caught sight of Shannon and her companion, they gave the prince a quick bow.

"Good morrow, Prince. To what do we owe the honour?" asked a female Fomorian with interesting white streaks in her short black braided hair.

Shannon's fingers lifted to her own tangled locks tumbling down her back, tucking a snarled strand behind her ear. Braids were smart. Hell, she'd kill for a comb at this point. Gods, what she'd give to take a shower and to actually brush her teeth and hair. She shifted on her feet and forced her hands down, clasping them together. She was a disastrous hot mess next to this tidy woman.

"I need to send an encoded message to the Queen," Elatha said.

The woman stepped away from her station, allowing him to take her position. Elatha entered a code on a screen that gave him access, wrote his message and when he closed the screen, a pulse of light shot out from the energy barrier, through the water and headed back in the direction they had come. Did they have some kind of light repeater system, like cell phone towers back home?

"Thank you, Commander Mara. My guest, Princess Shannon of Asgard, and I will stay for a rest period and meal before continuing our journey," he said.

"Certainly, my prince. Welcome, Princess." Mara smiled and eyed Shannon curiously while giving her a shallow bow. "As we are only at half visitor capacity at present, you have your pick of rest chambers."

"Perfect. The nautilus wing, then. The view from those chambers is splendid."

"Very well, my prince." Mara inclined her head. "I'll alert the staff to expect you."

"Thank you." Elatha gestured for Shannon to follow, and they descended the stairs, much to her relief. Instead of returning outside, they curved around at one landing into an open hallway that connected this central tower and one wing.

The top of the hallway was clear, with nothing obstructing the view of the water above and surrounding the energy dome. With the glowing green vegetation growing profusely in the waters outside the energy dome, there was an abundance of sea life swimming by.

"If you like that view, you'll love the view from the rest chambers," Elatha said, breaking into her reverie.

She hadn't realized she'd stopped partway down the hallway to stare at the spectacular sight. "I'm looking forward to it," Shannon replied with a smile. It was absolutely mesmerizing.

When they continued on, they entered what she took to be the nautilus wing. The building had an open central spiral staircase and on each level, many doors led to what Shannon assumed to be rest chambers. After gritting her teeth to follow him up the stairs, Elatha led her to the top level. He placed his palm on a dark circular door scanner on the wall next to a silver door. With a flash of blue on the scanner, the door swooshed open, sliding sideways into the wall.

He led her to the next door along the hall. "Put your palm on the scanner to code it to you. The staff will reset it when we leave. It's how you'll open your door and control everything inside."

Following his instructions, she put her palm on the scanner until it lit up blue and her door opened.

"I'll give you a quick tour before heading to my chamber." After leading her inside, he showed Shannon the bathroom and kitchen, including how to select a prepared meal or beverage from something he called the AMP, or to request grocery supplies on the screen in the kitchen. Elatha demonstrated the lights and the privacy shades for the windows. In addition, the entire top of the suite was the same transparent material as the hallway they'd walked through. With the privacy shades engaged, she could still see out, but he assured her no one could see in.

"Thank you," she said as he finished the tour. "You were right. The view is spectacular."

Elatha grinned. With a thumb pointing at the room on her right, he said, "I'll be right next door if you run into difficulties, need anything, or just want your curiosity further assuaged." The unmistakable glint in his eyes suggested he wasn't referring to her intellectual curiosity.

Damn it. He'd caught her checking him out. It'd been hard not to stare at his ass as they'd climbed the stairs, and hell, he had a nice one. "Thank you for your kind offer, but I'm sure I'll be fine," she said firmly, but politely. Gods, she'd have to be dead not to notice his inherent sex appeal and incredibly toned body, even as she tried not to. But her heart belonged to Loki.

Elatha's lips twisted in a rueful half-smile. "Can't blame me for offering. Fomorians are a polyamorous people. Our women take multiple consorts, as our natural population sex ratio is distinctly male-biased." He ran an admiring glance over Shannon's form. "Loki is a lucky, lucky god. I'd be happy to share if it meant being with you."

Her libido wasn't quite getting her heart's message as an image of Elatha and Loki both wrapped around her in an erotic embrace short-circuited Shannon's thoughts for a few seconds, leaving her open-mouthed and blinking. Damn. So hot. Almost whimpering, she couldn't help her arousal.

Until her brain kicked in. Guilt churned that the idea tempted her.

"Ummm... I'm confident Loki doesn't share," she said breathlessly, even as heat flushed her cheeks. Flustered, she needed Elatha to leave before her exhaustion led her to do something stupid.

"The offer is there if you change your mind. You are a rare pearl, Princess Shannon."

Another appreciative look from him did nothing to calm her confusion. Rather than that uncomfortable, unclean sensation when a man leered, Prince Elatha was charming and warm in his obvious admiration. It had her heating in an entirely unacceptable way.

No. Not happening. Even if he was absolutely delicious and those full lips... Shannon dropped the illusion hiding her well-rounded pregnant belly. Surely, that would put him off. "While I thank you for the compliment, Prince Elatha, Loki and I are soulmates and expecting our first child," she explained as she got a grip on her wayward thoughts. *Don't be a fool and cause some kind of diplomatic incident! Hormonal idiot!*

Elatha's unusual silver starburst irises widened, eating the black surroundings, and he blinked several times, mouth gaping. "You are even more desirable and radiant with child, Princess," he said in a reverent tone before his face grew stormy, fury snapping in his gaze and a muscle ticking in his jaw.

The silver looked like bursts of lightning crackling in a night sky. So beautiful and distracting, Shannon almost missed his words.

"Those elves and dwarves must have a death wish! There is no greater dishonour than hurting a pregnant woman. I'm shocked all of Asgard isn't combing every inch of Tír na nÓg to find you when you carry an heir to the Asgardian throne," he snarled.

His tone conveyed an appalled fury that had her stopping in her tracks, her next words forgotten. Although their brief acquaintance suggested the Unseelie' and dwarves' actions would disgust him, the level of his response was far beyond what she would have predicted. "To be fair, they didn't know," she mused, then added, "I've been hiding my pregnancy with an illusion, as you just saw. The Wild Hunt did seem to target pregnant mortals when I was taken. Even if they'd known, I don't think it would have stopped them." Her fists clenched, voice clogging with tears. Those women... gods, those poor women and children.

Elatha spat, lips twisted in disgust. "Crom Cruach is the most depraved elf I've had the misfortune to ever cross weapons with."

"Who is Crom Cruach? The old elf leading the Wild Hunt?" That cruel face with the sick look in his eyes haunted her dreams. Just recalling him had nausea churning and an acidic burn in her throat.

"Yes," Elatha snarled. "He'd be the old one, but it's actually Llew that leads and controls the Wild Hunt. If you didn't see him, he was probably in his white stag form."

Shannon frowned, a hand on her belly. She'd seen that stag. But the name... she'd heard that name before. Where?

Elatha sank to one knee, and a thousand butterflies erupted into flight in her stomach as her thoughts scattered.

Oh, gods! What was he doing?

With his left hand across his chest and his right on his trident on the floor in front of her, he spoke, "I swear on my honour and the trident of the Sea Peoples that I will do everything in my power to help you return to your mate Loki and your home." Oddly, it had the wording of a formal vow, with a ring of magic to it, and the seriousness of his face confirmed it.

Quietly and with relief, Shannon released the breath she'd held when he'd knelt. "I thank you for your vow, Prince Elatha." She wasn't sure what else to say, but it seemed to satisfy him.

Holy cow, she'd thought he was proposing. Talk about cultural differences. If he wasn't still standing in front of her, looking like he wanted to say something further, she'd smack herself in the forehead. Instead, she gripped the wall, her heart still thundering.

But how was she to know? Sheesh... it wasn't like she knew marriage proposals customs between the different immortal races. Did they even kneel? Was that just a human thing? This whole learning by stumbling into it was *not* a sustainable educational paradigm! For fuck's sake, she'd not been given any choice with her soulmate bond. It had just happened, snapping into place after she'd had sex with Loki during her transition. Next thing she knew she was a princess and consort. Immortals were so damned confusing with their unexpected customs.

She choked down an almost hysterical laugh as Elatha picked up his trident and backed away. If more humans were at risk of mating for life by having unprotected sex, sexually transmitted diseases would be extinct.

Elatha opened his mouth to say more, but then closed it and nodded as he retrieved his trident and backed towards the door. With the green rim eating the golden brown within her widening eyes and the way her olive skin had blanched when he'd knelt, it was clear he'd already trespassed more than she was comfortable with. She blinked rapidly, her hand rising to cover her mouth. Yes, he'd overstepped. No way would he upset her further. Not in her fragile condition.

Bowing, he said, "I will see you on the morrow's rising, unless you have need of me earlier. Good resting, Princess Shannon," and stepped out the door, closing it behind him. He thunked his head on the wall of the corridor. Could he have been any more of an octopus in an oyster bed? Recalling her alarmed, almost panicked expression at his vow, he winced. Had he committed some cultural mistake by trying to reassure her? Seastars, but she'd scattered his brain cells when she'd revealed her pregnancy.

And not just pregnant—she wasn't far from full term if the size of the child was anything to judge by. Especially on her slender frame. Shells, her belly was bigger than the succulent, giant melons their plant tenders grew, swamping her thin body. No wonder she'd gotten winded climbing the stairs. Her rasping breaths had him considering calling a healer, wondering about an injury, until she'd revealed the real reason. Should she even be climbing stairs and swimming about so close to term?

Maybe he should still offer to take her to the healing chambers?

He dragged his hand through his hair. No, not unless she asked.

She had healthy meals and a safe place to rest—more than she'd probably had for however long those sick bastards had had her. And she knew how to contact him. He had to give her space. She'd call if she needed help, right?

Still, he'd check on her tomorrow. She might need more rest before they continued their journey. Shells, how had she managed to get so far while carrying her baby? No way would Fomorian women be able to expend such effort and energy as Shannon was—not this late in their pregnancy.

He rubbed a hand over his face. Beautiful. Every part of her was absolutely incredible. What he'd give to be one of the men privileged enough to tend to her. If only she needed him. A heaviness grew within him, his ribs constricting as his shoulders drooped.

But he wasn't. She'd made that clear.

All he could do was fulfill his vow to get her safely to her consort.

Chapter 18

FANTASY & DIPLOMACY

Shannon fanned herself after the door closed, almost giddy as adrenaline continued to surge through her veins from her mistake in thinking he was proposing.

Gods, call her a hopeless romantic, but she *wanted* to be asked, to be given a choice about a lifetime commitment that would last thousands of years. Elatha hadn't known he was jumping on one of her hot-button issues with both big feet when he'd knelt for his vow, but yeah, the idea of a marriage proposal, of being wanted for herself and that her opinion mattered...uh huh, it was a *big* fucking deal to her.

Loki had called her his wife, but she'd refused to accept that title or his claim—they were *not* married. Not on Earth and not on Asgard. He'd had a wife before. Sigyn had been a Valkyrie and no pushover, according to Kara, so it wasn't like Loki wasn't aware that he hadn't bothered to ask Shannon.

And bless Frigga when Shannon had tearfully complained about having no choices, thinking being a consort meant she'd never get the chance to choose her spouse. The queen always seemed to know the right thing to say, explaining that soulmates were always each other's consorts since the connection was unbreakable except by death, but that they could formalize their binding as well in a ceremony similar to the marriage customs Shannon was used to on Earth.

Shannon made her way to the kitchen, poured a glass of cool water from the tap—a luxury after her captivity—and selected a light meal of shrimp vegetable stir-fry from the list on the AMP's screen.

According to Frigga, not all soulmate relationships worked out. Rarely, the mates blocked the bond and denied the connection. Odin and Frigga were formally bound in addition to being soulmates, and damn it, that was what Shannon wanted eventually, too. To be asked. To have her choice matter. To not be taken for grated or it be assumed that she wanted the relationship. She wasn't a fucking possession, after all. And after being tormented by the dwarves who'd treated her like an object, taking from her whenever they wanted, and ignoring all but the most basic of needs, the idea of having no choice, of being forced, struck home that much harder.

The food prep unit chimed. Shannon removed her plate, taking it to the small round table overlooking the gardens. Her fingers tightened on her fork.

No, Loki hadn't asked for her hand. Nor had she'd been ready for him to—not when she'd only known him for a grand total of seven weeks, with barely more than four weeks of actual time spent together when he wasn't gone all day and night recording music or making movies. Her fault for taking off after her transition, true. Nevertheless, if she'd spent those first five months of her pregnancy with him, would she feel ready to choose him as her one and only?

She loved him. No doubt about that. And when the bond was open between them, she felt his love for her. But after so little time together, was it a love that would last centuries? There was still so much she didn't know about him.

Hell, there was so much she still didn't know about the immortal worlds. She snorted to herself as she took a bite and chewed. Even to the point of customs she could get herself in trouble with by still thinking like a human—the image of Prince Elatha kneeling before her flashed into her thoughts.

She swallowed and rubbed a hand over her belly. Gods, this kidnapping had opened her eyes in so many ways. When she returned to Asgard, she needed to focus on learning as much as possible about the realms, *all* the realms. She had to be in a position to protect her son. Knowledge was power, and she needed it. Her fist tightened on her fork. She never wanted to be a victim again.

And yeah, realistically, it meant giving up her beloved mortal career as a scientist and professor. Her next bite was like ash in her mouth, tears pricking her eyes. Damn it, she'd fought hard for her success, but this was a matter of survival as an immortal. This whole experience had highlighted the risks of being unprepared. She was already way behind the learning curve. As much as she hated the idea, she could always return to her career sometime in the future, reinventing her mortal identity. When she wasn't so vulnerable.

She forced herself to finish her plate, the first actual meal she'd had in several days. After withdrawing her armour and clothes into her torc, she crawled into the massive bed, sinking into the pillowy softness.

Despite her exhaustion, she fell into a fitful sleep.

Nightmares disrupted her rest—visions of the women and children she couldn't save from whatever horrors the Unseelie had planned for them, the pain of the dwarves sucking her life's energy, slashing her body and harvesting her blood, and her fears for her son if she couldn't get them to safety. She woke tangled in the sheets, sweat covering her body and a cry on her lips. No, she never wanted to be anyone's victim again. Not ever.

With no idea of the time, she gave up on more rest and dragged herself out of bed. She'd been up multiple times already to use the bathroom when her son bounced on her bladder. That aspect of pregnancy was not enjoyable, but at least it disrupted some of the nightmares. Despite the sleep she'd managed, some sadist was trying to crack her head open from the inside with spikes of pain every time she moved too quickly. Eyes sunken in dark purple circles stared back at her in the mirror.

Was that really her?

She'd lost so much weight that she barely recognized her gaunt face. A weak laugh echoed in the pristine white bathroom—her asshole ex-fiancé Trent sure wouldn't have anything to say about her size now. Once bodily needs had been taken care of and after finding supplies to properly clean her teeth, Shannon convinced herself that she was still alive, if not particularly perky.

A repeating chime broke the quiet of the suite before she could turn on the shower. Hand to her pounding head, she searched for the source. That damn noise needed to stop. Not finding anything, she tried saying, "Hello?"

"Good ris—" the rest of the words choked off in a low strangled groan.

Still searching, it took Shannon another minute to find the large screen by the front door. Once she got close enough, she spotted Prince Elatha with his back to the screen.

"Hello? Can you hear me? I don't know how to work this. I'm sorry." Why was she seeing his back? Did she need to flip the camera around? In frustration, she rubbed her temple, trying to think past her headache.

Elatha's voice was deep and rough when he answered. "It will respond to your voice controls, Princess. It shows audio and *video*." He cleared his throat, still facing away from her.

With the thumping in her brain, it took Shannon a second before she glanced down at herself.

Oh. Oh. Gods. She was naked!

Blushing, she apologized as she called her fighting leathers to cover her.

"It's safe to look now," Shannon replied, cringing in embarrassment. She wanted to smack herself. For fuck's sake, was she determined to cause some kind of diplomatic disaster between Asgard and Atlantia? Ugh.

Elatha cleared his throat again. "I'm not safe to look at right now," he muttered as he turned, his hands held in front of him.

She blinked, sure he hadn't expected her to hear that. She blinked again as her mouth lost all ability to speak, her brain misfiring even as her pulse pounded in her veins and her core spasmed.

Holy fucking shit.

She'd thought he looked hot yesterday, but today, oh good gravy. Elatha wasn't wearing his armour, just the skinsuit. Every muscle was clearly defined. In distinctive glorious delineation. There wasn't an ounce of fat on his tall, athletic body. Not one. Especially not the thick erection his hands were doing a terrible job at hiding.

"Good rising, Princess. Would you like to have breakfast with me?" he asked politely, his tone still gravelly.

Although Shannon heard his words, it took her a few long seconds to get her voice to work. She had to swallow several times and drag her eyes up to finally meet his heated starburst gaze.

"Thank you, but no. I was about to take a shower," she managed in a husky croak.

His eyes darkened further, eyelids lowering with predatory intensity.

Fuuuck.

There was no way she could fail to notice how his cock leapt at her words, that gloriously proud beast straining at the thin fabric leash. A fresh flush of moisture drenched the already slick heat between her thighs. She had no business looking there. Oh gods, why did he have to wear clothes that didn't hide a damn thing? She could not drag her eyes away. It was magnetic. She looked away, only to find her eyes pulled right back.

Through the fog of her desire, she heard him groan. A shudder of reaction rippled over her, and she squirmed. Elatha groaned again, gripping that exquisite cock through the tight but stretchy material.

"Shannon, I'm sorry to be so blunt, but if you aren't interested in another consort, you need to stop staring." Elatha pumped his hand a couple of times.

A moan escaped her, and she clenched her thighs together as she leaned against the wall. She couldn't look away. Yet, she couldn't answer.

"Or you could let me inside if you've changed your mind," he growled as he pumped his hand again.

Literally going up in flames, heat flowed through her veins like molten lava, searing her nerve endings. Hell. Oh gods, she was in hell. She was definitely damned.

She couldn't let him in here. No. No way. If she did, she'd be fucking him in seconds. She wanted that magnificent thick cock inside her with a feral intensity that had her whimpering.

Don't do it. Don't do it. Don't.

With a hand out, she shook her head as if to keep the image of him away, desperate to keep him out of touching range. Yet, she could not tear her gaze away. She licked her lips as she panted.

Elatha snarled, "I will talk to you later, Princess," then stalked out of view.

"Oh my gods," Shannon moaned, dropping to her knees. Her hand reached out to touch the screen, sagging as it finally turned dark.

She sat there, panting, for a good five minutes, shivering as desire raged through her veins. Finally rising with a groan, she withdrew her fighting leathers into her torc and walked naked into the bathroom. As she replayed her conversation with Elatha, she sat on the edge of the jacuzzi tub, exhausted and overwhelmed. Pain pounded behind her eyes, making it difficult to think. With two fingers, she rubbed her aching temples. She didn't understand her response, her attraction to him. Was it just pregnancy hormones running amok?

She loved Loki.

She missed Loki.

Gods, she wanted Loki.

However long it had been, it felt like forever since she'd seen him. Ages since they'd made love. That must be it. A combination of pregnancy and being a fertility goddess. She needed and craved Loki, his body on hers.

In all their time apart, she'd not touched herself. While a captive, there'd been no privacy to use the chamber pot, let alone anything else. The leering looks Galar had given her when she couldn't wait until they'd left the workshop had creeped her out. No way was she going to do anything with those perverted dwarves looking on.

Of course, now that the thought had occurred, she could think of nothing else. Even her headache and exhaustion couldn't compete with it.

Stupid pregnancy hormones.

Aroused and insistent, her body demanded satisfaction. She didn't know if it would help her goddess powers, but perhaps she'd feel less edgy if she took care of it now while she had privacy. Or at least, the boost of endorphins might help her damn headache.

Maybe then she'd be able to stop noticing how fucking sexy Elatha was.

After dialing in the temperature she wanted, the tub filled rapidly, and she carefully climbed in. With it up to her chin as she leaned against a reclining seat, the heat soaked into her muscles and aching joints. The control panel gave options for different jet configurations. After exploring each setting, she found what she wanted. The powerful jets pulsed, hitting exactly where she most needed them.

At the stimulation, her pulse picked up, and arousal flared anew. As she panted, Loki came to life within her mind and his clever fingers played her body. Her fingers became his slick-coated fingers, teasing her as fine tremors started, nerves sparking.

Writhing as she grew closer, the mental image became more vivid and detailed. The jets in front of her became Loki, while the jets behind her became Elatha. Both males pressing hot and rigid against Shannon, driving hard into her, hands and lips exploring.

Loud moans escaped her lips.

Heat built, searing her with its wildfire spread.

Caught at the precipice, breath held, her hips writhed until the stimulation was just right. With muscles spasming, lightning exploding up blazing nerve endings, and gasping for air, she rode out the intensely glorious release.

Minutes later, sated and with a relaxed lethargy seeping into her bones, she fumbled for the jet controls, turning them off. Despite the climax, her head still pounded. But at least it had backed off to a dull thumping instead of an ice pick driving through her brain. While she floated in the water, she let her mind wander.

Gradually, rational thought returned. She bolted upright with a sudden realization.

Oh. Flying. Fuck.

She'd fantasized not just about Loki, but Elatha as well. And not just an insanely erotic fantasy about both of them, but also the most intense orgasm she'd ever given herself.

Shannon couldn't believe it. What the hell had she done? How could she mentally cheat on Loki? Tears sprang to her eyes, pain welling in her chest. The idea of hurting him, of betraying him like that, had her sobbing into her hands.

Loki was in her heart and soul—her literal soulmate. That she desired someone else to the point of fantasizing broke her. She hated herself, and she'd never hated herself before. Not even when her loathsome ex-fiancé had tried to shred her self-confidence.

Riddled with self-loathing, Shannon's heart squeezed with despair and disgust. She'd thought she known who she was inside. But this desire she couldn't escape, couldn't deny or get rid of... it shredded her self-respect and self-worth right down to her soul. She was going to the deepest level of hell reserved for cheaters and betrayers.

Shannon dragged herself to the shower, and in blisteringly hot water, she scrubbed her body roughly from head to toe. As if she could wash what she'd done from her skin and mind. Dirty, unclean, and unworthy. Finally collapsing onto the hard surface, she cradled her abdomen and let the water wash away the salty tears pouring down her face.

Time had no meaning as she sat there, sobbing. Body and soul ached with the cold of dead expectations. By the time she finally turned off the water, eyes aching and nose stuffed up, her head pounded worse. Her limbs were as stiff as the grave.

With slow, exhausted movements, she dried and wrapped her body in a heavy tunic and leggings to cover everything to her wrists and ankles before leaving the shower. In the kitchen, she forced herself to eat a meal despite the sick churning in her stomach. Too wrapped up in her misery and guilt, she didn't notice what she ate. Just that she did. Each bite was chewed and swallowed with all the mechanical enjoyment of an automaton.

When her plate was empty and cleaned, she made her way to the bedroom, ignoring the door that had started chiming again. Pulling the pillow over her head in an effort to shut out the world, she tried to sleep.

Elatha shuddered as Shannon's moaned words chased him down the hall to his suite's door. The image of her naked body burned his mind like staring too long at a thermal vent in the ocean floor—dark honey skin, dark reddish-purple nipples on high, full breasts that would fuel his fantasies for years, and by the first shell, she was fertility personified with such a lush belly. So perfectly round. Would that she'd ask him to provide for her and her growing child. Shells, if only he were so lucky.

He didn't lack experience in his thousand years of life, but never had he been fortunate enough to be with a woman carrying the next generation. To take care of their needs was a joy every Fomorian consort hoped for.

Shannon was spectacular in her ripeness, and his primal reaction inevitable in the face of her glorious form. He groaned, gripping his shaft after his suite door closed behind him. The way her hazel eyes had devoured him. Shells, the sight of that little pink tongue licking her lips—

Unable to wait any further, he tore open his skinsuit, stroking his engorged shaft and gliding a thumb over the leaking tip. Fuck. Was she in the shower right now with water gliding over those luscious peaks? Those tits he ached to weigh with his hands, feeling them overflow his palms? His hand moved faster as he leaned his forehead against the wall, panting.

And her ass, the way it had flexed when she'd turned, trying to find the source of his voice.

In his mind, she lay back on a pile of cushions, a fertility goddess in full bloom, splaying those silken thighs to tease him with glimpses of flushed, moist depths below the small patch of reddish-brown curls.

"By the shell, I would give pretty much anything to taste you," his fantasy self growled, watching her glistening fingers move. "Show me that pretty pink pussy while I come," Elatha demanded as he stroked harder.

Moans left her lips as she panted, working her fingers in and out of her sex, widening her legs as she began to orgasm, lush body writhing.

"Fuck. Oh fuck. Fuck. Fuck!" Elatha groaned, eyes closed as the scene played out behind his eyelids. "Shannon! I'm going to—" His body jerked, legs trembling as he spurted, come jetting in bursts of pearly white onto her thighs, sex, and round belly.

Still quaking as pleasure hummed throughout his nerves, Elatha opened his eyes to find the spattered wall. "Shells," he cursed, tucking his now spent cock back into his skinsuit. Forcing his thoughts from the delicious woman next door who'd turned him down despite her apparent interest, he went in search of a towel.

If he continued to dwell on Shannon, he'd soon be adding to his clean-up.

After finding what he needed in the bathroom, he returned to the suite's entrance and mopped up, then headed to the kitchen to make breakfast. Despite his best efforts, he couldn't stop his thoughts from wandering back to her. "Damned sea squirts," he cursed as he nicked his finger while cutting vegetables. He'd foregone the ready-made meals, needing the distraction of cooking. So much for that idea. All it did was have him injuring himself.

Blood welled, and he washed it away, wrapping a quick bandage around the minor cut. In short order, he had an omelette on the table. As he ate, his thoughts again drifted to her. Had she eaten? Rested? Did she want to leave today? Unable to stop himself, he rang her suite's door after he finished his food and tidied the kitchen.

But she didn't answer.

Shoulders slumping, he left and checked in with the outpost commander. There'd been no reply from his mother, but he hadn't expected her to when he'd told her he would be leaving again right away.

Shannon didn't answer when he tried again in the mid-afternoon.

Fighting the need to ring the door multiple times, Elatha left the outpost to check on nearby coral plantings. When he returned that evening, Shannon still didn't answer the door.

Nor did she answer the next day.

Or the day after that.

Anxiety twisting his insides into knots, he couldn't abandon her to distract himself with more work. Instead, he sought the outpost steward. "Can you please verify that my guest, Princess Shannon of Asgard, is using meals and water resources? I don't want to force my way in if she still needs more time to rest before we continue onward, but she's pregnant. I have to know she doesn't require the healer," Elatha asked the man in the tower's housekeeping office. He couldn't stifle his guilt that he'd attacked her, a pregnant sea goddess, and forced her to defend herself. Bile rose in his throat every time he recalled his actions when they'd met.

The man pulled up a control panel. "Yes, she's eating and has not activated any requests for help. Would you like me to keep you notified if her status changes?"

Elatha's chest loosened at the offer, his breath washing out in a long exhale. "Yes, please."

"Certainly, my prince. Is there anything else? Are the meals and guest suites up to your standard?" he asked, eyebrows raised in hopeful anticipation.

Elatha patted the steward on the shoulder. "Everything is wonderful. I can't think of a thing you would need to improve on. The ready-to-eat meals are excellent."

The man bowed, a grin on his white-and-black patched face. "Thank you, my prince. I know we aren't a big outpost with as many resources or variety as our cities."

"I have no complaints," Elatha reassured him before departing. Shannon was alive and he couldn't do anything more until she let him.

Chapter 19

THE ROAD TO HELL IS PAVED WITH GOOD INTENTIONS

In a deepening depression, Shannon woke, showered, attempted to scrub away the fantasies of Elatha that continued to plague her dreams—better than the nightmares reliving her torment at the hands of the dwarves or her fears about her baby's health, but traumatic in their own way—cried, dressed, ate, and returned to bed. Over and over, she repeated the negative spiral. All the while, ignoring the chiming door that periodically announced itself and taunted her with the possibility of fulfillment.

Eventually, her anxiety about her child's lack of activity had her answering the door. Surely, she had suppressed her unreasonable attraction to the sexy Fomorian prince.

"Shannon? Are you okay?" Elatha asked, stark concern in his gaze as he looked her over. "Do I need to call the healer? It's been four risings since you answered the door."

"No, no, I'm not, but I need to ignore it for now and get home. I can't keep wallowing," she replied in an unemotional, flat monotone. She'd grown more tired by the day, exhaustion plaguing her every waking moment. Had it really been four days? She'd thought maybe two. Her headache had built to excruciating proportions—it hurt to open her eyes, and no position was comfortable despite the fluffy mattress. Her fingers gripped her belly. And her child... her child hadn't kicked since the second time she'd woken in these plush surroundings. Was he okay? Was he—

"Wallowing? I upset you. Shells, I'm sorry. What—"

Shannon interrupted his apology, holding up a hand. A shaft of guilt speared through her, breaking the numbness she'd cultivated. Her fantasies weren't his fault or his responsibility. None of this was his fault.

"No, Elatha. You didn't do anything wrong. These types of relationships are normal for your people. You aren't the one already in a monogamous relationship. That's me. This is on me. I should not have returned your interest. I did. This is my responsibility. I have to deal with the consequences." The words hurt, but she couldn't hide from them. She didn't have the energy to even try.

Elatha opened his mouth, then closed it, shaking his head. He frowned and finally said, "I don't... We didn't... I'm not sure what to say, Shannon."

"It's okay. I just need you to guide me to the surface waters," she replied, trying to keep her inner turmoil in check. She had to get back into the energizing saltwater, to get some kind of energy for her son. Despite her hopes, the chance for real sleep in safe surroundings and food hadn't done her or her son any good.

"I vowed to see you to your home or your mate. I'm not going to break that vow," Elatha said sternly.

Shannon's heart squeezed. She wanted to be away from the temptation of Prince Elatha, but he wasn't making it easy. Especially when she needed his help. It was becoming clear she couldn't make it on her own. Fuck, she could barely get around the suite without hanging onto the walls. Surely, this lethargy and the joint aches would lift once she was in the ocean again. Maybe even the damned headache. *Please, please let her baby be okay.*

"Very well," she answered quietly. "I'm ready to leave."

Elatha opened the door, and she saw him in person again for the first time in days.

Time hadn't lessened his impact. The punch of arousal ripped through her like a physical blow to her sternum, stealing her breath and leaving her heart pounding. At least this time, he had his armour on, so she didn't have quite as good a view of every rippling muscle of his tall, impressively athletic physique. Unfortunately, she had an excellent mental image of what was underneath that armour.

His scent, that fresh, clean rain smell that she'd thought was the air of the outpost, wrapped around her, teasing her with its comforting familiarity. Even as it burrowed inside her sea goddess essence, pooling in her lower abdomen, she clenched her teeth against the rawly sensual temptation. The sooner they got into the water and her overloading senses had something else to focus on, the better.

With him guiding her through the outpost, even with her stumbling gait—she refused to ask for help walking—it took only a few minutes before they reached a water gate.

Before re-entering the underground sea, Shannon modified what she wore. Fighting leathers and Asgardian-style armour were all very well on land, but something more streamlined and less bulky worked better in the water. If she could reduce the water's resistance on her body, it would conserve her energy. And gods, she needed every scrap. After observing the sleek design of his armour and skinsuit, she concentrated and shifted hers to replicate his style, but in shades of blue, ignoring the sharp spike in her headache.

Elatha nodded his head. "That's impressive. You can replicate any design and materials with a thought?"

"Yes. It was a gift from Odin, with some additional modification by Loki." She fidgeted, staring at the silver ring. The energizing touch of saltwater was so close.

"Very useful. A bubble isn't needed to exit from this side of the barrier. We can just walk through. Watch me go through first and follow," he instructed.

He strode through the gate and melted into the water on the other side. She wasted no time in copying him. It was as easy as it looked, and she sighed, shoulders loosening as the tingling saltwater fed her energy-starved body and the blessed buoyancy relieved the baby's weight from her aching back, hips, knees, and ankles.

Elatha frowned slightly as Shannon simply hung in the water, but she didn't have the words to reassure him. She just needed a little time to gather enough strength to start swimming. As the tension eased around her lungs, she set off, correcting her direction as the prince pointed the way.

A few minutes later, she increased her speed, and they soon left the light of the outpost and its surrounding vegetation in their wake. Minutes built into hours at their continued easy pace, with awkward silence their third companion, even as they took several stops to eat. After a longer break to sleep partially submerged on a rock ledge with a bit of a beach, the fog around Shannon's mind cleared enough for her curiosity to awaken.

"With your outposts underwater, are the Fomorians the source of the mermaid/merman myths on Midgard?"

Elatha's lips twitched, and he met her gaze briefly before searching the dark depths ahead with the glow of his trident. "Partly. We certainly get some of the blame when a Midgardian has a tale about humanoids breathing underwater. But the sea gods and goddesses, the selkies, and even some of the sea demons get rolled into those myths as well, depending on what part of Midgard we are talking about. Around the ancient territory of the elves on Litauī, what is now the United Kingdom and Ireland, the Northern Atlantic, and Arctic Oceans, it's usually selkies, sea gods and goddesses, and sometimes, sea demons. On the west coast of North America, it's usually the selkies. On the other side of the Pacific and Indian Oceans, it's the Shen."

Shannon considered his answer. No way would the bunyip she and Loki had tackled on Australia's Great Barrier Reef be mistaken for a mermaid, but Manannan? Or the Shen? Yeah, she could see how they'd contribute to spreading the mythology. "The other day, you mentioned outposts and surface waters. Alfheim has seas not just below ground like this one, but also above? How does that work? Why doesn't all the water fill this space?"

Elatha grinned. "You'll see when we go through the Tunnels of Glass up to the surface. It's the tunnel shape and that the surface seas, while extensive, are considerably shallower than our underground seas, equalizing the pressure. The dwarves add pressure equalizers to their tunnel systems, and particularly, their air slides. Not only does it allow them to manipulate air pressure within their kingdoms, but also the weather down here. We aren't impacted by their weather, but the Unseelie are. It's my understanding that's a big part of why the Unseelie don't mess with the dwarves."

Shannon's eyes widened. It sounded like the dwarves had the dark elves over a barrel, technologically. No wonder Galar and Fjalar hadn't been worried about stealing her from the elves. Bastards. She kicked extra hard, wishing it was their faces she was pummelling.

Shoving them from her thoughts, she returned her focus to the prince eyeing her curiously. What were they talking about? Oh right... "But the surface seas are still deep enough to hide outposts at the sea bottom?"

"Indeed. We have many outposts within the surface seas. Some have even grown into small cities, just as they have on Litauī, although we still call them outposts. Still, our largest cities are here in the deeper underground seas." He gestured around them. "We've left the Sea of Lantia and reached the Sea of Uaithne. It won't be much further before we stop for a longer rest period at one of our waystations."

Shannon's chest ached at the thought of sleep. Even with the energy of the water, her head pounded. Every stroke of her arms and kick of her feet was a strain on her muscles and joints. But the nightmares... the memories.

And her child still hadn't moved.

He had to be okay. He had to be. She swallowed against the lump in her throat. "So where are your people on Ear—Litauī?"

"Our outposts range from Antarctica, around Australia, around Africa, South America on both the Pacific and Atlantic sides and into the Caribbean and Mediterranean Seas."

"With as busy as the Caribbean and Mediterranean Seas are, I'm amazed that you can maintain outposts there undetected."

"You're correct. We moved them out of those two seas more recently. We left the Mediterranean about five hundred years ago, and the Caribbean about two hundred and fifty Midgardian years ago. They were getting too well travelled by the Midgardians. Too many of our people were being spotted. Avoiding detection is the best way to avoid conflict with the more primitive land-dwellers."

She nodded. "That's a wise move. Having been raised human, I agree. Humans attack anything they fear, and whatever they don't understand, they fear." Too many alien movie plots revolved around that premise to think the human race as a collective would respond otherwise. They absolutely weren't ready to know life existed on other planets, especially much more advanced beings.

Elatha started to say something, then stopped.

"Go ahead and ask." She had a pretty good idea what he wanted to know.

"How is it you were raised thinking you were human?"

Yep, that was what she expected.

"The story I got from the woman who adopted me, my mom, is that my birth father found them and claimed he was a fisherman like my dad. He said he needed to return to the sea and asked my human parents to take me, to raise me. They did, although my adoptive father died over a decade ago. My remaining human family has no idea I'm not human."

In another few minutes, they arrived in front of a water gate at the mouth of a large cave. After triggering the bubble, Elatha led her inside. It was a surprisingly bright cavern. Glowing plants grew over the outside surface so that the many windows on the walls and ceiling let in bright light and views of the richly diverse surrounding sea life. There were several interconnected rooms, including multiple bedrooms, a sitting room, and a kitchen, all in a bright white, further adding light to the space. The floor had sea shells embedded into the smooth surface in pinks, blues, oranges, and browns. They stopped between the sitting room with its plush yellow couches and glass side tables and the lively kitchen with gleaming silver appliances, including an AMP, and white storage nooks filled with all kinds of bottles, jars, and bins of spices, oils, and foodstuffs.

"By the first shell." Elatha shook his head, eyes wide. "It must have been such a shock to find out you weren't human. I can't even imagine what that must have been like."

She smiled, a wry twist of her lips, and shook her head. "Shock is an understatement. It's been quite the... do you know what the date would be on Midgard right now?" Frowning, she rubbed her wrist. Damn, but she missed the watch Loki had made her. Her sense of time was completely skewed without it.

"Sure." He tapped a couple icons on his trident, peered at the readout, then said, "It's February twenty-second, twenty-twenty-three on Litauī." He pointed out the bathroom and then started towards the kitchen. "Let's get some foo—"

Shannon's breath seized in her lungs. She halted and grabbed the edge of the nearest couch. Six—*six months* since her girls' weekend? She'd been a captive for... Holy shit. She gulped, a hysterical giggle rising in her throat that she fought back. Of all days, it was her birthday. But no—she stared down at her belly, letting her armour recede—it couldn't have been anywhere near that long or her son would have been born. Surely it was only a couple of weeks. A shiver travelled down her spine as she cradled her abdomen with one hand and wheezed out, "What's... what's the time conversion between here and Asgard or Midgard?"

"The same as between Asgard and Tír na nÓg, both five times slower than Litauī," Elatha said, frowning and stepping back beside her.

August first to February twenty-second... two hundred and six days divided by five, times seven days a week—"I've... I've been gone from Asgard for five-and-a-half, almost six weeks?" She blinked, staring at Elatha when he nodded to her. "I'd thought maybe half that. Holy crap. I'm thirty-three-and-a-half weeks now," she whispered.

Concerned, she eyed her belly, rubbing her abdomen. If her son came on his due date, she only had six weeks. She began panting, pulse racing. Shit... he could come sooner, especially with all the stress. Oh fuck. Oh gods. She was still at least a week and a half from getting back to Asgard. Oh gods... She clutched her belly tighter. What if he—

"What's wrong? Are you okay? Is your baby okay?"

Elatha rapid-fired questions that Shannon only heard in a fog. Tears pricked her eyes. Talk about rotten birthday presents. Not at all how she'd wanted to celebrate her thirty-sixth... no, wait, she'd missed one while on Asgard. Did that make her thirty-seven? Or was her birthday counted by when she was born on Alfheim? What did that make her... seven? Or eight? Her vision blurred and a laugh that was partly a sob burbled out.

Elatha approached, putting a hand on her abdomen. With his hands on her body, the arousal she'd been doing her best to ignore roared back to life like a live electric current circling between them.

She blinked, trying to focus on his face. "What—what are you doing?" she managed through a hiccupped cry.

"You didn't answer so I'm checking to see if you are having contractions."

"No," she said, even as the heat of his hand penetrated through the skinsuit to her greedy skin. Of course, the baby kicked hard right then.

Elatha's eyes widened. "Your child is strong!"

Shannon's laughter took prominence, chasing away the sobs. Lightheaded with relief, her knees buckled. Elatha caught her against him, staggering until they half-fell, half-sat on the nearby couch with her on his lap.

She laughed again, tears soaking her cheeks. "Yes, he is." She moved Elatha's hand directly to the underside, slightly to the right and below her belly button, where her son kicked the hardest.

Elatha chuckled, rubbing circles as he leaned down and told her son to have patience, to stay in there a while longer, and to take it easy on his poor mother. Elatha was smiling when he glanced back up at her. At the same time, both realized his fingertips had paused, brushing over the junction of her thighs.

Her breath froze as their gazes locked. Desire and guilt churned, fighting each other. Part of her insisted that she move his hand off. But the desperate wanton within craved moving his touch just a fraction lower to where she ached. Not trusting which words would come out of her mouth, she bit her tongue. Her body strained, muscles trembling.

She needed to get off his damned lap. Now. Right fucking now.

The same awareness was in Elatha's eyes, the conflict as he fought with himself. His chest rose and fell with each quick breath.

Closing his eyes, his hands on her shoulder and abdomen flexed.

Lightning shot through her as the tip of his longest finger managed to hit just right. Fiery need was a living, breathing dragon burning up her insides, shattering her control like a toddler-driven tantrum in a room made of glass. Unable to stop herself, she moaned, hips jerking into his hand, driving his finger deeper—the thin skinsuit no barrier to his touch.

"Fuck!" he swore as his hand moved to fully cup her, his fingers dancing over the taut nub that demanded attention.

She gasped, keening with need as her hips moved against the pressure of their own volition. Instincts snarled, lunging for satisfaction, even as her heart screamed to stop. Yet, desperate desire refused to be restrained, overthrowing her every attempt to rein it in. It was a thirst, a craving that was undeniable.

"Please!" burst out of her mouth, despite her attempts to stifle it.

"Fuck!" Elatha swore again, his fingers finding a faster rhythm over her skinsuit-covered mound.

"Yes!" she snarled, her entire body writhing in animalistic reaction. Molten desire was a fire in her blood, scorching her with its intensity.

"Shells, you are so damned beautiful," Elatha growled into her ear.

Shannon screamed, shaking as the heat of her climax tore through her. The savage inferno incinerated her nerves, blasted through her blood, and exploded out her skin, even as the waves of pleasure remade flesh and knit her back together, one atom at a time while she slumped and consciousness faded.

Elatha groaned, catching Shannon as she collapsed against him. Her body still quivered with orgasm, but as he lifted her into his arms, her eyes were closed and face lax.

Her chest rose and fell. She'd passed out? Had he hurt her? He didn't think so. But shells, he'd attacked her when they'd met. Bile rose to coat the back of his throat, and he swallowed hard.

She seemed to be disappearing before his very eyes. When she'd answered the door yesterday rising, his heart had clenched at the gauntness haunting her face. She'd gone from the extreme slenderness revealed when she'd removed the illusion to a skeletal frailty that had his stomach churning. Numerous times yesterday, he'd almost turned around to take her back to the healer, but she'd seemed to be better in the water.

Shells, she'd almost seemed perky after waking on the beach this rising, despite the primitive rest stop that had him cursing they'd not created more frequent waystations. She deserved more comfort, and he couldn't stifle his need to see to her care. Yet, she hadn't noticed how slowly they'd swum, taking over forty hours to get here, or how often he'd stopped to push food on her. Indeed, they should have stopped for another resting hours ago, but he'd wanted better than a sandy beach for her this time. It'd be the last comfortable bed he could offer until she returned to Asgard.

How had she lost so much weight in the four days she'd locked herself in her room? She'd eaten, and eaten well, according to the records he'd viewed. And whatever rest she'd gotten hadn't helped her either.

He still wasn't sure why she'd secluded herself for those days. If her comments were to be believed, some sort of misplaced guilt for what... thoughts? An admiring glance and natural body reaction? The idea was unfathomable to him. His stomach twisted—would she react the same way to the climax she'd just enjoyed? From the speed of her body's reaction, she'd desperately needed the relief. Shells, it had been such a minor pleasure to provide when she suffered constantly. Her every wince and pinched expression he caught when she thought he wasn't looking told the story she didn't want to admit. Even if he couldn't give her energy like a pregnant Fomorian, the endorphins had to give her some respite from the pain she carried. If only he could do more for her.

As he laid her on the bed, he put a hand on her abdomen. The babe still kicked, and he seemed healthy enough, if overlarge on her tiny, vulnerable frame. Was something wrong with her or her child? Was Shannon ill—a wasting sickness her immortal healing couldn't deal with? Did she have some injury that was sapping her strength or something those barnacle-blighted dwarves had done to her? Had they damaged her immortal healing? Her ability to renew the energy within her? He scrubbed a hand over his face and into his hair. What could he do? How could he help her? All he had were questions and no answers. Fuck. He *had* to help her.

Shells, he should have brought a healer to her before they'd left the outpost. He was a damn fool. Why hadn't he insisted?

He tucked her into the blanket. Maybe higher-nutrient foods or more food? He rose and opened the bins in the kitchen, perusing the options while keeping her in sight. If he sent a message to the outpost, they could restock if he wiped out all the travel rations of nuts and berries. And there were ingredients to make nutrient-dense spicy seafood rolls. They'd be good for her and the babe. She'd liked the one he'd given her earlier in the day.

After removing what he needed from the food stores, he spent the next few hours preparing six times what he'd normally take with him on a week-long trip. They still had a nine-day—he glanced over at Shannon—perhaps a fourteen-day swim to the plains between the Summer and Winter realms where the Asgardian Bifrost could pick her up.

When he finished, he eyed the pile of rolls, berries, and nuts. Surely, that would be enough. He pulled out a set of wraps and spread them with a chocolaty nut butter his little sister seemed to adore, then rolled them into tubes. Hopefully, Shannon would enjoy them, too.

He loaded the extra food into a pack that wouldn't impede his swimming or access to his weapons, then returned to Shannon. She'd rolled onto her side, and he lay beside her, listening to her breathe. Bold perhaps, to share her bed, even with them both fully clothed, but she was in his care. The idea of leaving her to rest in another room had his belly churning and a pit opening in his chest.

He couldn't do it. Not while he didn't know how to help her, and how she'd declined the last time he'd let her out of his sight. No, he had to keep an eye on her. Hearing her breathe beside him settled the nerves that rose just thinking of being apart from her.

Within minutes, his breathing matched hers, and he rolled to place his hand on her belly. The child moved under his hand, and keeping his voice to a low murmur, Elatha sang a lullaby his mother had sung when he was young. He'd keep them safe. He'd sworn it.

Chapter 20

SILVER CITY

Duplicating himself to search the tunnels for Shannon had worn Loki's energy lower than he'd realized. With sleep eluding him, he'd resorted to telling stories to Eitri and Brokkr to boost his natural recharge. The rest of the time, Loki paced the shoreline like a wild beast caged for too long—panic a metallic taste on his tongue that he swallowed down repeatedly. Every minute, every hour, Shannon got farther and farther away. Mist talked him down daily, convincing him to wait, but even she had begun staring into the water for long periods.

Loki's pulse sped as Manannan rose from the water on their seventh day of waiting. Had he found her?

But the sea god was alone as he strode up the steps leading to Eitri and Brokkr's workshop to join him on the top of the landing. "Prince Loki." Manannan inclined his head. "I was already on Tír na nÓg when I got Mist's message. After talking to you on Litauī, I believed I'd be of more use here. Unfortunately, I didn't find any sign that Shannon has reached the surface Ocean of Ceobhran, but I put out word with the selkies and dolphins, as well as my fellow sea gods and goddesses, to keep an eye out for her."

Loki exhaled and shoved fingers through his shoulder-length hair, pushing it off his face, even as he fought the sinking sensation in his belly. Too much to hope that Manannan had already located her. "Thank you, Manannan. I appreciate it. We missed her by less than a day, it seems, before she set off into the Sea of Lantia." At least they could finally follow Shannon. Surely with the Atlanteans' help, they'd find her quickly.

"Our best bet would be as you suggested. We need to talk to the Fomorians. Since I wanted to speak to you first and not keep you waiting, I haven't stopped there yet," Manannan said.

The door to the workshop opened behind them, and Mist emerged. "Are you able to take me with you to talk to them?" she asked. "Unlike you two, I can't shapeshift or breathe underwater."

"Although it will slow our progress, the trade-off is you will learn what we know at the same time we do. It would allow us to change where we go depending on what we find," the sea god mused.

Loki weighed the pros and cons. While he could continue without her, the Valkyrie knew Shannon in ways he didn't. Best friends shared different things than consorts, and he appreciated Mist's insights.

"Mist can run along the water's surface until we need to dive. That should allow us to still make good time and talk to the Atlanteans together," Loki proposed.

"I hadn't thought of that. Sure, it works," Manannan agreed, flashing a smile at her.

Loki left them on the shore, returning to the workshop to say goodbye to Eitri and Brokkr. "Thank you both for your kind hospitality."

"Make sure you bring your beautiful Shannon to visit us. I can't believe you have offspring on the way! Talk about chaos!" teased Brokkr.

Eitri cuffed his brother on the back of the head. "We really are very happy for you, Loki. I hope you are reunited with her very soon," he said with a kind smile on his ugly face. Turning serious, he added, "If there is anything else we can do to help, let us know. I'm still ashamed of what those sacks of basalt did to your consort."

Brokkr nodded his agreement, eyes downcast.

"I will. Thank you."

Loki rejoined Manannan and Mist. "Ready to go?"

"Yes. I'll stay close to the surface so Mist can track us until it's time to head into the depths," Manannan said before he plunged into the waves.

Loki followed until he could dive underwater and shift into a dolphin form. Jumping into the air, he spied Mist already running above the waves. Back in the water, Loki put on a burst of speed to catch up with Manannan. That sea god was no slouch. He was moving at a good clip, lighting the way with his trident. To keep up with him, Loki had to exert himself—something he couldn't have done if he'd left a few days ago. Perhaps it had been wise to take those days to recover.

As they travelled, the trio swerved around pillars of white stone that stretched down into the depths and passed fields of glowing green vegetation rich with sea life. Loki took advantage of these to gulp down tasty striped yellow fish that Manannan indicated were fine to eat. Although Loki tossed a few into the air for Mist, she waved them off. There were still some dried provisions in their packs to keep her going.

Every six hours or so, when Manannan found a dry spot above the waterline where they could stop, they took a brief break to check in with each other. Since only Manannan understood Loki as a dolphin, Loki shifted back during their rests to talk. On their third break, sitting on a ledge of rock jutting out above the water from a curving wall of a massive pillar, they took turns keeping watch and getting a few hours of sleep. The Asgardians were using a lot of energy to keep up with Manannan. At least the nightmares didn't plague Loki with such brief naps.

"We've been in Fomorian territory, what they call Atlantia here on Tír na nÓg, for the past few hours. If we don't get stopped sooner, we'll reach their capital city of Hy-Brasil by this time tomorrow. I've been giving their outposts a wide berth since I'd prefer we go directly to talk to Queen Edniu," Manannan said.

"It's rare for Asgard to interact with the Atlanteans. We don't even have an ambassador for them. Does the queen still have two sons and a daughter? I thought we'd received word a while ago that she'd given birth to a daughter." Loki hadn't met any of their royal family. He'd met a couple of their outpost commanders on Midgard over the years, although not since they'd chosen to lower their outposts beneath the water's surface. Usually Thor interacted with the reclusive but friendly race. As far as Loki was aware, Asgardians had never been invited to one of their cities on Alfheim. To be fair, Atlanteans had never been invited to Asgard, either, and it was rare to see them travelling on other planets or space stations in the galaxy.

"Yes, Prince Elada is the eldest. Prince Elatha is only one hundred years younger than his older brother, but it is Princess Eriu who is the heir to the throne. Still a child, relatively speaking, she's only two hundred compared to Elatha, who is around one thousand if I remember correctly. But then, the queen herself is only three thousand, so no doubt she will have more children." Manannan smiled with an expression that seemed to hold secrets.

What wasn't the sea god telling them?

"They are matriarchal then, if the young daughter is the heir to the throne? I know very little about how their society is organized," Mist admitted.

"Yes. No surprise with their skewed population sex ratio. Many more sons are born than daughters. It's almost five or six sons for every daughter born. Because of that, their culture developed into a polyamorous society where females rule and take numerous male consorts. When children are expected or present in the household, the grouping is often formalized into a marriage."

Mist grinned. "Hey, I think I like the sound of that! I have a new proposition to bring up to the All-Father. To heck with the typical one-partner thing! Elves and Atlanteans know how to do it."

With a laugh, Loki shook his head. "Don't you already have that, Mist? I'm sure I've heard rumblings among the Einherjar that you aren't willing to settle down with just one. Or is that hurt male egos talking?" he teased.

Mist smirked and put a hand on her hip. "I make no promises and tell them no lies. Variety is the spice of life."

Manannan eyed her with interest.

She winked at him.

Loki smirked. "Not to interrupt your mating rituals, Mist—you know I'll be your wingman anytime—but I would like to get to Shannon as soon as possible."

Mist grinned and thumped him on the shoulder. "Thanks, Loki. That's a nice offer." Her eyes lost the sparkle of amusement as her smile disappeared. "I'm worried about her, too. Let's go."

Loki and Manannan dove into the water while Mist followed them from above. The rest of the journey continued to be uneventful. They didn't see any Atlanteans as the trio approached the capital, but the sea god had explained that he was a relatively frequent visitor every few years. Likely, they'd marked their presence and were watching, but letting them approach since the Asgardians were with him.

The light of the city was visible before it came into sight. A bright green glow lit the depths and everything around it. The sea teemed with life nearby, taking advantage of the light.

When they got close enough to see details, Loki blinked. Perhaps it was a good thing Asgard had never come into conflict with the Atlanteans. A multitude of silver towers were encased in overlapping green bubbles of energy, like soap bubbles linked together in multiple rings. It was impressive shield technology, easily on par with Asgard's defensive city shields. Or perhaps more advanced, given Asgard's city shields weren't constantly activated, nor holding back the pressure of water at these depths. How did the Atlanteans power them?

Manannan brought Mist below, wrapped in her own bubble of air, and Loki followed. Down they swam, farther and farther. It was deeper than it looked, which had Loki's admiration for the Atlanteans' technology growing. No wonder they'd been so willing to retreat beneath the waves.

Manannan seemed to be angling toward the nearest bubble of energy. As they approached, Loki spotted a metallic silver circle overlapping the wall of energy with the sea floor. Manannan gestured for Loki to come into the circle where he and Mist stood. When Loki joined them, the energy wall moved over the trio to the edges of the metallic circle, pushing the water out and leaving them surrounded by air.

Quickly, Loki shifted back to humanoid.

A pair of male Atlanteans with black-and-white patched skin and hair, in black scale armour, complete with swords on their backs and tridents in hand, waited for them just inside the energy barrier. One lowered a palm from a holographic control pad on the side of the barrier. Several other guards stood a short distance away. Manannan walked in unconcerned, so Loki followed. Once Mist had joined them inside, the energy wall snapped back from the silver circle, returning the barrier to its original configuration.

An Atlantean raised a hand. "Manannan Mac Lir, welcome back to Hy-Brasil. Who is it you have with you?" he asked in a light baritone voice with an accent that reminded Loki of ancient Greek.

Manannan gave the guard a brief nod. "This is Prince Loki of Asgard, and Mist, Valkyrie of Asgard. We seek an audience with Queen Ethniu, and the assistance of the Fomorians in locating Princess Shannon, Prince Loki's consort."

"Very well. Follow me." The Atlantean led them down a path toward the interior rings of the city. Two more guards fell in behind.

The city was beautiful. From his few visits to their outposts centuries ago, Loki had known the Atlanteans were technologically advanced, similar to Asgard in that respect, but the scope of what they'd created here was breathtaking. If he hadn't just come in from the sea, he'd almost not believe they were underwater. Had Thor seen this? Or had he only communicated with the Atlanteans on the water's surface? Silver twisting spires of towers reached up into the heights towards the energy barrier, surpassing the heights of even the tallest Midgardian skyscrapers. Parks with tidy paths, fruiting trees, grass and well-maintained landscaping provided enormous areas of green space. Long stretches of raised gardens overflowed with fruits and vegetables. There were fountains with children laughing and playing, splashing in the water.

The Atlanteans themselves were a colourful people. Besides the range of striped and patched skin between black, silver, and white, they wore bright colours, typically in skinsuits with a range of styles of floating, gauzy fabrics overtop. The only ones who didn't seem to reflect this colourful palette were the guards in their all-black armour. Once in a while, Loki spotted other guards in black-and-white armour.

The most intriguing sight were the water bubbles. As they walked on a white stone path, Loki wondered why there were so many fountains, but then an energy bubble emerged from the centre of one. When it receded, an Atlantean stood there. The woman stepped out of the fountain and shed the water from her skinsuit and top as she walked.

It had to be some form of transportation within the city.

Loki's pulse quickened when the guard led them into one of the larger fountains. Wonderful. He almost bounced on his toes as his curiosity peaked.

"Stand close to me," Manannan advised.

As water surrounded them in a bubble of energy, Loki and Mist moved to either side of the sea god. Manannan had been expecting it, clearly, as he'd wrapped air around their heads. The bottom below them opened to show what seemed to be a network of water tubes. Manannan swam down one, following the guard and towing Loki and Mist with him. The other two guards swam behind them.

Much faster than walking, they jetted along the tube, passing Atlanteans whooshing by in the opposite current on the other side of the tube, until the guard stopped again and shifted out of the current. He pressed a seashell-shaped button, and above them, a portal opened and filled with water. When they swam up, the water bubble was held in place by green energy. After they were all within the bubble, the floor closed. The bubble with its water receded, leaving them standing in a fountain in a large ornate silver chamber.

An impressive transportation system. Loki wasn't sure the distance they'd travelled, but it had been quick and efficient, with directional currents that allowed travellers to switch where they were going mid-stream or divert into a new pipe at the junctions. How did they generate the currents? And their shield technology was so versatile. He had so many questions. Perhaps they'd let him visit again once he'd saved Shannon.

Loki climbed out of the fountain and dried himself with a flick of seidhr, as Mist did beside him. Manannan and the guards seemed to simply shed the water, leaving damp hair behind. Was that why all the Atlanteans wore skinsuits?

The guard led them from the chamber, down several halls, up a silver stone staircase to the third floor, and opened the door to a suite of rooms. "Please take your rest. I will inform the queen of your request. When it is time for your audience with her, you will be summoned." After leaving the trio inside, he closed the door and left.

"Is this normal when you visit?" Loki asked as he and Mist explored the bright white rooms.

"Yes, it's not usually too long before I'm called. But it will still be plenty of time for us to clean up and have a meal," Manannan replied. He gave the Asgardians a tour of the five bedrooms, a large common room with brightly patterned sofas and an oval glass dining table with curved silver chairs. He stopped in the kitchen to flick through a control pad on some kind of appliance with prepared meals they could request.

"That sounds lovely, but I'm calling first shower!" Mist said as she headed down the hall to the bathroom.

"Right. Well, I'm going to have a good meal. Raw fish is fine as a dolphin, but after a while, I need more variety." Loki browsed the options. "Got any favourites?"

"Yes, I'm partial to the shrimp noodles with seasonal vegetables. It's lovely," Manannan recommended.

"That sounds great. Two?"

"Please. And a light ale as well."

"Now you are talking." Loki selected both and was impressed the entire order was ready in less than a minute. Did they have a form of energy-matter conversion technology similar to his conjuration? However they did it, it was exceptional. "What is this device called? Do you know how it works?"

Manannan took the bowls while Loki carried the ales to the table where a large window provided a view of gardens. "I don't know how it works. Atlanteans are more protective about their technology than even the dwarves. They call it an AMP—an Autonomous Meal Procurer." He chuckled and shrugged. "Not the most inventive name, but it's descriptive."

"It's also efficient and convenient." Quickly digging in, Loki couldn't believe how hungry he was. The first bites exploded flavour on his tongue in a spicy burst. The noodles were an odd texture with a little more crunch than he'd expected, but held the sauce well. "And good."

Manannan murmured his agreement.

Within minutes, Loki had eaten the entire meal. "Wow, that was great," he said as Mist joined them.

"Huh! I wasn't even long and you're already done?" She eyed his empty bowl and Manannan's almost empty bowl as the sea god took his last few bites. "What'd you have? It looks good."

"Shrimp noodles with seasonal vegetables and the light ale. Highly recommended," Loki said, tipping his mug to her.

He smiled into his ale. What would Shannon do with these kinds of options? When he'd joined her at mealtimes, he'd conjured whatever she was craving, but she'd love this. Norns, but he'd wasted so much time, missed so many meals with her.

His chest tightened, guilt at his frequent absences to Midgard a leaden weight. Why had he thought recording the new album with Raven's Chaos and filming his movie sequel was more important than being with his soulmate?

Especially with their relationship so new. He shifted in his seat. Why hadn't he appreciated the time with her more? Damn it, he should have made spending time with her more of a priority.

A vision of her emaciated form, so shocking in comparison to her lush pre-pregnancy curves, had him rubbing his sternum against a sudden breathlessness squeezing his lungs. Nausea churned, the pleasant meal not sitting so comfortably as he recalled what those bloody dwarves had fed her. Did she have food now? How was she managing? Her sea goddess powers were surely helping her, right? Yggdrasil's roots, he had to save her. He *had* to.

"Damn, what a selection! Can you imagine what Shannon would do with this?" Mist called out.

"I was just thinking that," Loki replied, his voice cracking.

"Has she been having lots of pregnancy cravings?" Manannan asked with an amused smirk.

Mist returned from the kitchen, carrying her plate and mug of ale. "Pickles. She was eating lots of pickles. Not in weird combinations, like pickles and ice cream or anything. Just lots of snacking on pickles. Actually, anything with salt, too. Norns, I made so many trips down to Midgard to get her plain rippled potato chips or Hawkins Cheezies. It had to be Hawkins." Mist shook her head, grinning.

A small bark of a laugh escaped Loki, even as he frowned. "Yeah, but also, chocolate. The only way I could get her to drink any dairy was to add chocolate. So many chocolate milkshakes I made for her." Why hadn't he known she'd been craving salty things? She'd never asked him to get her any potato chips or a particular cheese snack on his three or four daily trips to Midgard. Why? Why hadn't he offered? Bor's beard, he was a selfish git. Why hadn't he taken better care of her? Heat built behind his eyes as he ducked his head.

Mist put her hand on his arm, waiting until Loki met her gaze.

"We *are* going to find her. She's fine! You'll see. She escaped those assholes. Our princess is smart and tough." She didn't let him look away until he nodded.

With a casual hand, Loki swiped at his eyes. "Okay, my turn for the shower now." He rose and left the room.

In the shower, the tears came hot and fast, washed away by the water. The bond hadn't changed. She was there, somewhere. Shannon was alive.

By the Nine, he missed her. He missed her so badly. It was an unrelenting ache, a need based in the deepest depths of his soul. Sobbing under the cover of water, he released the anguish he'd been holding back.

When he finally calmed, he reminded himself that she was here, on the same planet, within reach. If it wasn't for the damn cloaking mists, he'd be able to feel her and speak to her through their bond. Slowly, Loki pulled himself back together, rebuilding the walls to keep his chaotic feelings contained.

By the time he stepped from the shower, he was in control again. After summoning court attire for the upcoming audience, he considered the next steps, depending on what they found out from the queen.

"Are you ready?" asked Manannan from the other side of the bathroom door.

"Yes," Loki replied, opening the door.

A guard in silver-and-black stood waiting at the entrance to the suite.

"Queen Eithnu is ready for us," Manannan said, and turned to follow the guard out the door.

"Good!" Loki followed, with Mist right beside him. Whether the Atlanteans helped them or not, he needed to search for Shannon, not be stuck in one place. He had to be doing *something* to save her.

The guard led them up two flights of stairs and through several gleaming white halls before stopping at a double set of silver doors inlaid with two tridents crossing over a large seashell. A pair of guards stood on either side, and they opened the doors. After leading the trio in to the large throne room with its high clear ceilings and silver arches, the guard walked the length of the room to stop, bowing at the raised platform where an attractive Atlantean woman reclined on a silver padded throne.

Queen Eithnu had midnight-black-and-silver skin, with long silver-and-black hair plaited into intricate braids. A silver tiara sat on her head, nestled into the braids. She wore a silver low-cut skinsuit that showed off her long, fit and curvaceous body, with high black boots and a black wrap that floated carelessly half-on, half-off her shoulders.

Manannan bowed, and Loki and Mist copied him, although as fellow royalty, Loki kept his bow shallow.

"Manannan Mac Lir." The queen rose from her throne and stalked around him, trailing her hand up one of his muscular arms, across his back, then down his other arm. She smiled, then wrapped both arms around his neck and pulled him in for a long, thorough kiss.

Loki and Mist glanced at each other and tried to stifle their smirks.

The queen pulled back from him with a leisurely gaze down his body, cupped his now obviously hard erection in her hand, and smiled. "We've missed you. It's been too long, Sea God, since your last visit." With a stroking caress and squeeze that had Manannan biting off a deep groan, she released him and stepped back.

After heading back to her throne, she sat carelessly, with one leg thrown over an armrest. "Please introduce me to your guests, Manannan," she purred.

"Queen Ethniu, I'd like to present Prince Loki of Asgard and Mist, Valkyrie of Asgard," he managed, after clearing his throat.

"Welcome to my realm, Prince Loki and Valkyrie Mist. What brings you visiting our territories?" she asked.

"Thank you, Queen Ethniu. My consort, Princess Shannon, was taken by the Unseelie, then by dwarves, who stole her blood and life essence for perverted magic and power. She escaped them and fled into the Sea of Lantia. We believe she is trying to get to the surface, but I missed her by less than a day before she entered the sea. Asgard would be grateful for any assistance you can provide to help find Princess Shannon," Loki said.

The queen sat up.

"Before I provide assistance, do you have proof of the dwarves' actions? Those are serious charges. Although we have run afoul of those disgusting practices by the Unseelie, we are currently at peace with the dwarves." There was no hint of play or seduction in her tone now. This was the real monarch of the Atlanteans.

"Yes, but it was only the actions of two dwarves, both now dead by my hand. We informed their king, gave our evidence, and were assisted in the apprehension of the perpetrators by dwarves we consider friends. These are the memories taken from the criminals." Clenching his teeth against the anguish of recalling the horrific images, Loki projected the memories into the open space above the white, seashell-embedded floor. Yggdrasil's roots, it was brutal watching Shannon's torture again as those foul bastards treated her worse than a pet, like a fucking battery to be used up and depleted. Beside him, Mist had her fists clenched, breathing hard as she, too, knew what was coming.

The queen stood, fury etched in her features and in the rigid line of her body as she watched Shannon's degradation. Both Manannan and Queen Ethniu cursed when they saw Shannon's arm slashed over and over as Loki sped through the memories. The final image of Shannon standing soaking wet in the small tub, unnaturally frail, with her pregnancy fully visible, while the dwarf discussed selling her and her upcoming horrific death was what had the monarch snarling.

"They are dead?" she asked in an eerily calm voice compared to her thunderous expression. Narrowed silver-and-black eyes flashed as a muscle ticked in her jaw.

"Yes," Loki bit out, having a difficult time answering. Fury and nausea competed, churning within him. Every cell of his being felt polluted—coated in a sick miasma from his skin to his soul—after again experiencing the dwarf's callous emotions and disregard for Shannon through the fucker's memories. He caught sight of Manannan out of the corner of his eye—the sea god had his jaw clenched and hands fisted, chest heaving in fury.

"How is it she didn't appear pregnant earlier?" the queen asked, again in that deceptively calm voice.

Mist met Loki's gaze, and he flicked a Valkyrie sign, telling her to answer as he swallowed. Then swallowed again, fists flexing, fighting to keep his chaos in check, to not roar or spew his meal on the floor.

"Prince Loki made her a ring to allow her to hide her pregnancy when she visited Midgard if he wasn't with her," Mist explained. "Princess Shannon has only been an immortal Asgardian goddess for less than a year. She grew up on Midgard and didn't know her heritage. When the Wild Hunt attacked us on Midgard, she was still learning about the immortal worlds."

"Those *disgusting Unseelie*!" the queen yelled, giving vent to her fury. "Those *sick* bastards prey on pregnant women. She was wise to hide her condition, or it could have gone even worse for her. It's why we went to war with the shell-bent sea cucumber fuckers."

She paced for a few minutes before turning back to them.

"Thank you for sharing your evidence. I see how hard it was for you to show me, Prince Loki, and how much you care for your consort. Especially after viewing that, I'm sorry I made you wait to tell you my good news, but I needed to verify the information I had."

She walked over, put her hand on Loki's arm, and smiled kindly at him before continuing.

"My son, Prince Elatha, sent intelligence that the dwarves had delved into the twisted practices of the Unseelie. He'd received it from one Princess Shannon of Asgard, who he was escorting to the Tunnels of Glass and Ocean of Ceobhran, as she'd requested passage through our territory. Elatha said Shannon believed she'd be able to find her consort, Prince Loki of Asgard, if she could get to the planet's surface."

So great was Loki's relief that his knees buckled. As he hit the floor, he closed his eyes, trying to stop the tears that formed. Mist slapped him on the back, hauled him to his feet, and grinned when he opened his watery eyes.

"When..." Loki cleared his throat, emotion choking him. "When did he say he was escorting her there?"

"The message was received from him six risings ago, and I was told they left the outpost the rising before yesterday. As that outpost is a three-rising swim from here, you are five risings behind them. They'll be passing through the Tunnels of Glass today or tomorrow, then up to the surface ocean."

Loki bowed deeply. "Thank you, Queen Ethniu. Asgard is exceedingly grateful."

She smiled, pleased. "Princess Shannon is quite safe with Prince Elatha. My son will ensure no harm comes to her and stay with her until you can reach her. Take a good night's rest and leave next rising so you can make speed on your swim."

Although Loki would have preferred to leave right then, he knew he couldn't insult her offer after the Atlanteans' help. Despite the urgings of his heart, he had too much experience with inter-realm politics to make such an error.

Loki bowed again. "We appreciate your hospitality, Queen Ethniu."

The guard led Loki and Mist away while Manannan remained. They followed the guard back to their suite of rooms and once the door closed behind their guard, Mist burst out laughing.

"So I take it Manannan is conducting inter-realm negotiations? It's clear he's willing to penetrate the depths of diplomacy." She smirked.

Loki chuckled at her pun and returned her grin. "That was quite the greeting he got."

Mist snorted in amusement. "Their queen is gorgeous. Kara would be in lust."

"Not jealous you aren't getting to ride the wood Manannan was sporting?" Loki teased. As a fertility god, he knew when sparks flew, and yeah, he'd seen the interest Mist displayed.

Her lips twisted in a half smile. "Look here, God of Mischief, don't start with me. I'll jump that in my own good time. Manannan is going to have to work for it." Eyes twinkling, it was clear she had some plan afoot.

Loki's hands rose in surrender. "Alright. Just let me know if you need a wingman in this game." With a wink, he said goodnight and headed to bed. Knowing Shannon was safe, well taken care of with an ally who knew the planet and had a kingdom's resources at his disposal, had taken an auroch's weight off Loki's chest. Although she still wasn't in his arms, it was only a matter of time now.

For the first time in weeks, he slept without nightmares.

Chapter 21

THE JOYS OF BEING FEMALE

When Shannon woke, the first thing she noticed was the lack of immediate pain. That relentless headache pounding at the back of her eyes like daggers gleefully slicing into her brain was down to a mild ache. Her head didn't weigh her neck with tension, and most amazingly of all, she hadn't jerked awake, gasping from a nightmare. How wonderful. She smiled at the comforting warmth of Loki behind her, his arm wrapped around her, cradling their child who was currently kicking up a storm right on her bladder. He'd tucked her into the curve of his body. Gods, she'd missed this, missed him. It had been so very long.

Although, why was she dressed? She never slept clothed. Her eyes fluttered open, and she went to caress his arm, but froze with her hand in the air. The arm cradling her was black and silver, not pale white. The hard body tucked tight against her, morning wood snuggled against her ass, was not Loki.

Even as the previous day's actions flashed through her mind and her body grew wet with remembered pleasure, she was flinging herself away from him and rolling out of the bed.

"No!" Her hand covered her mouth as her heart squeezed in horror. In denial, she closed her eyes to not see the gorgeous, but fortunately clothed, man sprawled in the bed, gazing at her sadly.

Shannon caught a sob as it started to escape and ran to the bathroom. The speed and ease of her body's movement mocked her, taunting her with her guilt. In the punishing heat of the shower, she scrubbed as hot tears flowed unchecked. Although she scrubbed and scrubbed until her skin was pink and raw, she couldn't make her shame wash away. It was a knife to her heart, a wound that would not stop bleeding.

And she'd done it to herself.

Bad enough fantasizing about him, but she'd let him put his hands on her. As much as she wanted to, Shannon couldn't run from her own choices.

Elatha flopped his forearm over his eyes as Shannon fled to the bathroom, a sob echoing with the slamming of the door, then water running in the shower. He'd cherished the gift she'd given him yesterday, but it was now like ash in his mouth. The sound of her regret scoured his senses with the harsh scrape of barnacles.

Why had he hoped she might feel differently? She'd seemed to castigate herself for simply seeing him aroused at the outpost. The very idea was an anathema to his culture, especially in her condition, when a Fomorian woman would be demanding frequent satisfaction for her growing energy needs. Were pregnant elves so very different? Maybe she didn't need the energy, but orgasms provided so many more health benefits for her than just an energy boost. Was it Shannon's mortal upbringing? Surely Asgardians weren't so prudish as to punish themselves for seeking pleasure. Elves certainly didn't, with their public consummation ceremonies and numerous fertility rites. He'd been with a few mortals during visits to Litauī. They'd not reacted like this. Why did she feel pleasure between them was wrong? Did she react badly after she and Loki had sex, too? Or was this something specific to him?

He sat up, fingers tunnelled into his hair as his elbows rested on his knees. What could he do? How could he help her? Everything he tried went wrong.

She'd rested well, it seemed. Far better than she had at the outpost on her own, so that was something, at least. But perhaps he should have risen before her to make breakfast. Was finding him in bed with her what had distressed her? Or was it just that she'd allowed him to touch her, to bring her pleasure?

He released a long sigh.

Never had he found a woman so compelling and so confusing at the same time. Was this why so few of his people mated outside their race? Navigating cultural differences was like trying to walk barefoot through a sea urchin bed. There was certainly no bias on his end against bringing in outsiders as mates or consorts. She'd be more than welcomed in Atlantia.

He rose, cleaned his face and teeth in the kitchen, and readied his pack. When she emerged from the bathroom armoured and ready to go, he swallowed his questions and let her set the pace.

The sooner Shannon got distance from Prince Elatha and this uncontrollable desire, the better. Only speaking when she absolutely had to and staying as far from him as practical, she let him know she was ready to leave.

But it wasn't him. It was her she didn't trust.

This was her fault entirely.

Elatha must have understood well enough to not try to make conversation, but simply showed her how to exit the water gate at the cave entrance.

Leading the way, but checking to ensure she stayed by him, they sped through the water. This sea differed from the previous one they'd travelled through, with a greater diversity of different coloured glowing plants and sea life, as well as large meadows of flowing sea grasses where turtles and rays gracefully glided. If she hadn't been so wrapped up in her mental anguish, she would have enjoyed the beauty of it.

There were also fewer wide open spaces. Instead, it was more like huge interconnected caverns with large tunnels between them in a web of space. There were more rock walls and fewer pillars. All of her attention was required to ensure she took the correct turns and didn't end up separated from Elatha or in the wrong tunnel. She couldn't afford any more delays, any more wallowing in her misery. She had to get back to Loki, and the remaining time before her due date ticked in her mind like the countdown of a bomb.

At least her son was lively today. She rubbed her belly as he kicked, keeping her eyes on Elatha as she followed. Despite the relative ease with which she kept up with him today, Elatha still made them stop every few hours for a short nap and food from his pack. She wasn't sure why they were stopping so frequently now, but she had no complaints as long as they continued onward. The seaweed rolls were tasty with a nice zip that left her mouth tingling. The juicy berries were lovely, bursting with flavour on her tongue. After the slop the dwarves had fed her, she appreciated every bite of the Fomorian food.

Within the first couple hours, Elatha recognized the lethargy still plaguing Shannon. Although she made no complaint, her progress was noticeably slower when he let her set their speed. The food he'd prepared seemed to help, perking her up every time they stopped to take a break, but he started insisting she take a nap, too. Shells, but he was glad he'd made as much food as he had. Her appetite was substantial, and he couldn't help but offer more and more, delighting in her expression as she savoured the rolls he'd made.

He hid his sigh under his breath. At least he'd done that much right.

Every time he considered asking what he else he could do to help her, he bit his tongue. She wasn't talking and hadn't asked any questions as she had every other time they'd swum together. If she wanted peace to think her own thoughts, he didn't want to intrude.

She had to come to him, to specifically ask. He rubbed at his chest. Anything else hurt too damned much.

Finished her food after waking from her nap, Shannon jumped back into the water from the rock ledge. Sitting still for any length of time was not an option. She motioned for Elatha to lead on and dove under the water. He joined her, gazing at her with concern, like he wanted to ask something, but then pressed his lips together and set out. She ignored his look, not inviting conversation.

As the passageway got narrower, she followed closely. She didn't want to brush up against him by swimming beside him. She was determined to not make the same mistake she'd made the previous day. If she didn't speak, except when necessary, and she kept her distance, then it was easier to ignore the constant arousal in his presence.

Of course, her body wasn't getting the message. It craved more of what it'd had yesterday, especially as the day dragged on and her headache returned with a vengeance.

After a couple more hours, he stopped and pointed at a passage up ahead.

"This is the entrance to the Tunnels of Glass and the surface waters. We'll take a longer break here to sleep and eat. We need to be alert to pass through the confusing route." He rose to the surface and directed her to a dry ledge, then settled himself a metre away.

Her back ached, cramping with knotted muscle when she woke, wiping drool from her mouth. Lovely. She glanced over at Elatha but he was digging into his pack. Hopefully, he'd missed that ignominious moment. Like she needed more ways to embarrass herself.

"Here, eat up." He handed her one of the tasty seaweed rolls. "You will need to stay very close behind me in the tunnels so you don't miss one of the sharp turns. The walls are reflective due to the type of rock and the polishing action of the water over time. It can get confusing, so keep me in sight."

She nodded her agreement, and as soon as she finished her roll, they set out.

Within a short distance inside the tunnel, they had to dive to follow its curve. Keeping his warning in mind, she focused on his legs. The shiny black walls of the tunnel were visually disorientating, and she had no idea how he knew which path to take when they reached forking tunnels. As they continued, she realized they were swimming straight up now, then they curved around and down again. It seemed like their route was a series of sharp s-curves, double-backing on themselves into more than 180 degrees, if her inner ear was working correctly.

Although she lost track of time, judging by the growing pain in her limbs, it felt like many hours before they emerged in wide-open blue waters with a glow far above. They swam up to reach the surface. When she broke through the water into the air, a twilight sky shone above her. For the first time in more than six weeks, she gazed up at the twinkling of stars.

"So beautiful," Shannon found herself saying as she floated, resting her body, and staring at the sky.

"Yes," replied the quiet voice of the prince next to her.

When she glanced over, he wasn't looking at the sky. Instead, Elatha's gaze met hers. She flushed and turned away. "We should find land, and then I need to get to the Summer Realm."

He pointed towards the darkness. "The closest land is there, but it is still in the Winter Realm. If you want to avoid the Winter Realm entirely, the Summer Realm is at least a week's swim away. Or we can go to shore and walk."

"As much as I hate to return to the Winter Realm, they are the ones who took me as far as Asgard knows. It's the most logical place for Loki to search for me, and I don't want to miss him."

"It's your call," Elatha agreed as he set off towards the dark shore.

Shannon forced her body to follow. Despite her logical argument, everything in her rebelled—muscles trembling and breath hiccupping—at the thought of returning to the Winter Realm, of potentially being captured again. But the ocean was right there. They'd stay by the shore, able to retreat into the safety of the waves. She caught up to the slow pace Elatha had set while he waited for her to join him.

In less than two hours, they stood on the desolate sandy shore with the waves lapping at their feet. The land was foreboding, stark in its shades of grey twilight, with mountains in the distance and rolling hills of scrubby grass, shrubs, and the occasional sparse tree. Two moons overhead provided a little light. She shook, rubbing her arms against the chills washing up and down her back. A metallic taste coated her tongue. No way did she want to go further inland. Instead, she forced herself to turn her sight from the landscape that had her holding back screams. Gaze focused on the bright light of the Summer Realm on the horizon, she walked along the shoreline. Surely the light elves had to be better than the dark elves and their sadistic creatures.

Elatha fell into place beside her, keeping himself between her and the land.

Gods, she wanted to kiss him for it. He was protecting her so she'd have time to retreat to the water. Every step took effort she had to fight to achieve. She tripped frequently on the sand, and he caught her, releasing her when she had her balance again. She was slow and uncoordinated, unable to hurry. Her breath rasped in her lungs. Even as she tried to not be moved by his consideration, she appreciated it. And damn but she needed the help.

Yet, by the same token, his care made it harder for her to keep her distance, to not like him more. Despite the spike pounding into her eyes and dizziness that began plaguing her within an hour of them reaching land, she continued to lust after him. Damn it, she didn't need to like him as well.

When she found herself admiring the way his tight ass moved in his skinsuit as he walked slightly ahead of her, she took a long, stumbled step sideways towards the water. Fucking hell, but she needed a godsdamn cold shower. A bucket of ice water. Something.

The damn guy oozed sex as he walked, and she was having a really hard time not noticing his swagger. So much more pleasant to focus on than the wave of fear that hit every time she glanced toward the ominous Winter Realm. For fuck's sake, who was she kidding? It was impossible not to notice the way he walked, that cocky confidence she suspected he deserved.

Shit. Don't think about the other day. Don't think about the other day.

Of course, the more she tried not to, the more she remembered the way he'd brought her to such a strong, fast orgasm in less than a damned minute through her clothes. And fuck if she didn't crave another hit of that pleasure to take away all this fucking pain that throbbed and ached and bit at her self-control.

Her nipples were hard under her skinsuit and armour, rubbing with every step. They'd gotten more sensitive as her pregnancy progressed, driving her mental. She'd tried sports bras and loose tops. It didn't matter when they got like this. Nothing seemed to work. She'd thought they were bad before she was captured. They were so much worse now, hard stiff points that pulsed. Shannon let Elatha get a few more steps ahead of her as she cupped her breasts, trying to discretely pinch them to get some relief.

Of course, he stopped and turned to look at her right then, his eyes drawn to her hands.

"What's the matter?" He returned to her side.

Shannon didn't answer. What was she going to say? Her tits were driving her bonkers with ridiculous pregnancy hormones? She was a complete fucking idiot.

"Are your breasts bothering you? Is it the pregnancy?" Concern creased his brow as she continued to cup her breasts.

"It's just pregnancy hormones." *Please drop it. Please.*

But of course, he didn't.

"We have a week-long walk. If they are bothering you, we need to fix it so you aren't uncomfortable the whole time."

She huffed. Uncomfortable? Not fucking possible. Every part of her damned body was uncomfortable, achy, and a right pain in the ass. She was never ever doing this again. Loki could carry their next kid, damn it. Still, Elatha wasn't wrong. She couldn't deal with the constant rubbing on top of all her other complaints. It was both irritating and constantly arousing. But the solution was what? Go topless? Hell, no.

"Come on, Shannon, what is the specific issue?"

"Ugh! My nipples are rubbing as I walk, okay Prince Nosy?" For fuck's sake. Why had she blurted that out?

"And this hurts?"

"Oh my gods!" She threw her hands up before sinking to sit on a log. Finally, she just growled, "It's uncomfortable and keeping me constantly turned on, okay?"

Elatha blinked, tried not to grin and failed. "Take your shirt and armour off."

"I am not walking around with no top on!"

"Why not?"

"Because it's... it's... not decent," she spat out, unable to come up with a less ridiculously prudish thing to say. She wanted to smack herself at the level of foolishness coming out of her mouth.

Elatha rolled his eyes. "Well, I'd hate for them to get chaffed and raw. They will *really* bother you then. But if it's the constant arousal that's bothering you, I'll wait while you take care of that. Or I'll take care of it for you. Whatever you would like. I'm here to help."

His lips twitched, trying not to grin.

"Alternatively, if you don't want to go completely topless, then adjust your skinsuit and armour to just have your breasts bare. At least while we are walking. I'd promise not to look, but well, that would totally be a lie." He shrugged, not repentant even the slightest at his admission. "I'm going to look. You have gorgeous tits."

194

Shannon shrieked and stomped her foot. This was an impossible, ridiculous situation. Between the fucking headache, her back, feet, and godsdamn it, her annoying tits, she was ready to lose her shit completely. She would *not* masturbate in front of him, damn it. Nor was it a good idea to let him anywhere near her again. That way led to much badness on her part. She had no willpower.

Was letting her breasts hang out a ridiculous idea? It was. It was nuts, but maybe it was the lesser of all the evils? Ugh. She'd look like some ridiculous fantasy chick out of a porno magazine.

She sat picked up a handful of sand, and threw it.

Seriously, this was stupid! Stupid body. Stupid pregnancy. Stupid damn tits! Ugh! Why was being a woman such a fucking pain in the ass at times?

Reluctantly, she redesigned her skinsuit and armour to open across her breasts. As the armour shifted, she had an idea and reformulated it to create a pocket of space above her breasts and still cover them.

Shannon smirked. The skinsuit left her breasts free in the air, but the armour almost entirely hid that from sight except for small openings from the side.

Elatha reluctantly nodded when he saw her solution, then helped her rise. "Not what I would have chosen, but it works. Damn. I was really hoping you'd either get yourself off or tell me you needed me to suck them every hour or so."

Shannon bit off a moan as she grabbed her breasts, clenching her thighs together, then she deliberately walked away from him. Focusing intently, she practiced some yoga breaths. Fuck, but she wanted to scream. Okay, she wanted to throw something at his idiot, arrogant, far-too-sexy head.

Everything was fine. She was managing to keep herself in check. Then Mr. Too-Sexy-For-His-Pants had to blurt out something so fucking hot, it punched the arousal right back into her thoughts.

And it wasn't the first time he'd done it, the asshole.

It was a trait Elatha shared with Loki. Was it taught as an elective to wickedly sexy princes? Being able to say something so completely unexpectedly rawly erotic then returning to normal while leaving her panting in the meantime was so unfair. It wasn't the only damn trait they shared. Now, if Loki would share her as well, she'd have them both.

Damn.

Shannon couldn't believe she'd just thought that.

She was trying so hard not to think about that.

It was like a melody she absolutely couldn't get out of her head.
Fuuuck.

Chapter 22

THE LAW OF CONSERVATION OF ENERGY

After another hour of walking, Shannon was done. She tripped and fell more and more frequently. Elatha had taken to staying within arm's reach to help her. Still, she'd scraped her palms several times. Her knees throbbed like a rotted tooth, even with her armour covering them from the abrasive sand and rocks. That drawing sensation sucked at her chest again, and she needed rest. She had no reserves at all. None. The ice pick dug at her brain. And gods, it hurt to keep her eyes open. She squinted despite the low light.

When she tripping yet again—Elatha catching her before she could tumble to the ground—she stopped and panted. Some large driftwood had washed up on the beach further ahead. "Let's take a break for some sleep, okay? I need a rest." She pointed at the logs.

"That's fine. I'll keep watch while you take a break. You are carrying two, after all." Elatha smiled as he glanced down at her belly admiringly.

It was odd it didn't bother him in the slightest that she was huge with another male's child. In fact, he found it arousing. She shook her head, wincing at the sharp spike of pain at her inadvertent action. It had to be a cultural difference.

But was it specific to Fomorians? Or was her lack of understanding due to still thinking like a human and not an immortal? Both Loki and Frigga had cautioned her numerous times that her mindset had to change. It could put Shannon or her child in danger. She had to adapt to immortal life more quickly, to understand their culture, starting with thinking of herself as an immortal—something she struggled to remember.

She sure as hell didn't feel very immortal at the moment. More like a bag of smashed assholes. What the fuck did that expression even mean? It was one Trent had liked to use and fit her current mood.

Shannon dragged her wandering thoughts back on track. As a member of the Asgardian royal family who'd be expected to represent Asgard in diplomatic missions in the future, she had to do better. She needed to adapt faster and be more accepting of other immortal cultures. Accidentally teaching her child poor attitudes or inadvertently causing a war or offense that could cost lives was not how she wanted to start her immortal life. Continuing in ignorance wasn't okay.

Yet, she didn't know how to shed mortal thoughts and values that she'd spent thirty-five—no... seven?—years learning. Sure, that was a blink of an eye to an immortal, but she didn't have the benefit of those long years of experience. Instead, she was an adult in immortal worlds where someone wasn't considered to have reached maturity until they were closer to a century. But she didn't have sixty-odd years to catch up.

There was no choice. She had to do better. She had to. Her child deserved her best. She couldn't fail at this or at learning about other immortal cultures... starting with the Fomorians, since she had the opportunity right now.

Hesitantly, and after swallowing while trying to ignore the butterflies in her belly, she took the leap. "Why do you find my pregnancy arousing when it isn't your child?" Maybe by being blunt, she could avoid any flirtatious aspects that might bite her on the ass. She muffled her snort. Great. Even her brain was throwing innuendos at her.

Elatha blinked twice, then frowned. "Umm... why wouldn't I? Immortals don't reproduce very often. Every pregnancy is celebrated as it is a rare event. A woman might go hundreds or even thousands of years before becoming pregnant or between children."

His response stunned her, and she considered the ramifications. Those kinds of time scales were hard for her to put into perspective. How could she wrap her mind around a concept she had no real frame of reference for? But once she considered it, the logic made sense given the sizes of immortal populations. Of course they had a low fertility rate.

Shannon reached the grey, water-smoothed logs, and sighing noisily, she lowered herself to the grey-brown sand. "Okay, I can understand why pregnancy would be celebrated, but why does it turn you on?"

Elatha smiled. "It's not pregnancy itself that turns me on, dear Shannon. It's *you* being pregnant that turns me on."

She scowled and flicked her fingers. "Why? The child isn't yours. It's proof that I've had sex with another. For humans, that is a distinct turn-off. Men rarely want a woman who has been with someone else, or at least, they don't want the visual of it."

He rolled his eyes and scoffed. "Then human men are selling broken shells."

Selling broken shells? Shannon blinked, then understood the expression.

"Fomorian males don't want virgin females. Why would inexperience be a prize in any gender? Are crafts built by apprentices more highly sought than those by skilled masters?"

"I've never considered it that way," Shannon murmured. Recalling some of the highly unsatisfactory experiences she'd had, the Fomorians had the better viewpoint.

"We like our woman to know what they want, when they want it, and how they want it. When our women have high sex drives, it's a very attractive quality. We do everything possible to encourage it, in fact. The more consorts a female keeps drained, the more attractive she is in our culture."

Polyamorous relationships weren't unheard of on Earth but they were rare. How did everyone get along? "No one gets jealous or possessive?"

"No, never. Not to say there aren't disagreements within a household group, but never over intimacy. It's freely given. If someone is unhappy, they can leave to join a new household." Elatha sat beside her and took her hand. "It's also a function of biology. A pregnant Fomorian has an elevated sex drive because sex during pregnancy transfers energy to her. The more the pregnancy progresses, the more energy she needs for her and her growing child. Fomorian consorts play a critical role in helping the woman care for the child by having sex with her and giving her pleasure to recharge her energy, regardless of which male actually provided the sperm to create the child. All benefit from her increased energetic demands."

His answer was so unexpected that Shannon mused over the physiology for a few minutes, the scientist in her intrigued. The biological and evolutionary pressures that would create that kind of interaction were interesting. As she considered the idea from various aspects, it made perfect sense. Of course, it would be true for any pregnant female of an immortal race that gained energy from sex.

Oh—Oh gods.

She was such a fool!

Was that why her arousal was off the charts around Elatha? It certainly wasn't around any other male immortal except Loki. Being a fertility goddess and pregnant, did her body know what it needed to get enough energy for herself and her child?

Shannon cradled her belly, staring down at the basketball-sized bulge in her otherwise lean body—a body that used to have curves and what she would have called some extra padding. Not anymore. Her only remaining curves were her breasts and her baby. The ring Loki had given her wouldn't even stay on her thumb now. Too large for every other finger—it had fallen off twice when she wasn't paying attention—she'd tucked it into a pouch on her fighting leathers before they'd left the outpost. No way did she want to lose it.

But... why was Elatha capable of recharging her and other immortal males weren't? Or was it that she hadn't been as energy deprived when the Sidhe took her? Were the dwarves not compatible? Or were they, but something else was going on? Her captors had been disgusting. Maybe that made the difference? Even the thought of the two dwarves made her stomach revolt. There had to be more to it than a simple biological compatibility.

Was it something to do with her being an elf?

Neither Frigga nor Healer Moja had warned Shannon that attraction to another to meet her energy needs might be an issue. Why? Because Loki was a fertility god and could easily supply the energy she needed? No one could have anticipated Shannon would be away from him for weeks on end—gods, more than six weeks now—especially in her third trimester, when she needed his help desperately. The most Healer Moja had said was to monitor her energy levels and to recharge when necessary.

Although... that wasn't strictly true.

Moja *had* been concerned before Shannon was kidnapped, worried about weight loss and energy levels. Shannon hadn't had any of Idun's apples to boost her energy and nutrients since she'd been kidnapped, and Moja had wanted her to eat one of the special apples every day. Damn. The healer had warned Shannon that they might have to restrict Shannon's activities if she couldn't get enough energy.

She just hadn't paid enough attention to the implications.

What did that mean for her now?

Each hour, Shannon tired more quickly. Being in the sea had helped, but she was still losing weight—muscle, since little fat remained except her breasts—on top of what she'd lost during her captivity. She felt herself getting weaker, struggling to move, to do everyday things like walk. Her son had been active when she woke beside Elatha, but had grown quiet during her swim and hadn't kicked since before her uncomfortable sleep on that rock ledge yesterday. Her heart sped, a frantic thundering in her chest paired with the spiking agony in her temples. What was it doing to him to be so deprived of energy? The sea on its own wasn't supplying enough. Nor was rest. Or food.

Damn. The sea on its own wasn't enough. Not enough energy. Fuck.

She searched her surroundings. The sand turned into dune grasses on rolling hills with the occasional shrub. A few sparse trees, half of them dead, appeared as the land turned rocky further inland. There might be a forest off in the distant mountains if she was willing to delve deep into the Winter Realm, but a shiver down her spine and panicked fluttering of her heart forestalled that idea. Given what she'd fought in the Wild Hunt when the Unseelie had captured her, did she really want to attempt to find a forest in that forbidding land?

"Did I upset you? You look very serious," Elatha said, meeting her gaze with concern.

"No. You didn't upset me, but it did help me understand some of what is going on with me," Shannon replied as she tried to work out what she needed to do. Her brain understood the necessity, the logic, yet her heart had a harder time with it. Her stomach churned with the impossible choice.

But it wasn't a choice. Not any longer.

There was no way she could knowingly allow her child to suffer, to starve within her. What had her lack of knowledge already put him through? By delaying at the outpost, trying to recover with rest and food while indulging in guilt? By not asking for what she needed when Elatha had first expressed his interest? Recalling the seriousness of Healer Moja's warning about energy so many weeks ago, the answer scared Shannon. Guilt was a fucking luxury she couldn't afford. Not when the cost was her son's health. Oh gods. She was a horrible mother! What had she done? Why had she delayed? She was starving her baby... no, oh gods, no.

She swallowed, her pulse thundering in her ears. "Loki and I are both fertility gods. Do you know what that means? Do Fomorians have fertility gods?" she asked, not looking away from the handsome man with his unusual silver starburst eyes.

"No, we don't." He shrugged, then grinned. "I've heard of them, but only in the simplest of terms, that like us and the elves, they like lots of sex."

Of course. She almost laughed, but mirth died as she fought back her churning emotions. "It's not that simple. Just as pregnant Fomorians get energy from sex, so do fertility gods. They also have high sex drives. They can have sex over and over repeatedly, without getting tired or needing to recover because of the energy they get from it."

Elatha nodded. "It sounds like the way our physiology works, but for all Fomorians, not just a few."

She agreed and continued, "But I'm not just a fertility goddess. I'm also a goddess of the forests and seas, so I get energy from being around forests and in saltwater."

"Okay, that should be a good thing, right?" He frowned, eyes scanning her body, then meeting her gaze. "You have multiple ways of recharging yourself."

"Yes, it should. But just like what you told me about pregnant Fomorians, I need an increasing amount of energy to support myself and my child as he grows. Loki and I knew this before my capture. We ensured I was getting an energy boost one way or another at least once a day during my second trimester. But then I got kidnapped. My captors didn't know I was pregnant or a newly transitioned immortal. They hooked me up to power their forges with my life energy and drained me faster than I could recharge. Since then, I've lost more weight than I can spare."

Elatha's frown deepened as his gaze travelled over her again.

She winced, also eying her thin arms and legs, the bones jutting in her wrists and ankles. Why had she *ever* complained about her weight? She'd been perfectly fine, healthy even, at the size she'd been. "At the point the dwarves finally gave me a saltwater bath, I could barely stay conscious. For all these weeks, I've been at an energy deficit that my child has had to draw entirely from me. The saltwater alone isn't recharging me sufficiently. I'm still losing weight, losing muscle. It's why I'm getting more and more exhausted, faster each day, each hour." Shannon stopped, needing to blink back tears from eyes gone hot as the full horror of what her child was experiencing hit her. "It's why my son is less and less active each day. I have no energy reserves left to draw on, so he's grown lethargic and unable to move."

Oh gods. Her baby. Her poor little boy. Shannon took a shuddering breath, trembling as she clutched her belly. She had to save him. She had to.

"What are you saying, Shannon?" Elatha's tone was carefully neutral even as his eyes kept flicking to her abdomen, worry starkly apparent, before returning to meet her gaze.

"Unless we find Loki today, I think..." She paused, swallowing, the lump in her throat making it hard to say what she needed to. "Elatha, I—I need you to recharge me. My baby isn't active the way he should be. My lack of energy is hurting him. Please, I need you to save my child," she quietly pleaded, battling her conflicted emotions.

"Are you sure about what you are asking, Shannon? Have no doubt, I'm completely willing. I'll help you in whatever way you need. But I hate making you cry. It hurts to see you so upset. Please be sure, okay?" Elatha gently took her hand, stroking it. "I'd do anything for you."

"I'm not going to lie. This is hard for me. I'm holding out for Loki. But I can't let my child suffer... or worse." Her voice cracked on the last few words before she swallowed and continued, "If we don't find him today, I'm asking you to save us. Both of us. Please, Elatha. I can't lose my child." She lost the battle to hold the tears back as they spilled down her cheeks.

Elatha blinked hard, his beautiful starburst eyes sad as he nodded his agreement. "I will, I promise."

Gratefully, she leaned against his shoulder and closed her eyes.

Chapter 23

HOT ON THEIR TRAIL

Manannan was back and sporting some interesting hickies when Loki rose early the next day. Putting his plate of breakfast on the table, Loki gave the sea god a grin as his eyes flicked to Manannan's neck and back to his face. Loki sat, starting to eat his omelette.

The sea god's lips twitched in amusement, and he shrugged, continuing to drink his tea.

Mist snorted when she joined them and caught sight of him, her eyes twinkling. "Keeping up diplomatic relations, Manannan?"

He just gave her a half smile and sipped his tea.

In a deceptively innocent tone, she asked, "Not too hard, I trust?"

"Not currently," he said with a sly smirk.

Loki coughed to cover his laugh. "Enough flirting, you two. Let's get out of here."

"Ready when you are," Manannan said.

"I've heard that before," quipped Mist.

Loki shook his head. Those two just couldn't resist. They were definitely headed for a pelvic collision with the sparks flying between them.

Upon leaving their suite, a black-clad guard escorted the trio down to the bubble chamber and within half an hour, he had them back to the outer wall of the city. Manannan took Mist with him through the wall, keeping a bubble of air around her as they shot upward. When Loki stepped through, he held his breath as he shifted to a dolphin, then sped after them.

Once up at the surface of the sea above the city, Mist rose into the air, and they set out, staying shallow so she could track them.

As they had on the way to the Atlantean capital, they took a break every six hours for Loki and Mist to take a quick nap. Despite Manannan's lack of rest at the city, he seemed to have no shortage of energy. Even though Loki was still having a hard time keeping up with the sea god's pace, he didn't want to slow down. To save time, they'd already decided not to stop at the city between the capital and the outpost they were aiming for. Instead, they rested for a couple of hours that night on a rock ledge, then continued onward.

Although they managed to cut several hours off the journey to the outpost, there was no denying they all needed a longer break by the time they arrived three days later. Loki was dragging, and Mist seemed as bad as he when they entered the silver water gate.

"Welcome Manannan Mac Lir, Prince Loki, and Valkyrie Mist of Asgard. Rest chambers have been prepared for you," a black-uniformed guard said after they'd passed through the gate. "Please follow me."

As Loki had expected, the outpost was much smaller than the capital city and the guard led them along a white stone path towards a set of shorter towers. After entering one building, they climbed several flights of stairs in a central staircase before he showed them to a set of rooms. Instead of a multi-bedroom suite, they each had their own single bedroom suite this time. To individually key the respective rooms to them, he had them put their hand on some type of door scanner. Fascinating the high level of technology the Atlanteans used.

Once inside, the layout was similar to what they'd had in the capital and with the same colour palette and amenities. To recharge with some carbs, Loki ate noodles in some kind of rich green sauce from the AMP, then took a shower and collapsed on the bed.

Hours later when he awoke, he found he hadn't even pulled the covers over himself. Either way, he'd slept well and without nightmares. He was more than ready to continue their journey. Two more days and they'd be in the Ocean of Ceobhran, hopefully to find that Thor had already found Shannon.

Quickly, Loki wolfed down a savoury breakfast seaweed wrap and went next door to knock on Mist's door.

She didn't respond at first, so he pounded on it.

The door was flung open, and she scowled at him. "You know they have doorbells, right?"

Loki shrugged. He'd grown up with Thor. Sometimes pounding on something got the job done.

She rolled her eyes. "I'll be ready in just a few minutes."

"Okay, I'll see if Manannan is ready and meet you downstairs in fifteen?"

"Sure."

She closed the door, and he walked to the next door. Smirking, Loki triggered the panel and doorbell.

Manannan appeared on a screen on the door. "I'll be right out." The screen darkened. A minute later, his door opened, and they descended the stairs to the ground level.

As they stood outside, Loki appreciated the view. The outpost was a tiny version of the capital in terms of architecture but without the fountains. Probably no need when the entire outpost was within a reasonable walking distance. With lower central silver spiral seashell-shaped towers, unlike those in the capital, it was easy to see the diversity of sea life swimming around the outpost. It was beautiful and impressive.

Mist joined them, and they set out for the water gate. As he'd done previously, Manannan took Mist through the gate and up to the surface while Loki followed.

They set out at a good clip, Manannan establishing a brisk pace. Twelve hours in, after their second break, the topography changed. Rock pillars were broader, longer. There were more walls, and they changed direction more frequently.

When they stopped for their third break, Loki asked Manannan about it.

"We've left the Sea of Lantia and entered the Sea of Uaithne. It becomes quite the maze before we reach the Tunnels of Glass—still another thirty hours of travel from here. At that point, it will be important for us to stick together and for you to keep us in sight, Mist. It's easy to take a wrong turn here. There are many dead-end areas that would have you backtracking to find us again."

"Good to know," she said.

"We'll travel for another six hours before we break for a rest. There are a series of caves that the Fomorians have put water gates on where we can catch some sleep. It'll be better than a nap on a rock ledge."

"Lead on, Sea God," Loki said, and they set out again.

Besides the topography changes, the sea life changed. Several species of turtles grazed in a meadow of gently swaying yellow sea grasses as the trio passed. Glowing red vines with large bladed leaves grew from the sea floor, stretching up almost to the surface like a forest. Sleek bodies of sea otters dipped and swerved amongst the vines.

When Manannan rose to the surface by a wall, Loki marvelled at the diversity. Before he could rise to join Manannan, the sea god returned, bringing Mist down in a bubble. They'd reached the cave with a water gate he'd mentioned. Loki dove to join them, pushing through the barrier and changing back to humanoid.

Not huge, but it was nice. The entranceway led off to several rooms that included bedrooms, a kitchen, and central seating area with couches and the dining table and chairs, and two bathrooms. In numerous locations, energy barriers provided windows out into the sea, giving a view of the life surrounding the cave.

"I'm taking a quick shower," Mist announced. "Whatever you guys decide for dinner is fine with me."

Loki looked at Manannan, and he shrugged. "Let's go see what our options are."

Settling on a seafood vegetable and grain stir fry after browsing the AMP's selection, they sat to eat. Before they were half done, Mist joined them.

"There is no water's surface through the Tunnels of Glass. It's going to take us seven hours to get through the tunnels. You are going to have to trust me to pull you along and make sure you have air. Do you trust me, Mist?" Manannan asked, his eyes serious.

Mist cocked her head, meeting his gaze and not responding for a minute. Then she grinned. "I trust you to get me through the tunnels and not drown me. Not sure about other things," she teased.

Manannan rolled his eyes and turned to Loki. "I'll need to do the same with you. As a dolphin, you can't hold your breath for hours unless you want to shift into a different animal?"

Loki shrugged. "Although I can shift into a fish or shark, I wouldn't be able to keep up with you. Even as a dolphin, I can barely keep up with you."

"Well, it's probably better that I tow both of you, anyway. The tunnels are disorienting. They twist and turn, and are made of black obsidian. The walls are smooth from the wearing of water and extremely reflective, which can make you think you are going one way when you are actually going another due to the mirroring effect and the sharp bends," he explained.

"Sounds interesting. I'm looking forward to seeing them tomorrow. For now, I'm off to shower and bed," Loki said as he left the table.

Mist yawned. "G'night. I'm crashing now, too."

"Then I'll see you both in the morning." Manannan stayed at the table as he continued to sip a mug of tea.

Loki turned on the shower and stepped under the hot spray. As early as tomorrow evening, he could be back with Shannon. It made him grin, heart light, and he sang a song Raven's Chaos had recorded on their new album.

Thor and Thjalfi could cover a huge amount of ground between the two of them. Shannon should have reached the surface four days ago. Surely, they'd found her. He just had to meet up with them, which shouldn't be too difficult once they could travel freely by air.

Singing, Loki scrubbed and imagined Shannon in his arms again. It had been far too long. He couldn't wait to hold her, kiss her, hear the sexy sounds she made as he drove her wild.

Groaning, he gripped his cock, remembering the last time he'd taken her in the shower. The thought of her, clamped tight around him and slick with arousal, had him spilling in minutes. After rinsing, Loki dried off and found his bed. Tomorrow couldn't come soon enough.

Chapter 24

DELAYING TACTICS

E latha gazed down at the woman who'd fallen asleep immediately, her breath deepening. How had he not realized the problem when his own people needed energy to make it through pregnancy safely? Her continued weight loss and the deepening bruises under her eyes made so much sense now, as did her lethargy.

And she was a newly transitioned immortal. What strain did that put on her?

He'd heard of Sidhe and Vanir that hadn't been given food from their native planets. Such a rare occurrence, but one his instructors had mentioned during his boyhood lessons because it never happened with his people. Whether raised on Tír na nÓg or Litauī, all Fomorians had the ability to manipulate water, breathed air or water, lived thousands of years, and shared energy through sexual intimacy—a curious difference they'd claimed was evidence against Sidhe and Fomorians having a common ancestor. Some believed the Fomorians had once travelled the universe extensively and had colonized Litauī and Tír na nÓg, not evolved here in the Nine Realms as others thought.

Yet no one had said transitioning affected energy levels.

How could he let her continue to suffer when the solution was so simple, so easy to provide? Shells, his very physiology was designed to aid her. But she resisted and had made it a last resort. Why? Was it him? He didn't think so, but that kernel of doubt sent a quiver through his belly. Why couldn't she accept the heart was big enough to care for more than one consort? It was a mystery he didn't understand, didn't make sense with what he'd known and experienced, yet he'd respect her wishes. He had to. She'd captured his heart and meant the ocean to him.

In the meantime... he glanced over at the waves lapping at the sand. Scooping her into his arms, he stood, then strode into the water and sat, cradling her in the energy-giving saltwater. If nothing else, it would give her a better rest, staving off the time when she'd have no choice but to accept him.

Unless Loki found them first.

Shannon woke in the water, waves lapping against the skinsuit and her armour in a gentle rocking motion. Confused, she went to sit up and realized that Elatha had her head cradled in his lap, in the shallow depths of the ocean.

She met his silver gaze. "How'd we end up here?"

Elatha smiled gently, reaching a finger to brush her hair from her forehead. "Well, I realized you would recharge your energy better by sleeping here than up on the beach without the saltwater."

Returning his smile, she reached a hand up to cup his cheek. "Thank you for thinking of that. I do feel more rested." In the buoyancy of the water, her back and hips didn't ache, but she didn't want to admit the continued throbbing at her temples or lethargy that had her limbs still leaden. If only she could continue to float like a stray piece of seaweed. But they had to get to the Summer Realm. She had to get to Loki, to save her child.

"Are you ready to—"

Biting her lip to stifle her groan, Shannon used an incoming wave to roll to her hands and knees. Elatha sprang to his feet and held out a hand to help her up. She took it, but as she rose, blackness crept in from the side of her vision and her legs buckled.

Elatha caught her as she collapsed, lowering her back into the water. His heart clenching, he brushed the hair back from her face and checked her pulse, then her breathing. This was no sleep. She was unconscious.

"Fucking sea squirts!" he cursed. He'd wanted her to accept him, but blasted barnacles, not like this. Not because she was forced to, and he was the only available source.

He tugged at his hair. Regardless of why she'd chosen him, he'd do everything he could to save her and her child, to make it good for her, and maybe she'd eventually want him. Not because she had to, but because she actually wanted him. He could hope, at least.

His fingertips coasted over the soft skin of her cheek, admiring the sweep of her lashes. As he leaned down to kiss her, he froze. With her unconscious, sex between them wouldn't transfer the needed energy. She needed to orgasm. Not only that, but she still wore her armour and skinsuit. No way could he get through that armour, nor did he want to try. He glanced around them. Would the saltwater be enough to rouse her? He rubbed at his breastbone and the tightness building within. He *had* to save her and her child.

But how?

An hour later, a frown creased her brow and her eyes flicked back and forth rapidly beneath her eyelids. "No," she pleaded, her voice barely audible. "Not again." The whimpered cry struck at his heart as she started to thrash.

Shells, he had to break her from this nightmare. He cradled her to him, brushing her hair back and singing the lullaby he'd recalled last night, until finally, after long minutes, she calmed. Heart still pounding from the broken sounds she'd made, it took him a while to realize the implications of her slumber.

Now that she was asleep but dreaming, might he be able to help her, to shift her away from nightmares and into more pleasant thoughts? If he could get her to climax even once, he could get some energy into her. Maybe enough to wake her, at least. It had seemed to help her sleep last night.

"Remove your clothes, Shannon," he murmured into her ear. Even if he couldn't rouse her enough to give her a big boost through intercourse—and he wasn't taking advantage of a sleeping woman, damn it—surely direct skin contact with the saltwater would be more effective than soaking through her layers and give him access to her body to bring her pleasure and the energy she needed.

A small sigh escaped her lips, and like the revealing of a present, the fine silvery blue scales receded, drawn up to... was that a torc? Fine craftsmanship, for certain. As he admired the styling and runes in the gold metal circling her neck, her skinsuit also retreated into the torc, leaving her bare to his gaze.

His breath caught. His memory hadn't been faulty—she really was spectacular. As the warm weight of one breast leaned against the arm he had cradled to him, he licked his lips and his cock rose, hard and ready. In the cool water, her nipples tightened, and he groaned, unable to resist cupping the enticing fullness.

Damn, he'd been right.

Her tit more than filled his hand, and when he flicked his thumb over the peak, she moaned. Had he really made her moan? He repeated the caress, and again, a breathy moan came from her lips—a much better sound than the whimpered cry of her nightmare.

Hope lightened his chest. Maybe he could do this, could revive her by keeping her in the saltwater and pleasuring her.

He tugged on her nipple, and she arched her back slightly, both breasts rising from the water. Shells, it was a glorious sight with those red-brown tips and honeyed skin in perfect round floating globes. He leaned down and drew one into his mouth while his hand continued to tug on the other, groaning at the feel of her.

Movement at the corner of his eye caught his attention and his head lifted. Her hand shifted between her thighs. Was she—

His mouth dropped open, pulse thundering. By the first shell, she was! Her fingers delved between her thighs and her hips shifted.

Damn. He took her nipple into his mouth, drawing hard, as her moan deepened and her fingers continued to move. Watching her, helping her bring herself to orgasm, was the most erotic thing he'd ever seen. When she came, writhing in his arms, he trembled, awed at the beautiful sight.

She calmed afterwards, and he gave her a few minutes' respite before beginning again, repeating the process over and over. Each time, a healthier flush grew on her face.

Hours later, her eyes opened, hazel gaze staring up at him.

She frowned. "Am I still in the water?"

He smiled, taking the first deep breath since she'd collapsed. Thank the Ancestors she'd awoken. "Yes, I've been coaxing energy into you."

"Coaxing?"

His smile turned into a little half grin. "You haven't noticed yet, but it wasn't exactly a hardship for me to hold you and admire the scenery." He looked down her body, and she followed his gaze.

Her eyes widened. "Did we…"

"No. Well, not really. When your son got active, I rubbed your belly and talked to him. Okay, I do confess to playing with your breasts." He tugged one nipple.

Shannon bit that lower plump lip, eyes darkening as her pupils dilated. "Was that all you did?" Her voice was a bit husky, like she was holding back one of the moans he loved drawing from her.

"Almost," he said with a small grin. "I also did this."

Elatha leaned his head down to capture the other nipple in his mouth, tugging gently with his teeth before sucking. This time, he got the moan he was after, and she arched her back, raising her chest towards him.

A smile curved his lips as he released her nipple with a pop of sound. "And that's what you did in response," he said with a wink.

"Just that?" she asked breathlessly.

His eyelids lowered halfway. "No actually. You slid those beautiful fingers down and worked yourself to orgasm. It was incredible. I'll admit, I got you aroused numerous times while you slept, not just to play with these gorgeous breasts of yours and give you some energy, but because it is so fucking hot seeing you make yourself come."

His hand continued to caress her other breast, and she shifted restlessly.

"Will you show me again, now that you are awake? Granted, it's only a tiny energy boost, but it's still something and staves off having to go further. I know you're trying to avoid that," he said as his head lowered again to take her nipple into his mouth. Shells, he could play with her breasts forever and be happy.

Shannon's right hand was already resting on her inner thigh, and it took only a slight shift for her fingers to find that hard bud she'd caressed numerous times over the hours. Her breath caught, and from the flush coming over her cheeks, he knew her arousal had to be building.

His gaze fixed on her fingers, and when she opened her thighs, he groaned, his cock like a sea pillar. As a reward for her gift, he sucked harder and tugged a little rougher in the way he'd noticed she responded the best.

Shannon gasped, moving her fingers faster as her hips rose and fell.

She caught her breath and her hips froze, her body arched as her fingers frantically played her sex. It was the cue he'd been waiting for, and he bit down and pinched her other nipple at the same time.

"Oh *fuck*," she shrieked as her body convulsed. Eyes glazed, she panted, trembling in his arms.

"Damn! That is so much hotter when you are awake," Elatha growled, fighting to not lift her over his aching cock. Not yet. First, he wanted to see how she responded to what they'd just done, to know whether she would condemn them again. Heart bruised, he'd do what he had to in order to save her and her child. He never wanted to hear her pleading and crying out in pain again as she had in her nightmare, or to again fall unconscious in his arms. This precious, unique, complex woman had carved a place inside him. But he couldn't take the idea that she might hate, might reject him again.

As he gently stroked her body, soothing her, she fell asleep again. He continued rocking her in the waves, bringing her to dreamy pleasure over and over as he kept the nightmares from haunting her. He'd have to wait to find out her reaction.

No sooner had Shannon opened her eyes than Elatha asked, "Hey, sleeping beauty. Are you ready for us to try to make some headway on getting to the Summer Realm?"

He smiled down at her, but there was almost a... wariness... to his expression, like he was waiting for her to bite his head off. Fair, she admitted. She hadn't exactly been kind to him when she'd woken in his arms at the Fomorian waystation.

When she stretched, his eyes followed her movement. She was still naked, after all, but some of the lethargy was gone from her limbs, and the headache, although not entirely gone, wasn't trying to gouge out parts of her brain.

"I don't know about ready, but we need to go, regardless," she finally answered.

Elatha supported her, helping her rise, and she couldn't fail to notice his prodigious erection in the thin material of his skinsuit. It outlined every thick detail, and damn, but she wanted to feel him.

Trying for a casualness she didn't feel, she asked, "Did you enjoy the show?" and gestured to his cock.

"You can see that I did and continue to," he said with a smile. "If I wasn't concerned about putting some distance behind us and getting out of the Winter Realm, I'd be doing something about it. I let you sleep for almost two days in the water."

"What?" Her mouth dropped open as she blinked at him. They'd lost two more days? She spun around, searching the sky, land, and sea for any sign of the Asgardians, of Loki, but it was as empty and desolate as before.

"Shannon, you needed it. You are dangerously low on energy, and your son is lethargic. Don't deny it as you've told me so yourself. I know you've noticed. The options were to either let you rest for that long, playing with your body to give you little bits of energy over a longer time, or to fuck you thoroughly, completely, and repeatedly until you are fully recharged. The last would have been much faster, but I'm trying to respect your boundaries and sensibilities as much as possible," Elatha growled, pulling on his armour in rough impatient tugs. "And there was the added complication that you need to be *conscious* for my orgasm to give you energy when I fuck you. Otherwise, it's no different than bringing just you to climax. I sure as shell won't fuck you when you are unconscious solely for my enjoyment."

Shannon didn't know what to say. Part of her wanted to bend over the nearest log and tell him to just take her already. There was no doubt her body wanted it—needed it, in fact—and was more than ready. She was sure she'd enjoy it. Mentally, she'd accepted the necessity of their intimacy, but he was correct. Emotionally, she still had difficulty with it. As irrational as it was to fight the laws of nature, she felt guilty.

And she hadn't known she had to be conscious for the bigger boost of a dual orgasm.

"Thank you," she murmured as she stepped from the water and called her fighting leathers and Asgardian armour. Elatha had given her this additional time to deal with her conflicted emotions and paid for it with days of frustration. He was entitled to be short with her.

Shannon needed to put on her big girl pants and suck it the hell up.

The time was quickly coming—fuck, it was already here—where she didn't have a choice. It was a simple energy conservation equation. She needed energy, and more importantly, her son needed energy. Her body had used up all the mass reserves it could convert to energy. Without more energy, they'd both die, and there was no way she'd kill herself and her son over sex. Surely, Loki would prefer her to do whatever she had to do to survive.

And if he didn't, then he wasn't the man she thought he was. Better she know that now.

Elatha sighed. "Such a damned shame to cover that gorgeous body."

Amused after he'd spent days ogling her naked body, Shannon smirked. With a sway in her step, she started walking down the beach toward the lit horizon of the Summer Realm. Immediately joining her, he stayed within arm's reach—reassuring to know he'd catch her if she fell. Again.

Shit, *when* she fell, more likely.

As soon as they put a little distance behind them, she needed to step-up, take charge, and seduce him. It was time to stop pussyfooting around the issue and take the damned bull by the horns. She grinned. Or the Fomorian by the cock.

After insisting she eat, he passed her some fruit to chew while they walked. A few hours later, just as her footsteps were beginning to drag in the sand, he put a hand on her arm and stopped them. His head cocked to the side, listening.

Eerie, unworldly howls and piercing screams shattered the quiet of waves lapping the beach.

"The Wild Hunt!" Elatha's eyes widened. "I'll hold them off. Run, Shannon!"

Chapter 25

NO MORE MR. NICE GUY

No. No fucking way was he sacrificing himself.

Shannon grabbed Elatha and wrapped air around them, lifting them to fly as fast as she could towards the Summer Realm. The screams and howls faded in the distance. Without warning, her power failed and they dropped. Reaching deep, she grabbed enough to keep them from smashing into the ground, but it was not a graceful landing.

The impact on the sand staggered her. She fought to stay upright with pain spiking up her ankles and knees. Gods, had she broken something? Elatha had been knocked out of her grasp, and as she reached for him, it seemed to get darker; the light fading. Again, she tried to reach for him, and everything went black.

Blink.

A rocking sensation. What was sitting on her chest? So heavy. Hard to breathe.

Blink.

Blurry shape above her. What?

Blink.

A voice talking to her. She knew that voice. Who was it? When she tried to make out the words, the voice faded.

Blink.

Her eyes. Why couldn't she open them? Concentrating, she managed to get her heavy lids ajar. Elatha stared down at her.

Blink.

A little clearer now when she opened her eyes, but still, that heavy weight on her chest. Again, Elatha was above her, forehead creased and eyes narrowed as he gazed off into the distance. Her thoughts seemed to wade through thick mud, bogging down before she could complete even one.

Blink.

The next time she regained consciousness, it took her some minutes to notice they were in motion and a swirling sensation flowed around her body. Was he pulling her? She was in water?

"Where? What happened?" Her voice was a bare wisp of sound. Had she spoken out loud?

Elatha's silver eyes flashed to hers, and he peered intently. "Are you awake?" Even in her fogged state, his urgency came through. "There is no time to waste, but it won't work if you aren't aware on some level."

"What?"

"Shannon, Princess, I need you to get rid of your clothes for me." His tone was serious with command.

"M'kay," she said drowsily and felt the change as cool water caressed bare skin.

"Good girl. Stay awake for me, Shannon. I need you to stay awake, okay?" he demanded.

Gritty sand scratched her skin with waves covering her lower half as he laid her down on the shore.

"Ohhh... kay," she murmured. Everything was floating away again.

"*Stay awake*, Shannon!" he barked.

His urgency jolted her eyelids open.

Elatha knelt between her legs. Shannon blinked, fighting to not give in to the lethargy pulling her under.

With a dangerous growl, he pulled her hips up and his mouth descended, attacking her clit with a ferocity that cleared the fog from her brain like a fall storm stripping leaves from trees.

"Oh! Gods!" Shannon gasped, grabbing his hair as he ground her pussy into his face.

This was no gentle teasing or slow build-up. Elatha ravaged her core with tongue, teeth, and lips, brutally demanding her response and revelling in her mewling cries. Heat blazed from her abdomen to wake nerves and set her body to quivering.

With unrelenting swiftness, he brought her screaming to orgasm.

No sooner was she spasming against his tongue than he shifted her back down to his hips, his cock surging inside, stretching her. A screech of keening pleasure erupted from her throat. She panted in time with the throbbing in her core. Gods, he was thick, and it had been so fucking long. She tightened down on him, clamping the fullness setting her sex ablaze.

"Shells, you are tight. I can barely get in with you squeezing me like that," he growled, driving his hips until they met hers.

"Oh, fuuuck," Shannon moaned between breaths. It was a delicious burn that had fiery need surging.

Elatha slowly withdrew before plunging back in.

"Oh gods, so fucking good," she moaned. "More."

He snarled his agreement and thrust faster.

"Yes, harder," she begged, and the searing pleasure increased as he complied.

Shannon's back arched, craving more. Her hands found her nipples, tugging roughly as she bucked against his strokes, urging him onwards. "Harder!" she yelled, with the pressure building.

Elatha started pounding into her in strong, punishing strokes, and the heat coiled inside her abdomen, drawn tighter and tighter like a spring reaching its tightest compression.

When her breath caught and her muscled turned rigid, Elatha slid a hand to her clit and pinched as he continued to slam into her.

"*Fuck!*" she screamed as she bucked violently, exploding sensation burning through her shaking body. Elatha's shout barely registered, but the twitching of his cock and heated flood had her sex clenching and spasming in another orgasmic wave.

Still with her breath sawing in and out and heart pounding its rapid tattoo, Elatha leaned down to capture her lips.

Pussy quivering with aftershocks and his cock buried to the base, he nibbled and teased her mouth, lightly stroking her lower lip before slipping inside. It was their first kiss, and she had no complaints about his skill. When he deepened his tongue's forays into her mouth, awareness grew of his hips and tongue matching rhythm. No real recovery time needed, apparently. His cock had regained its steely firmness and plundered her drenched core as his tongue dove into her mouth.

And gods, immortals knew how to fuck. Holy shit. A hand reached between their bodies to pluck at her sensitized clit. She spasmed around his cock as lightning flared along her nerves, re-sparking the building tension.

Elatha lifted his lips long enough to give her a wicked half smile, silver eyes glinting with dark pupils expanding, then his mouth descended again, demanding her carnal surrender. Strong hips pistoned, setting a punishing rhythm that had the heat rising quickly to scorch her nerve endings.

Ripping her mouth free, Shannon yelled, "Elatha, I'm going to—" She broke off into a long moan as she started to come, writhing.

He continued to thrust, fingers thrumming over her clit, keeping the waves of her orgasm cresting again and again.

Sensitive to the point of pain, she pushed his hand from her clit. Elatha responded by pinning her hands to the sand in an iron hold. With a quick change in position, he pulled out and bent his head to suck her clit in aggressive pulses, grazing his teeth over her.

"*Fuck!*" she shrieked, the intense pleasure-pain kicking her into another relentless orgasm that he rode out with his mouth on her, growling against her.

Shannon panted as he released her hands and impaled her once again, savagely thrusting as she bucked to meet him in a frenzied carnal dance. Each flex of his hips sent a shockwave of pleasure exploding down her nerves, until again, she detonated.

Shuddering in reaction, she moaned her encouragement as Elatha's cock swelled, then erupted in hot spurts.

When he pulled out a few minutes later, he flipped her over onto her hands and knees, pushing her head down to keep her ass in the air. Again, he buried his face into her core, licking and sucking her throbbing flesh as she squirmed, mewled, and shoved back against him. He growled against her body, his mouth vibrating and adding to the intensity.

Two fingers thrust into her pussy in a fast rhythm.

"Oh yes," she whined, hips unable to stay still as the heat built, spreading in a wave outward from her core.

While flicking his tongue hard and fast, he curled the two fingers to rub over sensitive inner ridges. He pounded them harder, his knuckles slamming against her entrance. She keened at the intensity—the sensations flaring and sparking as the arousal drew tighter and tighter. It was godsdamn perfect. Exactly the rhythm that drove her crazy.

Her spine bowed, and she clutched the sand, unable to breathe as he drove her quickly up to hover at the pinnacle. With a nip to her sensitive bud, he shoved her over the edge. Freefalling, Shannon screamed and shook. Everything turned starburst white for a few seconds, lightning scorching her nerve endings.

"You taste like fucking paradise. I can't get enough," Elatha groaned as his tongue delved into her drenched and twitching core, then reached further back, licking over her back entrance.

Shannon's breath caught as a slippery wet finger explored further, dipping just barely in and out where his tongue had just been. It raised gooseflesh on her skin.

"You like that," he confirmed.

She panted her affirmative, pushing back against his touch.

Elatha lowered his head again, his tongue flicking over her heated nub while that slippery finger slid in all the way to the knuckle before dragging almost all the way out.

"Harder," she moaned, the heat rising in her body at the darkly erotic strokes.

"Like it a bit rougher at times, do you?" He smacked her pussy with his free hand.

She gasped at the pleasurable sting and nodded.

Elatha did it again, drawing the heat tighter as lower down, that slippery finger stroked in and out.

"Please," she whined.

He chuckled, then took two fingers of his other hand and drove them into her wet core. Staying with his slow pace of withdrawal, he pounded in with each stroke. He alternated the timing between hands so that as his two fingers drove in, the single digit slowly retracted.

Lowering his mouth to her again, he teased her clit.

Skewered in place between his hands and mouth, the sensation coiled like a snake preparing to spring. She tried to plant her feet to get more leverage to shove onto his fingers. The wave kept building, but ebbing, over and over, with each alternating thrust of his hands.

She whimpered. She needed it faster, harder.

"Demanding, aren't you? Mmm... I love a woman that knows what she wants." He picked up his pace, roughly slamming into her with his fingers. With his mouth sealed against her clit, he sucked hard as his tongue flicked.

Electricity built, piling on itself in a chain reaction. Hard to breathe, her lungs almost seized with the intensity of it.

"*Gods!*" she screamed, her skin unable to contain the lightning. It overwhelmed her, bursting out from her centre to blast out of her head, feet, and hands in mind-blanking blasts.

She shook, convulsing with each wave.

As her senses returned and her breath eased, he slowed his movements before pulling his fingers from her body. His tongue licked over her core in long strokes, lapping her up. Despite the multiple orgasms, the tingle of arousal again drove her wild against his mouth. With a few last long licks, he rose and drove his cock inside her pussy. Every single long, thick inch until his hips pressed against her. Gods, he was so deep in this position.

Elatha stopped like that, not moving. Shannon whimpered, craving those pounding strokes.

His voice was low and threatening when he spoke. "You almost killed yourself with that stunt, Shannon. Both you and your son. Never, ever again. This is to make sure you remember to never, ever, do something so reckless again."

A sharp, hard slap on her ass cracked with a painful sting that had her clenching hard around him.

"I... am... *never*... letting... you... endanger... yourself... like... that... *again!*" Each snarled word was punctuated by a painful slap on her ass. "*Do you understand me?*"

"Yes, please Elatha, please. Yes." Begging and mewling with feverish need, she pleaded for him to fuck her. Her ass was on fire, pain and pleasure combined into a swirling, towering wildfire. Her core wept with joy and their joined fluids as she clenched around his cock, the excess dripping down her thighs.

In snapping movements to emphasize each word, Elatha thrust and growled, "I'm going to fuck you until you are completely and utterly topped up with energy and overflowing with it!"

Shannon lost her mind, coming so hard she blacked out.

"Are you back with me, my stubbornly foolish little goddess?"

Although she couldn't see him, amusement coloured his tone.

She moaned, blinking. Her cheek was pressed to the wet sand, ass in the air. Elatha's thick, hard cock was buried in her soaked, quivering cunt. And her body was a mess of flaring, sparking nerves.

"I'm not moving until I know you are back with me, Shannon. I want you to feel every single stroke of my cock as I plunder your body."

"Oh, gods." She shuddered at his words, clenching in visceral reaction.

"Yeah, you love it when I talk dirty to you. Do you know how I can tell? Your pussy strangles my cock."

"Oh my gods," she groaned, again tightening.

"Yes, exactly like that," Elatha said, voice rich with satisfaction. "What else do you like?" He began to thrust in and out.

Unable to find words and shivering at the delicious sensation, she moaned.

Fingers slid up her soaked thighs and over her wet lower lips, collecting a mix of his and her essences, only to move his now slippery digits over the exposed puckered flesh of her ass. He circled and coated the outside before working two in, timing it with the thrust of his cock.

Gods, she was losing her mind. Elatha played her body like a master, and she was helpless to resist. Nerves flared in delighted ecstasy, and a needy whine escaped her lips as she pushed back against him. Desperate fingers scrabbled in the sand to grip something, anything to hold on to as an anchor with the scorching pleasure burning up her body.

"You like that, don't you, my filthy wicked goddess?"

"Yes," she admitted with a whine. "Fuck, yes."

There was a dark, kinky side to this prince, and it was incredibly sexy. The idea of what carnal torments he and Loki might invent together made Shannon's core clench again, hard. As much as it made guilt swirl uncomfortably, she couldn't deny the thought of the two of them taking her together. The idea of being at their mercy, utterly helpless against their more dangerously sinful plans designed solely to drive her pleasure to new heights, was so intensely arousing that she shook, a fresh flood of moisture coating Elatha's cock.

"What fantasies are behind those gorgeous hazel eyes, Shannon?" He thrust harder. "Tell me!"

"You, Loki, taking me together," she panted. Oh gods, surely she hadn't admitted that out loud?

"Just that? Or is there more to it, goddess?" Elatha coaxed as she writhed on his cock and fingers, almost reaching orgasm. "Tell me, or I'll stop." He paused his thrusts.

"Don't stop!" she begged.

"Then tell me what you are fantasizing."

"Being at the mercy of both of you, helpless against whatever wicked, kinky things you want to do to me together," she yelled, desperate for him to move as the heat started to dissipate.

"Good girl," he praised as he renewed his onslaught, plundering her sex and ass.

Waves built higher and higher until trembling and shuddering, she froze. Time paused, stretched into infinity, held at the peak. With another hard thrust from him, she screamed her release.

Elatha followed, grabbing her hip and groaning. Hot streams filled her core.

"I could play with your gorgeous, tight, responsive body for days, wringing pleasure out of you over and over," he said, even as his fingers continued to fuck her ass. When he added a third finger, it was difficult to pay attention to his words.

"I'm going to take you again, in these tight little holes that crave Loki's cock and mine. Is he large like I am? Will we split you between us when we impale this ass and pussy together? Because I *am* going to make that fantasy happen for you, my dear."

"Oh my gods, yes," she breathed, helplessly coming again.

"Somehow, some way, I'll give you need. If he won't share until after he's finished filling this glorious pussy or ass of yours, I'll happily take you when he's done, in whatever way you'll allow. Think about that, think about us taking you together, my beautiful goddess."

As he growled the words, her mind supplied the intense sensory image. Loki, her love, holding her as he drove himself inside her, kissing her, lips on her neck on one side. Elatha, the wicked prince behind her, alternating his strokes with Loki as he thrust deep into her ass, biting her neck on the other side.

It was so vivid, so arousing, as they plundered her body together, impaled and writhing on their thick cocks. Lost in her fantasy, she screamed their names as Elatha drove her into a state of orgasmic bliss.

And just as he'd warned her, Elatha was thoroughly ruthless. Clever and observant, he used everything he'd learned about her to make Shannon come over and over. Even when she was a quivering pile of flesh, he still drove her body further, plucking orgasms out of her at will. If she passed out from the intense climaxes, he waited for her to regain her senses and continued. When she grew too slippery, he washed her in the waves.

With relentless desire, he took her every way he wanted, repeatedly, until intoxicated with endorphins, she fell into a healthy sleep.

Elatha sank in the water, cradling Shannon's sleeping body to his chest. She'd lost that bleached, grey colour her skin had turned after her flying stunt. Effective in getting them away from the Wild Hunt, but shells, the cost had been too high. His heart still clenched and pain racked his soul, recalling the way she'd collapsed, lifeless in his arms.

She'd stopped breathing. No heart had beat in her chest.

Terror had him giving her his breath and pounding on her chest, desperate to save her. He'd wept, thinking she'd killed her and her child—the child that also now squirmed under Elatha's hand. When she'd finally gasped, sucking in precious air and a rhythm met his ear, he'd wasted no time getting her into the water, carrying her through the waves until she'd woken enough for him to save her.

Thank the Ancestors.

Warm, breathing on her own and with her pulse reassuring under his thumb, he caressed her face and let the tears he'd held back fall. Shaking with the intensity, he swallowed his screams, his rage at the Unseelie and dwarves that had brought her to this state. Water trembled around them, responding to his power. But she needed a brief rest, to continue to come back from the brink of death's cold clutches.

Still, he fought to keep himself from waking her, from taking her again, from feeling her heat surrounding him, reassuring him that she lived as he filled her with energy. He'd already given her as much as she could absorb for the moment, sensing it in a way he couldn't explain but knew. Shells, he'd been foolish to not have sex with her when she'd collapsed the first time. What the fuck had he been thinking? She'd almost died, and it would have been his fault for not acting sooner.

He wouldn't hesitate again. He wouldn't risk her again. Not even if she screamed obscenities at him afterwards.

But they needed to get farther away from the Wild Hunt. Those blasted barnacles wouldn't give up. No doubt the creatures were still tracking them. Rising, he lifted her in his arms. He'd carry her until she woke.

Chapter 26

WHICH WAY NOW?

L oki gasped awake, jerking upright in his bed and clutching his chest where he would have sworn a snow griffin had pierced his heart, trying to rip it out with its talons. What in the bloody hell had that been? Another nightmare? The painful throbbing slowly dulled to an ache as he continued to rub his chest.

Norns. What a bloody awful way to start the day.

As the pain finally faded, the cold sweat coating his skin had him shoving away the bedding to head to the shower. The heated spray chased away his lingering chill and unease, relaxing him enough to sing a melody that popped into his thoughts—the genesis of a new song for Raven's Chaos, perhaps.

Mist and Manannan were already at the breakfast table when Loki emerged, dried and dressed for another day of travel.

"Want a breakfast wrap?" Mist held out a seaweed wrap like the ones Loki had enjoyed at the outpost. "It's some kind of seaweed with a spicy filling."

"Thanks." He finished it quickly, nodding his appreciation when Manannan poured him a cup of tea. Neither Mist nor Manannan objected when Loki urged them to leave. Despite the shower and food, a shiver ran down his spine. The sooner he found Shannon, the better.

After taking Mist to the water's surface, Loki and Manannan sped through the rich sea life.

What had Shannon thought of all the different vibrantly coloured fish, the interesting forms and colours of the glowing vegetation when she'd passed through these waters? A ray glided gracefully past him, and Loki couldn't help but recall his and Shannon's first underwater exploration together when they'd visited the Great Barrier Reef on Midgard. Despite being attacked by bunyip, they'd had fun playing with the dolphins and zipping through the water. Norns, he missed her. To be so close to catching up to her, yet still not with her... it was an agony of endurance.

They swam for six hours, took a short break, then another six. While eating during their second break, Manannan warned them that the route grew more convoluted ahead.

"Make sure you stay close, as there are some sharp turns. We've got another twelve hours before we reach the Tunnels of Glass."

"The vegetation is creating enough light in the water that visibility is pretty good," Mist commented. "I'm able to keep track of you without issue, but if we hit a dark section, I'll need you to either come closer to the surface, brighten the glow from your trident, or slow down for me."

"I will. Loki, you'll see Mist every time you breach. If you lose me, give a shout and stop. As a dolphin, your clicks will bounce off the walls, and I'll get the message so I can double back for the two of you. That way, you don't take a wrong turn, and I have to track you down."

"Reasonable precaution," Loki agreed.

Once they set out, despite Loki's impatience, they kept to a more moderate pace as the passages got progressively narrower until Manannan stopped and headed to the surface.

"This is the entrance to the Tunnels of Glass. I'll need to tow the two of you from here. Ready?" he asked.

Although Loki wasn't thrilled by the idea, he trusted Manannan would get them through. He changed back to humanoid and nodded.

"Frankly, I'd do anything to find Shannon," Loki said.

Mist smirked and shrugged a shoulder, while flicking her hair back with a careless wave of her hand. "I'm about to get squeezed through slick wet tunnels at the mercy of a hot sexy god, while holding another hot sexy god. What's not to love?"

Loki snorted in amusement. There was no attraction between him and Mist, but her continued teasing of the sea god was an entertainment he'd not curtail.

Manannan opened his mouth to say something, changed his mind, and his lips twisted in a wry smile. His eyes travelled over her body in a slow, thorough assessment, meeting her gaze with distinct appreciation.

Mist sat on the rock ledge, relaxed and not in the least disturbed by his lingering perusal.

"So should I let you two quench that obvious lust first, or are we going to penetrate these tunnels together?" Loki quipped.

Mist burst out laughing. "Nice one, Loki. Loving the visual."

Manannan shook his head, eyes glinting with humour. "Are all Asgardians like this? How have I not noticed?"

Loki laughed.

Mist snorted. "Please. God of Mischief." She waved a hand at Loki. "Expect it from him."

"And a fertility god, so I'll not let a good innuendo go to waste." He winked at her.

Manannan chuckled. "I need to hang around you Asgardians more often. You are my kind of people."

"Okay, on that note. Ready, Mist?" Loki asked.

"Ready!" She grabbed the hand he'd extended.

Manannan wrapped a single bubble of air around the two of them. "Here we go," he said as they descended towards the dark opening.

The tunnels were as disorientating as Manannan had warned. The reflective surface sent multiple twisted copies of their forms and the openings of other tunnel branches in the light Loki cast. It was like a series of distorted funhouse mirror images in those travelling carnivals on Midgard. Loki and Mist floated together, holding each other's forearms, as Manannan tugged them behind him.

They curved up and down in what felt like several corkscrews and doubled back in sharp s-curves for hours before they suddenly emerged into a wide open ocean. The water was a rich deep blue with a faint light above.

Able to move much faster, Manannan dragged them to the surface. They popped up like a cork out of a bottle. Loki took deep breaths of the clean, salt-laden air and appreciated the sight of the sky again. Although not claustrophobic, he didn't particularly enjoy being underground for long periods.

"Thor should have connected with Shannon by now. She's been up on the surface for six or seven days, including today," Loki mused.

"I agree. It makes the most sense to head to the treaty plains." Mist pointed across the ocean to the bright glow of the border between the Summer and Winter Realms in the far distance. "That's where Thor would go to wait once he's found Shannon."

Manannan frowned and eyed the horizon. "Okay, but if Thor hasn't located Shannon, which way do you think she would go? Through the water towards the Summer Realm? Or to the closer shore of the Winter Realm to walk to the Summer Realm?"

Loki shook his head. "The Winter Realm is riskier, and she can move through the water with ease." He slapped the water. "The ocean also gives her energy. I think she'd take the water route to the Summer Realm."

"True, but she might have taken the Winter Realm way if she thinks you're here looking for her," Mist argued.

Manannan gestured to the dim outline of the nearby shore. "If I encounter any of the Unseelie, they won't attack me. Why don't I search that route while the two of you fly directly to where you expect to find Thor? You'll be twice as fast in the air, cutting down the travel to about four days or less. I'll continue until I reach the treaty plains, but it will take me at least a week. Leave someone there with a message if you've found Shannon and taken her home by then."

"That's an excellent plan, Manannan. If I don't see you for a while, thank you. I can't tell you how much Asgard, and I, personally, appreciate your assistance. I am in your debt," Loki said.

Manannan held out his forearm, and Loki clasped it. "It's been a pleasure, Prince Loki. Although I would have helped Shannon regardless, I'm glad to have had this time with you. There is no debt between us."

Mist swam over to Manannan, paused, then slid her hand behind his neck and another into his long blue hair as she tugged him tight to her and kissed him.

Clearly not slow on the uptake, Manannan held her firmly with a hand on her back and the other on her ass while he took control of the kiss. A steamy, demanding melding, it had Mist writhing against him. Both were panting, chests heaving when they broke apart.

After pulling herself out of his arms and into the air, she gave him a little smile and salute. "Something to keep you warm at night and remember me by, Sea God," she teased a bit breathlessly, not unaffected herself if her still rapid breathing was anything to go by.

"Oh, we aren't done by a long shot, Valkyrie Mist. I will see you again," he growled up at her.

As Loki waited for them to finish their flirting, he teleported into the air and shifted to a raven, circling.

Mist rose to join him and with a last dip of his wings to acknowledge Manannan, Loki set off across the water towards the distant light on the far horizon and his consort.

Chapter 27

SURROUNDED

E very part of Shannon hummed, bonelessly relaxed when she woke. For the first time since she'd been captured weeks ago, nothing ached, her headache was completely gone, and that drained feeling in her chest had disappeared. A swaying motion rocked her and water splashed around her. It took her sleepy mind a while to realize why, and as she opened her eyes, she gazed up at Elatha, his focus on the horizon as he walked, carrying her through chest-deep water.

A wave of tenderness, appreciation, and desire welled, and she swallowed against the lump in her throat. Even at her very worst, he'd cared for her and asked for so little back. What had she given him but constant rejection and trouble, after all? Even when she'd shared her body, she'd done nothing but lay there, accepting the pleasure he'd brought her as he'd saved her, energized her. She'd been a burden, yet still, he carried her towards her destination, taking her when she couldn't manage herself. How had she been so fortunate as to find this selfless man?

She reached up and cupped his face. "Thank you."

He looked down and a small smile briefly flashed over his lips. "How do you feel?" His gaze searched her eyes.

Her son kicked sharply and twisted, more energetic than he had been in far too long. "Better than I have in ages." She winced at a particularly hard kick. "The difference in my son's energy is dramatic."

Elatha's gaze grew stern. "Shannon, you scared me. I almost couldn't revive you to save you. Don't *ever* do that again." His voice was rough with emotion.

Gently, she sat up in his arms and pressed her lips to his. "No, I won't. I'm sorry."

Elatha had saved their lives, and she certainly hadn't made it easy on him. Her ignorance and unwillingness to accept the realities of what her body needed sooner had almost killed her son and her. To have come within a razor's edge of never having a future or the opportunity to learn from such a harsh lesson was shocking. Immortal healing and rejuvenation meant nothing if she made such foolish choices.

Although she didn't know what it meant for her relationship with Loki, she couldn't, wouldn't, treat Elatha's care with rejection. He didn't deserve that, nor could she find it in herself to push him away again. During those long hours of taking care of her, saving her, he'd found his way into her heart. Soulmate bond with Loki or not, somehow she needed to find a way to accept that she cared for both incredible men.

Moisture touched her cheeks, and she pulled back to see raw anguish and torment in Elatha's silver starburst eyes. He blinked hard, looking away, and she turned his face back to her. With gentle care, she kissed each of his cheeks as her tongue caught the salty tears. Tears he wept for her and her child. How could she not fall for this wonderful man?

"Please, Elatha. I'm sorry. I won't do it again," she promised, then kissed him.

A shudder went through his body as he hugged her tightly. Returning his kiss, he gently traced her lips with his tongue. When she opened her mouth, he slipped inside and caressed with light, feathered touches. She basked in their connection.

As she broke the kiss, she gazed into his eyes. This beautiful, kind man expected her to stop him, to reject him. A pain lanced her chest. She didn't deserve his care after the callous way she'd treated him. But she could return some of his care by pleasuring him this time.

"Let me down, please," she asked. "I want to taste you."

His silver eyes widened, and he slowly lowered her feet to the sand as he moved to the shoreline. She reached and found him rigid and straining in his skinsuit.

"Please take these off?"

His hands flew to remove his armour and peel down his skinsuit. As his midnight-and-silver body came into view, Shannon bit her lip. She wanted to run her hands and tongue over each defined ridge of muscle, but it was his cock that captured her attention now. Like his skin, it was both silver and black, with the thick shaft a dark midnight black and engorged head a shiny, wet silver. Pearly liquid dripped from the tip, his heightened arousal evident.

Waiting no longer, she wrapped her hand around the silky shaft. Her fingers didn't meet. He was too thick.

She pumped her hand and elation shot through her when he groaned. She sank to her knees and licked him from base to tip. Like the sea, he tasted oddly familiar and comforting. She wanted more.

"Shells, that's good," he groaned.

After circling the tip, she flicked her tongue over the slit, and he jerked. Yes, she liked that, liked making him groan and jump. Satisfaction purred within her.

Barely able to get her jaws wide enough to suck his head inside, she wrapped her mouth around him. She rubbed her tongue over the flared head, enjoying the sensation. Elatha groaned, hips flexing in a shallow thrust.

Taking the hint, she swallowed him down as far as she could, relaxing her throat. She couldn't fit all of him. Instead, she used her other hand to pump the rest in time with her mouth. She wanted him to come, filling her with his taste.

Setting a rhythm, he thrust in and out of her mouth.

She hummed, vibrating around his delicious length. He groaned, his thighs trembling. He had to be close.

"Fuck," he swore as his cock twitched, salty essence filling her mouth and throat as she swallowed. He tasted like saltwater taffy. Gods, she couldn't get enough of him.

Greedily, she sucked—his panting music to her ears as he continued to jerk against her.

When he recovered, a growl was her only warning before he withdrew, tugged her to her feet to spin her around, putting her back to him. He grabbed her under the knees, lifted her, and impaled her on his still-hard cock.

"Oh fuck," she cried.

Gods, he felt so perfect. The delicious fullness stretching her drew a long moan from her throat. When he moved with slow, deliberate strokes, raising and lowering her over his shaft, shivers rippled over her skin.

"Beautiful. So beautiful, Shannon."

As his hips continued their exquisite rhythm, he kissed her neck and bit at the most sensitive spots. The sensual torture of his slow assault on her senses had her writhing. It was an insistent, relentlessly gradual build that held her quivering at the crest before she gasped, shuddering as she fell over the edge.

Elatha growled, then began thrusting faster.

As the heat built inside her, she writhed, unable to stay still, flexing at each stroke. Harder and faster, he drove her body until the heat flared wide, searing her with its intensity as it burst and left her gasping.

With a long, deep groan, Elatha pulsed.

Together, they panted, gradually catching their breath, and he lowered her to the sand.

Elatha brushed her hair from her face. "We have to get going."

"Yes." She stretched. The difference in how she felt compared to yesterday was like night and day. Her bones didn't ache. There was no twinge of pain as she moved. Her head didn't weigh so heavily, and her pulse didn't beat like an ice pick chipping at her temple. Even her eyesight cleared. Gods, she hadn't realized how much strain it had been to see of late. Effortlessly, she called water and ran a thin film over their bodies, drying them with a quick flick of warm air.

Elatha blinked and smiled as she teased him.

While Shannon called her fighting leathers and armour to cover her body, Elatha pulled on his skinsuit and armour. As much as she knew they had to get going, she regretted the necessity of him covering that gorgeous body of his. She'd barely begun to explore him.

"We will make much better time in the air than on the ground," she suggested as they began walking.

Elatha glanced at her, narrowing his eyes with a frown creasing his brow. "But you just about killed yourself moving us that way."

"That was only because I was so low on energy. I'm not now." She smiled. "In fact, I haven't felt this great since before I was kidnapped." No, she didn't blame him for questioning her. To push so close to killing her son and herself had been incredibly foolish.

"Only if you promise to put us down if you feel the *slightest* bit tired." His frown deepened as her smile widened. "I mean it, Shannon."

She bounced over and kissed him, a little amused, but truly grateful as well. "Thank you for your care and concern. I promise I will."

Elatha pulled her into his arms. "I can't go through that again, Shannon. I just can't. It was too close. You stopped breathing. Your heart stopped. You *died*. It was luck and desperation that my breath worked to fill your lungs, that my pounding fist started your heart beating again." He swallowed hard. "I know you don't feel the same way about me, but I care about you. I can't let you die, Shannon. Please, you can't risk yourself or your son again like that."

The stark fear clear in his expression had the lightness in her chest sinking, plummeting into a pit in her stomach. She hadn't realized how close she'd come. That he'd had to perform CPR. She wouldn't be alive, her son wouldn't be alive, if it weren't for him—this beautiful, powerful man who'd been reduced to someone who expected to be rejected, to be hurt. And that was her fault. Through her foolishness, she'd hurt him, and the pain of it made her heart twist.

She cupped his cheeks and met his gaze. "Elatha, I care about you, too. I don't know how it's possible when I'm soulbound to Loki, but I *do*. You're in my heart. To know that I've hurt you is like shards of glass inside. I appreciate you, I desire you, and I care about you. That much, I can tell you with absolute truth. I don't know what the future holds. I just don't. But I will be careful, okay?"

He let out a long, unsteady breath and gave her another squeeze. "Okay."

She wrapped air around them and lifted them off the ground. They flew towards the lighter horizon as she followed the shoreline. Passing over the desolate landscape quickly, they made good progress. After travelling for a good four or five hours, they were far from their starting point when she returned them to the sand.

"Okay, I need a break and a meal," she said with a smile. "I promised I'd stop when I felt the least little bit tired."

Elatha gave her a wide grin, lighting up his handsome face. "Thank you. There are nuts, fruit, some cheese, and the seaweed rolls you seem to like."

"Oh! Yes. I want seaweed rolls." Happily, she unwrapped one and bit into it when he handed it to her. They seemed to hit her favourite mix of tastes, being a little salty, a little sweet, but also creamy and filling.

In the midst of devouring a second roll, the hair on the back of her neck stood.

She stopped chewing, surveying the surroundings. Although she didn't spot anyone, she was uncomfortable. It was that same sensation she'd had in that valley with Kara and Mist a few days before the Wild Hunt attacked them. Worried, she stood and looked around.

Still, she didn't spot anything alarming.

Yet the warning didn't dissipate.

Shannon called her weapons, and they appeared on her arms and hips.

"What's wrong?" Elatha rose to his feet and looked around.

"Someone is watching us."

No sooner had the words left her mouth when fluttering in the sky caught her eye. Against the dark twilight, she couldn't make out what it was.

What they were.

Multiple dark shapes flowed and fluttered above them. But they made no noise. None at all. It was eerie. Disturbing. Unnatural.

"Shannon," Elatha's tone was urgent, and she followed his gaze to what had drawn his attention.

Dullahan, the headless horsemen of the Wild Hunt, had appeared out of the darkness, their silhouettes barely visible in the dim light that penetrated from the far-off Summer Realm and reflected from the overhead moons.

Unearthly screams shattered the quiet as the fluttering and flowing shapes dove from the sky. Finally, Shannon recognized them as banshees. The dullahan began galloping, and the howling of hellhounds echoed off the desolate landscape.

She wouldn't be able to outrun the banshees in the air. Instead, she created poisonous nerve gas balls. Would they affect the creatures of the Wild Hunt? No way to know but to try.

"Don't breathe this in, whatever you do!" she warned as she hurled them at the diving banshees.

They blew right through the poison gas, not even slowing.

Damn!

Elatha blasted arrows of water at the banshees. Far more effective, it forced them to scatter, swerving away.

Instead, Shannon threw gas balls at the approaching dullahan and hellhounds. Both the horses and hounds squealed as they inhaled the gases and spun back. Quickly, she launched more, and still more.

Redcaps and trolls thundered into sight, running right through the clouds of gas.

Water, air, and fire hadn't worked against the troll last time.

Fuck!

But she still didn't know how to make a miniature sun. Just light. Would it be enough?

Elatha was keeping the banshees at bay.

"What stops redcaps and trolls?" she shouted over the screams of the banshees and howls of the hounds.

"Cut the heads off redcaps. Can you create sunlight for the trolls?"

"No!"

"Then try to keep out of their reach while we fight the redcaps!" he yelled back. "We can retreat into the water. Trolls can't swim."

"No, we can't! They've brought kelpies!"

Out of the corner of her eye, she'd spotted the horse-shaped water demons galloping down past the dullahan, out of reach of her poison balls, and into the water. They were waiting, cutting off any retreat.

Elatha met Shannon's gaze, fury and sorrow in his eyes as the redcaps and trolls drew closer. They were ridiculously outnumbered, but neither she nor Elatha would go down without a fight. Not again.

She put her back to his and drew her sais.

The redcaps were faster than the trolls and reached them first.

Shannon spun out with two throwing knives, piercing two throats. They stopped running, gagging and struggling to get the weapons out.

As she darted into the air, Shannon spun over a redcap, slashing his throat with the edge of her sais before he could pull her down.

Elatha was fighting two, while keeping the banshees at bay with water blasts. Staying in the air, she flipped back to whip a throwing knife through the side of a redcap's throat, giving Elatha time to cut the other one's head off.

Dropping to a crouch at his back, she prepared for the next wave of redcaps. The trolls were lumbering closer, and Shannon wasn't sure she and Elatha could take out all the redcaps before the trolls reached them.

Damn, but she wished she'd practiced creating sunlight. Gods. If she was wishing, she wished they were anywhere but here!

Shannon stumbled as a rainbow of lights surrounded them. Reacting instinctively, she grabbed Elatha's arm as it sucked them into the vortex.

PART 4

THE FATES ARE B!THCHES, REALLY

"All changes, even the most longed for, have their melancholy; for what we leave behind us is a part of ourselves; we must die to one life before we can enter another."

Anatole France

Chapter 28

NOT ME

E latha floundered, mid-swing, as a swirl of lights and some kind of wind caught them up. He reached for Shannon, only to find her hand already clasping his arm. The blinding lights disappeared and—oh shells! They were falling!

But no, with a slight jolt, they stopped, floating in mid-air. Shannon smiled and looked down. Following her gaze, he winced as five redcaps plummeted what had to be at least one hundred stride lengths, if not more, to hit the ground in a messy, near-fatal impact. Damn, those barnacles were tough.

Shannon lowered herself and Elatha, and before the groaning redcaps could recover, the two of them cut the foul creatures' heads off.

Elatha glanced up at the sky. "What was that?" Would it come again? Where was the rest of the Wild Hunt? He scanned the horizon.

"It was like the Bifrost, but since we aren't in Asgard, it wasn't the actual Bifrost." Shannon frowned, also eyeing their surroundings.

The water was strangely calm, with only gently lapping waves on a black pebbled beach curving into a bay. By the scent of the water, they were still on the same shoreline. The dark twilight sky marked this as part of the Winter Realm, but the increased light on the horizon suggested they were considerably closer to the Summer Realm than they'd been.

She turned in a circle. "If I didn't know better, I'd say we teleported using Bifrost energy?"

He jolted and stared at her. "Do you have the ability to teleport? Because I sure don't." If only he had powers the way she had, more than just manipulating water and a little air. To fly? That was an incredible gift. But Fomorians didn't have those kinds of innate abilities. Instead, their technology gave them an advantage.

"No, not that I'm aware of. I'd expect Loki would have figured that out when we were determining the extent of my powers." Shannon began walking toward the lighter horizon.

Elatha scowled as he followed her. "Loki can teleport?" Why hadn't her consort found her if he could move great distances with such ease?

She shrugged. "Yeah. Not vast distances, but yes, a few kilometres at least."

Huh. Well, that made more sense then. Still, someone had to have teleported them, and if not her and definitely not him, could it be her child? Elatha caught up with her and stared at her pregnant belly, his eyebrows raised in speculation. What kind of abilities would a baby have with such powerful parents?

Shannon cocked her head, eyes flicking to her belly before they widened and she blinked. "You think my *son* teleported us?" She sounded incredulous.

Was it such a far-fetched idea? "Someone did, and it wasn't you or me, so that leaves him." He gestured to her abdomen.

"An unborn baby can use powers? Is that *normal*?" her voice squeaked.

He chuckled. "Not for Fomorians, that's for sure. But answer this, how strong are Loki's abilities?"

"Pretty damn strong. He's the strongest mage in Asgard."

"Okay, and how strong are your powers?"

She frowned and shrugged. "I don't know any other Tuatha Dé Danann. I've only met a couple and not really seen the extent of their magic."

"Compare yourself to Asgardians, then. How strong are you?"

She waggled her head back and forth, then nodded. "Pretty damn strong. Not as strong as Loki, but not far behind, I'd guess."

"So I'd expect your son to be powerful as well. At this point, he'd use his magic instinctively. He sensed you were in danger and got you out of there." It was the only explanation he could come up with that made any kind of sense.

She rubbed her belly. "I can't fault your logic. Or come up with a reasonable alternative. Damn. How will I keep up with a child that can teleport?" Her gaze met his with a wide, slightly panicked expression.

Elatha smiled and reached a hand over to rub her belly as well. "With your usual strength, patience, and grace, I'm sure. And possibly considerable cursing at Loki," He grinned. What he'd give to see her child born, running his parents ragged. Would he be allowed to come to Asgard?

Shannon laughed. "Yeah, you probably aren't wrong about that."

She resumed walking, and he fell in step beside her. Unwilling to relax his guard without knowing how far they'd travelled with the teleport, he stayed vigilant, checking their surroundings frequently. He didn't want the Wild Hunt to catch them again.

Without knowing where those blasted barnacles were or if they were gaining, Elatha didn't coax Shannon into a break or take time to clean the blood and gore from his body. He wanted her far, far away from the Wild Hunt, preferably in the Summer Realm, although that wasn't feasible. The light band of promise on the horizon was still days in the distance.

Instead, he handed Shannon some nuts to munch as they walked. She had to keep up her energy, after all. With the Wild Hunt at their heels, they had no time to refuel using sex. Not yet at least. Getting caught naked was far too dangerous. The creatures of the Wild Hunt were hard enough to survive with weapons and armour.

Still, it didn't stop him from recalling her surprising actions this morning, and he hardened. It hadn't been what he'd expected. Not after she'd reacted so badly before. Her words of caring curled around his soul. Even if she didn't truly mean them, he'd cherish them. Regardless of what happened, he couldn't see himself with another. She'd taken his heart, curling up like a warm glow inside him. In a thousand years, he'd never felt for another what he did for her, and in a thousand more, he didn't think he'd find another like her.

Shannon plodded on hour after hour, pushing herself further. The Summer Realm was definitely getting closer. She stumbled, falling forward until Elatha caught her.

Holding her upright, he brushed a lock of hair from her face. "Stop, Shannon. We've walked nonstop for ten hours on top of the teleporting. It's got to be far enough to take a short break."

She shook her head, stepping out of his arms. "I don't want to get found by the Wild Hunt again. We don't know how fast they can travel."

He halted her with a hand. "Yes, but you're pale again. You are pushing too hard, and you've used too much energy today. If you let yourself get too low, it will take too long to recharge you before they catch us. We don't have that kind of time. This needs to be quick."

She wrinkled her nose and eyed them both. "Okay, but I want to bathe in the saltwater." She walked into the ocean until she was hip-deep, then stopped. With her sais out, she cleaned them and did the same with the daggers she still had. Some of her throwing knives had been left in redcap throats when they'd teleported.

Blood was splattered and dried all over her armour. After sinking to her knees, the waves came up to her neck, and using some sand, she washed off the blood. The surrounding ocean was red when she finished. Yuck. She pushed it away, swirling a current around her until only clear water remained.

Again standing, she retracted her armour and leathers back into her torc.

Elatha was scrubbing the crimson streaks from his armour and skinsuit as well. His hands paused, starburst eyes heating as he looked her over.

Shannon grinned. "I like my men with less blood of their enemies on them. Keep washing, Elatha."

His lips twitched in amusement as he used his power to swirl water over him in a wave.

"Done. Blood free. Acceptable now, Princess?" He bowed and presented himself for approval.

"Almost." She paused, and he quirked an eyebrow. "You are wearing far too many clothes on that gorgeous, sexy body."

He smirked as he pulled off his weapons, armour, and skinsuit, tossing them to shore.

"Now, my princess?"

She took her time eying his ebony-and-silver perfection. Black hair curling slightly around his wide shoulders and those built, but not bulky, arms that were more than strong enough to lift her into whatever position he wanted. The chiselled eight-pack abdominals, lean hips, and trail of black hair leading to the proud, thick midnight shaft with its broad silver head. Standing tall, it was ready for action.

Her hands cupped her breasts, tugging on the nipples as she let him see the lust heating her blood.

He groaned, cock jerking.

She smiled. "Yes. Now, Elatha," in a voice gone husky with desire.

He stalked through the water, picking her up behind the knees and back to carry her closer to shore. Finally letting her feet touch after he slid her down his front, despite the prodigious curve of her belly, he held the nape of her neck. His lips lowered for a blisteringly passionate kiss.

Gods, but he could kiss. Hot and wet, teasing and dominating. Nothing else existed except his lips on her, the feel of his hard body pressing against hers, and those clever, clever fingers. As his mouth plundered hers, a hand explored her breasts, tugging and twisting, pulling a moan from her as the sparks of pleasure burst into a melting heat.

That questing hand moved lower, caressing over her belly, before dipping below to find her slippery and ready. When two long, strong fingers curled inside with his thumb brushing over the bundle of nerves, her legs buckled.

"Gods! Please, Elatha!" she whimpered, breaking from his mouth to catch a breath.

Her core quivered. Heat spread from her abdomen outward. She was so close, her thoughts scattering as she focused on the building sensations.

With effortless strength, Elatha pinned her to him sideways. His lips trailed over her neck and teeth scraped erotically over her pulse in a dangerous tease.

"Come for me, Shannon," he demanded before biting down on that sensitive spot between shoulder and nape that further weakened her knees.

"Oh, fuck!" she moaned, riding his relentless fingers, hips helplessly bucking with the orgasm smashing through her nervous system.

"That's my girl," Elatha growled as he laid her in the shallow water, holding her ass off the sand as he lined himself up and sunk to the hilt.

Shannon shrieked. Her eyes wanted to roll back as he worked that magnificently thick cock in and out. Lightning shot through her core at every stroke. The delicious friction quickly brought her to a shuddering orgasm again, but Elatha didn't slow and continued his pace, driving her higher.

"Come again for me, Shannon. I want at least ten orgasms out of you before we continue our trek. You can't let your energy wane."

"Oh, fuck," she moaned while coming and trembling.

At just the right angle to rub over her G-spot, he rode it again and again with wicked efficiency. Fuck, it was so godsdamn perfect.

"Elatha!" she whimpered as his pace increased, pounding a bit harder, and not slowing even as she convulsed around his cock. Squirming and shivering, electric prickles sensitized every inch of her skin.

"That's four, Princess," Elatha said, groaning and pouring into her in hot splashes.

After pulling out, he lifted her higher. That talented tongue dove into her pulsing core. Licking deep, he flicked before lapping up and over her clit. She shrieked, babbling nonsensical words at the flash fire roaring through her as he sucked the sensitive bud, then lathed with his tongue.

Elatha didn't stop until she was limp and quivering with aftershocks.

Lowering her once more, he buried his cock in her soaked depths again, stroking hard and fast to bring her twice more in quick succession. Between the screaming and panting, she could scarcely catch her breath.

He lifted her into his lap for a kiss. "How are you doing, Princess?"

"Good... so good," Shannon moaned, drunk with sensation. Everything was sensitized, but at the same time, floating.

Elatha kissed her deeply as his fingers plucked at her taut nipples, and she arched towards him. It was like her breasts and core connected as two ends of a live wire.

After flipping her to her hands and knees, with her face pressed down onto the beach, he entered her from behind. Gods, his cock was so deep in this position, and she fucking loved every stroke. Bracing herself with hands clenching the sand, she drove her body back to increase the force of each thrust.

Elatha growled and smacked her ass, drawing mewling moans from her as she shoved back harder.

With those clever fingers, he reached around to her aching breasts and plucked at her nipples as he rode her. It had her shuddering in climax within a few brief minutes. Elatha joined her, groaning out his pleasure.

After pulling out, he inserted two fingers, curling and twisting in her still-spasming core as his thumb caressed her ass.

"Do you want me to finish you here, Princess?" Elatha asked, his voice deepened to a sinful rumble.

"Yes. Gods, yes," Shannon panted, squirming with anticipation.

Withdrawing from her core, he pulled their juices to coat her ass, sliding those slippery fingers inside. At the same time, he pressed his cock in just enough to start to stretch her, then came. The sensation was so hotly erotic that as each pulse erupted, gooseflesh shivered over her skin.

Using the added lubrication to ease in further, he pressed first that wide silver head, then sank the rest of his thick midnight shaft right to the base.

Her limbs trembled, even braced with her forehead on the sand. Elatha was large and knew it, letting her adjust to the stretch before he started to move.

"How are you doing, Princess?"

"Gods, so huge. Don't you dare fucking stop," she moaned.

"Yes, and your tight little ass is gripping me with the force of an octopus clinging to its next meal." Starting slowly, he withdrew, then sank back in again, over and over. The sinfully erotic sensation had the goosebumps shivering up her spine in waves.

"Do you like that?"

"Fuck yes."

Those clever fingers plucked at her clit.

"Harder, please Elatha."

"Come for me once first, then I'll go harder," Elatha demanded, thrumming her clit as he continued his slow strokes.

In desperation, with the climax so close but hovering just out of reach, she grabbed his hand and guided those strong fingers in a rougher rhythm. Gentle wasn't getting it done, and he figured it out fast. The orgasm boiled out with a shriek and violent bucking of her spine.

As she tightened even more around him with each writhing movement of her body, he groaned. When his cock twitched and jerked, she knew he'd come as well.

Quickly recovering, Elatha increased the pace, slamming that exquisite cock in with every delicious thrust. Plunging two fingers into her pussy, he began alternating, fucking both.

Vision went hazy as the heat built, creating a tingling in her abdomen. Like being in a tunnel, she could hear herself keening with every impact of their bodies.

The tingling turned to sparks that landed on the dry tinder of her flesh. When it caught fire, the overwhelming inferno fried everything in its wake.

Chapter 29

FIRST IMPRESSIONS

Loki and Mist made excellent time to the windswept treaty plains between the Summer and Winter Realms. With short breaks on sparse rocky islands they found along the way, and not sparing any time to sleep for more than an hour, they travelled the distance in three and a half days. Excitement swelled within Loki as he beat his wings harder, not quite able to see past the cloaking mists.

In minutes, they passed the edge of the grassy plains, and while the fog still swirled at the edges and obscured clear sight into the bright Summer or gloomy Winter Realms, the centre was clear.

But only two people awaited them. Surely, one was Shannon?

After circling to land, Loki's stomach sank. She wasn't there—only Kara and Roskva waited for them. Loki shifting back from raven-form, reaching the two Valkyrie as Mist touched down beside them.

"You didn't find Shannon?" Loki didn't understand how he could have beaten her here. Where was she? Where was Thor? What could have delayed her?

Kara scowled. "No, but we haven't been able to look far." Her posture sang with tension.

Mist eyed her two fellow Valkyrie. "Why? Haven't you been here for days?"

"Aren't Thor and Thjalfi looking for her?" Loki asked, almost on top of Mist's question.

Roskva shook her head. "They had to return to Asgard. Crom and Llew escaped the dungeons."

"*What?* How in the Nine Realms did that happen?" Loki growled. The dungeons utilized highly advanced technology, reinforced by seidhr. There were numerous safeguards. And they were well guarded with a full shift of thirty guards. No one escaped their dungeons. That those two fuckers, who should already be dead, had escaped... no, no, it could not stand.

"I don't—" Kara started, but stopped as the swirling light of the Bifrost appeared. When it dissipated, Thor and Thjalfi stood there.

Thor radiated fury. Not only was lightning flashing in his eyes, but it snapped on his fingertips and over Mjolnir clenched in his grip, with the occasional bolt coursing over his body to hit the nearby ground. Grass smoked and sizzled around him.

"What's happened, brother?" Loki asked.

"Llew's wife, Badb, and Nemain got into Asgard somehow without Heimdall seeing them. We believe she killed a guard and imitated him to get inside the dungeons, then the pair slaughtered the entire guard shift without a single guard managing to raise the alarm." Thor's voice thundered like the sound of the sky being ripped apart. Birds took flight, abandoning the area.

He stalked a few tens of metres away, smashed Mjolnir on the ground, creating a crater and venting some of his fury before returning to continuing his story. "They broke Llew and Crom Cruach out of the dungeon and escaped Asgard. We don't know how. Ambassador Ogma is claiming complete ignorance, but we're confident they returned to Alfheim."

"Fucking politicians!" Kara snarled.

Thor snorted. "There are no living witnesses, but we got the two names from one guard who lived long enough to tell us. He died before we could extract the memory as proof."

This was bad. Epically, colossally bad.

That they'd gotten in and out of Asgard was unacceptable. That they'd done it, and Heimdall hadn't seen them was even worse. Asgard had a serious security problem.

"Vidar?" Loki asked, naming the Einherjar who'd betrayed them a few months ago, letting Isis into Asgard and the palace to make an attempt on Shannon's life. The bitch had almost succeeded, and both Isis and Vidar had escaped. If Isis wasn't the soulmate and wife of his oldest brother, Baldur, who'd died as a consequence of Loki's childish prank, Loki would have gone after her. But Shannon had trounced her when Isis tried again, so he'd left his widowed sister-in-law alone. Vidar, though—he was someone they very much wanted either dead or in the dungeons for his betrayal.

Thor sent a bolt of lightning forking into the sky. "Yes, it was probably him. We can't figure out how else they could have gotten in and out unseen, and bypassed the palace or city portal dampeners."

"They killed the entire shift without an alarm being raised?" Mist's tone was incredulous.

Thjalfi scowled. "Yes."

Loki frowned, glancing at her. Had Mist not fought in the last war against the Sidhe four hundred years ago? The Valkyrie was younger than him by a few centuries, but he hadn't thought she was that young. It wasn't surprising the guards hadn't been able to hold off those two Unseelie. They were an especially lethal duo who'd wreaked havoc in every battle. As highly trained as Asgardian guards were, they weren't Einherjar or Valkyrie. They were no match for war goddesses. Not without warning or advanced weaponry that wasn't issued to dungeon guards. And once they'd freed Crom Cruach and Llew, Crom could cloak them in mists that Heimdall couldn't see through.

Thor turned, his gaze searching. "We still haven't located Shannon?" His voice rumbled across the plain.

Loki pressed the heel of his hand to his chest, rubbing at the spot that held his sense of Shannon. She still lived. She had to be okay. But why wasn't she here yet? Where was she? He took a shaky breath before answering, "With Manannan leading the way, we met with the Atlanteans. According to Queen Ethniu, Prince Elatha, her son, found Shannon in the Sea of Lantia and was escorting her here. By the time we left the Atlantean capital city, they should have been six days ahead of us."

"Actually, we figured she'd be here with you when we arrived," Mist added, glancing around them as if Shannon might appear any moment. She touched her Valkyrie ear communicator. "Shannon? Shannon, can you hear me?" She shook her head, worry creasing her brow. "She's not close enough yet, but they should have reached the surface ten or eleven days ago. It's supposed to be only a week journey by land."

Was Shannon moving slower with pregnancy? His gaze turned back to the way he'd come. Was she just beyond communication range in that cursed Winter Realm, hidden by the banks of cloaking mists? "We flew directly here across the water from the Tunnels of Glass, the nearest passageway between the underground seas and the surface ocean. Manannan is taking the land route along the closest shore in the Winter Realm in case they went that way, but it will take him almost twice as long to get here."

"Well, if the two of you didn't see them on the water, then they've got to be coming along the shore, right?" Kara asked.

"It's possible we missed them by flying over them when they were underwater. Although I would have expected them to arrive faster if they'd swam, so that's less likely." Loki eyed the swirling fog. "Highest probability is that they are walking."

"Let's work our way back along the shore from here to find her. I don't want my pregnant sister travelling through the Winter Realm with just one protector when Crom and Llew are back on the loose!" Thor boomed. "Those fuckers could call the Wild Hunt after her again."

"Agreed, but someone still needs to stay here in case they took a different route, were slower under the water, or something we haven't considered," Loki mused, trying not to give in to his heart's rapid beating at Thor's words. The best-laid plans went awry. Unpredictable, chaotic things happened that could change outcomes. He needed to cover all their bases and not miss her this time. Not again.

And if Crom and Llew had gone after his consort, knowing who she was now? His fists clenched, chaos churning and surging in his veins. They needed to die.

Roskva sighed, "Oh, fine," then shoved a thick blond braid back over her shoulder. "Kara and I can stay since no one should be on their own in this cursed realm," she volunteered. "Plus, someone needs to be here to let the other search parties know."

Kara nodded. "You all can travel faster and search more ground by flying."

Loki let out a breath and agreed. The two Valkyrie could hold the plains and their retreat, if needed, with the Bifrost backing them up should the Wild Hunt attack or Shannon somehow reach them from a direction he hadn't anticipated.

Mist rose into the air, looking towards the ocean. "We should head that way," she said, pointing at the shoreline they'd crossed earlier. The landmass curved not far from here, and the shortest direction back to the ocean was to travel into the Winter Realm.

Loki shifted to a raven and joined her.

Thjalfi set off running, while Thor took to the air. The group spread out. With the cloaking fog making details difficult at any distance, the searchers had to stay in sight of one another.

It was several hours before they reached the ocean. Turning to follow the shoreline, they headed deeper into the gloom of the Winter Realm. Flying slower, closer together, and lower to the ground in the poor visibility, they couldn't go as fast, but Loki would rather go slow and not miss Shannon this time.

Every minute they searched, the tension wound tighter within him. Surely, she couldn't be too far away? Had something happened? Had she gone into labour early? Had the Unseelie or their foul creatures attacked to delay her? Where was she?

After eighteen hours, they stopped to take a rest break on a wide, grassy bluff overlooking the water. Despite his lack of appetite, Loki conjured meats, cheeses, and bread, while Thor shared a flagon of wine. Yet while the others dug in, then caught a few hours of sleep, Loki stared off in the distance, down the shoreline, muscles vibrating with the need to press on, to continue his search. Where was his goddess?

"I hope I encounter Llew or Crom out here," Thor rumbled when he woke. "No prisoners this time."

Loki nodded and gave his brother a fierce grin. "That's what I want to hear. Not just for the guards, but it didn't sit right that captivity in the dungeons was the only penalty after what they did to Shannon."

"Father agrees, Loki. He's ordered their deaths. We tried the diplomatic route," Thor said, lightning flashing.

Loki blinked and a warm glow wrapped around him for a moment before he swallowed and his gaze was drawn to their surroundings again. "But I hope they aren't out here, Thor. Shannon's too vulnerable. She's my priority. Once she is safe, I'll help you squash those cockroaches."

"As it should be. I don't like how long she's been out here on her own. She's in her third trimester, and I saw how difficult that was for Amelia. Even as an immortal goddess, I can't imagine how Shannon is dealing with it. I'm scared for her and my nephew, brother. I don't know how you aren't losing your mind." Thor shook his head, frowning.

A laugh that was almost a sob escaped Loki's control, and he wrestled the welling tide of emotion. "Well, for the last week, I'd hoped she was already with you, my big brother, and well protected. Now that I know she isn't, yes, it's scaring me. Both Queen Ethniu and Manannan assure me that Prince Elatha would protect her with his life, so at least she isn't on her own, but damn, Thor." Loki tugged at his hair. "I'm trying to keep it together and not panic."

Thor winced and patted his brother on the shoulder, but didn't say anything more. What was there to say?

The churning in Loki's gut bubbled, and he stuffed it back down, walling it off. If he thought too much about what could have gone wrong for her not to be here already, his heart thundered in his ears and chaos surged, curling around his fingers. His fists clenched and unclenched as he worked to calm his breathing, to think clearly.

Loki stood. He couldn't sit anymore. "Ready to press on?" he asked when the others woke and had some breakfast.

Thjalfi stuffed his last bite into his mouth and nodded, running through the grasses to where the bluff met the beach further down the shore. Thor rose into the air, and Mist sprang aloft beside him. Loki teleported into the air and shifted back to a raven, joining them.

Sweeping back and forth from the coast and in as far as they could without losing sight of the shore or each other, then back out over the water, they continued to work their way deeper into the Winter Realm. Hours passed as they searched. The tension wound tighter within his chest. Where was she? By the Norns, she had to be okay. She had to be.

Thor and Thjalfi were discussing another break when Mist shouted.

The closest to her, Loki swooped over to join her as she peered into the gloom in front of her. There. Was that someone sitting in the shallow water by the shore? Loki sped up, pulling ahead of the Valkyrie.

It was. It was two people.

He dove, shifting to humanoid at the last second, and landed a short distance from them.

Shock stopped him in his tracks.

Shannon was unclothed, armour and weapons missing, in the black-and-silver arms of the Norns-cursed Atlantean. This was the prince that was supposed to be protecting her? Helping her? He was... he was *kissing* her. Had his hands all over her. Had the fucker attacked her? *Forced* her?

Rage swelled, chaos bursting to swirl along Loki's body as he stalked closer, growling.

Shannon twisted, her gaze meeting his. "Loki?" She blinked, eyes widening as a blush covered her cheeks.

A blush as she covered her breasts from his sight, but not from the Atlantean's. No, she hid from her own soulmate, her consort.

He couldn't breathe.

He couldn't breathe.

His mind wouldn't process what he saw.

She—she cheated on him? His *soulmate* let someone else hold and caress that gorgeous body? Let that Atlantean—

How... How could she?

He stumbled, clutching at his chest, unable to look away. "You..." Nausea climbed his throat, and the words burned like acid. "You had sex with him? You *fucked* him, despite being *my* soulmate?"

But he didn't wait for her reply—the guilt was already apparent in her expression, in her hunched posture.

Heart breaking, he fled.

Chapter 30

SHATTERED

When Shannon woke from the third time Elatha insisted on recharging her energies since they'd escaped the Wild Hunt in an improbable teleportation, he was dressed in his skinsuit and armour, holding her naked body in his arms as they floated in the water.

She blinked up at him. "Any sign of the Wild Hunt?"

"No, not since we teleported two days ago, but I'll be glad to get moving again. We haven't travelled as far as I'd like since then. How do you feel?" He inquired, smiling down at her.

She took a moment to take stock. That relentless pounding headache had disappeared again, thank goodness, and so had the heavy lethargy. It had lingered yesterday, despite Elatha's best efforts, hampering their ability to travel. Her son's portalling seemed to use a massive amount of energy. She released a relieved breath. She wasn't confident she could have fought them off again if they'd attacked yesterday. At least now they had a chance if she could speed them through the air.

"Well energized," she teased, returning his smile. "I should be able to fly us some distance today."

Silver eyes glinted. "My pleasure, Princess, I assure you."

She laughed. It had certainly been for her. But more importantly, she had the energy to fight, to survive, to get out of this blasted nightmare realm and off this fucking planet. Her son kicked, almost as if he understood and agreed. Appreciation welled within her. She owed Elatha so much... not the least was her life and the life of her child. Sliding her fingers into his thick hair, she pressed her lips to his.

A blur dropped from the sky and landed on the beach, not five metres from where she floated. Shannon broke the kiss and froze, her heart pounding.

But it wasn't a creature of the Wild Hunt.

Even in the dim lighting, the athletic build with its broad shoulders and narrow waist in black fighting leathers, silver scale armour, and long black leather duster topped by tousled midnight hair framing a pale angular face was unmistakable. Black seidhr swirled around him, billowing in chaotic waves.

Could it be? Was he real? Oh gods, please tell her she wasn't dreaming. Her voice trembling like the quaking in her limbs, she whispered, "Loki?"

She blinked, afraid to he'd disappear, that he was a trick of her exhaustion. But he was still there, still not saying anything.

It took her another painfully long few seconds to realize Loki's eyes were wide, shocked, and glassy. Why was he... she blushed, recalling her naked state and covered her chest with an arm as she struggled to stand. She must look an absolute disaster, so thin, and good grief, without a hairbrush in days. Did he not recognize her?

Elatha helped her rise. But as she stepped out of the Atlantean's arms and towards the shore and Loki—the consort she'd fought so hard to return to—he stumbled, then blurted, "You... you had sex with him? You *fucked* him, despite being *my* soulmate?"

That was what he was most upset about? Sex? As if it had been a simple choice? As if she hadn't died? For fuck's sake, as if his child wouldn't be dead now if she hadn't? Could he not see her state, naked as she was? It wasn't like she was hiding her frailty, her dangerous weight loss, that she could barely stand on her own.

Still, his words stripped her more effectively than the loss of her clothes. Her blush deepened.

She hunched her shoulders as she fought to find her voice, to find the words to reply to such an inconsequential accusation when their baby's very life had been at risk.

But before she could reply, her soulmate, her love disappeared between one breath and the next. As if he'd never been there.

"NO!" She launched herself from the water to fall where Loki had stood on the pale sand. His footprints slowly filled with water—the only evidence he'd been real.

Mist descended from the sky, then Thor. A panting Thjalfi ran to stand on the beach.

Eyes streaming, Shannon sobbed and clutched the sand, the very spot where he'd been. He left her. Oh, gods. He left her. After everything... gods, he left her. Her heart shattered, pain spiking to every part of her body.

Elatha lifted her gently into his arms, and she cried harder, burrowing her face into his chest and the fresh rain scent that was familiar.

He left her. How? How could he leave her? She'd fought so hard to get back to him, gave everything to get back to him.

"What the hell is your brother playing at? Shannon came within a shell's width of killing herself trying to find him, to return to him, and he takes one look at her and bails? What kind of jellyfish does that?" Elatha shouted.

Thor shouted back, their words piling on top of each other's in a cacophony that pierced the singular thought repeating over and over in her mind—he left her.

Pushing away from Elatha, Shannon screamed, *"Shut up! Everyone shut up!"* She stood, shaking, breath heaving. "He left me," she whispered into the silence, blinking at them.

"Shannon?" Mist's tone was careful as she approached and reached a hand out.

Tears poured in such a constant stream Shannon could barely see her friend through the blurry mess. "Yeah?" she managed.

"Why do you have no clothes, honey?"

Mist's gentle, calm contrast to the snarling male voices was a balm to the pain and confusion of Shannon's thoughts. With a shrug, Shannon called fighting leathers and armour into place. "Better to recharge," she said wetly, as another sob caught in her throat. "It was the only way for Elatha to save me, to save my son."

Mist pulled Shannon into her arms and held her as Shannon cried.

"He left me. How did he expect me to survive?" Shannon laid her head on her friend's shoulder. "Why did he leave me? Did he really think I had a choice?"

"Oh honey, I don't know. Men are fools?"

A weepy laugh turned into another sob.

Thor approached and laid a light hand on her back. "Little sister, let me take you home."

The quiet tone, so unlike his usual boisterous self, had Shannon releasing her best friend and turning to hug Thor as she nodded agreement.

"Wait." Shannon pulled out of his arms.

Looking around, she found Elatha scowling and scuffing a foot into the sand. She cradled his cheek with her palm, the muscle flexing as he clenched and unclenched his jaw.

"Loki doesn't deserve you," Elatha grumbled.

Despite the despair weighing her down, she smiled. "And yet, he's my soulmate. I love him."

Silver eyes turned serious. "If Loki doesn't return, you are going to need help. If you want me, I will be there in any way you ask me to be. I love you, Shannon."

Her vision blurred with the renewed salty stream, and Shannon fought to find her voice through the lump in her throat. "Thank you, Elatha. I care about you, too. If it wasn't for you, I wouldn't be going home."

Elatha scowled at Thor. "Take her to your healers immediately. If they can't help her with her energy needs, saltwater isn't enough. It isn't enough, Thor. If Loki doesn't show up, come get me. Don't delay! Don't let her use any energy. None. Talk to your healers. You'll understand." Elatha held Thor's gaze until Thor nodded his agreement, even though he frowned.

Shannon wasn't in the mood to enlighten him. Not now. Not with her heart aching.

Elatha pressed a gentle kiss to her lips. "I will stay just offshore, off the coast closest to the Bifrost site so I can be in Asgard within a few hours if you need me, until I hear you've had your son safely." He pinned Thor with narrowed eyes. "You'll send word to me?"

Again, Thor's brow furrowed, but he agreed

Elatha kissed her again, this time thoroughly. "Although I've fulfilled my vow, I believe I will see you again, Shannon. You need time to work things out with your soulmate. When you do, I will be here."

He released her, and she almost grabbed him back, but fought the instinct. Gods, she was so messed up.

He stepped back and turned to Thor. "I'll swim to where I said I'll be. It will be faster for me. Be sure to tell your brother that he's a sponge-brained broken shell and doesn't deserve her, but I'll always respect her choice."

Without a single glance backwards, Elatha strode into the waves.

Shannon sobbed as he disappeared under the water, leaving her as well. They'd both left her. Fragments of her heart went with the Fomorian prince who'd saved her and her son. She hid her face in Thor's powerful arms, soaking his chest with her tears. Awkwardly, he rubbed and patted her back.

"Little sister, you clearly have some interesting tales to tell. In the meantime, let's do as the Atlantean suggested and get you home to the healers, okay?" Thor's voice was gentle, filled with concern.

Not raising her face, she nodded into his chest. He scooped her up, cradling her to his wide body as they rose from the ground.

It was different flying when she wasn't in control. But she trusted Thor. He'd cut off his arm before he'd hurt her. She wasn't worried about falling. In some ways, it was freeing, not having to be the one to concentrate. Instead, she tried not to think about how Loki had abandoned her. He hadn't waited for any explanation, just condemned her and teleported away.

Mist said it had taken a full day to get to where she was, but it seemed only hours to reach the plains. As they cleared the cloaking mists, the bond with Loki opened. Immediately, Shannon blocked it. After the way he'd left her, there was no way she was ready to deal with him or his emotions. Her soul ached, pain spiking whenever her thoughts turned to him. Would he have rather she'd died? That their son had died?

Kara and Roskva were happy to see her, but she just wanted to go home. Worn out, emotionally and physically, Shannon didn't have it in her to be social, to return their enthusiasm. Her headache had reappeared during the flight, gouging into her brain with renewed glee.

Unable to do more than nod at their words of relief, Shannon murmured to Thor, "Can we please go home?"

"Of course," Thor said. "Heimdall? Open the Bifrost."

The familiar lights swirled around them. Thor kept her tight against his body, keeping her from being jarred by the buffeting wind of the wormhole. Still, pain wracked every part of her, right down to her bones, and she gritted her teeth.

Focused on breathing, on keeping her screams inside, she simply blinked at Heimdall's greeting when the lights dissipated.

"I'm taking her directly to Healer Moja," Thor told the others.

They flew to the palace instead of walking, landing in the garden courtyard nearest to the Healers' wing—the same courtyard Shannon had first sat and talked with Frigga after learning she wasn't human, that she was pregnant... gods, fourteen, no fifteen weeks ago. How was it less than four months? With all that had happened since? Shannon had aged decades, not months, and her body ached to match the mental exhaustion.

Within a few minutes, Thor burst through the archway into the Healers' Hall and called for Healer Moja.

The dark-haired, round-faced woman emerged from a treatment room and gasped when she saw Shannon. "Put her in here, Thor." Moja gestured to a sensor bed in the nearest alcove as she beckoned them inside.

Thor laid Shannon down, and the green glow snapped on.

Quickly, Moja had an image of Shannon's son on the holographic screen. Moja smiled, her kind brown eyes meeting Shannon's. "He's fifty-eight centimetres in length and two-point-seven kilograms now. He's exactly where I would expect him to be at thirty-five-and-a-half weeks, given his father's Jotun heritage. Has he been kicking a lot? He's running out of room in there, but he won't get any taller, just heavier."

Shannon bit her lip, then grinned when her son moved. A swell of relief surged through her body. "Yes, he gets quite active." At least now that Elatha had saved them, had given them the energy they needed to survive. "Is my son really okay? There were times when he wasn't so"—her voice broke—"active."

"He's beautiful, Shannon. I can't wait to hold him." Thor smiled as he took her hand and gave a gentle squeeze before releasing her fingers.

"He's developing as expected, responding to external stimuli." Moja studied the screen, then frowned. "His energy readings *are* on the low side. That's concerning."

Shannon swallowed, grin faltering as her heart pounded. She clenched the sides of the bed, eying the holographic display.

Moja changed some readouts on the side panel and sucked in a harsh breath. "My dear, you need more energy. Now. A *lot* more. You aren't getting nearly enough, and your son is taking it all. You are far too young in terms of your immortality to be this" —she waved a hand at the screen—"depleted. Resting and eating don't regenerate enough yet for you compared with an older immortal." She pinned Shannon with a look. "You need to do everything you can to recharge your goddess energies and put some much needed mass back onto your frame. Did you figure out what you are a goddess of?"

Shannon cleared her throat. "Um, yes. Forests, seas, and fertility."

"Fertility," Moja snorted, turning her gaze back to the data and frowning. "Of course. I should have guessed, given how rare it is for an immortal to become pregnant at such a young age. Do you know why that is?"

"Because we don't have enough energy reserves and can't produce enough naturally for the baby and mother to survive the pregnancy?" Shannon guessed, based on what she'd deduced from her experience.

"Exactly. If you were a regular immortal with no goddess powers, we would have had to terminate the pregnancy to save your life. I didn't want to worry you at your last check-up. Although it was a strain on your body, you seemed to be keeping up with the energy demands within acceptable limits." Moja met Shannon's gaze. "I need to be blunt. That isn't the case right now, Shannon."

Thor sucked in a harsh breath. "What are you saying, Healer Moja?"

"I'm saying that if Shannon doesn't get considerably more energy every single day, immediately, as in *right now*, today, we'll need to deliver the baby early to save her life and hope the child survives." Her voice was firm, but not without care.

Shannon winced, but wasn't surprised. Moja's words simply reinforced what Shannon had already worked out for herself. Thor took her hand gently in his large grip, his blue eyes sparking with emotion in their depths, as they listened to Healer Moja continue her assessment.

"I'd like to get at least another week or two if we can. It would let your child's lungs fully develop to give him the best chance at survival, but you are well below acceptable energy levels." She turned to Thor. "Shannon is in danger of slipping into a coma at any moment. If she does, she will not recover unless we take the baby."

"Thank you for your honesty, Healer Moja." Shannon forced the words past the lump of emotion squeezing her throat. "I've been doing better the last few days, but it doesn't make up for the weeks of energy deficit when I was held by the dwarves. They drained my energy. Will that have a lasting effect on my son or me if I can get enough energy now?"

Moja moved to a wall unit, pressed several buttons and extracted a silver tube. "If you can get enough energy and hold off at least another three weeks before giving birth, both of you should fully recover. That's a big if. The likelihood of you making it the four-and-a-half weeks to full term is not good at this point. Unless you are doing what you need to get energy, I want you on full bed rest. High nutrient meals with one of Idun's apples at every meal and absolutely *no* use of your powers. None, Princess. I mean that. You absolutely can't afford the additional drain," Moja insisted as she brought the silver tube over and pressed it to Shannon's neck with a slight hiss and pinch.

"I'll ensure she rests." Thor's face was stark with worry and something else as he met Shannon's gaze.

She shrank, wrapping her arms around herself. Was he angry? With her? Great. Everyone hated her.

Healer Moja frowned, almost appearing puzzled when Shannon tore her eyes from Thor and met the healer's gaze, like the woman wanted to ask something, but thought better of it. "I will come to you with a portable scanner. Given your current situation, I'll be monitoring you at least twice daily and giving you supplement injections." Moja wiggled the silver tube for emphasis, then switched off the holographic display and the green glow disappeared. "No getting out of bed, even to come here."

Shannon agreed and quietly thanked the healer.

Thor lifted Shannon from the bed and carried her to the chambers she shared with Loki.

Her heart began to pound a frantic, uneven rhythm the closer they got to Loki's door. Heat pricked her eyes. She couldn't go in there. What if he was inside? He didn't want her. Shit, he'd abandoned her. Condemned her and abandoned her. She couldn't face more of that. No, no way. And even if he wasn't... she couldn't be there, surrounded by his things, their things. It was a dagger to her already fractured heart. After surviving her capture, the dwarves, her escape, having to make the choices she did? How was she supposed to deal with more? Panic blazed through her veins. How much more could she take?

Thor opened the heavy oak-and-blacksteel door, and she started to struggle, to get out of his hold. "No! I don't want to be in here, Thor. He abandoned me. He took one look, accused me, and left. I can't be in here! What if he's in here? I don't want to see him. Don't make me. Please. It hurts too much. Please! Please take me somewhere else? Anywhere else?" Tears streamed down her face as she trembled, not strong enough to escape his firm grip.

Lines furrowed his brow as Thor searched her expression, holding her tighter to his chest. "I—I..." He exhaled heavily. "Okay."

He carried her to a set of rooms across the hall. "Is this acceptable?" His tone was cautious, unusually quiet for him.

It was the same layout as Loki's chambers, but in soothing tones of blue and silver. She swiped the moisture from her eyes, then let out a breath she hadn't realized she'd been holding at the sight of the other rooms.

"Yes, this is fine. Thank you."

With gentle movements, Thor laid her on the bed, helping her into the covers. She'd already removed her armour for the scan and was in a simple long tunic and pants. After tucking her in, he sat on the edge.

Thor was quiet for a few minutes, staring down at his hands in his lap. Was he trying to figure out what to say? He had to have questions. Of course he did. She would have.

"The Atlantean knew, didn't he? That's why he insisted I take you straight to the healers."

Shannon wrapped her arms around her belly, shifting further down in the bed. She wanted to burrow into the bed, to hide. Gods, she couldn't look at him, to see the condemnation in his eyes. It took her a few minutes of nervous swallowing, her spit dried to non-existent, to raise the courage to answer. Even then, she barely managed more than a whisper. "Yes, Elatha knew. As a fertility goddess, my energy is recharged the same way it is for pregnant women of his race. Besides the skewed male sex ratio of their people, the other main reason their women have multiple consorts is so the men can provide the energy the woman needs to make it through pregnancy."

"But you are a goddess of not just fertility, but also seas and forests." When she finally met his gaze, his eyes held a question he wasn't saying out loud.

Yes, she'd tried every other way before she screwed Elatha's brains out.

Her heart squeezed. She wasn't being fair to Thor. His expression wasn't judgmental. In fact, his gaze held an understanding. It seemed he was trying to find out what she'd endured with careful consideration of her feelings. It was her own pain at being forced into choices she wouldn't have otherwise made that had her squirming. Just because she knew she needed to forgive herself and accept what she couldn't change didn't make it any easier to actually accomplish.

"Yes, I am, and when the Wild Hunt was tracking us, I would have died if Elatha hadn't saved me by having sex with me. I tried to maintain my energy from only what I could get from the sea, from resting, from food... everything I could do to not have to resort to my fertility powers and not feel like I'd betrayed Loki. It wasn't enough. The saltwater couldn't provide enough energy fast enough. There weren't any forests available nearby to try as an alternative." Her fingers twisted in the blankets. While true, it didn't explain the attraction between her and Elatha. Or the way she felt for him now. She didn't have an answer to that. But he'd done too much for her to deny it.

Thor took her hand, squeezing it with gentle pressure, before releasing it.

"Maybe if the dwarves hadn't been taking my blood and energy for a month, I would have been able to survive with just the sea. But it wasn't an option after what I'd been through." Exhaustion pulled at her, dragging at her consciousness even as she forced the words out to help Thor understand.

His lips flattened as his blue eyes snapped with lightning. "Those dwarves are dead. Loki killed them, and we destroyed all the mead we found. He killed the giant that taught the dwarves how to make it."

A weight lifted off her chest. "Good. I'll admit it makes me feel better to know they aren't still out there."

Thor sighed. "Loki loves you and will come around. He wouldn't want you to risk yourself or your child, Shannon. I'm not saying it's easy, but he would have wanted you to make the choice you did to live. But I think it was a shock for him to see you like that, to find you naked in the arms of another."

Tears escaped to trail down her cheeks as she recalled Loki's expression before he disappeared. "Elatha realized that the more skin contact I had with the sea, the greater the energy I absorbed, so even when we weren't recharging me *that* way, being naked in the water helped. The Wild Hunt found us again and attacked two days before you discovered us. We escaped, but I burned too much energy to travel any real distance."

Thor winced and hung his head, fingers lacing together behind his neck. "I'm sorry, Shannon. We had Llew and Crom, the two Unseelie that took you, in our dungeon. They had help from other dark elves and fled. They never should have escaped to attack you again. I'm so sorry I failed you."

Squeezing his leg to get his attention, she waited until he met her gaze.

"You didn't fail me, Thor. You found me and got me home. Take it from me, as it's a hard lesson I've learned recently. There is only so much you can control. You made the best decisions you could at the time, with what was available to you."

"Like the difficult choices you've had to make? I know you love Loki. I've seen how well matched you two are. And I can only imagine how traumatic this entire ordeal was for you. Just as I can see that you are still struggling. I am glad you made the decisions you did and survived, Shannon. This family would be greatly lessened without you."

The understanding in his eyes made the tears flow faster, drenching her shirt. How could she deserve his compassion, when she'd enjoyed everything she and Elatha had done? More than enjoyed. Craved it. Begged for it. And part of her wanted him even now. Part of her cared for him, perhaps even loved him. If she hadn't, then maybe she wouldn't feel so guilty. How could she love two men? Gods, but she hated these conflicted feelings.

A quiet knock sounded.

Thor rose to answer the door. A few murmured words later, he left, and Frigga entered. She sat where Thor had been only moments before.

Her kind emerald eyes looked Shannon over as Shannon's hands rose to her face. How could Shannon face her, Loki's mother?

"Oh daughter, you've had such a rough go of it." Frigga pulled Shannon into her loving embrace.

Shannon burrowed into her, into her warm apple-and-cinnamon scent, and cried harder.

One hand tenderly stroked Shannon's hair while she also rubbed Shannon's back. They sat there, with her comforting Shannon, until the sobs finally died down. Not letting go, Frigga continued to gently rock Shannon.

Finally, Shannon pulled away and looked up at Frigga with a tear-stained face.

Frigga gave her a sad smile, reaching up to wipe the tears away. "I'm so, so sorry, Shannon. So incredibly sorry. I knew the risks of your pregnancy and didn't warn you. This is my fault. I should have prepared you better, as I can see you are beating yourself up with guilt." Her voice was full of regret.

"How could you have prepared me for that? No one could have," Shannon said through her hiccupped breaths.

"That is not true, child. Have you forgotten I am a fertility goddess and soulbound? If anyone knows, it's I."

Shannon frowned. What did Frigga mean?

"Shannon, I was a two-thousand-year old goddess when I was pregnant with Thor. Even with all those years, I couldn't maintain my energy during my pregnancy with my other goddess powers. I needed the energy from sex, especially as I reached the third trimester."

Shannon stared at Frigga and blinked. It wasn't just that Shannon was young?

Frigga brushed a long black curl back from her cheek, tucking it behind her ear as she nodded. "Yes, I did. I'm going to be blunt since there are things you need to hear and understand." Her green eyes with their long dark lashes so like her son's pinned Shannon in place. "I needed sex multiple time a day in the third trimester, just to complete my day. That was without using my powers to escape and survive, or after a month of being drained of energy."

Shannon's mouth fell open. Frigga really was being blunt.

"And let me tell you another thing, my daughter. Thor, for all his powers, is not as powerful as your child will be with the melding of yours and Loki's powers. Your child requires even more energy during your pregnancy than Thor did during mine."

Shannon thought about that for a few minutes. "So what are you saying?"

"Both Healer Moja and I are thanking the Norns that you survived. We owe Prince Elatha an enormous debt of gratitude for saving you and your son's life. That there is *no way* you would have survived without having sex with him, and frankly, even though I've never met him, I absolutely love him for saving you. If I could adopt him right now, I would."

Shannon swallowed, then whispered, "So you are saying I made the right choice?"

"No, Shannon. I'm saying you made the *only* choice. It wasn't even a choice, to be honest."

Pain speared her chest like an ache that would never heal. "But Loki is my soulmate."

"Yes, he is, which is why it is a Norns-blessed miracle that Elatha could save you."

She stared at Frigga, then shook her head. "I don't—I don't understand. Wouldn't sex with anyone give me energy?"

Frigga smiled softly. "Is that what worries you? That you are a cheater and a betrayer?"

Shannon nodded, tears spilling in hot trails.

Frigga hugged her, then pulled back to look into Shannon's eyes. She gently wiped Shannon's cheeks. "I know you don't fully grasp what the soulmate bond means yet, but you shouldn't have been able to enjoy having sex with anyone else. Let me ask you this. Since binding with Loki, and except for Elatha, have you had any sexual interest, even mildly, in any other male?"

Shannon considered the question, but knew the answer instantly. "No, not even a little."

"Exactly. When you soulbond so tightly to another, it isn't possible to be attracted to anyone else. Yet, in order for the energy transfer to happen with your fertility goddess powers, you absolutely must be interested and aroused. One of you must reach completion and the transmission is most effective if you both do with physical contact. The greater the contact, or the more powerful the orgasm, the greater the energy transfer. If you hadn't enjoyed it, it would not have worked. That you could with Elatha, I can't yet explain." She shook her head, a frown marring her smooth forehead, before she turned back to meet Shannon's gaze. "But he has to be *very* special to you in some way, perhaps even the same way Loki is to you. Do *not* take that lightly. Don't dismiss your connection to him just because we don't yet understand how or why it works."

"So you are saying I'm not going to be suddenly lusting after random men?" After the way her lack of knowledge had bitten her in the ass so many times already, Shannon wanted to be sure she understood what Frigga meant.

Frigga grinned, eyes twinkling. "No. You aren't a succubus, Shannon. Your passions are reserved for two very specific men."

With a long sigh, some of the tension in Shannon's muscles relaxed. She hadn't realized how much of a fear that had become for her. Given the overwhelming intensity of arousal with Elatha, she'd been scared she would be out of control.

"Try to rest, sweetheart. I'll have food brought to you and be back to check in on you and answer any questions you think of." Frigga pressed a soft kiss to Shannon's forehead.

Sinking down in the bed, Shannon let her exhaustion pull her under.

Chapter 31

WAITING IN THE WINGS

Elatha's heart shattered as he left Shannon, her sobs chasing him into the waves and the water stealing the tears from his eyes. How could he leave her like her fucking soulmate had? Blasted barnacles, he couldn't believe Loki had bailed on her like that. But Elatha had to, hadn't he? He'd fulfilled his vow. She had Thor to take her to Asgard's healers. Shells, he'd offered to go, to be there if she needed him... or wanted him.

Still, with every length he swam away from her pain grew in his chest. He fought not to look back, but gave in and turned in time to spot Thor fly toward the plains with Shannon in his arms. Elatha rubbed a fist against his aching chest, watching until they disappeared, then he dove deep and powered through the depths towards the shoreline nearest the Summer Realm.

As he swam, images of Shannon flashed through his mind—her smile, her eyes glazed with passion or snapping with anger, the flush of her cheeks and expression as she climaxed, the peace on her face as she slept, and the anguish when he'd left. Had he made a mistake? Should he have insisted on going with her to Asgard? What if she fell unconscious on the way?

No, he'd given her a boost just before the Asgardians had arrived. Surely it would be enough to get her to the healers. Wouldn't it?

And she had her consort... if the sponge-brained sea cucumber wised up and returned to her. How could Loki have left her like that? Hadn't he seen how frail she was? Elatha hadn't known how she appeared before she'd gotten pregnant, but given how much thinner she'd become even in the twenty days he'd been privileged to know her and the dark circles that had deepened under her eyes, how could Loki not? It had to be a dramatic change. Hasn't she said it had been, what, more than a month she'd been held prisoner with those fucking dwarves draining her energy? His stomach twisted, and he increased his speed.

If Thor returned for him, he had to be there.

Instead of taking breaks, Elatha pushed through, swimming hard all day. By evening, he'd reached the far shore of the bay and the closest access to where the Asgardian Bifrost might bring news to him. He staggered up the sand and sank onto a log, pulling out a seaweed roll.

Would Thor keep his word and return?

Elatha surveyed his surroundings. This close to the Summer Realm, its light penetrated further, brightening the gloom of the Winter Realm so he could make out the dark trunks of trees with their evergreen needles covering a mountainside where the mists swirled and parted briefly. A chill breeze blew off the land towards the ocean. He didn't trust that relentless Wild Hunt wouldn't attack again, but this time, he could retreat into the water and fight them on his terms, not theirs.

As he ate the roll, he recalled Shannon's enjoyment in the food he'd prepared. The taste turned to sand in his mouth. How was she? Were the healers able to help her? Had Loki returned to her?

A sound reached him, and he sprang to his feet, spinning to search the land and skies.

Was it the Wild Hunt?

A speck in the sky grew in size, then resolved into Thor. Within a minute, the Asgardian had arrived and thumped down in front of Elatha.

"Does Shannon need me? How is she?" Elatha blurted, stepping towards him. "Has Loki—"

Thor raised a hand. "She's not worse, but she is critical. You knew that though, didn't you? That's why you wanted me to take her to the healers immediately?" Thor's narrowed gaze pinned Elatha in place.

Elatha dragged a hand through his hair. "Yes. In the three weeks she was with me, she grew weaker and weaker, losing mass no matter how much saltwater I or she soaked herself in, how much food I gave her, or how much rest she got. You had to have seen how thin she is now. Shells, it was terrifying seeing her waste away in front of me."

A muscle ticked in Thor's jaw, and he clenched his fists. "Yes. I almost didn't recognize her. She was shockingly light when I carried her, barely heavier than one of my children."

Elatha locked his fingers behind his neck, pacing. "You can't let her use her powers or expend any energy without recharging." He halted, meeting Thor's blue gaze. "She has to have sex. Nothing else works fast enough to keep up to her energy needs."

Thor's eyes narrowed. "Did you take advantage of her?"

Elatha dropped his hands, stiffening, vibrating with a rage that filled his entire body. He locked his jaw, forcing himself to not yell at the Asgardian. He drew air in through his nose, taking several heaving breaths before he trusted himself to answer. The man was just defending Shannon, and he had to respect that. Even if he wanted to break the arrogant sea urchin's nose.

"No, I did *not*. She stopped breathing. Her heart stopped. She *died*, Thor. Do you understand that? Fucking *died*," Elatha finally bit out.

Thor took a step back, face paling as his eyes widened.

"If we hadn't realized she was like the pregnant women of my race, that beautiful, complex goddess would have been a corpse by the time you'd found her. Her and her son, both. Her baby had stopped moving, stopped kicking for *days* until we found a way to save her." Elatha's voice rose, tears welling, and he fought to stay calm. "Where the fuck were you? Where was her damn consort?"

Thor swallowed. "We searched constantly from the moment she was taken."

Elatha swiped at his wet cheeks. "And yet Loki fucking abandoned her? Accused her of cheating on him, like that was the most important thing right then when she was barely surviving? When her life and her son's life were hanging by a fucking eelgrass? Why? His fucking ego? Because she'd done what she had to and accepted me as a second mate so she and her son, Loki's son, would live? What kind of prudish kraken shit is that, Thor? Are Asgardians really that backwards? Would Loki rather she be dead?" His voice cracked, breaking as he continued, "Because she was. For several minutes while I frantically breathed for her, pushing my air into her lungs, and pounding on her chest. Until I could revive her to yes, bring her to orgasm and give her whatever energy I could. She was *dead*."

Thor opened his mouth, swallowed, and closed it again. "I can't..." He shook his head and ran a shaking hand through his red hair. "I can't excuse what Loki did. I agree. He shouldn't have abandoned her."

"So I ask you again, Thor. Has Loki returned to her? She needs energy. Not tomorrow. *Today*. Fighting the Wild Hunt twice took every drop from her. It can't wait," Elatha said, firming up his voice.

Thor winced, looking away, before meeting Elatha's gaze again. "I'm sorry. Llew and Crom will die when we catch up with them."

"What about *Shannon*? She is my priority, Thor. Fighting them cost her energy she didn't have to spare," Elatha insisted. "You being sorry won't keep her alive."

"I will ensure Loki returns to her tonight, but if he doesn't, I'll come get you," Thor promised, putting his hand on Elatha's shoulder for a moment. "Thank you. Thank you for saving my sister and nephew. I can see how much she means to you. I'm sorry I implied—"

"As long as you promise Shannon will be taken care of, it's forgotten," Elatha interrupted. "I love her. I'll do anything for her. Anything, Thor."

Thor nodded and held out his arm.

Elatha clasped his forearm.

"Either way, I'll return once the baby is born to tell you, if I don't come for you sooner. The healer is hoping Shannon can carry for another couple of weeks, but we'll see. Moja won't risk Shannon. She'll deliver the baby sooner if she has to."

Elatha let out a shaking breath. "Okay. I'll be here."

Thor released Elatha's forearm, stepped back and launched into the sky. Within a minute, he was gone, and Elatha's knees weakened. He sank onto a nearby log, hands clenched in his hair as he bowed his head. Shannon would be okay. She had to be.

Chapter 32

HIDING IN DREAMS

L oki bailed.

No way to put it nicely.

He freaked out and escaped.

He didn't remember choosing to teleport away. His thoughts had descended into a chaotic fog of fury, pain, and confusion, torn between wanting to bloody the Atlantean that had dared put his hands on Shannon and screaming at her for being a faithless slut. How could she throw away the blessing of the Norns? Did she even realize how rare soulmates were?

Not even sure where he was, he blindly walked. Time lost all meaning as he stumbled through brambles, tripped on rocks, and fell into a creek. The water shocked him enough that he shifted to a raven and flew, but his destination was unclear.

After drifting on the breezes for hours, he found himself gazing down at the treaty plains. Desolate and empty, they reflected his mood perfectly. Dropping to the ground, he shifted back to humanoid and landed.

There was no sign of anyone. Fog crept along the wind-swept grasses at the edges, like the ominous draugar of Niflheim waiting to suck him into the eternity of their shapeless, formless depths. A walking death.

"Heimdall, please open the Bifrost." Loki's voice was harsh in his ears.

The swirling rainbow lights caught him and deposited him on the stone of the golden chamber. Its light seemed dimmer, lacking its usual sparkle. He caught his balance more by instinct than any actual intended thought.

"Prince Loki, welcome back." Heimdall's deep greeting came from his left.

Loki nodded without really looking at Asgard's gatekeeper. Instead, he shifted back to a raven and flew out the arching doorway and over the lake. Soaring on the familiar warm winds, Loki took his time heading to the mountains, to his cabin. It was where he retreated when he needed time alone, was hurting, or otherwise not wanting to be near others. Where he'd recovered from the loss of love before.

It was his secluded refuge where no one would bother him.

After landing in the meadow, Loki shifted and stumbled towards his cabin nestled in the tall fir trees. Someone thumped to the ground behind him, hard.

Not needing to turn, he knew who it was. "I can't talk right now, Thor." Barely audible, his voice came out raspy and strained.

"That's okay, brother. You just need to listen because *this isn't about you.*" Thor's tone reverberated with a thundering anger.

Mid-step, Loki halted as fresh betrayal shattered his numbness. His own brother? How would he feel if his soulmate... Loki couldn't finish the thought. It was too painful to say again, even in his head.

Loki spun, fists clenched with his fury rising. How dare he—

"*She. Is. Dying,*" Thor boomed, each word bitten off sharply with a crack splitting the air. "In truth, she *did die,* and he saved her. He saved her. He saved her son. *Your* son."

Everything stopped.

No wind.

No birds.

No breath in his body.

Loki sucked in a shocked gasp.

The world came back in a rush of confusing sounds, smells, and sights that all blurred together.

"What?" It came out as a whisper. A visceral denial of what he'd thought he'd heard. Thor couldn't have said that.

"Shannon is dying, you fool! Get your head out of your ass and use that massive intelligence of yours," Thor snarled.

"I don't understand. How can she be dying?" It made no sense. Surely, Thor hadn't said she'd died. That couldn't be right.

No.

She'd been fine.

Pain lanced through him at the vision of her naked in that Atlantean's arms. Kissing him. Blushing when caught in the midst of her infidelity.

No.

She'd been fine.

No wounds. No blood.

"You should understand this better than I, *Master Mage*! I didn't study the ins and outs of immortal energetics, conservation of energy, and all that the way you did. That's *your* expertise," Thor scoffed as his hands gesticulated wildly. "Or at least, it's *supposed* to be."

What? Loki still didn't understand. He stalked back to his brother and shook Thor to stop his ranting. "Thor! Stop insulting me and just explain! What do you mean?"

Thor stopped talking abruptly, crossed his arms, and glared at Loki. Lightning flashed in the depths of his eyes, discharging off his body and hitting the surroundings, including his brother. "Shannon is a baby immortal with minimal ability to regenerate energy, except at a baby's rate. You got her pregnant with your energy-sucking offspring. The dwarves spent a month sucking the life's energy out of her at the same time your child was."

"I know all that, Thor! Get to the fucking point!" Heat flushed through Loki's body, fury at the way his brother was talking like him was a Norns-cursed idiot. And bloody fucking hell, Thor's fucking lightning was pricking Loki's skin and his fucking temper.

Thor shook his head with a pitying smirk twisting his expression. "No forests in Nidavellir. The sea only provides a small boost. Maybe a little more with as much skin contact as possible."

"Okay. So? *What is your fucking point?*" Loki was ready to tear his hair out, yanking at it in frustration as he shoved his brother and his fucking sparking body away from him.

"Did you know Mother, an immortal of two thousand, needed to have sex with Father *multiple* times a day in her last trimester just to maintain her energy when she was carrying me, a decidedly *less* energy-consuming offspring than your giant-wielding intensive magic-using ass? Only her fertility goddess powers could provide the energy she needed. *Do the fucking math, Loki!* Did you even bother to actually *look* at Shannon? She's a fucking shadow of herself! I was scared I'd break her bloody bones just carrying her."

Thor flung up his hands, stomped around the clearing, swearing and cussing Loki's heritage, his intelligence, his choices, and even his boots. His boots?

As Loki watched his brother, his mind spun, trying to make sense of it all. It wasn't until he forced himself to bring up the memory of her, gritting his teeth against seeing her naked in that damn man's arms, that the pieces finally clicked into place.

Loki staggered. Oh, Norns. Thor was right. She'd lost a dangerous amount of mass even since he'd seen how slender she was in the dwarves' memories. Her face and limbs were practically skeletal, eyes sunken and lost as she'd stared at him, the blush highlighting her far-too-sharp cheekbones.

His chest tightened and bile burned at the back of his throat.

He deserved every single one of Thor's insults and more. How? How could he have forgotten? He'd known how frail she was after the dwarves. He'd already been worried about her energy levels. Fuck. And he'd seen the strain she was under before her kidnapping. Loki knew, *knew*, she'd struggled to get enough energy when he'd spent too much time on Midgard, too self-absorbed with his music and acting to make sure he was taking care of her needs.

Loki's knees buckled.

She'd gone weeks. Weeks with no way to recharge except saltwater, rest, and food. And that was after the dwarves had drained her. Helplessly, his mind raced through the energetic calculations with growing horror. No matter which way he did the math, she should be dead. Several times over. Had Thor really said—

"She died?" Loki whispered, his voice cracking.

"Yes," Thor snarled.

That she wasn't... Yggdrasil's roots, it was a miracle. A truly undeniable miracle.

"Our child... our child still lives?" Shaking, he hardly dared ask the question as bile climbed his throat.

Thor glared and snarled, "Yes, you undeserving boneheaded selfish git."

Fuck, he should be kissing Elatha's boots for saving her, for saving their son.

The thought of the handsome Atlantean twisted Loki's gut, and he shied away from thinking too much about those details. Elatha kept her alive. Loki had to keep remembering that. Elatha kept her and her baby alive.

Shame swamped him as he realized now what he'd been seeing when he'd found her. Elatha had been holding her naked in the sea, letting her rest and absorb energy. Mid-kiss or not, Loki should have thanked the Atlantean, not responded like a jealous little boy with his favourite toy taken away.

Even if they'd been mid-coitus, it didn't matter. *Fuck.* Elatha brought her back, revived her, and kept her alive. Loki should have thanked him. Norns, Loki should have grabbed her in his arms. Not fucking bailed on her like an immature asshole who didn't know better and couldn't do basic fucking energetic calculations a bloody apprentice mage learned.

Why had he not truly considered how desperate Shannon's need would be? For fuck's sake, it wasn't like he hadn't helped destroy that disgusting equipment the dwarves had used on her. He'd known they were draining her energy. What the bloody hell did he think would happen to her?

She'd died.

He shuddered, his heart thudding.

She'd died, and he hadn't been there, hadn't saved her. Instead, he'd bailed on her.

He tore at his hair.

"Getting it now, are we? Bloody great wanking fool. You are supposed to be the brilliant son. Some fucking genius." Thor wasn't holding back on his opinion.

Bor's balls, Loki didn't blame him in the slightest. "Where is she?"

If Thor was right, Loki didn't have time to castigate himself. He needed to take care of Shannon. Now. She had to be on the threshold, critical. That she wasn't... fuck, he owed that Atlantean a debt he'd *never* be able to repay.

"I put her in the suit of rooms across from yours. She panicked at the thought of being in your rooms. You fucking broke her when you accused her, then rejected her, after all she's been through to survive. You made her feel guilty for surviving, you fucking asswipe. If you weren't her soulmate and she needed you to keep surviving, I'd keep you far, far away from her so you couldn't hurt her again. Brother or not, I kind of hate you right now, Loki."

Thor's words struck home, exactly as he'd intended. Loki felt every blow. He deserved it.

"You're right. I am an asshole. I hate myself, too."

"You don't deserve her."

"No, I definitely don't deserve her."

Thor glared, but didn't say more since Loki was agreeing with him. With his arms crossed over his chest, he waited.

Loki looked at him. What else did his brother wanted him to say?

Finally, Thor rolled his eyes. "Well, what are you waiting for? Go save my little sister and nephew!"

"Thank you, Thor. I don't deserve you either."

He huffed, and Loki caught a tiny twitch of Thor's lips as his brother suppressed a smile.

Too far to teleport directly to the palace, Loki teleported into the sky, shifted to a raven, and flew to the palace as fast as his wings would take him. After shifting back as he landed on his garden terrace, Loki turned invisible and teleported into her rooms.

Shannon tossed and turned, whimpering, "Stop, please stop." It tore at his soul. He crawled onto the bed, gathered her stiff body against his chest, and hummed a song she'd liked from his first Raven's Chaos album. A little frown wrinkled her nose, then she slumped, relaxing as the nightmare left her.

He exhaled and catalogued the toll the time had taken on her—Norns, over eight weeks since he'd last held her. Her cheekbones protruded and dark purple circles ringed her sunken eyes. One arm rested outside the covers, and he winced at the loss of muscle that left little flesh around her collarbone, shoulder, and wrist—the outline of bones visible the length of her limb. Even her almost skeletal hand tucked by her cheek told the tale of how desperately she'd fought to survive.

Except for her rounded belly. Even laying on her side the way she was, their baby was almost obscenely large on her dangerously diminished frame. He'd been a complete idiot to have missed her condition.

Tears pricked his eyes. Everything swam in front of him. Loki swiped the moisture away angrily. There was no time to deal with tears or his guilt. Shannon needed energy, fast.

But how? Every minute he wasted, he risked her falling into a coma and beyond his reach.

On his way back to the palace, he'd checked their bond. No surprise she'd blocked it when he'd been such a fuckwit. Shannon didn't want him sensing how she was. What could he do?

Wake her and try seducing her?

He didn't hold out much hope of that working, given the way he'd accused her then bailed. For the energy transfer to work, he needed her aroused and orgasming. Not furious and hurt.

But did he need her awake?

If they were in a dream, would she be more likely to ignore real-world issues and let herself enjoy? Even if she'd blocked their bond, his telepathy would let him into her head, to join her dream. As long as he could get her to actually climax, it shouldn't matter for the energy transfer whether she was awake and aware, or asleep and having an erotic dream. The bond and her fertility goddess powers would still carry the energy between them.

Touching his lips to her forehead in a gentle kiss, Loki let part of his consciousness sink into Shannon's mind. With the slightest use of hypnosis, he coaxed her to open the bond a bit to allow him further into her mind without needing to constantly touch her head.

Like a flower, her thoughts and feelings opened to him, and his feelings flowed to her.

Despite the temptation, Loki stayed at the surface of their connection, stayed within her dream. If she chose to share memories, he wanted her awake and aware. They weren't his to take. Norns, bad enough he was invading her dream without permission.

After removing his clothes with a thought, he pulled back the covers and carefully slid in behind Shannon so their skin-on-skin physical contact could aid the flow of energy between them. With his arm wrapped around her, he relaxed into her dream reality, finding them also in bed but in their suite of rooms.

"I missed you, Shannon," he whispered.

She sighed. "I missed you too, Loki. Sing to me some more." With the glide of her fingers, she lifted the hair from her neck, looking back in invitation.

Not slow to take the hint, he feathered kisses up and down, licking and blowing air over her sensitive neck as he murmured song lyrics to her. Goosebumps rose on her skin.

Using his teeth where he knew she liked to be bitten, Shannon gave a little breathy moan, shifting back into the curve of his body.

"You are so gorgeous, my sexy goddess. Norns, I want you," he murmured in her ear. Loki trailed his fingers over her inner wrist, circling her pulse. Shannon turned her arm to give him better access. He couldn't help smiling, relief easing the tension in his chest at her response. He continued, lightly teasing her soft, supple skin with his fingertips while he continued to seduce her neck.

Shannon pushed back her ass against his hips a little more insistently. "Loki," she complained.

He shuddered. It seemed like forever since he'd had her in his arms. Yggdrasil's roots, but he'd had missed her.

Trailing over her collarbone, Loki kissed the dip, despite knowing the faint shallowness was a dream illusion. It was her mental memory of her body. Her physical state was so much more dire, but he blocked those negative thoughts from travelling into her dream as he let his fingertips glide to the curve of her breasts—breasts that lacked her current pregnancy fullness. He forced his mind to ignore the disconnect. This was her dream, and he wouldn't shatter it. She needed energy.

She stirred restlessly as he teased. He knew what she wanted. He sensed it every time he neared those sensitive nipples that had tightened into taut, proud peaks.

"Do you want me to touch you here?" Loki murmured into her ear.

"Please, Loki," Shannon begged as her chest rose towards his hand.

He plucked one peak, and she shuddered, the delight rippling through her. He plucked the other, moving back and forth between them as she moaned.

Lowering his lips, he sucked one succulent tip into his mouth, using his fingers on the other. Shannon squirmed, starting to pant. He could make her climax just like this. His goddess was so responsive.

A start, at least, to fill her needs.

As her skin grew flushed with arousal, her pulse pounded and breath rasped. Damn, he'd missed the gorgeous sight. When she came, shaking in his arms, he rejoiced.

As her orgasm started to wane, he continued to suck, bite, and tug on those responsive nipples he could never get enough of. Caressing her abdomen, no sign of their son in her dream, his love for both of them swamped his senses. He blinked back tears.

Reminded of his purpose and the frailness of his beautiful consort, Loki yanked his emotions back on track. This was about her, not him. He shifted his hand down to the pulse pounding between her thighs.

At the lightest brush of a finger, her hips jerked.

Loki smiled. It was time to play.

After rolling her onto her back, he moved between her legs, widening them to fit his shoulders. With a light, teasing touch of his fingertips up and down her outer lips, she squirmed.

"Loki," Shannon complained.

He smiled and spread her, blowing soft, cool wafts over heated flesh.

"Loki!" she whined again as he continued to tease.

Lowering his head, he sucked that aching little button into his mouth, tongue flicking fast and hard. Shannon shrieked, exploding in orgasm in seconds, but he continued to torment her sensitive flesh even as she tried to push his head away. He needed to keep her on the knife's edge so he could bring her again quickly, over and over and over, building her energy each time. He kept her orgasming until he felt the heavy, sated sensation in her limbs.

It was time to trigger additional nerves endings. The larger the orgasm with more synapses firing, the greater the energy transfer. Plus, his Shannon was a finely tuned instrument that had an incredible range for pleasure. Exploring ways to play different songs with her body, in different combinations, was always arousing. Her moans were music to his ears.

Leaving her clit to recover, Loki turned to her glistening core.

"Please, Loki. I need you."

With a shift of her body onto her side, Loki moved behind and lifted her top leg onto his. Hand tweaking her nipple, as his mouth nibbled her neck, he eased his cock inside.

"Too slow. Harder. Fuck me harder," she complained.

He grinned as he rolled his hips. Always so impatient, his goddess.

Sheer bliss. So hot, wet, and tight. Yggdrasil's roots, he'd missed being inside her. Not that he really was, but damn, the physical dream memory was so vivid.

Loki kept his slow rhythm as she moaned. Picking up the speed as he monitored how close she was to orgasm, he drove her over, groaning as she clenched tight around him. He continued to thrust as he tugged harder on a nipple, triggering another rolling wave of climax through her body. Still, he continued, fighting his release to give her more energy by waiting, building his arousal higher.

Twice more, Loki managed to hold on through the orgasmic squeezing and quivering of her hot little quim, wrapped so snugly around him.

Despite the temptation and her pleading, he kept his pace moderate, gritting his teeth when he sensed her cresting again, and knowing this time, he wouldn't be able to hold back his building release.

As she cried out his name, Loki let go, jerking uncontrollably as the warm gush filled her and a burst of energy flowed between them.

Panting, he cradled her to him, and her dream started to fragment as she shifted deeper into sleep.

Loki sighed with conflicted relief as he withdrew from her mind, and with a flick of seidhr, removed the evidence of his wet dream from her ass where he'd laid pressed against her. Her skin had taken on a healthier tone. He'd give her a few hours to descend deeper into sleep before he returned to join her dreams again. He was going to see to her pleasure and energy resources multiple times tonight if he could keep her asleep long enough.

Which is exactly what he did.

Returning to her four times in the twelve hours, Loki managed to disrupt her nightmares and keep her asleep while he boosted her energy, before she eventually woke, well-rested, and with a sparkle in her beautiful hazel eyes. Hidden as he was in the room's corner, invisible, he observed as Healer Moja checked her over, telling her she was doing better today.

With a sigh of satisfaction, Loki popped back to his rooms and slept.

Chapter 33

THE JIG IS UP

Over the next two-and-a-half weeks, Shannon slowly went stir-crazy. She was not used to this level of prolonged inactivity. Even before she transitioned to a goddess, she'd never been one to lie around for days at a time.

At least she got the occasional break from the monotony of her rooms and nightmares that wouldn't leave her alone.

Thor took her to the nearby forest each day for a morning picnic. Shannon loved spending time in the Mimameidr Woods. The energy of the massive ancient redwood trees soaked into her body like rain on parched ground. While she reclined in the peaceful surroundings, listening to the wind through the branches, the trickling of a nearby stream, and the chatter of squirrel-like rodents, she could forget everything bothering her. Thor was great company as well. He had lots of stories, and kept her amused with the tales of his exploits, detailed history of Asgard and the Nine Realms, and funny gossip from around the capital city.

The one thing they never discussed was Loki.

Shannon still hadn't seen him, and that pain was a constant torment in her chest. Every time her mind strayed to him, she tried to push the questions of his abandonment away. She'd removed the charm bracelet that had served as a physical reminder of him during her kidnapping and escape. The happy tinkling was agonizing when it was clear he wanted nothing to do with her or their child now. And in the dark of night, waking from dreams of her soulmate, she spent far too many hours sobbing over the love she'd thought they'd shared. As much as she ached to find him, to be in his arms again like the erotic dreams that haunted her, tormented her when she woke alone and forsaken, she was conflicted.

Split in two like she'd never be whole again.

That he'd rather she'd died, rather she'd let their innocent child die, than do everything to survive. Gods, after he had been the one to insist she be ruthless and do whatever it took to protect herself and their child, had made her promise—going so far as to say he wouldn't let her leave Asgard until she swore to do so.

The unfairness of it ignited a rage burning within her soul. It was a visceral betrayal so deep that if she allowed herself to dwell on it, she'd scream until the world shattered.

But another part of her cowered, gut twisted. Shame was a slick coating on her skin she'd never be able to wash away.

She'd fallen for another man.

Part of her heart ached with the loss of Elatha, missing him as deeply as she missed her soulmate. Hell, she'd spent three weeks with Elatha and barely more than twice that with Loki, especially considering Loki had been gone recording his new album, then filming his sequel for four of those weeks. Okay, so she'd spent some of those days with Elatha days unconscious, but still... she'd not spent much real time with either man.

Despite Frigga's words, Shannon couldn't reconcile the two emotions. She found herself crying over the loss of Elatha, then furious with herself for it, then crying over the loss of Loki, before raging at his callous abandonment of her and her son. When she wasn't dreaming about Loki, she was dreaming about Elatha. Or fuck, both of them together. Better than the nightmares, but torturous in their own way.

Yet, as the days dragged on, she began to wonder if perhaps she shouldn't go to Elatha once her son was born. He'd been more than accepting of being with her in whatever way she would agree, regardless of Loki's presence or not.

And how could she stay here in Asgard, knowing she'd see Loki at some point and he wouldn't be hers? The idea of disgust, of the kind of disdain she'd experienced from Trent, twisting Loki's face as he denied their child, denied her... no, she wasn't strong enough to face that on an ongoing basis, even with the support almost everyone else continued to show her.

Yeah, she'd seen the cruel glee on some of the palace elite as Thor carried her through the halls to or from the palace hangar when they went to the forest—those who'd glared when she'd been announced as Loki's soulmate and consort. No doubt they were already making moves on him. Had he taken a new lover? Accepted one of them into his bed? A spear of agony pierced her, and she wept, shuddering at the loss.

On the positive side, between the daily forest visits, the saltwater baths, rest, injections, and eating one of Idun's apples at every meal, Healer Moja was pleased with Shannon's progress, but wouldn't release her from bed rest. Moja insisted Shannon's energy deficit was still critical, even if Shannon felt she had energy to spare. Rising from her bed no longer made her joints ache, and she hadn't had a headache since the day after she'd returned to Asgard. Day by day, the dark sunken purple rings around her eyes were disappearing.

Mist and Kara came by daily, telling Shannon stories of events in the palace, capital city, or in the wider realm. Relations were still unsettled with the Sidhe after the daring prisoner escape from Asgard. The people were on edge, not knowing how the Unseelie had gotten into Asgard to free Crom and Llew. Shannon agreed with Mist and Kara. It was probably Vidar.

Still, she looked forward to their visits, and the two Valkyrie had brought her books from the palace library so she could continue to read about the creatures across the Nine Realms... and so she could research baby names in the Elven language. Since Loki didn't care to visit, she didn't feel she needed to consult him on the names she was considering.

Given her son's parents, she was expecting a little firecracker, especially with him exhibiting powers while still in the womb. It seemed fitting when she discovered little fire translated to Áedán, her current favourite choice for her son's name. Although Tàire, meaning trouble, was another name she was considering. She might be setting her son up for mischief if she chose that, though, no matter how much she liked it. She preferred Bréanainn, too, but no way would she use it as a possible first name. Really, who would call their child Prince prince? That would just be asking to get him bullied, but she did enjoy the way Áedán Bréanainn rolled off her tongue. Was it odd to use a name that meant prince as a middle name when he would be a prince?

Odin came by a couple times a week, telling Shannon how pleased he was to have her safely back home. Her child grew rambunctious every time Odin took Shannon's hand, as if the baby would bounce right out of her womb and into the All-Father's arms. Little fire, indeed. Odin didn't stay long, fortunately, as her baby's activity got somewhat exhausting and painful when he kicked a rib, but she appreciated his visits, nonetheless.

Frigga visited every afternoon to brush Shannon's hair, read stories, and teach her Asgardian board games. It made Shannon's time on bed rest bearable, and she told Frigga so when she arrived that afternoon.

Frigga frowned, head tilted, with an odd look in her green eyes. "You said I've visited you *every* day?"

The hesitancy in Frigga's voice and the way she'd emphasized *every* had Shannon puzzled. Why wouldn't Frigga know how often she'd visited?

"Yes. It's made my time stuck in bed go much quicker."

Frigga took Shannon's hand and held it, meeting her gaze. "But Shannon, I haven't come to see you every day."

"Yes, you have." Bed rest hadn't made Shannon addled. Her brain still worked just fine, thank you very much.

"No, I haven't. What am I doing on days when I haven't been teaching you these board games?"

Frigga's question made no sense. How could she not know what she was doing? How could she not know how often she'd visited?

Shannon frowned. "You know what you've been doing."

"Please just tell me." Frigga stroked Shannon's hand in a soothing manner.

"You've been brushing my hair and reading stories."

Frigga sighed with a long exhalation before smiling and shaking her head. "No, I haven't. But someone who misses you, loves you very much, and is acting like quite the coward certainly has been."

It took Shannon only seconds. Her breath froze, heart clenching. "Loki—Loki has been visiting, pretending to be you to spend time with me?" Her voice cracked at the end, the emotion thickening her throat.

"Yes, it appears my son continues to be a fool."

"But—but why? Why can't he just talk to me?" All this time, Loki let her think he didn't want her, didn't miss her, didn't forgive her. She'd spent countless hours sobbing or raging at his absence. Every day. She'd cried over him every single day. She'd begun to think she'd have to leave Asgard, believing he hated her.

Frigga snorted. "You did hear the *fool* part, right? Do you still have the bond closed between you?"

"Yes," Shannon said cautiously, even as her heart stuttered, then pounded a frantic rhythm in her chest.

"Well, there's your answer. Loki doesn't know how you feel. He's afraid and insecure, worried you won't forgive him for his response when he found you. Do remember I said *fool,* right?" Frigga's tone was both exasperated and loving at the same time.

Shannon wheezed, her breath beginning to rasp. It hadn't occurred to her that Loki might fear her response. She'd been so wrapped up in her conflicted feelings, assuming he was angry and rejecting her. Could he really be afraid she'd be the furious one? Enough to leave her in the torment of not knowing? For this long? Really?

Frigga sighed and squeezed Shannon's hand to regain her attention. "I think, in light of this revelation, we should discuss what seems to be your miraculous energy recovery. Healer Moja has been mystified as saltwater wasn't sufficient to supply even maintenance amounts of energy. Even the addition of daily trips to the forest don't explain your rapid recovery. I suspect I know the answer. Have you been having dreams?"

Shannon frowned. Of course she dreamed. Everyone dreamed. She met Frigga's gaze and with a jolt, understood what the All-Mother meant. *Those* kinds of dreams. "You are asking if I've had any erotic dreams, aren't you? Not regular dreams."

"Exactly. Have you?"

Shannon blushed. "Yes. Frequently." Hell, she dreamt of sex non-stop—with Loki, with Elatha, and oh gods, with them both. A flush of gooseflesh rippled over her skin as she recalled the ones from last night. "I thought it was simply pregnancy hormones."

Frigga pressed her lips together. "No, I think someone has been playing Morpheus in your dreams, visiting you while you sleep."

Heat flushed over Shannon in a wave, skin prickling. "Loki has been coming to my bed, seducing me? Multiple times a night? Every night?" She couldn't decide if she was shocked, aroused, or angry. It was certainly a combination of all three after the incredible revelation that he was visiting her during the day, unbeknownst to her. What did he think of her dreams about Elatha? Oh gods. Or the ones about them both, together?

Now Frigga smiled, amusement gleaming. "My, my. Loki has been busy, hasn't he? Well, that certainly clears up a few mysteries. I couldn't understand how he was resisting seeing you. Apparently, he's spending hours with you every day. He must be sleeping during part of the day to be keeping up that kind of activity schedule to recharge your energy reserves."

Shannon's fists clenched, the bright burn of anger coiling in her gut. While she'd been miserable, lonely, and sobbing, he'd known he was spending time with her, seducing her. He'd left her to suffer in anguish as she carried their child, while she endured the aching need, the pain, and discomfort. The fucking backache that wouldn't leave her alone today.

Blood pounded in her ears.

If Elatha was to be believed, she'd died... She'd fucking died, and Loki couldn't even work up the courage to *talk* to her?

Nostrils flaring, she snarled, "So are you going to tell me next that Thor hasn't been taking me for picnics in the forest each day? That Loki has been doing that, too?" Shannon didn't think so, but was Thor actually available so often? Were Mist and Kara really visiting her? Surely he wasn't impersonating everyone?

Frigga eyes widened. "Oh my. Thor has been on Alfheim, trying to track down Crom and Llew. He isn't even on Asgard this week, Shannon."

How *dare* he? Heat enveloped Shannon's face as fury rose, hot and fast. Flexing her fists and panting, she tried to stay in control. She tried not to let her powers out. The open pages of books fluttered on the nightstand as a breeze spun through the room. Damn it, she wasn't supposed to be using her seidhr.

She grit her teeth, pain rippling through her body and down her back. Where was that chicken-ass rat bastard? He left her to suffer. Made her think he'd abandoned her. Her rage erupted. "*Loki!*"

A rainbow of lights surrounded her and then dissipated, leaving Shannon bare-foot with her long hair tumbled down to her waist and wearing only her blue silk empire-waisted nightgown in the midst of shouts, flashes of light, and people.

Too many people.

Disoriented after catching her balance and her vision tunnelling, the first thing she saw was Loki, standing with his mouth gaping, dressed in a gorgeous blue suit with the short red hair and pale ice-blue eyes of his Midgardian Tod Corvus persona. Her fury still riding her in a blinding red haze, she took the couple of steps to reach him and slapped him hard on his too-sexy dimpled face.

The smack stung her hand and brought her back to herself.

Eyes widening as she gazed around her, Shannon clapped a hand over her mouth. A sea of cameras, media, and fans stared at her in shock. She burst into tears, covering her face. Oh gods, how had she ended up here?

Loki took her shoulders gently. "Shannon! How did you get here? Are you—" he began, and a hot gush of fluid soaked her nightgown and thighs.

Chapter 34

FIERY LITTLE PRINCE

Shannon stared at her soulmate, almost unable to speak as horror evaporated the spit in her mouth. "My water just broke," she whispered, starting to tremble as her words—not nearly as quiet as she'd wanted them to be—broke the tense silence like a dam collapsing under overwhelming flood waters.

Questions were yelled at Loki about her, about the child, asking if it was his. Camera flashes blinded Shannon. No doubt they were recording every embarrassing moment. Why? Why did these things happen to her?

While her heart thundered and her knees weakened, Loki turned to the crowd with a brilliant smile. "Excuse me while I get my wife and child to a hospital. We're about to have a baby boy!"

The reminder of his lies stiffened Shannon's spine. She growled and ripped open the bond. <*I am not* your wife. You haven't even asked! Plus, you have a lot *of explaining to do, pretending to be your mom, your brother, and my dream lover! What the fuck was that, Loki?*>

<*I'm sorry! Really, really sorry! I will gladly beg your forgiveness, but please, please let me get you back to Asgard so our son isn't born on the red carpet or in a primitive Midgardian hospital. I want you home with Healer Moja to care for you and our baby. Please, darling. Please let me get you out of here.*>

His love and protectiveness flowed into her, filling the gaping wound in her chest after an absence of eleven long weeks. She tried not to let it affect her, but damn it, she'd missed him... hell, she'd fucking mourned him.

She let him guide her to the entrance of the red carpet, security holding everyone back while the valet raced to bring Loki's vehicle.

A contraction hit, doubling Shannon over as she held her belly, clenching her teeth to keep from screaming. Loki rubbed her back, murmuring something she was too distracted to hear as she sucked air through her nose and blew it out noisily.

The vehicle arrived in a few short minutes. Loki helped her in and got her buckled. He sped the distance to his flat in record time. As soon as the vehicle was parked, he teleported them to the roof.

"Heimdall?"

The lights of the Bifrost swirled as another contraction hit, rippling pain flowing like a wave from her back to her belly. She screamed and was still screaming as the lights dissipated.

Teleporting first to the city, then again to reach the Healer Hall enclosed in a lower wing of the palace, Loki carried her to Healer Moja.

"Here, put her here," Moja said as soon as she spotted them. She indicated something that looked like a partially reclining chair, but had stirrups for the legs and no actual seat, except on the very edges to support the thighs and hips but not get in the way.

Loki helped Shannon into it, and the healer flipped on the green scanning light. A fast, rhythmic thumping filled the room.

"Your son has decided he's done waiting. You are seven centimetres dilated already. His heartbeat is strong."

Another powerful contraction hit, and Shannon panted until she couldn't take the pain. Gripping Loki's hand harder, she wailed as the squeezing agony in her back and abdomen shot spikes up her spine and down her legs in an unrelenting, fiery burn.

"You can draw some of that pain away through the bond, Loki," Moja told him.

Shannon's head cleared, and the pain became tolerable. Loki's face paled as his eyes flared wide.

"Yggdrasil's fucking roots, trunk, and bloody leaves! How do women do this?" he groaned, his brow breaking out in a sweat as the contraction continued relentlessly. "I am never, ever having a baby."

Shannon glared at him, panting her way through it.

Healer Moja flashed him a small grin. "Just think, Loki. You are only taking part of the pain. Shannon was experiencing the full brunt of it."

Shannon sagged, releasing her grip on his hand, breathing easier now that the contraction was over.

"You don't need to convince me of how amazing and courageous Shannon is. I know it." He shook out his fingers.

Shannon side-eyed him. If he thought he could flatter his way out of trouble, he was dead wrong. "I just thought my back was aching earlier," she told the healer.

Healer Moja smiled and patted her shoulder. "Your labour pains were starting. You must have been in labour for most of the day. It would have felt like a backache that kept getting worse?"

"Yes, that's exactly it."

"You probably have at least another three hours," Moja said.

"Hours? Hours of this?" Loki asked, incredulous. "Can't you numb some of the pain for her? Even on Midgard, they have epidurals."

Moja gave him an amused smile. "That's what you are here for, Loki. Epidurals can have lasting side effects for both mother and son. We don't like to use any neural blocks when she has you to siphon off some of the pain."

Loki blanched, his eyes widening, and Shannon grabbed his hand again. "Don't you *dare* fucking leave me, Loki!" she growled. "Not again!"

"Is that the dulcet tones of our princess I hear?" Mist entered the room with a smile.

"Fuck off, bitch," Shannon snarled as another contraction hit, and both she and Loki gasped.

Mist smirked. "You are a badass warrior goddess. You've got this, babe," her best friend reassured her. She picked up a cool, damp cloth and held it to Shannon's forehead.

The stark contrast between the fiery agony of her abdomen and the cold relief of the cloth had Shannon blinking. She groaned between panted breaths.

"Now you, Loki. Get off your ass, use those mental powers you've been abusing, and talk to your son. Some reassurance wouldn't go amiss. He *can* hear you, you know." Mist glared at him.

Shannon blinked. He could talk to their baby? How was that fair? She was the one carrying their child. How come she didn't get to talk to their son?

Healer Moja nodded at Loki, and he moved to put a hand on Shannon's abdomen. After a minute, the fetal heartbeat calmed slightly, even as another contraction ripped a cry from Shannon.

Time blurred together, a confusing blend of exhaustion and pain, with brief periods of respite. Soaked in sweat, Shannon growled as she chomped on the ice cubes Mist popped into her mouth and glared at Loki. The fucking bastard groaned while she swore her way through another searing contraction that felt like her spine was trying to detach from her back and tear her godsdamned pelvis out.

"I fucking hate you right now, Loki!" Shannon yelled. "Your damn cock got me into this position! I hate it!"

"I hate it, too. We're never having sex with it again," he whimpered, his normally pale skin sheet-white with trickles of sweat as he panted with her.

"Godsdamn it. You can carry our next child," she growled.

"No. No way. We aren't having any more. Not doing this again," he panted.

Mist laughed. "I should record the two of you. Epic blackmail material." She grinned as they both snarled at her.

"Almost there, Shannon," Moja reassured her as the calm healer checked Shannon's progress. "I need you to push for me now."

The next contraction hit, and Shannon crushed Loki's fingers as she shrieked her way through the pressure. Light-headed when it eased off, her eyesight had sparkles. That didn't seem right.

"Breathe. In and out, Shannon," Mist coaxed her.

"One more big push," Moja instructed as the relentless tightening in her back and abdomen started again.

Loki and Shannon screamed together as the pain crested in a crushing wave, and then there was a sudden relief of pressure. Moja rose from her crouched position between Shannon's legs, their son in the healer's arms.

"Loki, do you want to—" she asked until he collapsed onto the floor. "Oh dear!"

Mist snickered, and Shannon couldn't help the chuckle that escaped between panted breaths as she leaned over to see him unconscious, despite the loud cries of their son echoing in the room.

"Guess he hit his limit," Mist teased, meeting her friend's gaze.

Shannon rolled her eyes, smiling now that the pain was gone. "So much for the vaunted and feared Black Prince."

Healer Moja cleaned off their son and laid him gently on Shannon's chest, distracting her from further comment.

With the press of warm skin against his face, her son calmed. His open mouth instinctively searched until Shannon got him latched onto her nipple. Her beautiful boy had his father's thick black hair and long limbs, but they wouldn't know his eye colour until it settled in a few months from the current newborn blue. Skin reddish and wrinkled like a little old man, she smiled down at his greedy sucking as his tiny fingers clutched at her.

So involved was she in watching him, that it took her a few minutes to notice Loki had recovered his senses to join them, an arm wrapped around her as he watched their son nurse at her breast.

"Beautiful, just like his mother," Loki whispered, his voice low and rough, lacking its usual smooth purr.

"He's got your hair, and I expect he's going to be tall like you," Shannon said, glancing at Loki to find tears leaving salty trails down his cheeks. He looked awestruck, unable to tear his gaze from his son. The love coming through the bond was an overwhelming wave, swamping every other feeling. She and Loki had things they needed to discuss, but not at this moment. This moment was perfect in its harmony between the two of them and their child.

"What's his name?" Shannon had never seen such a tender expression on her best friend's face as Mist gazed down at the child.

"Áedán Bréanainn Lokison." Shannon glanced at Loki to see his reaction. She'd asked Frigga if immortals used last names after recalling how Isis had made fun of her for having more than one name. The genealogy of children were recorded at birth, but last names weren't common. Still, it was a cultural tradition from Earth that wouldn't be detrimental to her son—an acknowledgement of how she'd been raised human—but she hadn't liked the sound of Shannonson as the alternative naming choice here on Asgard.

Loki's lips twitched, before he laughed, a big full-bodied howl that echoed in the room. Their son stopped nursing to listen, eyes wide. Shannon caressed his soft head and his eyelids fluttered closed, even as he nursed occasionally. Áedán was falling asleep after all the excitement.

Quieter in his amusement, seeing their baby's drowsiness, Loki kissed her forehead. "Fiery little prince is the perfect choice for our son, darling. I love it."

Mist snorted. "Yeah, because both of you are such quiet, meek personalities."

Shannon grinned and stuck her tongue out at the Valkyrie. Hey, at least she hadn't gone with Tàire.

Mist laughed. "Exactly my point."

Chapter 35

TIME TO FACE THE MUSIC

The next two weeks passed in a blur of sleeping, feeding, and changing diapers, with occasional visitors. Shannon moved her and Áedán back into the rooms she'd shared with Loki, although she hadn't yet put Áedán in the nursery. He still slept in a bassinet next to the bed so either she or Loki could lift him out to bring to her to nurse every two-to-three hours. Exhaustion and headaches plagued her, with barely the energy to get out of bed to take care of Áedán or herself.

"Shannon needs more from you, Loki. Look at her. Look! She's not recovering the way she should." Frigga's voice penetrated Shannon's sleep, and she opened her eyes to see the All-Mother holding Áedán, rocking him as she burped him on her shoulder.

Shannon struggled to sit, everything aching. Air chilled her chest, and she pulled the blanket over her mostly unbuttoned nightshirt. Loki must have been letting her sleep, holding Áedán to her breast so their son could nurse.

"What's wrong?" Shannon asked as Frigga frowned at her.

"You and Loki need to resolve your differences and get your relationship back on track. You've lost weight again since giving birth. Both Healer Moja and I are concerned about your and Áedán's health. You didn't have any spare weight to lose, as you were barely recovering as it was. This has to change *now*."

Huh? Still foggy from sleep and a lethargy that dragged at her, Shannon didn't understand Frigga's meaning. She blinked, rubbing at her temple.

Frigga let out an exasperated sigh. "I'm talking about sex, Shannon! Loki needs to provide energy for you and Áedán, like he did when you were pregnant. Just because Áedán isn't inside you, doesn't mean he isn't still getting all of his energy from you."

Shannon shrank into her pillows. How had she failed to learn this lesson? Once again, she'd fallen into thinking like a human and forgot the energetic demands of immortals.

Loki paced, tugging at his black locks. "I told you I didn't want to force her or deceive her again, Mother."

"You are a master mage, Loki. You *know* the energetic demands, yet you haven't even been taking her to the forest or helping her into saltwater baths. She's so weak she can barely get out of bed," Frigga scolded. "What does it take for you to wise up? For her to die again?"

Loki blanched, staggered to grab the back of a chair, opened his mouth, shook his head and closed it again.

It wasn't until Shannon saw his body language that she realized he'd restricted the bond to hide his feelings. Why hadn't he said anything? How had she been so stupid? She could have asked him to help her into a saltwater bath or to take her to the forest. "I'm sorry, Frigga. I guess I still haven't adjusted my thinking from being a mortal," she apologized, rubbing at her head.

Frigga laid a now sleeping Áedán back into the bassinet and came to sit beside her on the bed. The All-Mother stroked Shannon's hair with one hand as she spoke. "Darling daughter, I do not blame you. I can only imagine what an immense adjustment all of this has been. You've been through so much. I admire your perseverance and strength."

Turning, she scowled at Loki. "Now my son, on the other hand, has no excuse! Loki has let you suffer exhaustion and energy depletion since you gave birth because he's been too afraid to discuss this with you. I've had enough of his cowardice."

Loki flinched at her harsh words and hung his head.

"You two are going to work this out right now. I'm taking Áedán with me, so you can make all the noise you need to. I won't blame you if you feel the need to throw something at Loki, Shannon. He deserves it." After lifting the bassinet within a nimbus of golden energy, Frigga left the room with it floating beside her.

Frigga's harsh condemnation of Loki left Shannon open-mouthed. Sure, Shannon had been furious with him when she'd discovered his deception, pretending to be Frigga and Thor, and seducing her in her dreams. She didn't like feeling like a fool or that he'd let her think he didn't want her or their child for two-and-a-half heartbreaking weeks, but then, he'd had quite the shock himself, seeing her with Elatha. She winced. And continued to see her with Elatha in her dreams.

"I'm sorry, Loki." She swallowed, clenching the bedding in her fingers. "It was never my intention to hurt you when you saw me with Elatha. I wish there had been another way. Gods, I'm—I'm so sorry I hurt you."

Slowly, Loki came over and knelt on the floor by the bed. His eyes were downcast, not meeting her gaze as he reached carefully for her hand and gently pried the covers from where they were twisted in her grip until their fingers interlaced. Tears pricked Shannon's eyes as heat built behind them at seeing her normally confident soulmate act so uncertain.

It took him a minute before he spoke, and he swallowed a few times, his mouth opening, then closing, then opening, as he struggled with what he wanted to say. Finally, his eyes met her, and she sucked in a sharp breath at the pain and vulnerability in the emerald depths.

"Shannon, I'm... I'm so sorry." Loki's voice broke. "I acted like a bloody arse. I never should have..." His eyes grew glassy with unshed tears as he blinked hard.

"Loki—" she started, and he stopped her with a quick finger to her lips.

"No, please. Please let me get this out. I have no excuse for abandoning you like that when we found you on Alfheim. You'd been through the fires of Helheim to get back to me. I betrayed you by judging you without giving you a chance to explain. The pregnancy would have killed you." Tears escaped and dripped off his cheeks, his voice cracking. "It di—did kill you. You and our son. If not for the Atlantean prince and the choices you made, I would have lost both of you." He kissed her hand. "Instead of telling you how proud I was of you for escaping and surviving, saving both of you all by yourself, I threw it back in your face by accusing you, then abandoning you. I'll never forgive myself for that." His green eyes glowed, black lashes glistening with diamond-like droplets clinging to them as he met her gaze.

She pulled his finger from her mouth, holding both his hands instead.

"I blamed myself, Loki. How can I be angry at you when I already felt guilty?"

Loki pressed his lips together, biting back a sob, and then released her hand to swipe angrily at his cheeks. "That's just it, Shannon. You have *nothing* to feel guilty about. Absolutely nothing. You did exactly what you needed to do. And you made the right choice, the *only* choice. You saved yourself and our son. It's what I made you promise you would do, and I'd want you to make the same choice again."

"Really?" Her voice was barely a whisper. A weight lifted off her shoulders she hadn't realized she still carried. "But my dreams... I know you've seen—"

"Nothing is more important to me than you and our son," he interrupted. "Nothing. I know I'm possessive, but I can't lose you. If I had to share you with one hundred others to ensure your survival, I would learn to deal with it, and you'd have my entire support. Please darling, please put the blame where it belongs. Don't feel guilty about this anymore. I love you more than anything in the universe. Nothing exists for me without you in it. I can't lose you."

His heartfelt declaration eased the last of her tension. "I think you overestimate my stamina if you think I could juggle one hundred and one men, Loki," she teased, reassured by his earnest expression. She'd be more than content with just her one Asgardian and one Atlantean.

Amusement twitched at the corners of his mouth, and he shook his head, his eyes starting to sparkle. "By the Nine, I love you. I can't make quite that many copies of myself, but I'll try if you want to see exactly how many you can juggle."

Arousal shimmered through the bond between them. She shifted, squirming at the thought of him and Elatha together. But as erotic as it was, it was tenderness and intimacy she wanted right then, not screaming hot sex. She'd missed the way Loki held her, touched her, and missed the connection between them. They'd not made love since she'd had Áedán. Not even in her dreams. She missed Elatha, too, but couldn't yet see how to resolve her love and need for both of them, despite Frigga's advice and Loki's seeming acceptance of her past actions. He'd never once indicated that he'd share her now that her survival didn't require it. Not with him there to take care of her needs.

"How about just one of you makes love to me now, and we can discuss those possibilities later?" She pulled his hand to tug him up off his knees, and he crawled onto the bed beside her.

"I can agree to those terms," Loki replied in a voice deepened into a sensual purr.

With a gentle hand on her cheek, he feathered kisses on her lips, along her other cheek towards her ear, down her neck and back again. Goosebumps broke out over her skin at the light teasing touches, and she dragged her fingernails through his hair and over his scalp. Loki shuddered, a soft groan against her skin, as he worked his way back to her lips. She loved the way her touch could elicit such a reaction from him, and did it again, just to hear those sounds.

"I missed you, darling. Yggdrasil's twisted trunk, but I missed you," he whispered between licks and nibbles at her mouth.

"I missed you too, Loki. Kiss me, please," she asked as she tugged on his hair.

Tongues glided in a sensuous dance. Cool air shivered over her skin when his hands made quick work of the remainder of her nightshirt, sliding it off her shoulders. Teasing fingertips glided lightly over one arm, down to her fingertips, then up her inner wrist and the charm bracelet once again encircling her. His fingers tinkled the new charm to celebrate their son's birth gleamed—a crowned black flame with the colours of the Bifrost. His touch continued up to her elbow, and over her collarbone.

Breaking their kiss to breathe, she tilted her head back, even as she tugged his head down. His lips turned into a smile against the tender skin of her throat, and one hand cupped her breast.

"What is it you want, Shannon?" Loki teased, as he kissed his way down between them.

"You know what I want. Stop teasing."

"Even with the nursing? They aren't sore?" He licked and nibbled his way over the enlarged curves. "Damn, they are gorgeous."

She squirmed, aching to have his lips on her. "Not sore. Just extra sensitive. Please, Loki." She'd no sooner gotten the words out than he sucked a taut nipple into his mouth, drawing hard.

"Oh gods." Her eyes wanted to roll back in her head. The pleasure had her arching towards his mouth, even as her toes curled. "Gods, don't stop," she moaned, clutching his hair to hold him to her. It was indescribably more arousing than before her pregnancy. Each pull of his mouth had her panting faster. His grip tightened as he groaned and rocked his hips against her thigh.

"Loki, oh gods. Don't stop, please!" She was so close, racing towards that precipice, until her breath caught in a frozen moment, body rigid.

His next deep draw had her shuddering in his arms, waves of energy rippling through her body. Loki groaned, the hard ridge of his cock like a steel bar pushing into her leg even as he jerked against her.

Releasing her nipple with a pop, he met her eyes, his pupils blown wide as he panted.

"Damn woman, you taste fucking incredible! Bloody hell, that was so insanely sexy. Do you have any idea how long it's been since I lost control and came in my pants? Yggdrasil's roots, Shannon!"

As she caught her breath, she revelled in the intense pleasure surging through her at his admission. She loved she'd made him lose control. Giving a little sensuous wiggle, she smiled. "Well love, I do believe I have two breasts, and the other is feeling quite neglected right now."

Lust burned in his eyes as he smirked. "I swear the Norns created you just for me. You are perfect." A wave of black seidhr rolled over them, leaving them naked, and Loki moved to shift his hips between her thighs. "But this time, my darling, I'm going to feast on you with my cock where it belongs. Inside your hot, wet little body."

"Oh gods," she whimpered when he slowly pushed inside until his hips were flush against hers. She didn't know what techniques they used after childbirth on Asgard to aid in recovery, but she was damn glad they did. Every inch of him stretched her walls, and it was fucking glorious.

Loki smiled, watching her reaction. His own cheeks flushed. She squeezed around him, drawing his groan. With long, slow strokes, he began to move even as he held her gaze.

"Please, Loki." It was so hard to look into his eyes when she wanted to yank that talented mouth of his to her other breast. The seductive glide of his body against hers had her pulse pounding and heat flaring from her abdomen. Yet she craved his mouth, and her back arched, pushing her chest toward him.

With the corners of his lips twitching, he lowered his head, scraping her nipple with his teeth.

She tightened her core, and his eyes turned half-lidded. Yeah, two could tease.

With a hand under her ass to tilt her hips, he thrust against her G-spot.

Shannon gasped, and then moaned, the electrifying sensation building, as he began sucking hard at her breast. It was like a cord connected the two spots of her body, and he drew them tighter with every pull of his mouth and thrust of his hips.

Starting to tremble, she couldn't help but demand harder, faster. She was a spring wound ever tighter, ever higher.

"Please, Loki! Gods! Please!"

Loki growled, hips pounding as her breath caught. Her body was rigid, right at the cusp, until the next cresting plunge spiralled her over. She screamed. Bucking in his arms, the pleasure seared her nerves, bursting from her body and bathing her in bliss.

Loki thrust through her orgasm, before holding himself deep and groaning his own release, muffled against her breast.

He propped himself up on an elbow over her as they caught their breath. Once they had, he rolled them over onto their sides. "Sleep, Shannon." Loki flashed a wicked little smile. "I'll let you recover for a few minutes before I ravish you again. After all, the queen has ordered it."

Shannon snorted, even as her eyes closed. As if Loki needed an excuse. Gods, she'd missed him, missed this. Yet, being so connected with him again, without the stress she'd carried, had her relaxing into his body and drifting off into a dream of being held by two sets of arms.

Chapter 36

FEARS

L oki paced, shoving his hair back with a frustrated hand. "Short of having sex with her every hour of the day, including when she's feeding Áedán, I can't give her more energy than I am, Mother." He frowned, gesturing. "I've tried saltwater baths while she's sleeping, and spending time in the forest while she's feeding Áedán. Shannon is still losing weight. To see her getting so thin again scares me. I don't know what to do."

Mother stopped him with a hand on his arm. "I've spoken to Healer Moja about it. She's also worried. Áedán is growing well, exactly as we would hope for a six-month-old. But with his ability to manipulate portal energy, he's drawing more energy from Shannon than she can supply as a new immortal herself."

Loki snorted. Yeah, his son was powerful and a right little pain in the ass. Loki had installed dampening fields around their suite of rooms, including on his crib. Every time Áedán wanted something, or someone—usually his mother—he created a portal to pull himself to her. Unfortunately, his son didn't understand what he was doing was dangerous. It was still instinctual, with no real control.

The first time he'd portalled out of his bassinet and into her arms at only a few weeks old, it had freaked both Loki and Shannon out. Fortunately, she caught Áedán when he appeared in the air in front of them, but still, it was shocking. When the little troublemaker started leaving his crib every time

311

he didn't want his nap, Loki installed a barrier that would prevent his son from portalling out. With a flexible range depending on what they needed, the dampening field could be as small as Áedán's crib or as large as their rooms. It was the same technology used to secure Asgard from unexpected visitors.

"I know that. And you know that. But I need your help convincing Shannon that she can't keep this up. Please, Mother," Loki begged. "She'll listen to you." Whenever he'd tried to have the conversation with Shannon, she refused to discuss it.

When she nodded, his breath escaped in a relieved sigh. Leading the way, he brought Frigga out to the gardens stretching the length of the suite of rooms Loki and Shannon shared. His goddess sat on the grass with Áedán sprawled and rolling around, trying to chew a fist-full.

"Well, I see Áedán already knows what I've come to talk to you about," Mother said as she sank onto the grass beside him.

Stomach churning, Loki paced around them. Mother had to get through to Shannon. She had to.

Shannon gazed from Mother to Loki, frowning. Her red-brown curls lacked their usual luster and those beautiful hazel eyes had dark circles under them. Loki's heart pounded at the sight of the hollows in her cheeks again.

Their son was literally draining the life out of her.

"What do you mean, Frigga?" Shannon asked quietly.

"You know exactly what I'm talking about, Shannon. You aren't blind to your condition. This can't continue. Áedán is doing very well. At six months, he can transition to other foods in addition to breast milk," Mother said in her firm but unyielding way.

"But everything I've read says I need to feed him for at least the first year," Shannon protested, turning a scowl towards him. *<Why are you undermining me and siccing your mother on me?>*

Loki bit his lip, staying silent to her telepathic complaint. Shannon would listen to Frigga instead of getting defensive, as she did when he'd tried to bring the issue up over the past month while she grew thinner and more exhausted.

"You don't have to stop nursing him. He needs to add eat other foods so he's getting energy from more than just you. If you don't, you'll be dead. What good will you do Áedán if you are dead, Shannon?" Mother said bluntly.

Loki sucked in a breath as his heart pounded. He hadn't dared get *that* blunt with her.

Shannon glared at him.

"Don't blame Loki." Frigga gestured to Shannon's body. "Go look in a mirror. You're a walking skeleton right now."

Shannon's back slumped, and Loki sank to his knees beside her. She was such a good mother. Norns, he hated to see her struggling. "Please, Shannon. Áedán and I need you."

"Fine," she conceded, reluctance in her tone and set of her shoulders.

Mother conjured a bowl of the local starchy fruit, mashed to a fine puree. "Let's see how Áedán likes musa." She put a tiny amount on a soft spoon and touched it to Áedán's lips.

His little face scrunched as he rubbed his lips together, sucking the bottom lip into his mouth. The cute expression had Loki holding back a laugh.

Mother put another tiny amount on Áedán's lip, and he did it again.

The third time, she timed it just as he opened his mouth, so she got a bit more into him. Áedán's eyes widened, showing the current progress of gradual change from newborn blue to green within his irises. Although he mushed the fruit around in his mouth, he seemed to like it.

Through trial and error, he ate several spoonfuls before Mother called a halt.

"He seems to like it," Shannon said as they watched Áedán squish it, smacking his lips.

"Indeed, he does. Over the next day, he may run a bit of a fever. It's fine. Feed him some of this first, then nurse. You'll see he doesn't drink as much with a bit of food in his belly," Mother told her. "Keep him on this for the next couple of weeks, and then we'll try another food."

"Why will he have a fever? That isn't in any of the baby books," Shannon asked.

Even as Loki tried to relax her by rubbing her back, she sat stiffly, spine tight. She seemed to eye Áedán carefully. What was she so worried about?

"Áedán will be transitioning to an immortal. It's much less stressful on the body to do it as a baby. As another benefit, it will mean that he also starts drawing tiny bits of energy from his environment. That further reduces the demands on your system, Shannon. Finally, you can start to really recover," Mother said with a gentle smile.

"He won't need anything... additional to transition?" Shannon had blanched, eyes wide, gaze darting between Áedán and Frigga. He was happily trying to grab grass in his little fists.

Loki's breath caught. Was that why she'd been so resistant to consider giving Áedán solid foods? Bloody hell, he was an idiot to have not anticipated her worry. But it hadn't entered his mind that she'd think Áedán's transition would require anything of a sexual nature. Loki already knew how immortal babies transitioned. Shannon didn't. Of course she'd be upset at the idea. It was disgusting.

Mother smiled, eyes understanding. "No. No, there's nothing like that. Only the rougher transition of an adult has those sorts of side effects. Babies, even ones with a mix of yours and Loki's genetics, transition much more effortlessly since their systems are still developing, and Áedán is already primed for it by feeding on your breastmilk."

"Is that why he exhibits powers, even at his young age?" Shannon asked, her shoulders losing their tension. Finally, her hand found Loki's in the grass.

"Yes. All breast-fed infants born to two immortal parents do until they are weaned. If they aren't given immortal foods at that point, their system goes into a form of hibernation, like yours did until Loki gave you the mead." Leaning over, Frigga snagged Áedán from the grass, tickling his side and making him giggle. "Now, I'm going to take the little prince with me for a few hours so Loki can recharge you."

"Thank you, Mother," Loki told her gratefully, even as Shannon echoed his sentiment.

When she disappeared through the doorway, Loki pulled Shannon back against his body, between his legs. Gently, he traced his fingertips over the delicate skin of her wrists, arms, shoulders, and back down again.

With a sigh, Shannon leaned her head on his shoulder, tilting to give him access to that graceful neck. Norns, but he loved biting right where her nape and shoulder met. It always seemed to make her pliant and wet, willing to give him whatever desire he had in that moment.

Sitting like this, teasing her and watching the gooseflesh rise, it reminded him of their first time together at the movie theatre. She'd been like trying to tame wildfire, burning in his arms. Scorchingly hot, she'd incinerated his control. He'd barely kept the illusion around them.

His hands shifted from her arms to reach under, plucking at pebbled nipples. Her breath caught. Loki couldn't help but smile against her neck as he continued to kiss and lick over the soft flesh. Even with her lost weight, these breasts stayed full, supplying their son. And bloody hell, the taste drove Loki wild. If ever there was a nectar of the gods, damn, her breasts were it.

Whimpered moans escaped her lips, and she shifted against him, rubbing that sexy ass of hers against his aching cock.

"What's the matter, Shannon? Is your little quim empty?" Loki purred into her ear.

Her cries grew louder. The filthier he spoke, the hotter she got, and playing with her tits like this, he could make her come just by talking. Norns knew, he loved driving his goddess wild.

"Are you hot and wet for me? Aching to have me to pound into those soft, tight depths? You love it when I slam my big cock in, don't you, darling?"

She whined, squirming as he tugged hard on her nipples. Milk dripped, soaking her body, and sweetness perfumed the air. The scent had Loki's pulse thundering, lust raging. He wanted to flip her over, bury his cock in her soaked pussy and devour those glorious tits.

Fuck. If he wasn't careful, she'd have him coming before he was ready. But he was determined to make her climax like this first.

Even if his cock was harder than Laevateinn.

"Let me hear how wet your little quim is for me."

As he instructed her, she fucked herself with two fingers, and the spectacular scents and sexy wet sounds had Loki groaning with her. She was keening, little breathy gasping moans that told him she was close. He just had to push her a little farther.

"Or is it your ass that's aching for my cock today? Have you missed me stretching it on my hard cock? Would you like me to fuck that tight ass of yours with your fingers playing with that needy little quim?"

Her surge in arousal was so blisteringly hot, it set the bond between them on fire.

An image flashed into his mind through their soulmate connection—him pounding into her ass, hard and fast, while another—that fucking Atlantean—ploughed her pussy with his huge black-and-silver cock. She was stretched between them, screaming in pleasure. So incendiary, so wickedly erotic, the fantasy catapulted them into a shared mind-shattering, body-shaking orgasm.

When Loki regained his senses, they were collapsed on the grass, breath sawing in and out of their lungs. Shannon lay partially on him, partially on the grass, and Loki had once again come in his pants.

He was speechless.

When she'd first returned, before Áedán was born, she'd dreamed of the Atlantean. Loki had known she fantasized about them taking her together. He'd joined her in those blisteringly hot dreams, used them to give her energy. But he hadn't realized she still thought of the damned Atlantean, that she still fantasized about him six months later. What claim did the handsome fucker have on her heart... on her dreams?

Did she know he had picked up on her fantasy? No, not likely.

Fuck, he wasn't even sure how he felt about it. Part of him was insanely jealous that she'd thought of the Atlantean while with him. Yet, it made him wonder. Had she fantasized about this when she had been with the Atlantean? It had been... well fuck—it had made him lose control, even hotter than when it had been in her dreams.

Shannon stirred, and Loki put his musings aside. She needed more energy, and he was suddenly feeling he should remind her of his creativity. They didn't need some third wheel mucking up their relationship. With a thought, their clothes were gone, and Loki had her on her back. Relentlessly, he plundered his beautiful goddess, teasing her mind and body with numerous orgasms, until she glowed with healthy satiation.

Chapter 37

I DO, BUT I CAN'T

The glee on Loki's face as Frigga took Áedán left Shannon laughing. She'd expected to take their son with them on their weekly jaunt to the nearby ancient redwood forest. Despite her expanding knowledge of Asgard, the western mountains were still her favourite place to explore outside the capital city.

With Áedán old enough now at ten months to be primarily eating solid food and only nursing twice a day, it had given her the freedom to venture further afield. They'd visited numerous towns and villages within a few hours by hovercraft so she could meet more people and learn Asgard's geography and industries in person. She had a thirst for knowledge, for practical details of the various regions of Asgard, it's main imports and exports, and how that related to the rest of the Nine Realms. And maps... she spent hours examining maps of every realm. Never again did she want to be lost and unable to find her way.

"Thank you, Mother. We'll be back in time for the evening meal." Loki handed over their son's favourite toy—a hammer-shaped stuffie with googly eyes that Thor had given Áedán, much to Loki's annoyance.

Frigga smacked a kiss on Áedán's giggling cheek. "Good. Your brother is joining us tonight."

"That's wonderful. Will he be staying for a couple days? He's been promising to teach me to better control my lightning strikes." Shannon had read that lightning was particularly useful against redcaps and kelpies. Or dwarves. She was determined to never be taken captive again.

After finally gaining back her pre-pregnancy weight, Shannon had restarted her training last month. It seemed to take forever to return to fighting shape, but she'd fought through it. With the nightmares still plaguing her, she needed the reassurance of defending herself. Although Kara and Mist insisted she'd surpassed her previous levels, even to the point of being proficient at creating a miniature sun—no fucking troll would take her again—Shannon continued to drive herself to improve. Not having to adjust for a constantly changing centre of gravity certainly helped.

Still, Loki wasn't yet willing to spar full-on with her. Maybe she'd be able to convince Thor to spar with her, and they could battle with lightning. The idea had her bouncing on her toes.

Frigga smiled. "Yes, I believe he plans to be here for a few days."

"Let's get going, darling. The huckleberries are calling." Loki's eyes glinted as he fought his grin.

With a huff of exasperation, Shannon rolled her eyes and stuck out her tongue. He liked to make fun of her, but it was true. She'd been excited last week to see the huckleberries were almost ripe. Some should be ready to pick this visit.

Laughing, he tugged her into his arms, then teleported them to the palace hangar. The transition from the quiet of their rooms to the hangar's cacophony was jarring—armour-clad warriors' boot hit the stone floor, workers shouted as they unloaded crates from the black spherical shuttles that transported imported goods from Skaikaup, the Asgardian spacestation, and technicians clanged tools repairing and prepping the skuta, the individual hovercrafts, and larger shuttles. But she'd become used to the hangar's chaos given how frequently they used one of the skuta to travel out of the city.

"Wow, you are impatient today. You must really want huckleberries," Shannon taunted.

He snorted. "Those aren't the berries I want. I'm after sweeter fruit." Playfully, his eyes flicked to her chest, then back to her face as he winked.

Shaking her head, she let him help her to a grey bench seat before he fired up the skuta. He'd taught her how to fly the little ships. But she enjoyed watching his fingers fly over the controls. He was always so graceful in his movements.

Distracted by admiring him, she didn't realize they'd arrived until she sensed the trees' energy. Ancient and rich with history and experience, they wrapped her in their embrace whenever she got close to them. Gods, but she loved coming out to this forest. All the forests on Earth, even the old-growth groves around her Vancouver home, felt young by comparison.

"Before you get mesmerized by the trees, let's fly to the waterfall," Loki suggested.

"Definitely! Do you want to fly with me today?" Only a month ago, they'd discovered the waterfall. Loki claimed he didn't know about it, that he hadn't spent much time in this forest until he met her. Not sure if she believed him or not, still she enjoyed the idea of them exploring and finding something new. The waterfall was far enough away, at least seventy kilometres up into the mountains, that they couldn't go unless they had all afternoon. There was no nearby clearing large enough to land the hovercraft, and it was well out of Loki's teleporting range. Yet with her ability to fly and his shapeshifting, they could travel the distance in about thirty minutes.

"Absolutely, darling. Take us away," he teased with a glint in his eyes. Although not needed, he pressed his body close, holding her around the waist.

As if she minded being held tight to his strong, athletic frame. She loved the feel of his body against her.

Wrapping air under them, she propelled them over the massive trees. When Áedán was a bit older and more independent, she wanted to try flying through the trees, like that scene in *Return of the Jedi* with the speeder bikes. She wasn't willing to risk being laid out for a few days with broken bones if she crashed full-on into one of the enormous trunks, not yet anyway. Perhaps she could get Mist to practice with her? It was exactly the kind of crazy stunt her best friend would think was a blast. At least, as long as Kara wasn't there to chide them on a lack of wisdom. She was the more cautious member of their trio.

Spotting the waterfall, Shannon brought them down at the edge of the dark blue pool that burbled and swirled with the force of the twenty-metre falls cascading into it in a rainbow of colours. Surrounded by the ancient trees, this hidden grotto deep in the forest had become hers and Loki's secret oasis—a favourite place to make love outdoors. It was a private haven where they could play, splash, swim, and scream their pleasure.

Although she loved watching the pool and majestic falls, Loki took her hand and turned her toward the forest. The glimpse of something blue caught her eye. Partly hidden behind a large sword fern, she walked forward to investigate. She glanced back at Loki as he followed. The small, secretive smile on his face suggested he'd planned this.

As she stepped around the fern, a gasp escaped at the scene in front of her. Little glowing balls of yellow light floated in the air like dancing fireflies. A thick, royal-blue blanket lay overtop a bed of dense moss. Pillows, in multiple rich jewel tones of blue, purple, and green, were scattered around the blanket. Some of her favourite finger foods waited on trays at the far edge of the blanket. A bottle of Argentinian malbec from her favourite winery sat with two glasses.

It was perfect in every detail.

And so incredibly thoughtful. Tears welled at the effort he'd made to please her. She spun to thank him, but when their eyes met, Loki held her gaze and slowly knelt on one knee. In his hands rested a black-and-silver scrollwork ring inlaid with diamonds and a central stone that appeared to be a swirl of both emerald and sapphire. She'd never seen anything like it. The gem was utterly unique.

Shannon's heart raced, booming like thunder in her ears. Her skin flushed hot, then cold, then hot again, as if uncertain of its choice. Caught, she couldn't look away from his serious emerald eyes, pulling her into their incredible depths.

"Shannon, I've lived a thousand years, yet my life didn't begin until I met you. You make the stars shine brighter, the sunlight warmer, and the melody of the universe sings when you are with me. You are the better half of my soul. I consider myself fortunate every moment I get to bask in your presence. I will spend the rest of our eternity trying to be worthy of you if you would do me the very great honour of becoming my wife."

There was absolutely nothing flirtatious or mischievous about his expression. Instead, a vulnerability she'd rarely seen lurked in his gaze.

Goosebumps broke out over her. Was he worried she'd say no? She'd known she'd have to choose eventually. Part of her mourned the loss of her Atlantean—a dream that had stayed alive despite the passage of time—even as another piece of her soul took flight, rejoicing in the love she felt for this Asgardian. She swallowed. Then swallowed again.

Desperately, she wanted to answer. But her throat was so choked with conflicted emotion that she was having a hard time speaking.

She blinked, and hot tears overflowed her lashes to trail down her cheeks. Nodding, a sob finally escaped her throat, freeing her voice.

"Yes. Gods, yes, Loki," burst out in a flood even as a hidden side of her heart cried.

Both grinned like fools when they stumbled back to the hovercraft on the fjord's shore. After not having had alcohol since her first taste of Asgardian mead a year-and-a-half ago, the wine had gone straight to Shannon's head. Yeah, it was also possible the numerous orgasms had something to do with her current euphoria. She and Loki had celebrated their engagement thoroughly and vigorously.

Fortunately, he was in a much soberer shape than she, since there was no way she wanted to be piloting a vehicle of any kind at present. The hovercraft lifted off, and he chuckled when she lurched in her seat. She burst into a fit of giggles at her uncharacteristic clumsiness.

"Don't worry about Áedán, darling. Your immortal metabolism will clear the alcohol out of your system within the next hour. You'll be clear-headed by the time we get back to the palace," Loki told her. "And it will be entirely gone before you feed him tonight. Of course, if you are worried, I'll certainly help drain you dry."

Her insatiable soulmate and fiancé leered at her playfully and only partly in jest. Not that she could cast stones. Even as sated as she'd been an hour ago, she found herself rubbing her thighs together restlessly at the thought.

After docking the skuta in the palace hangar, they meandered their way towards the throne room to let Odin and Frigga know they'd returned. In no hurry, Loki tugged her into a darkened room to drive her to screaming ecstasy with his clever fingers, tongue, and cock.

Still straightening her clothes as they continued through the palace, Shannon slapped his hands away with a laugh as he tried to waylay her again.

"Are you trying to see if you can take me in every room on our way there, love?" she teased.

"Now, there is a goal to aspire to!" Loki grinned and gave her a lascivious wink.

"Didn't you say we were running late?" They'd forgotten to ask Frigga if they were eating in the family quarters tonight or if it was something more formal since Thor was home.

Loki grumbled something about willpower and sexy goddesses.

Shannon had to admit, she absolutely loved teasing him. Especially if it meant he couldn't do anything about it at the time. Adding a little sultry sway to her hips as they strode down the hall, she used her torc to shift into court-appropriate attire. It would never do for a member of the royal family to show up unsuitably dressed when a simple thought ensured the change. Of course, the chance to get Loki riled up also put a smile on her lips.

Loki gave her a sly, knowing little smile. "Trying to seduce me, darling? You know how much I absolutely adore those tall boots and double-slit dresses. I always find them so... inspiring." His heated gaze travelled down her body, and she could tell he was watching the flare of the green-and-gold dress when each of her strides played peek-a-boo with the thigh-high black leather boots.

Shannon wiggled an eyebrow. "Perhaps. I wouldn't want you to get bored. Maybe I have fishnets under these boots and maybe I don't."

He groaned. "You are evil. Now I'm going to have to use an illusion to hide my hard-on in the throne room. If we weren't running late already, I'd have you on your knees putting that clever little mouth of yours to use."

"Promises, promises, Loki. Put up or shut up," she taunted, knowing he couldn't do anything about it immediately. They were only steps from entering the throne room, with the guards watching.

"Oh darling, you really shouldn't have taunted the God of Mischief." His eyes had darkened with promised retribution before he hid it behind a polite façade and passed between the guards to enter the large golden space.

<Why so many guards?> More than double the usual number were posted along the walls.

<Someone must be here that Odin wants to impress. Perhaps an ambassador, since Mother didn't mention the visit.>

As they drew closer, she spotted a tall, lean, golden-haired male surrounded by six of their Einherjar. He wore golden armour and a grey cloak. Loki stiffened beside her.

She frowned. <*Who is it?*>

<*The Sidhe Ambassador Ogma. What the fuck does he want?*> Loki snarled.

Shannon's heart thundered, bile coating the back of her throat as they walked around the Ambassador to stand at the side of the steps to the throne, both bowing to Odin and Frigga.

"Rise, my children." Odin's voice was deep and resonant with anger, and a scowl furrowed his brow. Frigga's eyes were narrowed, lips pressed together, and Thor, who'd arrived while they'd been gone to the forest, had his arms crossed, a muscle ticking in his clenched jaw. The atmosphere in the room was tense, to say the least.

"Ambassador Ogma, I don't believe you've met Princess Shannon, my daughter, Loki's consort, and soon-to-be wife," Odin added.

Shannon eyed her new fiancé. <*You told them before we left for the forest?*>

<*Mother knew what I planned. I guess they assume my powers of persuasion are effective,*> Loki teased.

<*As if you thought I'd say no.*>

Even missing Elatha and mourning the relationship that would never be more than the brief weeks they'd had, Shannon never considered saying no to Loki. Not after the months she'd spent getting to know him better. She loved both men, each holding a part of her heart, but she'd loved Loki first. He was the father of her child. Despite his words of sharing and Frigga's advice to not deny Shannon's connection to Elatha, the reality was she had to choose. Even when it hurt.

<*It could have happened. It wouldn't be the first time you've surprised me, nor will it be the last.*>

"Princess Shannon, it is lovely to meet you," the Ambassador said with a bow. "I come on behalf of your paternal grandparents, and with greetings from the Kings and Queens of the Summer and Winter Realms."

Shannon inclined her head. "My grandparents?" She raised an eyebrow.

Ogma met her gaze with no change in his expression. "Gwydion and Arianrhod of the Winter Realm."

With effort, she tried not to wrinkle her nose as her spine stiffened. The Winter Realm. Those fucking bastards. "I have no desire to have anything to do with the Winter Realm or those individuals. I don't recognize them as family since they tried to kill me. They sent the Wild Hunt after me multiple times." She didn't bother to hide her disgust as her fists clenched.

Not very diplomatic of her, but she didn't see why she needed to be polite to those assholes after what they did.

"Indeed, that was regrettable. Unfortunately, your family lineage was not known at the time of those events. Your Uncle Llew greatly regrets the kidnapping at the hands of the Wild Hunt." Ogma's tone was polite, like he was apologizing for spilling her tea.

Fucking politician.

"Right. Does he also regret trying to kill me with the Wild Hunt after I escaped?" she scoffed, disdain leaving a sour taste in her mouth. She still had nightmares every night. *Uncle* Llew could take his regret and shove it up his fucking ass.

"It was a misunderstanding. Llew was only trying to find you to help return you to Asgard," the Ambassador explained.

Shannon's jaw dropped. Had that bullshit actually come out of Ogma's mouth? Truly, the elf was a politician in every worst meaning of the word. "Sorry, but did you really just say that to me?"

Ogma inclined his head. "I'm afraid I can only pass on what I have been told, Princess."

"That's unbelievable. Perhaps Llew should have explained his goals to the redcaps, hellhounds, trolls, dullahan, kelpies, and banshees that attacked me." She crossed her arms, fingernails digging into her skin. "After all that, why would Gwydion and Arianrhod think I want *anything* to do with them?"

Ogma held her gaze, maintaining his neutral expression. "To celebrate your nuptials and consummation ceremony."

Confused, she glanced at Loki. *<How could they possibly know when you just asked me?>*

Loki frowned. *<They couldn't.>*

"Asgardian weddings don't have consummation ceremonies." Frigga narrowed her eyes further.

"Oh, well yes. There does seem to be some confusion." His eyes flicked to Frigga, Odin, then Loki, while shifting his stance as if he wasn't as comfortable as he was attempting to appear. "Although it's certainly not a problem for the Sidhe, it is my understanding that neither Midgardian nor Asgardian laws permit multiple-partner marriages."

Again, Shannon glanced at Loki. Was she missing something? What the hell was the Ambassador talking about? Why on earth would that matter?

Loki's expression darkened, his fists clenching. "Explain," he demanded.

"Princess Shannon is already wed to Prince Elatha of Atlantia. The consummation ceremony is scheduled for Samhain, fifteen days from today."

Shannon staggered and blinked, mouth agape. Her eyes met Loki's furious gaze.

The story continues with Origin, Book Three of the Triquetra Prophecy within the Gods Among Us universe.

CHARACTER LIST

<u>Asgardians</u>

Áedán Bréanainn Lokison - God of Portals. Prince of Asgard. Son of Loki and Shannon. Born on Óðinsdagr, the 10th day of Mörsugur, in the 8000th year of Odin's reign as All-Father.

Baldur/Osiris - God of Light & Summer Sun. Eldest son of Odin and Freya, and crown prince until his death. Soulmate to Isis, with whom he had one son, Horus. Born in the 5000th year and died in 7200th year of Odin's reign as All-Father. His death and loss of access to the Asgardian throne infuriates Freya, sparking Freya's War between the Sidhe and Asgard.

Frigga - All-Mother, Queen of Asgard. A fertility goddess. Soulmate and wife of Odin since 6743rd year of Odin's reign as All-Father. Shares two sons with Odin, Thor, their natural-born son, and Loki, their adopted son. Born 4900th year of Odin's reign. Racial origin is Vanir. Had a twin sister, Revna, the birth mother of Loki.

Heimdall - God of Boundaries, Road, & Sight. Asgard's guardian and gatekeeper. Racial origin is half-Jotun and half-Aesir.

Hemrod/Hermes - God of Communication. Asgard's mage in charge of messaging systems. Spends considerable time on Earth and responsible for the development of social media. Racial origin is Aesir.

Kara - Goddess of the Hunt & Battle Strategy. Valkyrie. Shannon's best friend. Born 6200th year of Odin's reign as All-Father. Racial origin is Vanir. Has a twin sister, Sjofn.

Loki/Tod Corvus - God of Chaos, Stories, & Song. A fertility god. Asgard's strongest mage. Second son of Odin and Frigga. Adopted from Frigga's twin, Revna, as a baby. Father unknown. Younger brother to Baldur (deceased) and Thor. Racial origin is half-Vanir, a quarter fire-Jotun, and a quarter frost-Jotun. Born 7000th year of Odin's reign as All-Father. Married Sigyn in 7595th year of Odin's reign, but widowed five years later. Becomes Shannon's soulmate in 8000th year of Odin's reign. Known as Asgard's Black Prince due to his lethal chaos powers and black seidhr that killed many of Asgard's enemies in the two recent wars between Asgard and the Sidhe. Songwriter and lead singer/guitar of Raven's Chaos, his rock band on Earth. Actor in popular Assassin series movies on Earth, playing the assassin Sicarius. Also known as Set, Bastet, Eris, Hermes, Hephaistos, Raven, Coyote, Tezcatlipoca, and Kokopelli in Earthly mythologies as he has spend considerable time on Earth.

Mist - Valkyrie. A fertility goddess. Shannon's best friend. Born 7200th year of Odin's reign as All-Father. Racial origin is half-Aesir, a quarter Vanir, and a quarter Elven. No siblings.

Moja - Masterhealer of Asgard. In charge of Healer Hall in Asgard's palace.

Odin - All-Father, King of Asgard. Soulmate and husband to Frigga since 6743rd year of his reign as All-Father. Shared one son with Freya, Baldur, deceased. Shares two sons with Frigga, Thor, their natural-born son, and Loki, their adopted son. Born 9000th year of Bor's reign as All-Father and became All-Father at 1000 years of age when his father, Bor, fell in battle against the Sidhe Wild Hunt. Married Freya in political alliance with Vanir and Sidhe in the 3000th year of his reign, then divorced her in 6700th year of his reign. Racial origin is Aesir. No surviving siblings prior to his birth.

Roskva/Beth Olive - Goddess of Minerals. Valkyrie. Married to a human, Bobbie (Robert). No offspring. Friend of Loki's. Plays keyboard and vocals for Raven's Chaos, Loki's band on Earth. Born 7350th year of Odin's reign as All-Father. Racial origin is Vanir. Twin sibling, Thjalfi.

Shannon Murphy - Goddess of Forest & Seas. A fertility goddess, scientist, and university professor. Adopted daughter of Rose and Thomas Murphy (humans) at the age of approximately one in the 7994th year of Odin's reign as All-Father, and grew up in Hope, British Columbia, Canada. Birth father is Dylan, a summer elf. Mother unknown. Discovers she is not human but Elven. Becomes Loki's soulmate in 8000th year of Odin's reign. Human siblings from her adopted family, Liam and Heather.

Sigrdrífa - Valkyrie. Childhood friend of Thor's. Racial origin is Aesir.

Thjalfi/John Olive - Einherjar. God of Speed. Friend of Loki's. Plays drums for Raven's Chaos, Loki's band on Earth. Born 7350th year of Odin's reign as All-Father. Racial origin is Vanir. Twin sibling, Roskva.

Thor/Tempest Corvus - God of Thunder & Battle. A fertility god. Crown prince of Asgard since his elder brother's death (Baldur). Oldest son of Odin and Frigga. Older brother to Loki. Racial origin is half-Aesir, half-Vanir. Born 6900th year of Odin's reign as All-Father. Married to a human, Amelia, with twin daughters. Retired Winger for Leicester Tigers in Premiership Rugby, now an action movie actor and owner of Sidney Wreakers rugby club in Australia on Earth. Also known as Set, Zeus, Thunderbird, Talok, and Xolotl in Earthly mythologies as he has spend considerable time on Earth.

Vidar - Einherjar. God of Space & Vengeance. Born 2997th year of Odin's reign as All-Father. Family unknown. Racial origin unknown, but presumed to be Aesir.

Atlanteans/Fomorians

Elada - Prince of Atlantia. First son of Queen Eithnu. Commander of Fomorian outposts on Earth for 500 years. Born 6900th year of Odin's reign as All-Father; 1900th year of Queen Eithnu's reign.

Elatha - Prince of Atlantia. Second son of Queen Eithnu. Born 7000th year of Odin's reign as All-Father; 2000th year of Queen Eithnu's reign.

Eiru - Crown Princess of Atlantia. Daughter of Queen Eithnu and Manannan Mac Lir. Born 7800th year of Odin's reign as All-Father; 2800th year of Queen Eithnu's reign.

Eithnu - Queen of Atlantia. Sole ruler of the Fomorians, or the Sea Peoples. Born 5000th year of Odin's reign as All-Father, became queen during 6000th year of Odin's reign. Has numerous consorts and includes Manannan Mac Lir as her occasional lover.

Mara - Outpost Commander nearest to the Tunnels of Glass.

Dwarves

Brokkr - Master Weaponsmith. C0-creator of Mjolnir, Thor's warhammer. Brother to Eitri. Friends of Thor and Loki. Lives on the Shore of Lantia near the Howling Falls Wharf in King Sudri's kingdom.

    Delling - Master Builder. Mated, has a young daughter. Worked on builders guildhall with Loki in King Vestri's kingdom, but lives in King Sudri's kingdom.

    Einhenda - Ambassador for King Sudri.

    Eitri - Master Weaponsmith. C0-creator of Mjolnir, Thor's warhammer. Brother to Brokkr. Friends of Thor and Loki. Lives on the Shore of Lantia near the Howling Falls Wharf in King Sudri's kingdom.

    Fjalar - Journeyman Chemsmith. Convicted criminal. Lives in the lowest habitation level in King Sudri's kingdom, sharing a workshop with his best friend, Galar.

    Galar - Journeyman Chemsmith. Lives in the lowest habitation level in King Sudri's kingdom, sharing a workshop with his best friend, Fjalar.

Humans/Midgardians

Amelia Corvus - Thor's wife, but only knows him as Tempest Corvus, a human. She has twin daughters with Thor. Youngest of four siblings, she's the only girl. Her older brothers all play rugby. Lives in Sidney, Australia.

    Basil O'Keefe - Actor. British friend of Loki's, but only knows him as Tod Corvus. Enjoys Raven's Chaos' music.

    Bill - Department Head of Environmental Management at Victoria Charles University in Vancouver, British Columbia, Canada.

    Brian - Professor from University of California. A former grad school friend of Shannon's.

    Christine - Secretary, Department of Environmental Management at Victoria Charles University in Vancouver, British Columbia, Canada.

    Colin Rivers - Shannon's uncle, her adopted mother's brother. Lives with her mother, Rose, in Hope, British Columbia, Canada. Moved in six years after Rose's husband died.

Elise Chapelsworth - Movie director. Married to Harry Chapelsworth, with whom she has four children. A new friend of Shannon's. Lives in London, United Kingdom.

Harry Chapelsworth - Actor. Married to Elise Chapelsworth, with whom he has four children. A long-time friend of Loki's, but only knows him as Tod Corvus. Lives in London, United Kingdom.

Heather Murphy - Hair salon owner. Shannon's older sister in her adopted family. Six years older than Shannon. Twice divorced with no kids. Lives in Hope, British Columbia, Canada.

Jay - Government scientist from Miami. Friend of Shannon's from grad school.

Kristen Parker - Professor at Mackenzie University in Ottawa, Ontario, Canada. Shannon's friend and former roommate during graduate school.

Liam Murphy - High School History and Music teacher in Hope, British Columbia, Canada. Married to Sarah Murphy. No kids. Shannon's older brother in her adopted family. Seven years older than Shannon. A fan of Raven's Chaos. Lives in Laidlaw, British Columbia, Canada.

Lynda Warden - Owns Warden Marketing. Single. No kids. Shannon's best friend from high school. Lives in Vancouver, British Columbia, Canada.

Mary - Dean of Applied Sciences, Victoria Charles University in Vancouver, British Columbia, Canada.

Mike - American ecology professor that constantly hits on Shannon despite her refusals.

Nancy - Secretary to the Dean, Faculty of Applied Sciences, Victoria Charles University in Vancouver, British Columbia, Canada.

Rick - Professor from Hawaii. Went to grad school with Shannon.

Rose Murphy - Shannon's adoptive mother. Widowed. Husband Thomas died ten years prior. Mother of three: Liam, Heather, and Shannon. Lives in Hope, British Columbia, Canada. A single brother, Colin, moved in with her four years ago.

Sarah Murphy - Wife of Liam Murphy. Shannon's sister-in-law. No kids. No siblings. Lives in Laidlaw, British Columbia, Canada.

Shannon Murphy - see entry under Asgardians.

Tempest Corvus - see entry under Asgardians - Thor.

Tod Corvus - see entry under Asgardians - Loki.

Trent - Professor at Charles Victoria University in Vancouver, British Columbia, Canada. Former hockey player. Shannon's abusive ex-fiancé.

Jotuns

Gunnlod - Suttung's daughter. Mountain giant (Bergrisa). Lives with him and guards his divine mead.

Hrungnir - Extremely strong mountain giant (Bergrisa) in Thrymheim.

Hugi - Forest giant (Fyririsa) known for their speed. Used as messengers on Jotunheim. Assigned to Lord Thiazi in Thrymheim.

Suttung - Mountain giant (Bergrisa) that dabbles in blood magic. Told Fjalar and Galar how to steal powers from immortals using their blood. Lives in the Gudbrandsdal mountain range.

Thiazi - Lord of Thrymheim. Rules over the Bergrisar, the mountain giants. Located in the Gudbrandsdal mountain range.

Shen

Ao Guang - Dragon god. Brother to Ao Qin and Ao Shun. Also known as Quetzalcoatl in Earth mythology. Enemy of Loki.

Ao Qin - Dragon god. Brother to Ao Guang and Ao Shun. Enemy of Loki.

Ao Shun - Dragon god. Brother to Ao Qin and Ao Guang. Enemy of Loki.

Lü Dongbin/Derick Lang - Leader of the Eight Immortals. Actor. Fan of Raven's Chaos. Friendly to Loki.

Seelie/Summer Court Elves

Aine - Queen of Summer Court elves (Tuatha Dé Danann), Ruler of the Summer Realm Sidhe. Married to Nuada. Racial origin Elven.

Dylan - God of Selkies. Shannon's biological father. Brother to Llew. Son of Gwydion and Arianrhod. Racial origin Elven.

Manannan Mac Lir/Poseidon - Sea God. Numerous children, including Eiru. Lover of Queen Eithnu, but has many lovers. Friend to Asgardians and Atlanteans, but no friend to the Unseelie. Racial origin Elven.

Math Mathonwy - Master Mage. Loki's former lover. Racial origin Elven.

Nuada - King of the Summer Court elves (Tuatha Dé Danann), Ruler of the Summer Realm Sidhe. Married to Aine. Lost a hand in the last war with Asgard and has no desire for war again. Racial origin Elven.

Ogma - Sidhe Ambassador to Asgard. Represents both Elven courts. Racial origin Elven.

Unseelie/Winter Court Elves

Arianrhod - Sky Goddess. Mated to Gwydion. Has two sons, Llew and Dylan. Shannon's grandmother. Racial origin Elven.

Badb - Goddess of War. Mated to Llew. Had two sons that were killed by Loki in the last war against Asgard. Twin sister to Mene. Shannon's aunt. Best friends with Nemain. Racial origin Elven.

Cailleach - Hag of Béara. Raises Cŵn Annwn spectral white hellhounds and Cŵn Cyrff black hellhounds. Racial origin Elven.

Crom Cruach - Former fertility god. Marks prey for the Wild Hunt. Prefers pregnant women as prey. Racial origin Elven.

Freya - Goddess of Rivers. Ex-wife of Odin. Sister to Cernunnos. Mother of Baldur (deceased). Married Odin in political alliance with Vanir and Sidhe in the 3000th year of Odin's reign, then he divorced her in 6700th year of his reign after her repeated infidelities. Racial origin is half-Vanir, half-Elven. Daughter of Njord, King of Vanaheim. In her fury over Baldur's death and the lost access to Asgard's throne, she convinced her brother to go to war with Asgard—Freya's War.

Cernunnos/Freyr - King of the Winter Court elves (Tuatha Dé Danann), Ruler of the Winter Realm Sidhe. Married to Mene. Brother to Freya. Son of Njord, King of Vanaheim. Racial origin is half-Vanir, half-Elven.

Gwydion - Master Mage. Warrior Mage. Mated to Arianrhod. Has two sons, Llew and Dylan. Shannon's grandfather. Racial origin Elven.

Llew - Horned God. A fertility god. Leads the Wild Hunt. Mated to Badb. Had two sons that were killed by Loki in the last war against Asgard. Shannon's uncle. Son of Gwydion and Arianrhod. Brother to Dylan. Racial origin Elven.

Mene - Queen of the Winter Court elves (Tuatha Dé Danann), Ruler of the Winter Realm Sidhe. Twin sister of Badb. Best friends with Nemain. Racial origin Elven.

Nemain - Goddess of Panic & Fear. An assassin. Best friends with Badb and Mene. Racial origin Elven.

Vanir

Horus/Helios/Apollo - Sun God. Son of Baldur and Isis. Grandson of Odin and Freya. Grandnephew of Cernunnos and Mene. Struck from Asgard's royal family and lost Asgardian citizenship when sided with Freya during the war. Racial origin is half-Vanir, a quarter Aesir, and a quarter Elven.

Isis - Goddess of Women & Children. Soulmate to Baldur, with whom she had one son, Horus. After Baldur's death, she blamed Loki and left Asgard. Racial origin is Vanir.

Revna - A fertility goddess. Twin sister to Frigga. Born 4900th year and died (murdered) 7200th year of Odin's reign as All-Father. Racial origin is Vanir. Birth mother of Loki.

ABOUT THE AUTHOR

Melody Grace Hicks writes spicy science fantasy romance. She'd apologize for the increase in your lingerie replacement budget, but really, we both know it's those darn wickedly sexy characters that bring you back for more, right? Born and raised on Canada's West Coast, Melody has travelled the world and brings the diversity of her heritage and travels into her fiction. An award-winning internationally published scientist and professor in her day job, she's an enthusiastic masher of mythology in the evenings, using her pen name to tell tales of soulmates, secret identities, unknown origins, betrayals, and magical powers.

For updates and new releases, please subscribe to her email list on her webpage (www.melodygracehicks.com).

Melody loves interacting with her readers and you can follow her on Twitter/X (www.twitter.com/melodyghicks), Tiktok (www.tiktok.com/@melodygracehicks), Instagram (www.instagram.com/melodygracehicks), and Facebook (www.facebook.com/melodygracehicks). Or, if you want to check out the first draft of her stories as she writes them with all kinds of bonus content, including uncensored one-shots and excerpts, join her on Ream (reamstories.com/melodygracehicks).

ALSO BY MELODY GRACE HICKS

Confessions of Mischief – Episode 12
Fiction's Embrace – BT4W Season One (Episodes 9-12)

OTHER BOOKS

30 Days To Save The World – Short Story Anthology

ACKNOWLEDGEMENTS

Thank you to my many beta-readers who provided feedback during the development of this story. Your comments and reactions helped me take my first draft and weave the threads into a cohesive series. Thank you to the sensitivity readers who helped guide my word choice for authenticity regarding specific cultures, dialects, and diversity groups. I can't express my appreciation enough for my editor, Brenna Bailey-Davis at Bookmarten, who pointed out those dangling modifiers, cheered on my quirky chapter and part titles, and gave wonderful suggestions to ensure the tension didn't fizzle.

This book wouldn't exist without my daughter's steadfast enthusiasm and support. She helps me create the covers and critiques my designs. She's my main cheerleader and my sounding board. When I delve deep into the science of my planets, my races, or my magic system, she's right there to hear about it. When I'm wading through mythology, she wants to know every detail. And when my characters make me cry, she's handing me a box of tissue.

My oldest brother introduced me to Anne McCaffrey's *Dragonrider* series when I was a young teen—an incredible blend of science fiction, fantasy, wonderful characters including strong female leads, amazing world-building, and even some romance. I fell in love with that mix of hard-science backing fantasy ideas and never looked back. Not even when he scared me silly letting me watch Ridley Scott's 1979 *Alien* movie at far too young an age. No wonder I tend to write strong female characters. Thanks for the inspiration, big brother.

www.ingramcontent.com/pod-product-compliance
Lightning Source LLC
Chambersburg PA
CBHW032234010726
47494CB00002B/485